SAMURAI CRUSADERS

TED TAKASHIMA

Translated by

ALEXANDREA MALLIA

MUSEYON

New York

Library of Congress Cataloging-in-Publication Data

Names: Takashima, Tetsuo, 1949- author. | Mallia, Alexandrea, translator.
Title: Ranshin : samurai crusaders / Ted Takashima ; translated by
    Alexandrea Mallia.
Other titles: Ranshin. English
Description: New York : Museyon, [2022]
Identifiers: LCCN 2022030327 (print) | LCCN 2022030328 (ebook) | ISBN
    9781940842684 (paperback) | ISBN 9781940842691 (ebook)
Subjects: LCSH: Hōjō, Tokimune, 1251-1284--Fiction. | Kublai Khan,
    1216-1294--Fiction. | Mongols--History--Fiction. |
    Japan--History--Fiction. | LCGFT: Historical fiction. | Novels.
Classification: LCC PL862.A424144 R3613 2022 (print) | LCC PL862.A424144
    (ebook) | DDC 895.63/5--dc23/eng/20220629
LC record available at https://lccn.loc.gov/2022030327
LC ebook record available at https://lccn.loc.gov/2022030328

Editor: Francis Lewis
Cover illustration: Cheolsa Kim

First published in the United States of America in 2022 by:
Museyon Inc.
333 East 45th Street
New York, NY 10017

Museyon is a registered trademark.
Visit us online at www.museyon.com

Printed in USA

RANSHIN

The word "**Ranshin**" comes from the *Analects of Confucius*, and refers to supernatural power.

To all the people on Earth who currently fight for freedom, dignity, and their homelands. And to the people who support and fight alongside them.

"How can people attain peace when the fire of their life goes out? They have no land, no status, no fortune. And God doesn't offer them salvation. All that's left is a story of how they lived," Edward said almost as a whisper.

"Are you denying God? That is not very like you."

"I accept Him. Only God knows my life."

FOREWORD

February 2022—the month in which Russia invaded the Ukraine—will be talked about for a long time to come. As I write this three months into the assault, a country that was expected to submit to its aggressors in only a matter of days continues to fight for its sovereignty.

In 1274, Japan found itself in the same circumstance. A powerful foreign army had invaded our shores. The samurai of Japan risked their lives to resist and drive back the sudden and horrendous invasion. In this story, the armed forces of a foreign god, the Crusaders, join the samurai to save Japan, which is at a horrible disadvantage when it is invaded for a second time in 1281. What do these European soldiers, who have grown weary from their long battle in the Holy Land of Jerusalem, discover in this Asian country?

At present, there is much strife across the globe. The greatest victims are those who live at the center of conflict. I pray we can swiftly return to a world of peace.

—Ted Takashima

CHARACTERS

Edward Gawain . . . . English knight and Crusader
Alan . . . . Edward's attendant and best friend
Zafir . . . . Saracen merchant loyal to Edward
Thomas . . . . Genoese captain of the *Bel Oceano*
Enrico . . . . Chief navigator of the *Bel Oceano*

Hojo Tokimune . . . . Regent of the Shogunate in Kamakura
Adachi Yasumori . . . Advisor to Tokimune
Adachi Morimune . . Military commander and son
of Yasumori
Takakura Haruno . . . Courtesan
Xie WangSheng . . . . Foreign trade merchant
Nichiren . . . . Buddhist priest who preaches the
Lotus Sutra

Gaue Shun . . . . Associate professor of anthropology at
the University of Kitakyushu

CONTENTS

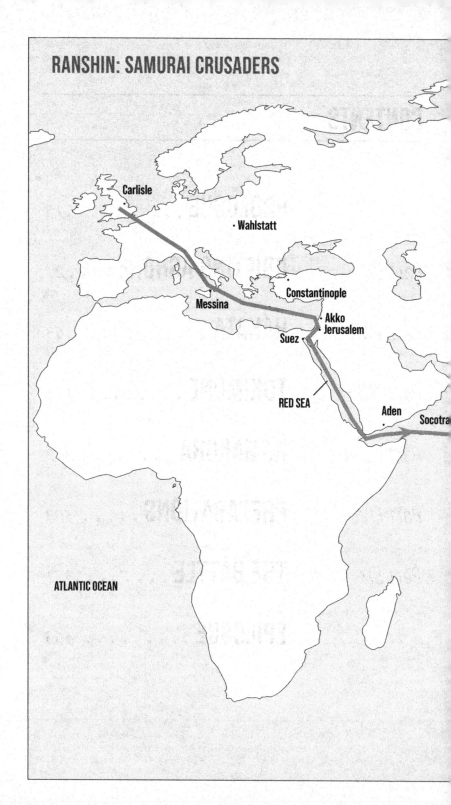

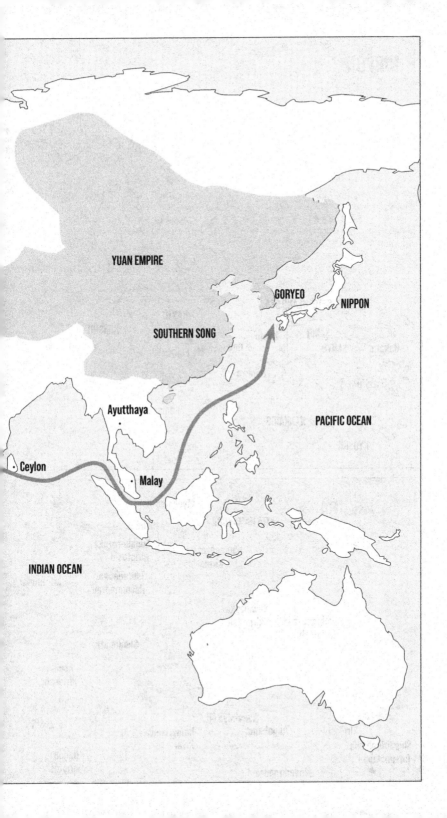

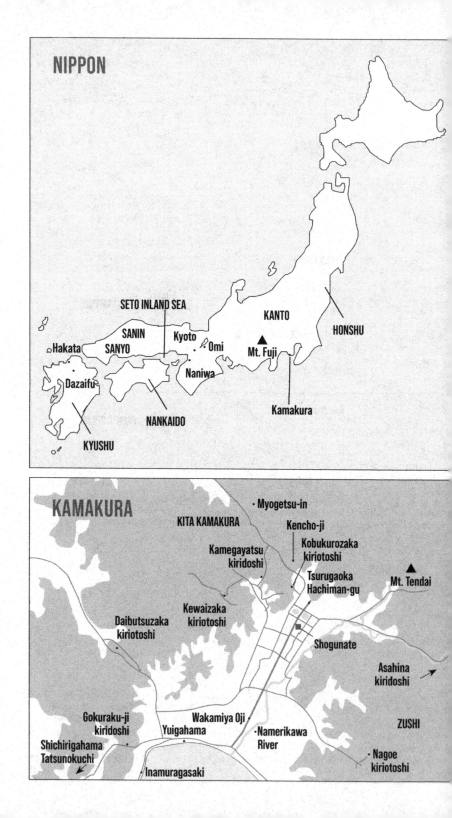

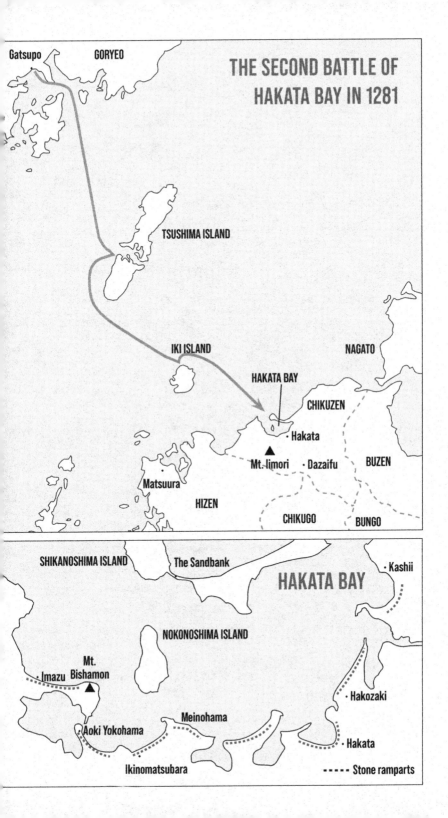

THE SECOND BATTLE OF
HAKATA BAY IN 1281

Gatsupo
GORYEO

TSUSHIMA ISLAND

IKI ISLAND

NAGATO

HAKATA BAY

CHIKUZEN

· Hakata

Mt. Iimori · Dazaifu

BUZEN

Matsuura

HIZEN

CHIKUGO

BUNGO

SHIKANOSHIMA ISLAND   The Sandbank

· Kashii

HAKATA BAY

NOKONOSHIMA ISLAND

Mt.
Bishamon

· Imazu

· Hakozaki

Aoki Yokohama   Meinohama

Ikinomatsubara

· Hakata

----- Stone ramparts

PROLOGUE

The smell of mold tickled my nose. This was the second time I had entered the centuries-old, white plastered storehouse on my grandfather's estate. I grimaced, but not because I thought it was an unpleasant smell. In my fourth year of elementary school, a girl came up to me when I didn't recoil from the musty scent and asked, "Shun, do you like mold smells?" Embarrassed, I turned away without responding. I didn't hate it. I don't hate it. I find it rather comforting. However, I knew then that such a feeling is not the norm. So, to fit in, outwardly at least, I deliberately make a face every time I smell mold.

We lived in Tokyo because of my father's work, but every summer we would spend two weeks in his hometown of Hakata. The first time I sneaked into my grandfather's storehouse, its thick wooden door was ajar, and I could just make out the shadowy interior. I crept inside.

Suddenly, a silhouette appeared in the soft light behind me. Startled, I stifled a scream. My grandfather was towering over me. I rushed outside, where the sun's radiance blinded me.

"A ghost lives inside the storehouse, and if children enter it, they will be whisked away to a faraway place," my grandfather said, but I did not believe him.

After that, I would always look for the chance to enter the storehouse, and today I once again found the opportunity to go inside. I slowly climbed the stairs in the dim light coming from a small window near the ceiling. My sneakers left faint footprints in the thick dust. I wasn't worried, though. I could get rid of them when I went back down.

On the second floor were all sorts of old wooden boxes of different sizes. "The boxes up there haven't been burned since the War," I remembered my grandfather telling my father one day over drinks. I wormed my way between the boxes, venturing deeper into the overcrowded space. A twelve-inch square vermillion lacquered box, sitting atop a dust-covered desk, caught my eye. With its color faded and the lacquer peeling off, I could tell it was not only very old, but different from the other boxes around it. It had an air of secrecy that aroused my curiosity. I removed the lid. Inside was a rectangular box. I took its lid off. Something was wrapped in a black cloth.

A dagger. And a cross about the size of a child's palm. My palm.

I knew that my grandfather had been in a kamikaze unit in the Imperial Japanese Navy and that the War had ended before he could fly on a suicide mission. Kamikaze pilots strapped daggers to their waists. I had never seen his dagger before, so I wondered if this could be it. I took the dagger in my hands. It was a lot heavier than I expected. A lion had been carved into the hilt. It didn't look Japanese.

My heart began to furiously beat in my chest. The lion's eyes were staring straight at me. I remembered what my grandfather had told me, and I instinctively shut my eyes. I felt like I was about to be snatched away to a faraway place. A place I could never come back from.

I heard the heavy door opening below.

"Shun, are you in here?" my father called out.

In a panic, I quickly shoved the dagger and cross into their box and replaced the vermillion lid.

MEINOHAMA COAST, HAKATA, KYUSHU

Around ten young people were huddled together on a half-collapsed rampart, a protective stone wall built parallel to Hakata Bay during the Kamakura period as a defense against the Mongolian invasion of Japan. Shun Gaue, associate professor of anthropology at the University of Kitakyushu and their tutor, squatted among them. Gaue's fair skin, chiseled face, and elegant long nose made him especially popular with his female students. "Were some of your ancestors from Europe?" people would ask. "Generation upon generation of my family are Hakata-born," he would respond, intentionally putting on a Hakata accent.

"Be careful," Shun advised his students. They had made it this far, he didn't want any mishaps.

Before them was a rod-shaped object, twenty inches long, two inches wide, and smeared with dirt and mud. The students carefully cleaned off the grime with brushes. After an hour of work, a broken Western sword appeared. As more mud was brushed away from the pommel of the sword, carvings emerged. The students grew tense. Professor Gaue delicately moved the sword to a cloth he had laid next to it.

"That's from the Middle Ages in Europe," one of them exclaimed.

Professor Gaue took a dagger wrapped in velvet from his bag and placed it next to the sword.

"They're identical," he said, looking at the roaring lion engraved on each.

He let out a small sigh of relief, while the students cheered with joy.

"You've done it, professor! You've finally solved the mystery of the dagger. This discovery will rewrite Japanese history!"

"We're not there yet, but we are one step closer," he said quietly, his voice nevertheless brimming with excitement. "The other half of the blade should be in this area," he continued. He got to his feet and once more looked down into the three-foot hole they had dug.

Later, Shun stared at the broken sword in his office. Close to eight hundred years of history were etched there. His gaze shifted to the dagger lying across from the sword on his desk. It was the same dagger he had first seen twenty years before in the musty recesses of his grandfather's storehouse.

When he was at university studying history and archaeology, he researched the dagger and cross. They dated from the 13th century and were English. But everyone in his family, including his now-dead grandfather, knew nothing about them.

"No one told me we had such things," his father explained. "Our family descends from the samurai during the Kamakura period, so it wouldn't be unusual for us to have katanas. But a Western dagger? A Christian cross? . . . Well, perhaps one of our ancestors got them by chance, put them in the storehouse, and then forgot all about them."

DRIFTING ASHORE

CHAPTER

1

The ship had been at sea for two and a half years. Sailing upon seasonal winds from the Red Sea, she had voyaged past Aden, Socotra, Ceylon, and Malay, dropping anchor just long enough to plunder ports for food and water.

"We can't say we are the Army of God now, can we?" Crusader Edward Gawain, third son of the House of Gawain, reflected.

For generations the powerful House of Gawain controlled northwestern England, defending the border of England against Scotland. When Edward was twelve, he was sent to live in a distant relative's remote castle. His cousin, who was a knight, took him in as his squire and trained him rigorously. Once he was nineteen, Edward became a knight serving under the crown prince of England. When France's virtuous King Louis IX of the Christian armed forces invited the crown prince to join him on a Crusade to rescue the Holy Land from the infidels, Edward went too. But the army's actions as they marched to Jerusalem were far from those of soldiers of God. They looted villages and inflicted pain, even death, on those who dared to stand in their way, all in the name of God. For surely to suffer in life is to receive God's divine retribution.

When they arrived in the Akko region of Palestine, the crown prince, greatly tired from the journey and fearful of assassination at the hands of the Saracens, returned to England, abandoning Edward and his fellow Crusaders in the pagan-ruled territory. The Saracen army pursued them on land as far as the Red Sea, where a sympathetic merchant named Zafir helped them escape on board the *Blu Oceano*, a trader refurbished from a Roman warship and equipped with two small catapults. To evade the Saracen flotilla, the *Blu Oceano* turned eastward bound for India.

When Edward first departed from his homeland, he had eighty soldiers under his command. Twenty of his men were killed in action against the infidels. Of the more than fifty men that sailed with him on the *Blu Oceano*, only twenty-four survived; the rest either succumbed to disease or died in skirmishes in port cities. Those who remained were emaciated and, worse, their morale was low. The twenty-three sailors manning the *Blu Oceano* were also run-down and near breaking point. From the outset, they had been forcibly threatened by Edward and his men to stay on board and aid them in their flight from the Saracens.

No sooner had they left India than a storm swept the *Blu Oceano* off course, setting them adrift in waters not yet known to Europeans. As they sailed along the southeastern part of the Asian continent, the rain was so heavy there was no longer a separation between sea and sky. But when the rain stopped, weeks went by with no precipitation. The supply of fresh water was running out, and everyone was restricted to two cups of drinking water a day. The sailors resented Edward and his men.

"There will be a mutiny any day now," Thomas, the captain of the ship, warned Edward, who licked his cracked dry lips.

But then the ship began to sway violently. The wind was picking up.

"Edward, it's raining! Come up!" Alan's voice rang out as he looked down from the deck.

Alan was twenty-five, two years Edward's junior. He knew nothing of hopelessness. Slender, with chestnut-colored hair and a handsome face, he appeared delicate, but he was bold and daring. His skill with a blade was unmatched. Yet he would frequently surprise Edward with how reckless he could be. Since Alan was ten, he served as Edward's attendant. They grew up like brothers.

Edward felt as if the ship was plummeting down a big hole. The urge to vomit came over him, even though his stomach was empty. Slowly he climbed up the ladder to the main deck. Everyone was there, looking up at the sky and opening their mouths to catch what rain they could.

"Bring out the empty barrels and collect the rainwater," Edward ordered, as he spread his arms to feel the rain fall over his body.

Suddenly the life-saving rain turned torrential. Everyone felt as if they were being drowned. The ship rose and fell with the swell of waves.

"It's a tempest! Every man to his post and keep her steady, lads!" Thomas shouted at the top of his lungs as he staggered to the ship's helm.

CHAPTER

2

The storm lasted for two days. On the third day, the wind lessened, clouds parted, and rays of sun shone through. Plenty of fresh water had been collected, but the storm had torn the ship's sails, and a third of the damaged hold was flooded. The more it was bailed out, the more seawater flowed back in. It was only a matter of time before the ship sank.

"Most of the food supplies are under water," a sailor shouted. Not that mattered. There was hardly any food left.

"Where are we?" Edward asked Thomas, who was standing next to the helmsman, staring ahead, his arms crossed. The Genoese captain was the most reliable seaman that Edward had yet met. He had bronze skin tanned by the sun and black hair that danced over his face. He was a man of few words, but the sailors had complete faith in him. Edward had heard that he was forty-five years old, but his strong and sturdy body was closer to that of a thirty-year-old.

"I'm not sure. We may at some point reach Southern Song."

"Have you been there?" Edward asked.

"No man from Europe has crossed the sea to Song."

No matter how much their eyes scanned the horizon, they saw no land.

Five years had passed since Edward left Carlisle Castle in England. "The Army of Christ." "Christ's Soldiers." When he first heard those words, they made his heart skip a beat. He was ready to devote his life to God and the Catholic Church. To be a Crusader in the ninth army of God was a sure path to heaven. To drive Muslims from the Holy Land and recover Jerusalem where Christ had been crucified was a noble act—the ultimate devotion to the Lord.

That's what it was supposed to be.

The reality, however, was far different. Were not the deeds they had committed grave sins worthy of casting them into the eternal fiery inferno prepared by the Devil?

Just when Edward thought the time had finally come to pay for his sins, a sailor atop the mast yelled out.

"Land!"

There, in the distance on the horizon, where sea met sky, was the faintest black smudge.

"Hoist sails! Turn her so she's heading straight for land. Hurry now! Why are you moping about?" Alan yelled at the helmsman.

"The storm broke the rudder."

"Well then, fix it and turn us to land!"

"We're already heading in that direction," Thomas interrupted calmly. "The tide's current is taking us there."

The crew collected by the ship's figurehead and waited. After a few hours, the shadow-like black stain on the horizon turned into land.

"Do you know what country this is?" Edward asked Zafir, as he leaned over the gunwale squinting into the distance.

In the battle for Jerusalem, Christian soldiers captured Zafir Walid, a Saracen, and, just when he was about to be beheaded, Edward purchased him for two gold coins and a horse. His sunburned face, with deeply etched wrinkles and a gaze that looked like it could pierce a man's soul, set him apart from other Saracens they had encountered. Zafir had been traveling with Edward for four years since his rescue. Originally a merchant of Constantinople, he was now Edward's good friend and close advisor. They had long since passed being master and slave. When asked his age, Zafir responded that he was probably over forty years old, but he was not sure. He possessed a deep well of knowledge in astronomy and meteorology, as well as medicine and religion. Wise and insightful, he took a profound interest in all things the world offered and was the only person on the journey who actually found enjoyment in it.

"It is not on my map," Zafir answered, his eyes fixed on the stretch of land.

His mind sorted through all its knowledge, trying to come to a conclusion about where they might be.

"Most likely," he started to say, but then took a moment to ponder further before continuing.

"This is east of the Asian continent. We likely were dragged east from Malay by the storm and the ocean's current, then headed north, and arrived here. We must have gone past Ayutthaya, so now we may be close to the eastern end of the Mongolian empire."

After several more hours, the current brought them to within a hundred yards of the shore, an alternating mix of sandy beaches and cliffs. Hills and smaller mountains stretched farther inland. As they looked over the side of the ship, the water was so perfectly clear they could see the seabed, which was becoming shallower.

"Prepare for impact!" Thomas yelled just as the bow of the ship rose up and rammed into a reef.

The crew lost their balance in the violence of the impact and toppled onto the deck. The ship listed to one side, but did not capsize. But every time a wave crashed into her, she swayed, making standing up difficult. The keel was irreparably damaged.

"If a storm comes, the old girl will be in pieces," Thomas said.

"Can you see any signs of people on land?" Edward asked him.

"No, but we must proceed with caution."

One month earlier, when they had landed on one of the scattered islands in the open sea to restock on water, they were attacked by the island's natives. Just as Edward and his men were dragging the rowboats onto the sandy shore, a slew of arrows painted with poison flew at them from the jungle. Two died. Out of vengeance, Edward and his men killed close to twenty natives. They withdrew without any water, but not before Edward questioned the point of the bloodshed.

"Shall we wait to assess the situation until tomorrow morning?" Edward asked Thomas.

Without responding, Thomas gazed up at the sky.

"There will be strong winds and high waves tonight. Best go ashore while we still have daylight."

"I leave it to you, captain."

They were eighty yards from the shoreline.

"Lower the rowboats!" Thomas ordered.

The ship swayed violently as the waves intensified. They needed to make haste.

Edward boarded the first rowboat to embark. Sitting in the prow, he kept his gaze fixed on the shore, his hand firmly gripping the hilt of his sword. The sailors put their backs into rowing toward the beach, but the strong tide hindered their progress. Violent transverse waves attacked them, lifting them high then lurching them downward. Seawater rushed over the men and flooded the boats.

"Abandon ship! Swim to the shore!" Edward heard Thomas yell out, just as a wave slammed into his rowboat, knocking him into the sea.

With his hand still clutching his sword, Edward desperately kicked toward the water's surface. But the undertow pulled him farther into the ocean's depths. He finally managed to rise to the surface and struggled to take a breath but his mouth filled with seawater. As he choked, the water rushed down his throat, and his body once again was shoved down toward the seabed.

I can't die here. What was the purpose of me joining Christ's Army?

Edward kicked with all his might, but still the undertow pulled him farther and farther to the ocean floor.

"Forget the sword! Swim with both your hands, you fool!" Edward thought he heard Alan's voice yell out before he lost consciousness.

CHAPTER

3

An ax dripping blood glinted overhead. Edward swept his sword to the side and cut the throat of the man confronting him. Blood gushed out as the man bent backward and fell.

Edward felt an intense shooting pain in his left shoulder. An arrow had pierced him from behind, its head passing through his flesh and out the front. Edward swung around and saw a Saracen archer fixing another arrow to his bow. He ran forward, slashing his blade, and decapitated the enemy. The head flew high before landing on the ground.

Pivoting, Edward saw a cavalryman charging toward him, a spear pointing directly at his chest. Edward crouched and readied his sword. Just as the spear lunged forward to hit its target, Edward jumped to the side and with all his might thrust his sword over his head. The point of the blade gored the rider in the stomach and, together with his horse, he collapsed.

"Kill them all!" Edward shouted, as he brought down his sword and stabbed the fallen man in the side. Barely taking a breath, he turned around and stabbed the man behind him in the gut. Blood spewed out, painting Edward's face and field of vision in red.

"Don't let a single one escape alive!" he yelled.

Suddenly, a hard blow to the head knocked him unconscious. Severely wounded, Edward teetered between life and death for nearly a week. Zafir mentioned that it was a miracle he had survived and that he must truly be loved by his God and that his God must have a plan for him to have lived through such an ordeal. Alan disagreed, saying it was because the Devil himself hated Edward and drove him out of hell.

Darkness dirtied his sight. And in that darkness, ominous black hands stretched out to grab his legs.

"No. Stop. I beg you. Please, stop!" he frantically screamed, but no sound escaped his lips. He tried to take out his sword and cut away the hands, but his sword was stuck in its sheath.

CHAPTER

4

Edward's eyes shot open. He was soaked in sweat. A bearded man peered down at him.

"You were having a nightmare," Zafir told him.

Edward turned and saw Thomas.

"How long have I been out?"

"Oh, just half a day," Thomas said teasingly, a broad smile spreading across his face.

Edward lifted his upper body and saw that it was day. Clouds covered the sky, but the sun's rays broke through their gaps. He looked toward the sea. The waves were rough, and farther out he could see the ship still stuck on the reef. Every time waves broke on the ship, it swayed dangerously and looked like it could capsize at any moment. Edward tried to stand, but immediately lost his footing. Thomas grabbed hold of him and supported his body.

"Is everyone all right?"

"One drowned, and two others are still missing," Zafir answered for Thomas.

Edward followed Zafir's gaze and saw the body of the drowned sailor lying on the sandy beach. Edward momentarily shut his eyes. He was tired of seeing corpses. For his first six months as a Crusader, he trembled every time he saw a dead body. But since then, he felt no emotion.

Noticing his sword was not in his hand, Edward frantically searched on either side of him.

I could have sworn I had it with me when I boarded the rowboat, but then . . .

"Don't worry."

Seeing Edward panic, Zafir placed the sword on Edward's chest.

"You sank because you were trying to swim with this."

"Who saved me?"

"You somehow made it to the beach on your own power. As for the sword, Alan grabbed it. Despite not being a skilled swimmer, he managed to bring it to shore. But he can regale you with the details himself."

"Where is Alan?"

"He is fine. He is out looking for fresh water."

Edward looked up at the sky. Through the clouds he could see that the sun was nearing its zenith. They had embarked in the rowboats in the evening, so it was true he had been unconscious for over half a day. The rain had stopped, but the ocean's waves still thrashed about and the wind was strong.

"There may be another storm brewing," Thomas observed.

"What became of the rowboats?" Edward asked.

"One of them sank, but we were able to bring the other one ashore."

"Then I'll take it back to the ship."

"I think it better to wait."

"We can't afford to wait," Edward insisted. "We have no idea when the ship might be washed away."

"Let's go," Edward heard Thomas mutter under his breath.

Edward managed to get to his feet and walked toward the rowboat. Thomas signaled to two sailors to follow them.

The violent collision with the rocks had created a gaping hole on the side of the ship. If the ship were to be dislodged, it would sink immediately.

"Grab everything you can," Edward ordered as they clambered on board through the hole.

"If you're talkin' about food, there weren't much left to start with, sir," one of the sailors said while eyeing the water in the bottom of the hull.

"Then load up weapons."

The armory in the stern held bows, arrows, swords, shields, and armor. Whenever they had to make port, these assets had saved lives time after time. They would once again come in handy, Edward reasoned.

After packing up some of the weapons, the two sailors rowed back to the beach on the first of several round trips.

"What should we do about the catapults?" Thomas asked Edward.

On the deck were two catapults designed for warships. They were small compared to those used for ground warfare. Even so, they stood close to six feet high. They could propel hundred-pound stones, and if oil-coated rocks were set ablaze and launched, they could bring down enemy ships. Even though Edward and his men had skirmished with the inhabitants in every port where they had docked, they had yet to use the catapults.

"Best to leave them behind. How would we even get them off the ship?"

"Do you think we could carry it?" Edward said, ignoring the captain's remark.

"It would be difficult, but not impossible."

"Then let's bring it. We have no idea what we might be facing in the future."

"Which one?"

"Both."

The four men detached the catapults from the deck, disassembled them, and after much effort loaded the pieces into the rowboats. By the time they reached shore, the sun had set. Alan and one of the other knights had already returned from their search for food and water.

"And here I thought you'd still be sleeping. Did you wake up to take a piss? You drank so much seawater your stomach was bulging out," Alan joked, then shrugged his shoulders as he noticed the weapons brought back from the ship.

"Did you run across anything dangerous out there?"

Alan set a leather bag filled with water next to the fire and a dozen plucked chickens.

"There's a river. I found the birds there."

"Any villages?"

"We were trying to be cautious, so we didn't see any."

He took a moment to search for the right words, before continuing.

"But this place is different from everywhere we've been before. You can tell that people live here, but I didn't seen a single person. Probably they noticed our arrival and are hiding."

"Hiding?"

"I can sense their presence even without seeing them."

The smell of roasting chickens began to waft through the air.

"Let's look into it tomorrow. Armed, we can go deeper inland," Edward said. "For now, let's rest. Double the usual watch tonight."

No one would say or admit it, but they were exhausted. They had spent a full three days in a storm, and just when they had found land, their ship was wrecked. Of all the men, only Zafir was energetically moving about. He busied himself observing the sea and investigating the forest's vegetation. He would jot things down in the notebook he kept close. His notebook was made of flax paper that he had tied together; he stored his ink in a small jar tied around his waist; and he made pens from common reed grass.

Edward had once stolen a peek at Zafir's notes. He found small grain-like characters in a script called Naskh tightly compacted on the pages. But Edward did not know how to read Arabic letters. Zafir had also drawn detailed sketches of plants and flowers, as well as small birds and bugs. There was even a sketch of Edward's sleeping face on one of the pages. Skimming through the pages, Edward felt he was looking directly into Zafir's mind.

CHAPTER

5

The next day, Edward, Alan, and a few soldiers headed inland. Thomas said that he wanted to return to the ship one more time to ensure that nothing useful had been left behind. Edward tried to tell Zafir to stay on the beach with the others, as his presence would only be a hindrance, but Zafir insisted on coming with them. This was unlike Zafir, who usually obeyed Edward's orders. However, since drifting ashore, Zafir was even more enthusiastic about exercising his deep interest in unknown regions.

Edward and his party walked from the coast in the direction of the nearest mountain. The May sunshine made it neither too hot nor too cold. A month earlier, they had disembarked on a tropical island where the sun blazed down so intensely that half of Edward's soldiers suffered heatstroke. Swarms of mosquitoes, with the potential of transmitting infectious diseases, also pestered them. They departed as quickly as they could. Compared to that island, this new land was welcoming and its climate perfect.

"This land appears more fertile than Europe," Zafir said, as he scooped up a handful of earth and sniffed it. "It's different from the jungle. There aren't any snakes, poisonous spiders, or scorpions either. Or at least we haven't seen any . . . yet."

"You would expect people to be living here on this island, or continent, or whatever it is. They have to be around somewhere. Perhaps they are watching us now as we speak," Alan said jokingly.

However, it did not entirely come off as a jest to the other men. The knights tightened their grips around the hilts of their blades as their eyes cautiously scanned the area. Edward also kept his ears alert for any new sounds. But all he could hear was the wind rustling through the trees.

The path led to a valley. They walked for another two hours, before encountering a river. Although 'river' was not the right word for it. It was more of a stream only several yards wide. Edward stopped just as he was about to head down the bank.

Several men were in the stream, fishing. They looked up and saw Edward.

"We will not harm you. We drifted ashore after being caught in a storm. So—"

Before Edward could finish, one of the men let out a scream and ran off, the others quickly following.

"Did you see their faces? They looked terrified. Did they think we were demons?"

"I'd say so. It looked like the bigger one was about to piss himself."

"I wonder if they thought the Saracens were coming to attack them?"

"They had Asian faces, so that must mean we're in Song, no?"

"We're at the eastern end of the main continent? We've drifted to one hell of a place."

"Now we know people live here. Which means there has to be a village nearby."

"Let's see where they went. But keep your wits about you! They may have fled, but there could be others who will attack."

Edward's men chattered on about this new discovery, as they walked farther inland. Alan, who led the party, suddenly came to a halt and crouched down low. He brought up his hand and signaled the rest to stop.

Edward rushed to Alan's side.

"There's a village ahead," Alan said, pointing to a narrow path leading to an open field. "But I can't see anyone. What should we do?"

"Let's take a look, shall we?" Edward said calmly even as he tightened his grip on his sword.

With bows at the ready, they inched forward.

"Now I understand why the men in the stream bolted," Alan said as they entered the clearing.

A shocking scene lay before them. The village had been attacked and burned to the ground. All that remained of dozens of houses were charred pillars.

"There's not a single soul around," Alan observed.

"After suffering such damage who would want to return here?" Edward commented.

"I wonder if the men we saw earlier were survivors from this village," Alan continued.

Thick weeds grew in the clearing.

"It's been quite some time since the attack. I'd say two, maybe three years. Nobody has been here since then," Edward said.

Zafir examined the charred remains.

"How cruel," he said. "They burned everything."

"Look!" Alan cried.

He pulled out an arrow lodged in one of the pillars. Half of the shaft was eaten away, and the other half was brittle. Rust covered the arrowhead.

"The Saracens didn't make this. I've never seen its like," Alan said as he showed it to Edward and Zafir.

"A short bow with considerable power fires this type of arrow," Zafir said as he examined the damage inflicted on the pillar. "The village was attacked suddenly. Not a single house was left standing. Those who tried to escape were shot down. Massacred."

Arrows littered the clearing, but they saw no bones.

"Do you think the men who ran away earlier may have buried the victims?" Alan guessed.

If they had stumbled across a scene of slaughter like this in Europe, skeletal remains would have been scattered everywhere. Once they had even come across a village that had a mound of skulls at its center. It was rare to find any corpses being buried.

"The path leads inland. There has to be another village where those men live. Let's search a little further." And at Edward's word, the party proceeded, leaving behind the decimated village.

As they continued, the narrow path widened, and they saw evidence that others had recently traversed the same road. They advanced another five hundred yards when the path narrowed again as it lead through a forest.

"Enemies!" Alan's sharp voice rang out.

Edward drew his sword. His soldiers followed suit, readying themselves for battle.

"No! Don't attack! If you do we will be killed!" Zafir cried out.

"Zafir's right. We're surrounded. Their bows are pointed straight at our hearts," Edward said. They could see rustling shadows within the trees and feel eyes piercing through them.

Edward cautiously re-sheathed his sword.

"Men, put away your blades," he ordered.

Edward's men slowly lowered their weapons.

"Let's fight! I have no interest in dying quietly," Alan growled.

"If they wanted to kill us, they would have done so by now," Edward snapped back. Alan put down his blade.

"Show yourselves! We are not here to fight. We drifted ashore by chance," Edward shouted into the thicket.

Silence. Then several men brandishing spears emerged from the trees. Behind them rode a man on horseback. He wore an ornate antlered helmet and equally ostentatious armor.

Footsteps brushed through the trees, and, as Edward turned toward the sound, he saw even more warriors armed with longbows taller than they were. Dozens of soldiers surrounded Edward and his men. The warriors in front carried a weapon that looked like a hybrid between a sword and a spear.

Edward had never seen such weapons and clothing. *Was the warrior atop the horse, with his strange vermillion armor wrapped around his body and a longbow tucked under his arm, their commander? But he looked so young*, he thought.

"We are not your enemies," Edward began in English. "We are travelers from Europe who drifted ashore to this land. We would be grateful for your help."

Zafir translated Edward's words into Latin first, then Persian, then Arabic, and finally Chinese.

Nothing registered.

The commander gave an order in a language that not even Zafir knew, and one of the warriors approached Alan and attempted to take his sword. Just as Alan pushed aside the approaching warrior's hand, another soldier bashed him over the head with the shaft of his spear.

"Stop!" Edward shouted as he dashed to aid the fallen Alan. Several spearheads were thrust in his direction.

"Do not move! Throw down your weapon! If you do, they will not kill you right away," Zafir pleaded with Edward.

"What makes you so sure?"

"If they meant to kill us, they would not have given you a warning. They would have attacked right away."

"Men, lay down your weapons. Slowly."

Once Edward's soldiers had tossed aside their weapons, the foreign warriors lowered their bows. However, the spears remained fixed on Edward. As Edward helped Alan to his feet, he saw that Alan had a dagger concealed within his tunic. Alan, following Edward's gaze, silently turned away.

The warriors collected the discarded swords and bows, tied them together, and loaded them onto a horse that had been brought forward. One of them grabbed Zafir's notebook and flipped through its pages.

"Please give that back," Zafir pleaded. "It is only a book in which I record strange new things and write memos."

The warrior carried the notebook to the commander and spoke to him in the unknown language. The commander took the notebook and stuffed it into a pocket.

"I beg you to return that. It is an extension of myself. Have this instead," Zafir implored. He removed a beaded necklace from his neck and approached the commander.

Zafir's usually calm demeanor had completely changed.

"Enough! Do you want to be killed?" Edward shouted.

"That notebook is as important to me as my life. No, it is even more important."

"Is it more important than the lives of all your companions here?"

Hearing Edward's words, Zafir composed himself and backed away, his gaze steadfastly boring into the commander.

CHAPTER

6

Edward and his men kept a close eye on the warriors as they were led through the forest. Eventually, they reached a valley with a village laid out on one side. Fields and thick green grass ringed dozens of houses. Townsfolk crowded around them as they entered, gawking and throwing hate-filled glances at these strange-looking foreigners. At the center of the crowd was one of the men they had seen fishing several hours before.

Was he the one who alerted the soldiers? Edward wondered.

All of a sudden, a fist-sized rock struck Edward's shoulder and landed at his feet. Edward turned to see where it had come from and saw a young boy at the front of the crowd. The boy picked up another stone and flung it. Edward leaned to the side and dodged it. He fixed his eyes on the boy, who yelled something at him. As if on cue, the rest of the villagers picked up rocks and threw them at the foreigners.

The commander angrily shouted at the villagers, and they panicked and hurriedly dispersed.

Edward and his party were brought to a house in the heart of the village. Across from the house was a hut, where between thirty and forty warriors with spears stood guard. Edward and his men were taken inside the hut.

"Thomas? Is that you? What are you and the sailors doing here? We left you on the beach," Edward exclaimed.

"Out of nowhere, these warriors came at us, surrounded us and brought us here. They had their bows fixed on us from the start. They didn't give us a chance to fight back."

"Is everyone all right?"

"Only one person was hit. As long as we didn't show any sign of fighting back, they did nothing."

"It was the same for us."

"We're forty men. Yet this land's soldiers managed to take us all captive. Now, do you think they'll slit our throats or enslave us until our last breath?" Alan quipped, while peering through a crack in the wall.

"It seems like they have no intention of killing us. At least, not for the moment," Edward responded.

"They can always change their mind."

"The warriors in the ornate armor were riding horses small enough to be ponies," Zafir said. "I have heard that cavalrymen in Asian armies ride horses of this size. They must be a light cavalry in the Mongolian army."

Someone audibly gulped. The rest were silent. Tales of the tidal wave of the Mongolian army annihilating the Kingdom of Poland and advancing on the plains of Hungary had reached their ears.

"I've heard that such an army would build mountains of decapitated heads and not leave a single grain of wheat or any livestock in the villages they passed through," one of the knights chimed in.

"I wonder if Mongolian soldiers attacked and burned the village we saw?" another added.

"Judging by the state of this village, I'd say this is a temporary garrison for their troops. We must have been captured by a scouting party."

"They don't seem all that tough. They seem as fragile as a woman. If we just had our weapons, we could kill them easily."

"Better to ask them where the hell we are."

"Whatever language they are speaking, it is the first I have heard it," Zafir interrupted the flurry of comments whirling among the men.

"Stop filling your heads with half-witted thoughts," Alan said as he lay down on a bed of straw in a corner of the hut. "We're still alive because they do not want to kill us yet. As long as they feel that way, we have a chance." Ever alert, he showed no sign of wanting to sleep.

"Someone's coming," Thomas, who had been keeping an eye on the state of things outside, warned.

Hearing that, Alan shot up and tightly gripped his hidden dagger.

"Stand clear of the door. Don't you dare do anything foolish," Edward hissed at him.

Shooting Edward an annoyed look, Alan crossed his arms and leaned back against the wall.

Accompanied by several armed soldiers, a short man, wearing wide hemmed clothes similar to a dress, and a bald man entered. The short man was the commander they had seen on horseback earlier. Now that he had taken off his helmet and armor he seemed as small as a child, and with a face as gentle as a woman's.

"Does anyone know Chinese?" the bald man asked.

"I have a fair understanding," Zafir said as he stood up.

The man told Zafir that he was a foreign trade merchant and that his name was Xie WangSheng. The Xie family of wealthy merchants, he pointed out, held considerable influence in this area. He also told Zafir that they were on an island east of Song, known as Nippon.

"This man is Lord Adachi Morimune, commander of the garrison here. Who is in charge of your troops?" WangSheng said, speaking for Morimune.

"My name is Edward Gawain. I am the knight in command of these Christian troops."

Morimune quietly consulted with WangSheng.

"Lord Morimune says that you and your men are foreigners who have come to invade this nation. Is that why you have come?"

Zafir explained how they sailed from Europe, ran into a storm, and drifted to this country. Zafir told them that Edward and his men meant the people of this land no harm, and that their intention was to leave and return to their homeland as soon as possible but that they required help to do so.

Zafir and WangSheng used a combination of English, Chinese, and Japanese to translate the conversation that followed between Edward and Morimune.

"We would like a ship large enough to carry forty people across the ocean and two months' worth of food and water."

"This is something I cannot decide on my own. We will return to Dazaifu and I will send a messenger to Kamakura, where our leader Tokimune resides."

"How long will that take?"

"I do not know. Even though he is the lord of Kamakura, Tokimune cannot make hasty decisions. You can wait for orders in Hakata."

"Where is Hakata? And what do you mean by 'orders'? We are the chivalric order of Christ's Army and seafaring men. We bear no hostility toward this land."

Talk ceased. After several seconds, Morimune gave a deep nod.

"I acknowledge that you are not our enemy," he responded.

Morimune scanned the room, gave a slight nod, and exited, leaving WangSheng to converse with Zafir. But soon one of the soldiers encouraged WangSheng to move along and leave.

"What did you talk about?" Alan asked.

Zafir turned to Edward.

"We are on the island country known as Nippon, which is east of both Song and Goryeo. They have been trading with Song for a very long time."

"So, there is civilization in this land after all."

"Two years ago, the Yuan Mongolian military forces attacked Nippon. The country suffered great damage. It was the Mongolians who burned that village we came through on the way here. They massacred everyone there."

"Is Nippon under Mongolian control? It does not seem to be."

"WangSheng mentioned that their forces are currently out searching for survivors of the defeated Mongolian forces. They mistook us for them, it would appear."

"I cannot imagine the Mongolian army being defeated by this lot," Alan interjected.

He had a point.

The warriors they had seen were of small stature and did not look strong. Their commander also seemed weak. It was impossible to think that such men could defeat the dauntless Mongolian army.

"Those men have been stationed here as guards," Zafir explained. "Apparently, a unit has just arrived to relieve them. WangSheng mentioned that they forced him to act as a translator after they had captured stragglers of the Mongolian army. He speaks the same tongue as the Mongolians."

"What is to become of us?" one of Edward's men called out.

"Eventually, they are going to bring us to a place called Hakata, a large port city where the main part of their troops is stationed," Zafir said.

Zafir told them what he knew about Mongolia and its empire. How several years ago, the fifth emperor, Kublai Khan, had conquered central China and renamed the new nation Yuan.

Just as Zafir finished, the door of the hut swung open, and several villagers accompanied by guards entered. The villagers placed before them a steaming pot, plates of air-dried grilled fish, wooden bowls, and a bundle of thin sticks. They gestured that Edward and his men were to eat, then exited. Understanding that for the time being their lives were not in danger, everyone realized how hungry they were. Each grabbed a wooden bowl and collected around the pot.

"How the hell do they expect us to eat this gruel? It's burning hot!" Alan's voice rang out as he stuck a finger in the pot.

"Use the bowls and chopsticks the way the people of Song do," Zafir said. He demonstrated how to scoop up the rice porridge with a bowl, place a piece of fish on top, and eat with chopsticks. Figuring out how to use these strange new utensils was a challenge, but eventually the Englishmen were able to follow Zafir's lead.

Edward took this moment to think through all the things that had occurred that day.

Stories about the Mongolian army's dauntless savagery had reached their ears in Europe. They heard that all the villages the Mongolian army passed through were burned to the ground, leaving behind only corpses and severed heads. They knew the stories to be true only after they had seen for themselves the burned skeletal remains of houses and the horrified faces of surviving villagers here in Nippon. Still, to be

told that the remnants of such an army were being hunted down . . .
that could only mean that the warriors of Nippon had won against the
Mongolians. Yet the soldiers they had met looked like children . . .

The sound of loud snoring spread throughout the hut and
roused Edward from his thoughts. It did not take long before he
too fell asleep.

CHAPTER

7

The next day Edward awoke to the sound of the hut door opening and the voices of the guards as they walked inside. The sun was already high in the sky. For the first time in a long while, Edward had slept soundly without any nightmares to disturb him.

Edward and his men were given the same meal as the night before and were brought outside after they had eaten. While they had been sleeping, their hosts had transported their belongings from the beach to the village square. Even though the hostility toward them from yesterday had vanished, the villagers still shot wary glances at these strange foreigners.

The village contained more than thirty houses. At its center was another hut where they stored the yield from their harvest. Across from that was what looked like an armory. Two soldiers carrying spears guarded its entrance.

Morimune and WangSheng walked toward them.

"Tomorrow we will be taking you to Hakata," WangSheng spoke for Morimune.

"Where exactly is Hakata?" Edward asked, with Zafir as his translator.

"It is more than fifty miles north of this village. A three-day journey. I advise you to rest all you can today."

"What will happen to us in Hakata?"

"You will wait there for instructions from the lord of Kamakura."

"And what is this Kamakura you speak of?"

"It is the seat of government where the lord of our samurai warriors resides."

"We don't want to go there. All we want is to repair our ship and go home," Alan interjected once he heard Zafir's translation.

"They could not find our ship," Zafir told him.

"The ship may have been damaged when we ran aground, but if we just had the materials we could—"

"Get hold of yourself, Alan," Edward snapped. "The ship has sunk. It would have been impossible for us to fix that much damage."

"These instructions are the will of the lord of Kamakura. Do not defy them," Morimune said in a menacing tone before he turned to leave, signaling WangSheng to translate on his way out.

Morimune's warriors began to prepare for departure in the village square, packing several loads onto horses.

"Do they not have any carriages here?" Alan questioned.

"There are too many mountain roads to use wagons, or so WangSheng told Zafir. Looks like we've come to a very troublesome place," Edward sighed in response.

Edward and his men returned to their hut.

"Men, gather round. I have something important to discuss," Edward said in a formal tone.

The hut fell silent, and everyone looked toward Edward.

"Tomorrow they will take us to a new location, a port city known as Hakata. We do not know what kind of place we will be walking into. We do not know if we will eventually be killed there or sold into slavery. Or if we will ever be able to return home."

"We should fight!" Alan yelled as he brought out the dagger he kept hidden behind his back.

"But they have taken our weapons," one of the knights complained.

Their swords, shields, spears, and catapults were under the close watch of a round-the-clock, three-man guard. The villagers and, least of all, Edward and his men were not allowed near the stash.

"If we wanted to take them back, we could do so whenever we wanted," another knight boasted.

"Forty soldiers at most occupy this village. If we had our weapons, we could overtake them," someone else added.

"Yes, if we flank the three guards and steal back our swords, then striking down the rest of the soldiers will be easy," yet another voice cut in.

"If you had noticed yesterday, we were completely surrounded by bows aimed straight at us. You should not think lightly of these opponents," Edward warned. "And even if we were to succeed in our fight against them, what then? We know nothing of this land's geography and its language. If we tried to stay here, sooner or later more troops would arrive and they would surely bring us down."

"We should still keep fighting," Alan countered. "I will die before I become a slave."

Edward sighed and looked at Zafir.

"What do you think we should do?" he asked.

"I think we should comply with what they want. There must be a reason they have not killed us yet. I dare say, we might be of some use to them. This could be to our advantage."

"Is there a guarantee they won't kill us?"

"I think they are at risk of being attacked from enemy forces again. Hence the reason they are still sending out scouting parties. They most likely wish to hear any foreign news we have. This may be the first time they have seen people who look like us. Perhaps they do not even know places such as Europe exist."

"Same as us not knowing a place like Nippon exists."

"Which is why I believe they have no intention of killing us anytime soon."

Ultimately, they decided to obey Morimune's instructions for the time being. Alan was clearly disappointed, but did not make any strong objections.

CHAPTER

8

That night, sounds of movement woke Edward. Soft rays of moonlight shone in through the skylight in the hut's ceiling, and he could make out faint figures in the dim light. Alan and a couple of the soldiers were at the hut's door.

"What do you think you are doing?"

"We're going out to piss," Alan said.

"I'll go with you."

"We're going to escape. If we end up being dragged to Hakata, or whatever that place is called, we'll lose our chance of getting back to England."

"He's right. I don't want to die in this pagan place," one of the soldiers piped up.

"Rather than being a pagan's slave until the day I die, I would rather die here fighting," the other agreed.

Edward sensed several more men rising from their sleep.

"I understand," Edward said, after considering what his men thought of their situation. "The armory is in the center of the village. We'll first strike down the soldiers on guard and retrieve our weapons. Then we'll assault the others."

"That nobody of a commander is a half-wit. He left only two men to guard the armory," Alan said.

"Thomas, stay behind and wait for our signal. When you hear it, come out with the rest," Edward ordered as he and Alan slipped out the door and disappeared into the darkness.

"Don't kill them. They haven't killed a single one of us," Edward whispered.

"Not yet," Alan replied sarcastically.

Together, they crept toward the armory. Two soldiers sat in front, with straight backs and alert eyes scanning the perimeter. They were more disciplined than Edward and Alan had expected.

"We have no choice but to kill them."

Edward reluctantly nodded his head.

"Let us get as close as we can, and on my signal, attack. If we give them the chance to scream, we're done for."

"Agreed."

Alan gripped his dagger, while Edward felt the weight of the rock he had picked up. *Is it possible the guards can lose consciousness without us killing them?* Edward thought.

"So, this is where you've been, Sir Alan. Everyone's been looking for you," a loud voice suddenly called out.

Zafir came stumbling toward them holding a bottle. The two guards stood up and pointed their spears at Edward and Alan. Zafir offered the bottle to the soldiers.

"Oh, look! Lord Edward, have you been with Alan this whole time? What I have in my hand is something called sake. Xie Wang-

Sheng gave it to me. It's not the same as wine, but it is still delicious. Come! Let's share it with the others."

When Edward, Alan, and Zafir arrived back at their hut, everyone immediately crowded around them.

"What the hell do you think you were doing?" Alan growled at Zafir as he grabbed him around the collar.

"Your weapons weren't where you were heading. Your opponents are no fools. They had already moved them to a different location and have prepared them for transport. The guards were decoys."

"Look outside," one of the soldiers whispered.

The situation around Morimune's hut had changed. Squinting, they could see soldiers carrying bows in the darkness.

"Morimune must have wanted us to think him a fool," Edward observed.

Zafir agreed. "Though, now I do not know if they truly intend to kill us or not," he confessed.

If that was their true intention it would have happened by now. They have been testing us. I can't help but ask who the true fool is here, Edward thought to himself. *At least these people of Nippon are not barbarians. Perhaps they are even wiser and cleverer than I and my men are.*

CHAPTER

9

"Did you rest well?" Morimune asked the next morning, as he and WangSheng escorted the Englishmen to the village square, where their catapults, crossbows, swords, armor, saddles, and even their compasses had been packed up and put on horseback.

"I have been ordered to handle them with care, seeing as they are your valued items."

"Is that why you moved them last night and kept them under guard?"

"It would be inexcusable if someone had stolen them," Morimune said once he heard WangSheng's translation. He looked right at Edward, a chuckle laced in his words.

"What is this?" Morimune asked.

"It's called a catapult. A weapon designed to fire rocks far distances."

The smile on Morimune's face disappeared.

"I saw something similar to this in the last battle against Yuan. One of their warships had one."

"If it were made larger, it could propel huge boulders over a thousand yards."

"I would like you to teach me how to use this machine."

"Unfortunately, it is broken. I wish I knew how to fix it."

The device used the potential energy from an enormous counterweight to launch a projectile into the air. Such weapons were said to have been used to repel the Roman army in the invasion of Syracuse. By modifying the heaviness of the counterweight, the firing distance could be easily adjusted with high accuracy. The largest class of catapult could fire a three-hundred-pound boulder a maximum of three hundred yards. Besides stones, catapults could also be used to propel the carcasses of plague-ravaged men and livestock. The smaller models relied on manpower rather than a counterweight to function. Several men would create tension by pulling down a rope attached to a throwing arm to release the projectile. Edward had heard the device had been first introduced by an Islamic engineer from Persia.

"Is everything ready? I want us to depart before the sun reaches midday," Morimune asked WangSheng to tell Edward, before ordering his own men to quicken the pace of their preparations.

In time, seventy men set off for Hakata. Ten soldiers, including Morimune, rode on horseback. The rest, carrying spears and bows, filed into ranks of ten in front and behind the formation. Edward and his men did as they were told and walked behind the packhorses.

CHAPTER

10

Hojo Tokimune turned his gaze to his garden. The early summer trees were thick with green and dazzling to his eyes. For the last few years, the trees had not moved his heart and senses, so preoccupied was his mind with the looming conflict between Nippon and Yuan. However, in time, his heart must have given him some degree of allowance, because he was once again able to experience and appreciate the changing seasons.

Tokimune was eighteen years old when he took up his duties as regent of the shogunate in Kamakura. His rise to power coincided with the arrival of the first diplomatic messages from Mongolia and the subsequent uproar they caused. In the nine years that followed, Tokimune never had a moment's rest. For the sake of weathering the national crisis that faced Nippon from abroad, he worked tirelessly to establish domestic order and unity. To that end, he had to kill his elder half-brother, Tokisuke. Supported by the court nobles in the capital of Kyoto, Tokisuke had rebelled against Kamakura.

No matter the personal cost, the samurai government centered in Kamakura had to prevail.

Three years after Tokisuke's rebellion, Yuan sent armed forces to Nippon. The army left enormous damage in its wake, yet somehow Nippon drove the invaders back. Or rather, the huge armada of enemy ships anchored in Hakata Bay suddenly vanished. Since the Mongol invasion, the Kamakura shogunate had been divided into those who wanted to take the offensive and send troops to attack Yuan, and those who wanted to take the defensive and fortify the country against future enemy assaults.

"Is there still anyone in the Hyojoshu Council of State who advocates an expedition to Yuan?" Tokimune asked in a composed voice for a twenty-seven-year-old.

"They are still debating, but those who strongly insisted on sending troops abroad have weakened," Adachi Yasumori reported. This both cautious and honest man was the elder brother of Tokimune's wife. Yasumori had supported the Hojo family since Tokimune was born. He was significantly older than his younger sister's husband, and now at age forty-five, he was committed to strengthening the reign of the Kamakura shogunate, with unwavering loyalty.

"Meaning their zeal has finally cooled down," Tokimune muttered.

It had been two years since the war with Yuan. Overnight, the Mongolian army, a force superior in the art of war, had disappeared from Hakata Bay. Since the Yuan warships that had once blanketed the sea's surface had vanished, the shogunate's government had been continuously arguing over defensive and offensive tactics. Like Tokimune, Adachi Yasumori was in favor of defensive doctrines. However, the people of Kamakura, drunk from the rewards of victory over Yuan, mainly supported the offensive position of Kanazawa Sanetoki and his followers.

"But we cannot simply sit here and wait to be attacked. A good plan would be to put our efforts into attacking the Yuan continent while we have this chance," Yasumori said.

"Have you read the letters from Dazaifu? They say the length of the Yuan warships surpasses forty yards. And that their advance fleet is nine hundred boats strong. How big and how many warships do we have?" Tokimune asked. "Furthermore, we did not get enough rewards from the last war, and the gokenin vassals are greatly unsatisfied."

"That is why it would be best to invade Goryeo and then send an expedition on foot to the Yuan Dynasty."

"Pipe dreams," Tokimune scoffed and then looked toward the mountains, which were also covered in fresh greenery.

It was said that the Mongolian army had initially attacked Hakata with the intention of assaulting Kamakura next. *The first thing we have to consider is how to defend Nippon against foreign invaders*, Tokimune thought.

"How is the construction of the stone wall in Chikuzen coming along?" Tokimune asked.

"I believe only twenty percent has been completed."

Having analyzed and discussed the details of the war with Yuan, Tokimune and the council had decided to build stone ramparts around the coastline of Kyushu to defend against enemy troops invading from the sea.

"We need to hurry. It won't be long before Yuan attempts to attack again." Tokimune said anxiously. "During the last war, why did the Yuan ships vanish so suddenly? Do we still know nothing about what happened?"

"I heard that the spiritual power of prayer summoned a divine wind and that it blew all the Yuan ships in Hakata Bay out to the open sea and sank them in a violent tempest. The monks and Shinto priests are thought to be our saviors, so now they are praying more than ever. However, there are some insolent monks who are spreading the word that if nothing is done, foreign forces will over-run our nation."

"Is it Nichiren? Ah, we are in trouble now," Tokimune said with a light sigh.

HAKATA

CHAPTER

11

The sea was calm as Edward and Morimune's party advanced along the intricate coastline of bays and capes. Morimune would occasionally halt the formation and write something down while looking over the shoreline. Since Morimune had deprived him of his notebook, Zafir had lost his usual exuberance and looked pitiful. Even so, it was clear that his curiosity could not be quenched, and he frequently asked WangSheng questions.

"What do you two discuss?" Edward wanted to know.

"Since we are both merchants, we talk about work," Zafir replied. "We also talk about this country, where we are being taken, and what will happen once we get there."

"You are not the only one collecting information. WangSheng must have been ordered to gather information about us as well."

"Would you not want to know as many details as you could about completely unknown strangers in your homeland? Keep in mind, we are not their enemy. And they are not our enemy. That is the reality of our situation."

They passed numerous villages on their trek, but half of those villages were in the same state as the first one Edward had come across. Burned to the ground with nothing left but the ruins of what once was. Other villages they saw were likely where survivors had fled and built themselves a new home. Morimune stopped at each of those villages and listened to the village chiefs.

Without exception, in each place folk would shoot hostile glances at Edward and his men. It appeared they held all foreigners in the same regard as Mongolian soldiers. But under orders from Morimune, his soldiers did not treat Edward and the men roughly, but politely and even gently.

The people of Nippon wore linen clothing, lived in wooden homes, and lived a simple and clean lifestyle. Inland villages grew crops in the fields on the outskirts of the village. Villages close to the sea made their livelihood through fishing.

"What are those?" Edward asked Zafir to ask WangSheng.

All along the roadside were slightly elevated mounds of earth.

"They are burial mounds for severed heads. It is a gravesite for Mongolian soldiers."

"A grave for enemies who have died in battle?"

"And those executed after being captured."

"So, the inhabitants of this land even bury their enemies?"

"It is most likely a religious custom. Or perhaps it is to stop the spread of disease," Zafir responded thoughtfully. Although it was clear that he, like Edward, was astonished.

Edward was reminded of the Battle of Wahlstatt. He had heard its story over and over again back in England. In 1241, the Mongolian army invaded Europe and all but destroyed the allied forces of Poles and Moravians. All the Mongolians' cruelty had been unleashed in that battle, a cruel reminder of the mountain of corpses the Mongolians left in their wake. After Wahlstatt, the invasion moved on to Hungary. The Hungarian army was similarly decimated, and its cities fell to plague. The army of death then headed to Italy. However, the Mongolian supreme commander, Ogedei Khan, died and the Mongolians withdrew and established the Golden Horde with Sarai in Russia as their capital.

"The Lord's divine protection has saved Europe," clergymen preached throughout the Continent, but Edward thought it was simple good luck that the enemy commander had died, allowing Europe to escape the calamity of imminent conquest. When he told this to his father, his father disagreed. "It was God who brought forth the good luck which led to victory," he said.

CHAPTER
12

Later that evening, after dinner, Zafir grabbed a twig and drew a map in the dirt for Edward.

"Here is your homeland, England," he said. "You crossed the channel between England and France, and came to the main continent of Europe. After reaching Italy, you boarded a ship for Syria. You and I first met in Lydda on the outskirts of Jerusalem, right? And I was captured here as I was coming from the port of Constantinople," he said, pointing to Anatolia and Thrace. "After that, we left Suez, passed through the Red Sea, and came to the Indian Ocean. It seems we went north after going through Malay and eventually arrived at this country."

"Then we are in a nation in the far east of the Asian continent?"

Zafir shook his head.

"We are not on the mainland of Asia. We are on an island. Which is why they have been able to preserve their own distinctive culture. But now the Mongolian army draws ever nearer. The culture of the main continent and the culture of this island are about to collide. We will see this piece of history as it unfolds before us."

Zafir's face was serious when he first began to speak, but his expression changed as he continued. He became more talkative, and a reddish tinge spread across his face. He was a man of limitless curiosity about the unknown.

"I have had my fill of war," Edward said.

He spoke true. Edward wished to see no more bloodshed. However, an assault by the Mongolian army would be as bloody as anything he had so far experienced. He had seen the burial mounds of severed heads. The warriors of this land were obviously worthy adversaries of the dauntless and cruel Mongolian army. Perhaps there was a hidden strength that Edward and his men had yet to recognize in the small-statured samurai who walked at the front and back of their formation. Still, it was difficult for Edward to understand why the people of this country gave their fallen enemies proper burials.

Edward recalled the tall mounds of unburied severed heads on the battlefields during the Crusades, where the pungent smell of rotting flesh permeated the air, and vultures and other beasts devoured the scattered corpses. When he had first witnessed the torments of war, he had to do his best not to retch. Soon he became numb and felt no emotions at all at such horrors.

"I believe that battles here take a different form than those fought in the world of Latin speakers. By all means, I want to witness that difference with my own eyes," Zafir said with a faint smile as he tried to quell the excitement building within him.

CHAPTER

13

The party departed the next day in the early hours of the morning. Gentle waves splashed on the glittering surface of the sea, and although the sun's rays were strong, the breeze that came off the water was cool and comforting.

"It is so peaceful, is it not? We could almost be walking along a riverbank," Zafir commented.

"Yes," Edward agreed. "It is not like England which is covered with thick gray clouds for more than half of the year."

"Look!" Thomas' voice suddenly rang out. He was pointing at the wreckage of a ship ten yards out in the ocean.

"I want to examine that ship. Tell WangSheng to inform Morimune," Edward said to Zafir.

Morimune must have guessed the meaning of Edward's words, because he signaled that he would accompany Edward and Thomas.

"She looks new. No more than a year since her maiden voyage."

"She must have been caught in the same storm that we were."

"This is a Mongolian vessel, is it not?"

Morimune nodded, as Zafir and WangSheng quickly translated Edward and Thomas' conversation.

"Does this mean they are still trying to reach Nippon?"

The ship's bow was pointed toward the shore, while its belly was pierced by the reef. The remains of the stern were not visible. It was hard to say if the ship had run aground whole, and then the waves and wind had broken the bow from the stern. Or if the typhoon had split the ship's hold in two, and what they saw was one of the sunken pieces that had washed ashore.

Edward and Thomas waded out for a closer look.

"It is large, perhaps a hundred and thirty feet in length," Thomas observed as he examined the wreckage.

"The hull is double-layered wood, but the deck looks to be only a single layer. And the planks that make up the ship are thin," Thomas said as he walked chest-deep in seawater around the hull. "If she were to be hit by any sort of catapult, she would sink before putting up much of a fight. She appears large to the eye, but her structure is poor. I wonder if the Mongols expect enemies to be without effective weaponry, or if they were simply hasty in her creation?"

"It looks like there were many cabins on the deck, but they are basically unrecognizable now. It also looks like there were four masts. Speed was likely her strong point," Edward said.

The two men crawled to the center of the ship.

"There were two auxiliary masts here. Although they snapped close to the base. It seems they were able to be taken down. The hold looks like it was divided by several planks. That way, if one part was damaged, the other parts wouldn't flood," Thomas muttered. "The basic construction is not much different from the *Bel Oceano*. However, they cut corners in building her."

"What makes you think this?" Edward asked.

"She may be new and large, but I would blame the crudeness of her design as the reason why the storm reduced her to such a state," Thomas stated definitively.

Edward wanted to respond, but stopped himself. He saw Morimune, submerged up to his chest in water, staring wordlessly up at them. In that moment, Morimune was most likely thinking what Edward was thinking: *If this ship ran aground in the same storm as the* Bel Oceano, *then where are the surviving sailors? Or did they all drown?*

Once on shore, Thomas came to Edward's side.

"There was no cargo left within that Mongolian ship," he told Edward.

"It could have been washed away when the stern was destroyed."

"Or they could have done the same as us and taken the cargo with them as they evacuated."

"You think the crew made landfall?" Edward said, lowering his voice.

"Or drowned in the storm? There are no corpses along this stretch of the beach."

"We need to be cautious. They could still be lurking around this area. Tell the rest of the men," Edward ordered.

CHAPTER

14

For two days Edward and his men walked close to ten hours a day. They were exhausted. However, the soldiers and infantry of Nippon showed no signs of fatigue.

"Tough bastards, aren't they?" Alan said as he walked next to Edward. "I guess their hardiness is what caused the Mongolian army to retreat. Looks like they are not to be underestimated."

Edward thought the same.

Walking behind the packhorses, Thomas and his crew began to fall behind.

"The sailors cannot keep up. Tell them we need to slow our pace," Edward told Zafir to tell Morimune.

"It is only half a day to Hakata," Morimune said after hearing WangSheng translate Edward's request.

"My men have been exhausted since landing on these shores after fighting for their lives in that storm. They cannot keep pace with you."

Morimune took a moment to look around, as if searching for a landmark.

"If we go through here, there is a stream. We will make camp there."

On the seaward side of the path were cliffs where waves crashed onto the rocky stretch below. On the opposite side were gently sloping hills and trees. Alan, who was walking in front of Edward, suddenly stopped.

"What's the matter?" Edward asked.

Without responding, Alan stared at the hills. When Edward started to walk toward them, Alan grabbed his arm.

"It's nothing. Just a hunch," Alan said.

The regiment abruptly halted. There was an ominous silence. The two soldiers on horseback behind Morimune galloped up one of the hills. When they returned to Morimune's side, the three of them spoke. Morimune came over to Edward and his men.

"Some of the soldiers from the previous war may be lurking about. We are going to investigate and contain these new invaders." Both Zafir and WangSheng exhibited worried looks as they translated Morimune's words.

"You think the enemy is out there?" Edward asked.

"I cannot be certain; but something does not feel right. If we were to be attacked where we are now, we would not be able to defend ourselves. We will take a different route."

"My sailors cannot go much farther," Edward said as he looked toward the sailors resting behind the packhorses.

Morimune kept his eyes fixed on the hills while he pondered the best course of action to take.

"What about the forest in front of the hills?" Edward asked.

"There is a high likelihood enemy soldiers are concealing themselves in the forest."

"The ship we saw was recently run aground. Which means it was beached by the same storm I and my company encountered. The crew likely disembarked."

Morimune did not seem surprised by what Edward said. He must have expected this. Yet again, Edward turned his gaze to the hills. He could not shake the feeling that something out there was watching them.

"If there were to be an attack, if would come from that direction." Edward pointed to the middle of the path that ran along the steep and jagged cliffs.

"Even if we were to go through the hills, we would be as vulnerable to attack as going through the forest," Edward added.

"It would put too much strain on the horses to force them through the hills," Alan said as he forcibly stepped up. "And the moment we decide to make a detour we will be attacked. No matter which way we go we cannot avoid an assault. Let's keep pushing forward, and figure it out as we go."

"Wait. We can't just jump into danger. We have to prepare."

Morimune thought for a moment, then split in two his group of samurai bodyguards.

"Those of us on horseback will lead. Then the packhorses. If anything happens, take the horses and ride to the hills. Half of us will move forward and the rest will stay behind to cover us! Those walking on foot, keep your arrows aimed toward the forest!" Morimune ordered.

Morimune turned his attention to Edward and his men. "If what lies ahead is safe, we will signal you," he said. "Wait for the signal before you proceed."

"Return our swords! We can also fight," Edward implored.

"You are under our protection," Morimune replied and rode off.

The horseman in front of Edward suddenly jerked and tumbled off his steed. An arrow had pierced his throat.

"Attack! Spread out!" Edward shouted as he took cover behind the horse.

All at once, the sound of an explosion reverberated and dirt from the hills flew around them. At the same time a torrent of arrows rained down from within the woods. The horses startled by the noise would not move, and one by one, the warriors on horseback were struck and crashed to the ground.

"Take the cargo from the horses! Use it to shield yourselves!" Edward yelled, as he jumped on the riderless horse and galloped up the hill.

Morimune followed, arrows bombarding his armor. They could see that a couple of horses had fallen off the cliff and into the sea. Several more soldiers on horseback raced up the hill. At that moment, tens of enemy soldiers ran out of the woods. Edward kicked one of them in the head as he rode past. Reaching down to grab a fallen sword, he narrowly escaped being slashed by an enemy blade. Edward returned the attack and cleanly cut the soldier's head from his body. Edward looked around and saw Alan struggling with an enemy soldier. Edward rode behind the soldier and neatly sliced him, kicking him away from Alan.

"Use this!" he said as tossed his sword to Alan, replacing it with the fallen enemy's weapon.

Edward looked down the hill and saw the *Bel Oeano*'s sailors cowering on the ground. He raced to them, avoiding an onslaught of arrows, dismounted, stabbed his horse in the chest, and pushed it to the ground.

"Take cover behind the horse!" he yelled before running back up the hill.

The Nippon soldiers found it difficult to handle their long-bows in close-combat battle. Every time they tried to stand up and shoot their arrows, the enemy archers counterattacked.

"Twenty to thirty men at best oppose us. If we can stop them from shooting arrows, we should be able to find our way out of this mess," Edward said once he made it back to Alan.

They could see the enemy leaning out to shoot from the shelter of the rocks between the path and the forest.

"It is time to go on the offensive!" Alan shouted. But there was not much he could do with only a sword and no bow.

"Give us our weapons!" Edward cried out to Morimune while miming the act of shooting a bow.

It only took a moment for Morimune to understand what Edward meant.

"They're on the packhorses!" he shouted.

Edward, with Alan and Thomas, rushed forward and untied their swords, crossbows, and quivers.

"Alan, Thomas, get behind the dead horses on our left and shoot down as many enemy archers as you can," Edward ordered after making sure they were all fully armed. "I'm going to the rocks."

On his way he encountered a horse with a dead soldier slumped over its neck. An arrow stuck out of the man's side. Edward pulled him off and mounted the horse. An arrow grazed his ear once he was up. Nippon horses were a head shorter than the ones he had ridden in England. Nevertheless, they had strong legs and explosive speed. Once he grabbed the reins, the horse followed his commands. Clearly it was well trained.

Lowering his chest to the horse's neck, he sprinted toward the archers hidden in the rocks. Arrows whizzed past as he swerved left and right, and he wished he had a shield for protection. Keeping a steady pace, he prayed his horse would not be hit.

Edward slashed at the shoulder of an enemy soldier in the act of fixing an arrow to his bowstring. He took a sidelong glance as the man's arm flew high into the air, before avoiding the spear of another soldier who jumped out at him. He countered the attack and sliced off his foe's head. After frantically dashing through the enemy soldiers, lifting his sword overhead and forcefully bringing it down on either side, he stopped and turned around.

A man on horseback was galloping at full speed toward him. It was Alan, swinging down his weapon while avoiding the thrusts of enemy spears. But it wasn't an English sword that he brandished. It was a sword that Nippon warriors wielded. A katana.

"I've killed three archers so far with this. There should only be about ten left. Come on! Follow me!" Alan called out to Edward, not even pausing to catch his breath before heading off to the next target.

Once the battle begins, this man truly forgets which of us is the master and which is the servant. Is it because Alan loves fighting beyond all reason? Or is he just too confident in his skill with a sword?

Edward laughed as he followed Alan.

The battle ended soon afterward. Having lost their archers, the enemy attempted to flee, but Edward and Alan stopped them. Heads flew, while others succumbed to the fatal injuries inflicted on them. The uninjured tried to escape to the sea, but the soldiers of Nippon pursued them. Twenty enemy corpses were scattered over the hill.

CHAPTER

15

Edward eventually dismounted and made his way to Morimune, who was receiving an injury report from a subordinate. Suddenly, Edward noticed something in the distance.

"Watch out!" Edward yelled and tackled Morimune to the ground. An arrow was speeding toward him.

Alan acted in a flash and fired his crossbow toward the hills. From out of the shadows an enemy soldier rolled into view, the crossbow arrow lodged in his forehead. The arrow intended for Morimune's chest pierced his arm instead.

"Don't move! The more you move, the more the poison will spread throughout your body," Edward told Morimune as he cut away the cloth around his arm.

Edward pulled out the arrow, but Morimune did not scream.

"My arm is burning. It is probably wolfsbane poison," he muttered.

"We will have to cut your arm off."

"Don't bother. If you are going to cut off my arm, you would be better off killing me," Morimune said using both Zafir and WangSheng to communicate with Edward.

On impulse, Edward removed a short sword from Morimune's belt and cut a cross in the wound. He brought his mouth to the wound, sucked, and spat out blood.

"You are truly a reckless fellow," Zafir said as he tied a cord around Morimune's upper arm. "The rest is up to God." Zafir removed a medicinal ointment from the pouch at his hip and slathered it on Morimune's arm.

Edward staggered as he stood up. His body was numb, and he had no strength.

"Go, rinse out your mouth, and then take this. It is an antidote."

Zafir brought out a black pill as he helped Edward stand upright.

"If we move him, the poison will spread more quickly. We have to camp here tonight," Zafir told Morimune's adjutant.

Morimune's forehead was covered in sweat, and his breathing was ragged. He was clearly fading in and out of consciousness.

"The fever is rising, but if he can pull through it, he should be fine."

"And if he cannot?"

"We shall cut the arm off. We may be too late for that, but it is better than doing nothing and watching him die. I'll keep watch over him tonight. You should rest. You absorbed quite a bit of poison yourself."

With Zafir's support, Edward staggered over to one of the packhorse loads and sat down.

"What became of the rest of the enemies?"

"They were almost completely annihilated. This nation's soldiers and Alan are hunting down any that remain."

"And our allies' injuries?"

"A total of seven Nippon soldiers were killed. Of the injured, five are in grave condition and three are slightly wounded. One of Thomas' sailors was stabbed in the stomach, but he will live."

Twenty enemy corpses were lined up on the hill, all of them sporting brand-new leather torso armor.

"They're Mongolian soldiers," WangSheng said. "But I don't think they are soldiers stranded here from the war two years ago."

Edward ordered that one of the corpses be torn open and its stomach examined. Inside were undigested pieces of meat.

"They've been eating well. And not on food from this country."

"A meat-heavy diet is characteristic of nomadic people."

These men were survivors from the shipwreck discovered earlier that day.

Alan and several others returned at last, accompanied by two Mongolian captives with their hands tied behind their backs. One was a young man with a wispy mustache, the other was an elderly man.

"Bring WangSheng over here!" Alan shouted out.

"Wait. Let Zafir talk to them first."

Edward indicated with his eyes for Zafir to approach the two men. If WangSheng were to converse with them, he would surely tell Morimune everything.

Zafir spoke to them, then turned to Edward and Alan and nodded.

"They can speak the Sino language."

"Tell them what I say as quickly and accurately as you can. If they do not follow my commands, there will be serious consequences," Alan told Zafir who did as he was asked, his face becoming ashen.

"Which one will it be?" Alan asked Edward.

"The old man."

Alan withdrew the dagger concealed on his hip and, without a word, stabbed the backs of the old man's hands. His screams rang throughout the hills. The samurai warriors looked on with faces blanched with horror.

"Well, there's no reason for you to wield a sword now, is there? Or pull a bowstring. It's not like you need hands—or eyeballs," Alan said darkly, pressing the dagger's blade close to the old man's right eye.

The man squeezed both eyes shut and desperately turned his face away.

"Now then, best you tell me everything you know. Until recently, you bastards were supposed to be on the other side of the sea, no?"

Zafir translated for Alan, but the two enemies clenched their teeth and said nothing.

"You must not have good hearing. Therefore, I can only assume you have no use for those ears of yours," Alan said holding his dagger against the older man's right ear. The man desperately tried to bend his head away and escape the knife.

"You better be watching closely, young man, and thinking of your response because your turn is next."

Before Zafir could finish translating, Alan cut off the older man's ear. Blood gushed out from the black hole where his ear used to be, and he screamed and crumpled to the ground. Alan picked up the ear from the ground and threw it to a dog, who caught it and ran off.

The younger man squeezed his eyes shut and curled his body inward. With his blood-soaked hand, Alan slapped the young man's cheek and ordered him to open his eyes and stand up.

"You are responsible for what I do to your senior next."

Blood oozed down the young man's cheek. A dark stain spread across his thighs.

"His nose! Then there are ten fingers and toes. And we cannot forget the legs and arms, and the eyes. Oh yes, I almost forgot about the tongue. I have no use for a tongue that does not talk. Should I take care of that first?"

Alan thrust his dagger into the young man's arm. His scream echoed out.

"You better think before you answer. I will keep you company until you remember."

"They say we have already started building ships in Goryeo," the young man stammered.

"How many ships?"

"I do not know."

Alan shoved the blade deeper into the young man's arm.

"There are more shipbuilders and craftsmen at work. They have raised taxes in the region and increased the number of forced laborers. They say you can taste the anguish in the deaths of the Goryeo people."

The young man began to talk just as he was ordered. His face was shattered, as if he had already lost his mind. Alan wiped the blood off his dagger on the unconscious older man and sheathed it.

The next morning, before sunrise, Edward, accompanied by Zafir and Alan, checked on Morimune. A concerned-looking WangSheng waited for them.

"All is well. There is no need to cut off his arm," Zafir said after putting his ear to Morimune's chest and checking his pulse.

The color returned to WangSheng's face, and he sighed with relief. Morimune no longer struggled for breath. His fever had gone down, and his face looked peaceful in sleep. Just as Edward was about to leave, Morimune's eyes opened, and he said something. WangSheng translated Morimune's words to Zafir, who passed them on to Edward.

"You saved my life."

Morimune looked up at Edward.

"And because of you my arm was spared," Morimune said to Zafir, before turning to Edward again.

"How are your men?"

"Only three were injured. Their wounds are nothing of concern. Thankfully, we had no casualties."

"We lost seven men. Thirteen are injured, five gravely so."

"Can you move?"

"For the most part."

Morimune groaned as he attempted to stand up, with Wang-Sheng for support.

"It's unwise for you to try to move. Remember, you are one of the gravely wounded. The wound itself is not of much significance, but there is still poison in your body. It will take another half day before it leaves your body and you will be able to walk again."

"We cannot stay here any longer. We do not know when the next Mongolian attack will come, and we are behind schedule."

Morimune called for one of his men and gripped his shoulder to help him stand. Zafir looked on astonished, but said nothing.

"We depart in an hour. Make sure you and your men are ready to leave."

Just then Morimune noticed the two Mongolian captives sitting under a tree and guarded by two soldiers.

"Who are they?"

"I captured them while you were sleeping," Alan answered.

"Did they tell you anything?" he asked, eyeing the old man's wounds and blood-soaked bandages.

"In England there is a saying that men are like oysters, you just need to pry them open to find the pearl inside. Those men were no different."

Morimune glanced at WangSheng, but said nothing. He mounted his horse with help, bowed to Edward and the rest, and took his leave to further investigate the state of his men.

"He must be in a great deal of pain. He is truly a great man. Even yesterday he did not let out a single groan or complaint," Zafir said under his breath, as he watched Morimune ride off.

CHAPTER

16

An hour later preparations for departure were almost complete as Alan gave his final instructions to Zafir.

"Tie them to the back of a horse," he said, pointing to the two Mongolians. "I still have many details to worm out of them. Tell them that if they try to run away, we will kill them."

The landscape changed as they neared Hakata, Kyushu's number one port. Mountains and forests gave way to fields. Occasionally they would see farmers tending to their crops, but the farmers kept their distance.

"It is the same in England, is it not? Village folk fear soldiers and do their best to avoid them," Edward observed to Alan.

"Yet the bastards come crying for us when enemies attack."

"They do so because they are heavily taxed."

"As they should be! We put our lives on the line for them."

"Is it truly for their sake? Or is it for the sake of whichever lord governs their land?"

"It is for God! I'm looking forward to the yet-to-be-seen reward from Him." Alan laughed.

As the sun reached its zenith, they heard a scream.

Edward and some of his men rushed ahead and saw the Nippon soldiers bracing their spears. An old woman stood before them. The middle-aged man protecting her identified himself as the chief of their village.

"The old woman stabbed our Mongolian prisoners," Zafir whispered.

She was breathing heavily as she gripped a rusty katana. Edward followed her gaze and saw the lifeless bodies of the two Mongolian soldiers lying behind a packhorse.

"What the hell was the old hag thinking? I was going to slowly torment them for more information!" Alan angrily barked.

"She claims they slaughtered her husband, children, grandchildren, and the rest of her family," Zafir told Alan.

"Where did she get the blade?" Edward asked.

"It appears she took it off a dead Mongolian soldier in the last war with the intention of one day avenging her family."

Morimune approached, listened to a subordinate while observing the woman, and walked away, without saying anything to Edward or the others.

"What did that man say?" Alan demanded.

"To pick up the sword and return her to the village. If it happened again, the village chief would be responsible," Zafir and WangSheng translated for him.

"What horseshit. No matter what she says about revenge, she just killed those two. Their hands were bound! Morimune is going to do nothing and let her go home?"

"What do you think he should have done?" Edward wanted to know.

"If we were in England, no matter how old the woman is she would be sent to prison. After that . . . well, she would be treated accordingly."

"Tell the village chief I want to hear what happened when the Mongolians attacked his village," Edward told Zafir.

The chief brought Edward to a hollow close to the hills. Edward let out an involuntary gasp. There were hundreds, if not thousands of human bones inside.

"Are they the enemies' bones?"

"The majority most likely are."

"You mean your comrades are also in there?"

"When I awoke one morning, large Mongolian ships covered the sea. There were so many ships I thought the sea between Hakata and the Goto Islands had become land. The Mongolians came for Hakata after they attacked Iki Island. Our village was caught in the raid."

"WangSheng told me that only two elderly women survived in Takashima when the Mongolians descended on that island after decimating Tsushima Island and Iki Island," Zafir said, transfixed by the sight of the hollow filled with bones.

The sun shone brightly over the gentle ripples of the ocean waves as the men talked plainly. Zafir and WangSheng translated for Edward.

"The Mongolian army landed in boats lowered from their ships. We did not have a single warrior in this village. All of them had gone to defend Hakata. The battle here was one-sided. We would run away, and the Mongolians would kill us," the chief said, staring hard at the sea.

"Then the bones in the hollow are—"

"Corpses that washed in from the ocean after the Mongolians left, corpses of women who were abducted, and corpses of our own warriors. The sea and beaches of Hakata overflowed with the dead. The waves stripped them of their clothes, and fish nibbled their bodies. We could not tell if they were friend or foe. We did not want to leave them out there, so we collected the remains in the hollow, and it became a mountain of bones."

Zafir's voice shook as he told the man's story.

"Will you not bury them?"

"We did not want to bury our comrades with the Mongolian enemies, so it ended up like this. To this day, the people of our village do not come near this place. No one wants to remember the dark horrors."

Even Alan listened to the tale in silence.

When they returned to their camp, Edward's men brought him a hand-sized cast iron ball they had found on the beach.

Zafir brushed away Alan's hand as he tried to touch it.

"I think it is a new type of weapon they use in China."

Zafir very carefully disassembled the casing. Inside the ball was a black rock-like lump.

"This is called gunpowder. If you add fire to it, it will let out a huge blast of smoke and sound. It is a truly dreadful weapon."

Putting aside the thunder crash bomb, Edward went with Zafir and WangSheng to ask the locals for more information about what had happened here. Zafir was surprised by what they heard.

"The assault from Yuan was exceedingly brutal. This country's soldiers and citizens were blindsided, since this was the first time they had battled foreign forces and encountered war tactics where enemy soldiers would surround a warrior and kill him using poison arrows and spears."

"The soldiers of Nippon also seem unfamiliar with fighting under the orders of a single commander," Edward chimed in as he remembered the battle yesterday. "The leadership necessary to defend against a surprise attack was nonexistent. Hence their forces were immediately thrown into chaos and suffered too many casualties."

After talking with the villagers, they walked back to camp. Zafir was uncharacteristically quiet.

"What's the matter?" Edward asked.

"The horrible things Alan did yesterday and that old woman killing those prisoners . . . It is overwhelming."

The sensitive pagan could not accustom himself to violence.

"Slaughter was a part of our everyday life in France, Italy, and Jerusalem. It is likely still going on. These wars are never ending."

"Then we should rid ourselves of war. Even a war in the name of God," Edward proposed. "Bloodshed will lead to peace, and a new world will dawn."

"I cannot believe that. People like to kill one another. That is the true nature of humanity. And if that is the will of your Christian God and my pagan god, then there is nothing we can do about it. We are doomed to destruction," Zafir confessed, a pained look spreading across his face.

At that moment, laughter roused them from their deep thoughts. Looking in the direction of the sound, they saw Nippon soldiers surrounding Thomas and his sailors around a bonfire.

"They are teaching Thomas' men how to use chopsticks," Zafir said.

Zafir's customary gentle face returned, and Edward saw him smile.

"The Nippon soldiers are finally opening up to some of us," Edward observed.

"In some ways the people of Genoa are like the people of Nippon. Both have small physiques."

"Where did you learn how to use chopsticks?"

"As a merchant, I had friends from Dai Viet, Song, and the like who crossed the Asian continent or set sail from India to Europe and Africa. Yuan dominated my friends' countries, and now that same Yuan has attacked this country and most likely will do so again."

Sadness washed over Zafir's face once again. War was inevitable.

Later that night, Morimune and WangSheng visited Edward and Zafir. Morimune was back to health. The man was stronger than he looked.

"I am greatly indebted to you for your aid in the battle. Many of our men were saved thanks to you," Morimune said and bowed deeply.

He took Zafir's notebook from his breast pocket.

"I return this to you."

A broad smile spread across Zafir's face. It was an expression of pure joy that Edward had never seen in Zafir. While others slept that night, Zafir opened his notebook and wrote in it by the bonfire.

The next morning, after not much rest, Zafir presented his findings and observations to Edward.

"It was the Mongolian Army that attacked this land. There is no doubt, judging by their armor, weapons, and the way they fought. The Mongolian light cavalry has unleashed their violence as far as Eastern Europe," Zafir slowly spoke as if he were digesting his own words.

"Over the last hundred years, the Mongolian Empire has repeatedly sent out their armies on expeditions all over the known world. They destroyed countless cities in Central Asia, including Samarkand, and murdered millions of people. Since Genghis Khan, the second Khagan, Ogedei Khan, lead an expeditionary force that overran all of Russia and part of Eastern Europe," he continued.

"I know of this," Edward said. "My father told me about them. They closed in on the Tatar army like a swarm and subjugated the whole country. To set an example they slaughtered the monarch and his entire family. Along with annihilating any nation that opposed them."

"Quite so," Zafir said deeply nodding his head. "They decimated the Moravians and Poles' allied forces over twenty years ago."

"The Battle of Wahlstatt."

"That is correct. If Ogedei Khan had not suddenly died, the Mongolians would have likely overrun all of Europe. By some stroke of good fortune Europe escaped from the catastrophe of subjugation." It was clear that Zafir, like Edward, also thought that it was not a god who had spared Europe, but simple good luck.

"The empire, under the fourth Khagan, Mongke Khan, then captured Baghdad. Two million lives were lost. And the Abbasid Dynasty, which had reigned for five hundred years, was destroyed. However, after such a 'victory,' a civil war split the Mongolian empire in four. One faction being the Yuan Dynasty of Mongke Khan's younger brother, Kublai Khan," Zafir said as he let out a sigh. His eyes gazed far off to the West.

"Ultimately, Mongolia created a great empire that expanded from the eastern tip of Asia to Europe. Because of this, East and West began to regularly exchange cultures. The East gained astronomy, the study of calendars, and gunnery. And the West acquired pottery and painting techniques. Truly magnificent." Despite saying this, Zafir's face darkened.

"I have heard a rumor that the Mongolian army has drawn near to France. That their cavalry is running through all of Europe."

"According to stories we heard in the village, during the battles in this nation, the Mongolians would always send in their cavalry. If that's true, how did they manage to transport so many horses? A cavalry without a horse is the same as a knight without a sword."

"We had embarked with horses, but—" Edward started to say.

After three days at sea, their horses were incapable of standing due to the sway of the ship; and after five days, all of them died because there was not enough water and feed to nourish them. The sailors happily ate the horses' remains.

"The reason the Mongolians were able to invade as far as Europe was because of their cavalry. And their powerful short bows and arrows. I have also heard that their infantry's archery is also not to be underestimated. In the battle two years ago, I do not think they had a chance to truly let loose the full impact of their power," Zafir said.

"Yet Nippon's army was victorious against them."

Edward studied Morimune, who was sitting on a rock looking out to sea, and then his warriors. He could not see in their serene forms the strength or willpower to overtake the ferocious Mongolian army. So, why did their enemy retreat? Edward's mind raced with speculation.

CHAPTER
17

They entered Hakata the next afternoon. The scene was the opposite of the blue sky, sparkling sea, and lush vegetation they had become accustomed to since arriving in Nippon. A long street now stretched before them, with shops lining both sides. People, with smiling faces, bustled to and fro. Edward did not trust his own eyes. The town was lively. It did not seem like a place that had been ravaged by war. In England and France, war-torn towns were filled with burned-out homes and littered with rotting corpses. Only a few surviving women, children, and elders made their way through that scene of death and destruction. But Hakata was different.

Brimming with curiosity, Zafir's gaze flicked left, then right. He saw that the shops were simple in design, with no walls and roofs supported by poles alone. However, within was an abundance of seafood, birds, rabbits, deer meat, rice, salt, vinegar, and honey. Other shops sold cloth and pottery.

As he walked down the street, the faces all looked the same to Edward, but it also seemed that not all of them were from Nippon. Everyone was animatedly going about their day, including suntanned and half-naked fisherman newly returned from the sea. What a contrast to the villagers he had met the day before.

"Does it not remind you of Messina?" Alan said in awe, remembering the Italian port city he had encountered en route to Jerusalem. It, too, was a meeting place for people of all races, religions, and nationalities.

"You are right," Zafir agreed. "Where sea routes intersect, people collect, prosper, and open the door to new cultures."

"But there are no followers of the Church or Islam that I can see here. This is a pagan town," Alan responded to Zafir's excitement-filled observation, as if to tear it down.

"I wonder if it is always this prosperous," Edward interjected. "Can you ask WangSheng?"

"He says the market is open on days that include the numbers three and six in the date. Today is one of those days. That's why it is so lively."

But in the shadows of the shops people puttered about wearing only scraps of cloth or wrapped in a straw mat.

"They are those whose only means of survival is from the charity of others. After the last war their numbers have increased drastically," WangSheng said, noticing where Edward's eyes had strayed.

"So, they are beggars. There were countless of them in my hometown in England and in Jerusalem. They are the people God forsakes," Alan commented.

"On the days the market is not open this place is merely a street of huts. Only dogs and birds wander along it. But because the huts can withstand rain and dew, they also serve as dwellings for the beggars," WangSheng told them.

Edward saw one of the beggars quarreling with a stray dog and throwing rocks at it. The dog stood his ground, and bared its fangs and growled at the beggar.

Morimune joined them.

"Feel free to take your time and explore Hakata. I, however, must return to the residence and report on our journey," he informed Edward and company.

"What will happen to us?" Edward asked.

"For the time being, we will wait in Hakata for Lord Kamakura's instructions. It is likely we will proceed to Kamakura once we receive his instructions." Morimune's tone indicated that Edward had no choice in the matter. WangSheng's look, as he translated, communicated the same. Edward turned and looked at the street.

"Did the battle not reach this place?" he asked.

"It did. The Hakata you see here was overrun by the Mongolians, who reduced it to ashes during their retreat," Morimune told him.

"Their retreat?"

"They had come close to reaching Dazaifu before they retreated. We must have been very frightening to them," Morimune said with a faint smile. It looked as if he himself did not believe the words he had just uttered.

Was Hakata able to rebuild itself because the destruction had not been severe? Edward wondered. *Or are the people of Nippon greater in strength and spirit than any misfortune that befalls them?*

"Are the residents aware that there are still stragglers from the defeated Mongolian army just a short distance from here?"

Zafir confirmed this and continued, "But would people gather if the town were so dangerous? The Mongolian invaders have been wiped out."

"Is that what the lord of Kamakura has been telling them?"

Zafir nodded.

"There is a proverb that truth is the will of the king. I do not sense discomfort among these people. Yet, they are not blind. If Yuan were to attack again, they would flee. The inhabitants and government officials are as astute as they come."

"Then they simply deceive one another. We should get the hell out of this country as soon as we can," Alan said and spat on the road.

As cosmopolitan as Hakata was, Morimune and Edward's entourage stood out from the crowd. At the head were the warriors on horseback, then Edward and his knights, followed by the infantry and the sailors. The packhorses brought up the rear. Exhaustion was written on every face. The townspeople gathered around to gawk and whisper. When Edward stared them down, they quickly averted their eyes and scattered.

"What are they gossiping about?" Edward asked Zafir to ask WangSheng, who shot a conflicted look at Edward.

"Whatever it is, do not worry. Just tell me," Edward petitioned. "With everything we have been through, whatever they are saying will not upset me."

"They are saying that you look filthy and smell horrible. They wonder if you are foreign beggars."

"Beggars?! Those savages," Alan's voice rang out.

But when was the last time any of them had bathed? It had been ten days since the storm at sea. Edward's skin was coated with a thick membrane of sweat and dirt that came off in clumps when he rubbed it; his hair was stiff with oil and dust. He sniffed his armpits, and drew back from the sour stench that assaulted his nose. Edward could not remember the last time he washed the clothes he was wearing. He looked down and saw that they were smeared with mud and riddled with holes. They truly looked like beggars or, worse, defeated soldiers.

"I think we might actually be the savages," Edward said full of self-mockery.

They were brought to a residence on the outskirts of the town. Enclosed by neither tall nor sturdy walls, the spacious compound of several buildings connected by long corridors was beautifully maintained.

"The estate belongs to a relative of Morimune," said Wang-Sheng, as translated by Zafir. "This is indeed a first. Normally, you would have been put in a jail cell, since you are suspicious foreigners."

"Please, wait a moment," Morimune insisted before opening a sliding door.

"You mean me?" Alan barked, realizing that Morimune was staring him down as he was about to enter the residence.

"He says that when you go inside a building you must remove your shoes," Zafir informed them.

Edward looked at his own feet. His mud-covered boots would certainly soil and damage the beautiful wooden floor before him.

"What, are the floors like a bed where a lady is waiting for me?" Alan retorted.

"The rules of our country and your own must differ. However, now that you are in our country you will follow our rules. While you may have doubts about some of them, I ask that you follow our customs while you are here," Morimune softly entreated through WangSheng.

"Of course. There are many things I have to learn about this land," Edward responded, bowing his head respectfully to Morimune. It was an etiquette he had quickly picked up since coming to Nippon.

"Pass the word about this custom to the men," Edward ordered Alan, Thomas, and Zafir.

The three nodded, but not in agreement. Dissatisfaction was evident as the order spread.

"We are about to enter the main residence. You may take off your footwear over there. Once you wash your hands and feet we shall go indoors. Please consent to this custom," Morimune said.

Alan grudgingly took off his boots while grumbling about Morimune under his breath. As the others removed their boots, an unpleasant smell wafted through the air. Edward washed his dirty, smelly feet in a bucket of water given to them. Alan and the others silently followed Edward's lead.

Upon entering the building, Edward noticed that the floor was significantly high off the ground. One side of the hallway did not have a wall and was open to an expansive garden with a small pond at its center. A long line of rooms stretched along the other side of the hallway. Each room had a tranquil beauty to it and was immaculately well-kept. Walking farther down the hallway, they were brought to a more spacious room. Another garden, surrounded by pine trees and with a small stream trickling into a small pond, lay outside this room. The garden appeared toy-like to Edward.

Edward and his men were given four rooms to use.

"You shall stay together in this residence for a brief period. It may be uncomfortable while you grow used to it, but please have patience," Morimune explained.

"Where do we piss and shit?" Alan demanded bluntly, causing the others to burst out laughing. Only Edward and Zafir frowned.

"Can we go into town, if we so wish?" Edward asked.

"For the time being, I ask that you stay within these grounds. If there is anything you need, we shall take care of it for you", Morimune said politely, before telling WangSheng something. Morimune then bowed to Edward and left.

"Who is Morimune?" Edward asked WangSheng.

"He is Adachi Morimune, a relative of the shogunate regent, Hojo Tokimune, and the son of Adachi Yasumori."

"Is he someone of high rank?"

WangSheng was taken aback by Edward's straightforward question, but smiled.

"Morimune is the cousin of the regent of the shogunate, Lord Tokimune. The regent governs this country under the Kamakura shogun. Morimune was sent to the Dazaifu office as the acting military governor of Higo province."

"Then he is related to the king? I thought he was a simple garrison commanding officer," Alan smirked. "That man does not look like his station at all. I thought he was a woman when I first saw him."

"And what about regent Tokimune?" Edward continued.

"He is the first-born of the Hojo clan that in essence run this country. He currently resides in Kamakura."

"Then he must be similar to the king of England," Edward commented.

"Actually, the emperor is the top reigning authority in Nippon, and he lives in the capital of Kyoto."

"There cannot be two kings in one country. It would cause conflict. Same as how it is unnecessary for there to be two gods in the world."

WangSheng shrugged after Zafir translated Edward's words.

"In a country in the West, there is both a king and a pope. They are seemingly the source of conflict there," WangSheng observed, almost as if talking to himself.

"For the time being, I request that you all stay within the residence. If there is anything you need, do not hesitate to ask," Zafir translated for WangSheng who left the room.

"What's to become of us?" a soldier asked.

"Sooner or later, they are going to kill us all. Until then, we should just sit back and relax," Alan joked before stretching out on the floor.

Edward also lay down. The wooden floor was hard but more comfortable than lying on stone. There was a warmth about the room, with a good and clean feeling to it. Both the ceiling and columns were made of wood. This country clearly possessed a culture different from England's with its castles made of hard, cold stone.

What is to become of us now? Are we all to be killed, just as Alan says? Edward's mind began to race as it reviewed images from their journey so far. The two Mongolian soldiers killed by that elderly woman, the mountain of bones piled in the ravine, the burial mound of severed heads, the busy shops lining the streets of Hakata, the beggars . . . but soon his thoughts grew hazy. And Edward's exhausted body was pulled into a deep sleep.

CHAPTER

18

Early the next morning the patter of footsteps padding up and down the long hallway in front of their room roused Edward.

"Are you awake?" a voice asked.

Edward rolled over and saw Zafir and WangSheng sitting across from him. The two merchants seemed to get along quite well and had formed a close bond.

"Lord Morimune will come by in the afternoon. He will likely discuss what is to happen next," WangSheng said.

"Are we to be Morimune's prisoners of war? Or perhaps slaves?" Alan asked as he raised himself up.

WangSheng glared at him.

"Not long ago, you were in a position where it would not have been unusual for you all to be beheaded. Yet, Lord Morimune has treated you with hospitality and made you feel welcome. I ask you to keep that in mind and hold your tongue."

Despite what WangSheng had told them, Morimune did not visit that afternoon.

"You said that Morimune was coming to decide whether we live or die," Alan demanded of WangSheng in the early evening.

"We want to know what is to happen," Edward said in a more measured tone of voice.

"Do you expect us to simply wait here for answers?" Alan boomed.

"At present you are guests of Lord Morimune and are being given the best treatment possible. I implore you to take these details into consideration," WangSheng said and deeply bowed his head.

He is right, Edward thought to himself. *But if things continue like this, I have no idea what trouble Alan and the others might cause.*

"Can we go into town?" one of the men called out.

"That would be difficult. However, you are at liberty within the walls of this estate."

"Oh, I understand. We will be in your 'care' for some time," Alan said with an edge in his voice.

"Is there anyone like us from Europe in Hakata?" Edward asked WangSheng.

"I do not believe so."

"Even though the town is so crowded?"

"Hakata is the busiest port in all of Kyushu Island. There are many people from Song and Goryeo who live here in their own settlements. Zhang is the most common last name among Hakata's Song residents. Hakata is also home to the Shofuku-ji Temple, which is most likely the first Zen temple in this country, built by a monk named Eisai. Furthermore, produce from the Kinai provinces is transported through the Seto Inland Sea," WangSheng began to explain. Zafir's curiosity was aroused, and he quickly wrote down all the information in his notebook.

Suddenly, loud cheers rang out. Some of Edward's soldiers and the sailors had seen movement in the garden pond. The estate's servants surrounding them looked perplexed and anxiously tried to tell the foreigners something, but the men paid no attention.

"Look there's a fish!" one of the sailors exclaimed and dived in. He caught a fish nearly as long as his arm. It was a freshwater fish that looked like it was growing a mustache.

"Light a fire. We'll cook it and feast!"

"There are more. Let's catch them all, lads."

"Stop!" Edward's voice sharply commanded. "Remember what Master Xie has told us. Whether we live or are killed depends entirely on the will of the rulers of this country. Do not forget that."

Silently, Edward's men hauled themselves out of the pond.

CHAPTER

19

The following evening WangSheng called upon Edward and told him that they would be meeting with Morimune.

"You are going by yourself?" Alan asked.

"Zafir will be with me. Without him to translate, I would understand nothing."

"It is dangerous. I will go with you," Alan said standing in WangSheng's way.

"That should be no problem. It is always necessary for nobility to have an attendant," WangSheng agreed surprisingly easily.

After walking for half an hour, they arrived at an estate surrounded by a moat and a wooden fence similar to the one where they were staying. The mansion itself, however, was considerably larger.

"This way."

A samurai, whom Edward had seen with Morimune when they first met, appeared and guided them to a large room. In the corner was a tub filled with hot water. Steam enshrouded the room.

"This is a bathhouse. A place to cleanse the body. With respect, you are quite— no—you are very filthy. We would like you to clean yourselves here."

Edward, Alan, and Zafir removed their clothes and entered the steam chamber. As they sat down, they began to sweat. When it felt like they could sweat no more, they were taken to another room. There they scrubbed their bodies with bundles of tied bamboo grass. The grime that covered their skin fell away. Next, they were guided to a room where they washed their bodies before soaking in a large tub filled with hot water. The heat of the water relaxed their muscles and eased their exhaustion. This was the first any of them had such an experience. When they exited the bathhouse, a middle-aged woman sat waiting for them. Naked, Edward could not help feeling embarrassed, but the woman offered them fresh clothes silently and without hesitation.

"What happened to my clothes?"

"They were burned. Lord Morimune said there was no way to fix the tears or rid them of lice," Zafir told Edward.

Zafir was also wearing a new Nippon kimono. The clothes seemed too small on both men, but Edward did not know if the small sizing was intentionally part of the design or not.

"Alan has also changed," Zafir said with a shrug, knowing that Alan would surely resist this new attire, which did not fit his slim physique.

"The others are waiting for us," Zafir told them via WangSheng.

CHAPTER

20

Edward, Alan, and Zafir stopped as they stared into the room they were about to enter. On each side were over twenty uniformed samurai. At their center sat Morimune. Edward recalled what WangSheng had said about Morimune being the relative of this land's ruler, Lord Tokimune.

"The new garments suit you very well. Come in. I have told everyone here how you bravely fought the Mongol soldiers and saved my life. Tonight, we shall share a meal and drink sake together," Morimune said.

"I am most grateful," Edward replied.

"Well, it doesn't look like it is poisoned. Not that I need to tell you lot that," Alan indicated, giving Zafir and the others a sidelong glance and a wink.

Edward sat beside Morimune while Alan and Zafir sat among the samurai.

"WangSheng tells me this is a most extraordinary experience. Lord Morimune is showing his gratitude to you for saving his life," Zafir told Edward in a hushed voice.

"Now, please, help yourself," Morimune told them with a smile.

Alan reached out his hand to take some food, but Zafir grabbed his wrist.

"It is uncivilized to eat with your hands."

"What the hell? You ate with your hands before we arrived here."

"Eat the way the samurai are eating."

"Meaning with those two sticks?"

"So, you complain about that, too? Thomas and Enrico have no issue using them. In fact, Enrico uses them just as well as the natives of Nippon." Enrico was the chief navigator on Thomas' ship. Growing accustomed to foreign cultures was likely easier for a sailor.

"Then it would have been better to bring them along," Alan snapped as he snatched a grilled fish by the tail and shoved into his mouth.

The samurai looked on in silence. Then Morimune reached out and took a fish by the tail and ate it the same way as Alan.

"These fish were caught in the Hakata Bay. They have a very distinct flavor. Can you taste it?" Morimune said, facing Edward but looking at Alan. "We are eating fish that feasted on drowned Mongolian soldiers."

Following Morimune's lead, the samurai also began eating with their hands. WangSheng looked on helplessly.

"I would like to have an audience with your ruler, and ask him to help us return to our homeland," Edward said to Morimune toward the end of the meal.

"Such a meeting will be granted soon enough. I hear that you were adrift for several years. There is no need to make haste. Rest here a while."

"Indeed, there is no hurry. And if I am being frank, I can see myself coming to like this place," Zafir said happily, his face flushed from drink. Beside him, Alan sat silently drinking sake. It was clear from his expression that he also did not completely hate being in Nippon, though that did not prevent him from swearing under his breath.

"I am grateful for the hospitality you have extended to us," Edward sincerely said to Morimune as he took his leave.

Edward and his two companions walked through the streets of Hakata accompanied by WangSheng and samurai bodyguards. The town was eerie late at night. There was no moon, and with only the stars for light, Hakata looked like a nest for goblins. Edward remembered what a villager had told him of the thousands of people who had been killed there.

Upon returning to the estate, Edward found his soldiers and sailors waiting with concerned looks. They were now wearing kimonos, and their faces were red from drinking sake. The group listened intently as Zafir recounted what had happened that night.

"We also drank sake," one of the men piped up. "At first glance we thought it was water, but it is more delicious."

"I prefer wine a hundredfold. I would like to teach these people what the proper taste of wine is," Alan shouted out, but no one paid him any attention.

"They are not planning on killing us then?" Thomas said with a sigh of relief hidden in his tone.

CHAPTER
21

The following morning, WangSheng came to see Edward. His gait was unsteady. Morimune had been generous with the sake the night before, and WangSheng had drunk too much.

"You and Zafir have been given permission to leave the estate whenever you wish, as long as I am with you," he told Edward and Zafir after confirming that Alan was not present. WangSheng was clearly not fond of rude and hotheaded Alan.

"Are the rest of our men not permitted to do the same?"

"There are no other people from Europe in this land. It is wise to slowly introduce yourselves. Let them wait a little longer before venturing out."

It was a reasonable request. Allowing Edward and Zafir to explore Hakata was indeed a special privilege from Morimune. He wanted them to be the first to know about his country.

"Everyone here sees us as savages!" Alan thundered as he entered."

Zafir turned around shocked at Alan's remark.

"Is it so unsightly to eat with your hands?" Alan continued.

"It seems to be the case. We are nothing but barbarians in their eyes," Zafir said.

"Then why don't they kill us? They have had more than enough opportunities to do so," Alan ranted.

"It would be killing without meaning. Doing so would be the height of savagery for them," Zafir said, although he gave the impression that he was trying to convince himself of this.

"They know nothing about catapults. And shipbuilding is beyond them. This estate's one-story wooden buildings would collapse under an attack. Ten of our soldiers could turn this whole place into a mountain of ash in half a day . . . or less."

"Is that what makes a civilization? This town is prosperous. Their clothes are clean and beautifully designed and made. If you get used to something that fits, you do not want to throw away such comfort," Zafir said.

"Yet there are naked and starving beggars here," Edward broke in.

"Our own countries have beggars. And Jerusalem has even more," Zafir responded with a sigh before continuing. "The food is also delicious and lovely."

At the mention of food, Edward realized that the usual amount of sand and dirt that had been mixed into their food when they were on the battlefield was absent here in Nippon. The food was simple, but the flavors were complex, so the seasoning could not have been salt alone. Miso soup was inedible at first because of the smell, but after a while he found its peculiar taste to his liking. The leisurely pace of a meal meant that it could be savored while peacefully enjoying a conversation. During the Crusades, Edward and his men did not have the luxury of such peacefulness. *As for sake, it was definitely more gratifying than wine . . .*

To occupy themselves when confined within the grounds of the estate, the soldiers and sailors used their knives to carve animals from blocks of wood, made dice, and gambled.

CHAPTER

22

Early one morning, a samurai bodyguard came to speak with Edward.

"Zafir, where is Dazaifu?"

"It is a two-hour ride to the south. WangSheng told me that it is the local office governing Kyushu. Its chief functions are diplomacy and defense. At one point, it was authorized to be called the Distant Imperial Court. Dazaifu oversees the judiciary and administration of the nine regions of Saikaido and the Iki, Tsushima, and Tane islands. However, people have been moving from Dazaifu to Hakata, because of the development of trade between Nippon and Song," Zafir explained in one breath.

Edward comprehended only half of what Zafir rattled off. Zafir was learning much about this country from WangSheng.

"We will be meeting a man in Dazaifu named Shoni Sukeyoshi," Edward said.

"When?"

"Now."

"You have begun to understand a fair amount of this country's language, have you not?"

"I mostly guess. If you were not by my side, I would be in trouble. Learning a new language does not come easily to me."

"I would not say that. Give yourself time, and you will be talking to the samurai guards. Obviously you have picked up the names of things."

"That is as much as I can do."

"Ah, but that is precisely the best way to learn a foreign tongue. It was the same for me," Zafir said with a gleeful smile lighting up his face.

Morimune, WangSheng, and the samurai were waiting outside with horses. Two hours later they arrived at Mizuki Castle in Dazaifu. There Morimune introduced Sukeyoshi to them.

"This is Lord Shoni Sukeyoshi, a supreme commander in the last war against the Mongolian army. He fought alongside Lord Otomo and Lord Shimazu's army," Morimune told them.

"So, these are the men who saved Lord Morimune's life. You have my deepest gratitude," Sukeyoshi said, bowing his head to them respectively. Morimune sat next to him, formally kneeling with the tops of his feet flat on the floor. Sukeyoshi was a higher rank than Morimune.

"And you have our deepest gratitude for bringing us to Hakata after we were lost at sea and drifted to this land," Edward responded.

"I hear you came from a far-off land called E-u-ro-pa before you crossed the great sea and arrived in Nippon. You must have faced a great many hardships on your journey. Two years ago, our country suffered great injury from the assaults of the Mongolian military forces. Because of this, our people are often hostile toward foreigners. I ask you to forgive them for this."

"I understand that Dazaifu has the responsibility of governing and defending Kyushu."

"Yes, that was the case once," Sukeyoshi said, with a tortured expression.

"In the previous war, Dazaifu almost became a battlefield. The Mongolians had annihilated our forces and were rampaging across Hakata, tormenting us with grotesque weapons and strategies we had never experienced before. Dazaifu was next. Then one night they set fire to Hakata, boarded their ships, and fled. To this day, I do not understand why," Sukeyoshi finished with a light sigh. It was basically the same story Edward had been hearing.

"What do you know of the Mongols?" Sukeyoshi asked Edward.

"My men and I fought to recover the Holy Land of my people. Our foes were the pagan Saracens. Thus, my knowledge of Mongolia is limited. However, I have heard that when Mongolians invade a country they massacre not only soldiers but common people as well. The women and children they do not kill are captured and turned into slaves. They sack the land's treasure and food, then leave. Mongols fight to the death for the sake of raping and pillaging. The cities and villages they pass through are set ablaze and turned to ash."

Edward felt dizzy as he told Sukeyoshi about Mongolian atrocities.

Were the Crusaders any better than the Mongols? Did they not do the same? he thought. *The noble purpose of reclaiming the Holy Land in the name of God soon vanished in the heat of battle. Was it truly noble to annihilate pagans? In the end, it was all an act of greed—and a matter of survival.*

"Send merchants to Goryeo or Song or talk to the Song merchants in Nippon. They have eyes, ears, and mouths. They can become a stream of information for you," Edward said.

"We have already exhausted those means," Sukeyoshi responded.

"Then you need to try again," Edward countered.

Edward did not speak of the news he had heard from the two Mongolian soldiers. Nor did Zafir. After dinner at Sukeyoshi's residence, they returned to Hakata, where Alan was waiting for them.

CHAPTER

23

"Where did you go?" Alan demanded.

"To Dazaifu."

"What does that lot plan to do with us?"

"We did not discuss that. They wanted to hear what we know about the Mongols."

"Isn't Kublai Khan preparing a second attack? That's what those Mongolian soldiers said."

Alan looked at Zafir for confirmation. Zafir had been his interpreter during the questioning.

"You have been going into town and making new merchant friends. And you have been talking to WangSheng. Any new information from any of them?" Alan questioned.

"I have also wanted to ask you about this," Edward said directly to Zafir.

Zafir took a moment to think and organize his words.

"According to what the merchants from Goryeo have told me, the people of Goryeo are building a large number of ships under orders from Yuan, the Mongolian Dynasty. The citizens suffer from the labor and taxation to create such ships."

"It is just as those two Mongolians said."

"Several thousand ships are being constructed. Far more than during their last invasion. Soldiers are gathering from all across the Southern Song Dynasty."

"When will they invade?"

"I am not entirely sure, but I believe as soon as preparations are complete."

"It takes time to construct that many ships. Perhaps three, maybe four years. Yet, in the meantime, this country carries on as if it did not have a care in the world. Are they that confident they will be able to drive back a force that size?"

"I think those in power are in a state of panic."

"You mean those in Kamakura?"

"That is why Sukeyoshi interrogated us about the Mongols."

"At any rate, all this talk has nothing to do with us. If they have no intention of letting us go, then I say we steal a ship and sail the hell back to Europe," Alan said as if this were easy to do. But as they well knew, Nippon did not have a ship that could withstand the rigors of traversing the ocean. At best there might be a ship that could handle crossing over to Goryeo.

"If we can get back to the mainland, then we can do whatever we want. We can travel by foot along the trade routes to Europe, or search for another ship and follow the sea route we took originally."

Alan looked at Zafir with a confident gleam in his eye. Zafir silently nodded.

CHAPTER

24

They had been in Hakata a week. During that time Edward and his men were slowly introduced to the town, and eventually Morimune granted both Edward's soldiers and Thomas' sailors permission to walk freely around Hakata. Whether it was because Morimune trusted them not to escape, or because he thought it impossible for them to leave Nippon on their own, Edward could not say. In any case, they had become accustomed to life in Hakata.

Edward looked up at the clear vibrant blue sky and took a deep breath. It was refreshing to be outside on this sunny spring day. Edward, Alan, and Zafir, with WangSheng as their guide, were walking along the Imazu Coast, where the Mongolians had once disembarked. The beach was filled with laborers carrying earth and stones. They were building ramparts to defend against the future Mongolian attack.

"They are simply piling up heaps of dirt and stones. The wall is too low. A single shot from a catapult, and it would fall to pieces in an instant," Alan observed.

He was right. The earthen walls were too thin, and the stones lined up were too small. If a soldier climbed on another soldier's back, he could easily scale the barrier and drop to the other side. The walls needed to be taller and thicker, and the rocks several times larger and heavier.

"If just one part of a rampart is weak, then the rest of it is weak. The enemy will always find and penetrate the weak spot," Edward said.

"Lay off it. Even if the people of Nippon were slaughtered, God wouldn't give a damn. They're only pagans," Alan said.

Continuing their walk, they met a fisherman. His left leg was missing, and traces of severe burns scarred his right arm.

"Ask him about the Mongolian invasion," Edward requested, turning to WangSheng.

When he did not reply to any of WangSheng's questions, the merchant forcibly held the fisherman's good arm to give him some money. The man pushed himself away, and several copper coins fell to the sand.

"We are going to strike down the bastards who did that to you," Alan yelled as he pointed to the fisherman's missing leg. After Alan's words were translated, he looked out to sea for a moment before he spoke.

"It was morning, and I had gone to the beach after waking up . . . I thought my eyes must have gone funny. The Mongolian ships filling up Hakata Bay looked like they covered the whole horizon. Those bastards had taken Iki Island and killed all the men. Women and children were hanging by ropes off the sides of the ships. The ropes ran through bloody holes cut in their palms. It was a picture of hell itself." The fisherman glared at the horizon as if he could still see the Mongolian ships.

"They killed my two sons and kidnapped my wife and daughter. When I tried to stop them, they stabbed my leg with a spear. I could not move, so they poured oil on me and lit me on fire."

Alan's face was unusually serious as he listened.

"What will you do if the Mongolians invade again?" he asked.

The fisherman was silent. He gripped his cane as his hands shook with fear, or perhaps anger. Edward could not be sure.

"We will protect you," Alan said in a low voice.

"What!" Zafir choked out.

The fisherman turned to go. His lips quivered, and he was muttering under his breath as he hobbled away.

"What did he say?" Alan asked, looking at both Zafir and WangSheng.

"He said, 'I will kill them all. Not a single Mongolian soul will leave here alive,'" Zafir translated from WangSheng.

"Did you mean what you said to the fisherman?" Zafir wanted to know.

"Did I say something?" Alan feigned ignorance, and Zafir knew better than to pursue the inquiry any further.

Edward and the others then stopped to speak to a samurai. He had fought during the invasion, but the reality of what he experienced differed greatly from that of the villagers and fisherman. The samurai regaled them with stories of courageous exploits as the samurai warriors, obsessed with glory, drove back the Mongolian forces. *Whom should I believe? What really happened during that first invasion?* Edward wondered.

Edward and his companions climbed to the top of a dune to get an overview of the bay. The rampart precariously snaked below them. The sea was calm and quiet.

"Why did the Mongolians not set up camp on land?" Edward asked, almost to himself.

The first thing they should have done after disembarking the ships was make camp inland close to the shore. The Mongolian army should also have pitched camp on the Hakata coastline. That way they could have transported food and weapons from the ship to their inland operations. However, from what Edward had heard, the Mongolians did none of this. The army simply invaded Hakata, and in one night set fire to the town and fled in their ships. *Why?*

"I gather the samurai did not know how to fight against Yuan and struggled in the battle on the coast. That said, they fervently resisted the invasion," Zafir told them.

"You mean Nippon's army was able to push back the Mongolian forces?"

"I do not believe it. If I had a hundred good men at my side, I could capture this country myself," Alan said as he watched the samurai giving orders to the workers constructing the rampart.

"Yuan may have been driven away because they underestimated the soldiers of Nippon, just as you are doing now," Edward responded.

"But look at those longbows," Alan said with some contempt. "They draw them on horseback! How accurate can they be? And that dress-like heavy iron armor. It would break a horse's back."

Edward thought the same. However, he could not help but feel that these samurai had an immeasurable power and emotional strength. In contrast, the Mongolian army may have simply been prudent. Their short bows were light. Their helmets were made of leather, not metal. They resembled the Roman army when they attacked and retreated to the sound of drums and gongs. With a capable commander they could be a formidable force, but without such a leader they were no more than a disordered mob.

"The Mongolian forces use short bows so they can quickly load arrows one after another," Zafir said. "But those bows lack power, so they make up for it by smearing the arrowheads with poison. Even if they graze a foe, they can inflict great damage. Like the arrow that struck Lord Morimune."

Back on the beach, Edward approached one of the samurai guarding the rampart construction. The samurai was cautious at first, but immediately became friendly once WangSheng mentioned Morimune's name. It seemed they were already well known among the Hakata samurai as the foreigners who saved Morimune's life.

"Lend me a bow," Edward said, as he mimed shooting an arrow.

The samurai shot him a curious look but understood his meaning. He took a bow from one of his subordinates and gave it to Edward.

"The design makes it difficult to load and fire arrows in rapid succession. The arrows are also too long, and you cannot carry very many."

"So, both bow and arrows are unfit for battle. Give it here." Alan took the bow and shot an arrow toward the sea. It flew out about thirty to forty yards before it fell into the water.

"You try it," Alan challenged the laughing samurai as he shoved the bow back into his hands. The samurai readied the bow and fired his arrow. The arrow flew far past the spot where Alan's arrow fell and eventually disappeared into the ocean.

"Looks like it flew over a hundred yards. The bow offers excellent distance, in spite of being hard to handle."

"However, as Zafir pointed out, its power is superior to that of the Yuan short bow," WangSheng said, defending the Nippon longbow. Edward took the weapon again and tested its balance. To master this bow clearly took power and skill.

"Lord Kamakura encourages the gokenin, vassals of the Kamakura shogunate, to learn martial arts. The arts of archery and horsemanship are the most esteemed. The Nippon military force is a rare army in this world. The standard size of the bows Nippon warriors use is seven and a half feet, and the arrows are three feet long," WangSheng further explained.

The bow was a head taller than Edward.

"We also have longbows in my country, but they are no longer than six and a half feet. Is not seven and a half feet too long for the people of this land?"

"They compensate for the difficult handling and imbalance with daily physical training. Both sides of the bow are carved from wood, then covered with two sheets of bamboo to maintain its toughness. The bamboo is carbonized which produces a strong, resilient force."

Alan crossed his arms and listened intently as WangSheng continued.

"Before Minamoto Yoritomo established the shogunate in Kamakura, there was a warrior with an exceedingly strong arm, named Tametomo. His bow was eight shaku and five sun—eight and a half feet—and his arrows were 15 bundles—four and a third feet—long. The story goes that it took eight men to string his bow, and that his arrow once pierced through the armor of three oncoming warriors at the same time. His legend may be exaggerated to some extent, but there is no mistaking the power and range of his bow. It was the best. Many warriors today use what is called a five-person bow, or even an eight-person bow, which takes four people to bend the bow and one person to attach the string to the upper and lower limbs while it is being made."

WangSheng paused and looked at the samurai standing on the coastline.

"It takes them many years to be able to freely use the longbows they carry. That is why they are so disciplined and train every day."

"So, Nippon longbows are powerful, but difficult to use. And Mongolian short bows are easy to handle, but lack power."

"Exactly."

"Then each has a strength and a weakness," Edward muttered.

CHAPTER

25

After dinner that night, Zafir took Edward aside. "Please ready yourself to go out," he whispered.

As they walked through the darkened streets of Hakata, Zafir grumbled.

"The warriors of this country are prideful and pigheaded. They think their culture and weapons are superior to all others and refuse to accept anything different."

"And here I thought they were supposed to have flexible minds."

Edward thought of Morimune, who had often listened to him.

"Religion is the only thing they are flexible in," Zafir griped. "There are too many gods in this country."

Zafir guided them out of the town as they talked. Eventually, they came to a watermill in the moonlight. Zafir stopped in front of the watermill's hut.

"This is—"

Edward gasped when he stepped inside. The torch Zafir held illuminated a mountain of bows and arrows.

"There are five hundred bows and over thirty thousand arrows here. In only one day, the Mongolians rained these arrows down on Hakata, first firing them from their ships at the samurai on the coast. There were some among the samurai who intentionally got hit by arrows as a show of bravery. But since no one knew that the arrowheads were poisoned, many were killed that day. Even after landing, the Mongolians continued to sweep people down with their short bows."

Edward could not tear his eyes away from the mass of arrows. Zafir nodded. Perhaps they were thinking the same thing. *Using this many arrows may have been the reason why the Mongolians retreated. They simply ran out of arrows. But why would they fire all their arrows on the first day of the invasion? No, they must have had a battle plan.*

"They can still be used," Edward said as he took an arrow from a bundle and examined it.

"A Hakata merchant I have become acquainted with was tasked by the government to dispose of them. He told me the Mongolian leather helmets and armor have been burned, and that their swords were melted down and turned into hoes and sickles. However, the bows and arrows remain intact, because the government would like to find some other use for them instead of destroying them. The 'use' he mentioned must be for the next Yuan invasion."

"Are these to be used by Nippon to fight against Yuan? Or are they to be given back to Yuan when they next invade Nippon?"

Zafir had no answer.

Edward examined a bow. The string had been cut, but if a new one were attached, the weapon would be as good as new. The arrowheads had become rusted and brittle, and half of the arrow feathers had fallen out, but if these were also fixed, they could be fired.

"Please be careful," Zafir cautioned. "Those arrowheads were once dipped in poison. It is best not to pick them up."

"What does your merchant friend intend to do?"

"What do you think he should do? He came to me for advice."

Edward was about to ask if this merchant friend was Xie WangSheng but stopped himself.

"This is an arrow befitting a nation of cavalry soldiers. The Mongolians have outdone themselves," Zafir commented.

"But to dip them in poison is—"

"There are no cowards or heroes in war. You of all people should know this," Zafir said calmly. They were the words of a merchant who had seen conflict everywhere he had traveled.

"If they are burned, the poison from the arrowheads will spread in the smoke. The best thing to do is bury them."

"It will take over a year for them to corrode if they are buried. The poison will end up polluting the land. I said we would find a way to dispose of them," Zafir said, turning to look again at the mountain of bows and arrows.

Edward silently nodded.

CHAPTER

26

"Prepare to leave," one of Morimune's subordinates informed Edward. "We depart for Kamakura early tomorrow. A letter has arrived from Kamakura. Regent Hojo Tokimune wishes to meet with you at once."

"We can leave immediately. We are ready," Edward said.

"Has the invasion begun?" Edward heard Alan shout as the sound of his approaching footsteps grew nearer. "They must want us to wash our necks and wait. Well, I am not going to just stand here and let myself be killed. I will take several of those samurai bastards down with me," Alan raged.

As the day progressed, the number of people visiting the estate increased. Stacks of boxes were piled in the gardens waiting to be packed.

At midday, Edward, Alan, and Zafir were escorted to Morimune's residence, where servants were also scurrying about and carrying out load after load to the packhorses. In the garden, Edward saw more than ten open boxes.

"These contain the items salvaged from your ship. We return them to you, with the exception of your weapons," Morimune said.

"If you exclude our swords, spears, bows, and arrows, all that is left are compasses and armor."

"We will look after your weapons."

"What will you do with the catapults? They are too big to transport. And have already taken a great deal of damage. Any more and they will be beyond repair," Zafir cut in as he examined the disassembled catapults.

"We will take the one with the least damage. Lord Tokimune seems very interested in this machine since he has heard of the slings that Yuan also uses. If we can bring the machine, he surely would be pleased," Morimune said.

"And what of the other one?"

"We will burn it," Morimune responded matter of factly, before ordering his subordinates to carry out the weapons. Edward noticed the faint exchange of looks that passed between Zafir and WangSheng.

CHAPTER

27

Later that night, Zafir asked Edward and Alan to leave the estate with him. They walked for a short time before seeing a light in the distance. Several men stood guard around an ox cart by the side of the road. They carried katanas, but they were not samurai. They bowed to Zafir the moment they saw him.

"What is this?"

"These are the servants tasked with the incineration of the catapult. You were disappointed it was to be burned, no?" Zafir said. He lifted a corner of the woven mat covering the cart and revealed the catapult that Morimune had ordered to be burned. "Thanks to the help of one of my merchant friends, we were able to salvage it."

There was no mistaking this 'friend' was Xie WangSheng.

They led the cart to the watermill Edward and Zafir had visited the night before, and carried the broken catapult to a corner of the hut and covered it with the woven mat. It blended in with the other rubble stored in the small room.

"This could be a great help to us in an emergency," Zafir said.

"We should bring it now. If we had it with us, I would be more reassured," Alan said looking reluctantly at the catapult.

"Not to worry, Alan. I have the blueprint to make another stored in here," Edward laughed and tapped his forehead with an index finger.

Thomas and the rest of the soldiers and sailors met them on their return.

"What is to become of us when we are brought to Kamakura?" Thomas asked Edward in a serious tone.

"I have not been told yet. But I think no harm will come to us in Kamakura just as no harm has come to us here in Hakata," he responded, even though he had no basis in fact for saying so.

"I have heard that last year an envoy from Yuan was summoned from Hakata to Kamakura, where he was met with a sword that cut off his head. He was apparently an envoy of high station. One of these days they are going to do the same to us."

There was truth in what Alan said. Nippon was a country whose land and people had been crushed by a foreign army. For them to spare the lives and send home a band of mysterious foreigners who happened to wash up on their shores seemed inconceivable even to Edward. If he were in their position, he would have decapitated all of them without hesitation.

"Then we should escape. If we could just steal a ship from the harbor, we would be fine," one of the sailors called out.

"Not everyone would be killed. We are seamen after all," Thomas said to calm the rattled sailor.

"Whether you are a soldier or a sailor, we are all the same to the bastards of this country. Would they even try to tell the difference? We are all foreigners, and therefore their enemy."

"I have a pregnant wife and three children waiting for me at home. I have to get back to them alive no matter what," Enrico, the usually jovial chief navigator, exclaimed as he fought back tears. He was known to talk of nothing but his family. Unrest spread among the sailors.

"Protest to the government officials of this land that we are different from the Mongolians," a sailor suggested, turning to Zafir who was the only calm one in the room. After traveling around the world for as long as he had, he was used to affairs such as these.

"The people here already know that we are different. Otherwise why are we still alive?" Zafir said.

"Then why won't they let us go home? Why do they need to bring us to Kamakura?"

"They wish to understand who we are and find out more about us."

"So, they have no intention of killing us?"

"That depends on whether there will be more profit for our captors to let us live, or more profit to kill us."

It might have been Edward's imagination, but he felt that the number of guards patrolling the garden had increased. A group of castaway foreigners gathering and arguing late at night was no trivial matter.

"Let us think more about this tomorrow. For now, I do not believe that there will be any significant changes to our circumstances," Zafir said to reassure the men. But they remained unconvinced.

CHAPTER

28

The next day they were roused before sunrise. More than fifty samurai were in the garden led by Morimune who sat astride his horse in full armor, just as he had when Edward first met him.

"Move out to Kamakura," he ordered.

Morimune marched the men to Hakata Bay, where three medium-sized ships awaited them in the harbor.

"Who will travel in each ship has already been decided," he announced. Edward and his men were then split into three groups and taken to their respective ships.

"Do you think they will send us to different locations?" Thomas asked Edward, worry written on his face. The two of them had been assigned to separate ships. Sensing Thomas' concern, Morimune spoke to the sailor.

"Do not worry. These ships are not much different from your own. We will first head to Naniwa. There we will secure more fresh water and food and then sail for Kamakura. We should arrive in

Naniwa in three days, five at most. The sea is calm this time of year. I hope you enjoy the voyage."

Edward, Alan, and Zafir had been assigned to the same ship as Morimune. Perhaps owing to Morimune's thoughtfulness. Or perhaps because he wanted to keep those most capable of dangerous actions and ideas close to him.

That night, Edward and Alan leaned over the railing at the ship's stern and looked out on the calm dark sea. The ship swayed gently. Compared to the journey they had experienced when they left Alexandria, this was like sailing on a lake.

"Let us commandeer the ship and get the hell out of here," Alan proposed.

"And if we fail, what then? Even if we succeed, we have no idea what would happen to the others on the other ships."

"Thomas and his crew must be thinking the same thing. The farther up the coast of this country we are brought, the farther away from our homeland we get."

"We meet with the ruler of this land in just over ten days."

"I have no desire to meet with the bastard."

"I will ask him to send us home. It has been five years since we left England. Surely you have the patience to wait a while longer."

"I am going to escape even if it means I have to do it on my own."

"Even if you take over the ship, where would you go with a ship of this size?" a voice from behind spoke out.

They turned around and found Zafir staring back at them.

"For the time being, your life is not in danger. If they were going to cut off your head, they would have done so by now. You should wait and see what opportunities arise," Zafir said in a quiet voice, taking his place between the two men by the railing.

"Lord Morimune is a wise man. He overlooks nothing."

Edward and Alan followed Zafir's gaze and noticed samurai with bows nonchalantly standing at the bow and stern. More samurai stood at the entrance to the ship's cabin. Morimune may have spoken comforting words, but he was nevertheless keeping an eye on them. Most likely it was the same on the other ships. *I pray Thomas and the others do not attempt to fight or make a run for it*, Edward thought.

Life aboard the ship was both unusual and surprising for Edward and his men. Many of the sailors' garments, hairstyles, and meals were new to them. Zafir, in particular, showed curiosity about everything and did his best to become acquainted with every new aspect of this culture. He wrote everything down in his notebook. The beautiful scenery observed from the deck, the sailors who operated the ship, even the weather and color of the sea were all of interest to him.

"Can this really be the ocean?" Edward observed. "It is more like a river with land to the left and to the right."

"We are currently on the Seto Inland Sea sailing between two bodies of land. Beyond this point is Naniwa, our first destination. Kamakura lies far beyond the land on the left," Zafir said with difficulty, attempting to include words from the Nippon language as he spoke.

"I learned from a sailor," he explained. "We began to talk while I was looking out at the mainland this morning. He has become a valuable teacher."

"You have a lot of teachers," Edward said.

He, too, had been picking up words on the journey. Whenever he could, he would ask the samurai and Nippon sailors questions about their clothes, footwear, hairstyles, katana, and work. By the time they made port in Naniwa, Edward was able to communicate in basic Japanese. This shocked not only Morimune, but also Zafir.

"So, it is not only combat you excel in, but scholarly talents as well," Zafir praised him earnestly.

CHAPTER

29

"The rampart in Hakata is only half-complete," Adachi Yasu-mori reported solemnly.

Tokimune recalled the topography of Hakata. He had never been to Hakata, but ever since the envoy from Yuan had come, he had studied the map of the port city countless times and had etched it into his memory. He knew every cove, hill, and stream. In the last war, when he received word from Hakata, he summoned that sight again and again. Hakata Bay, stretching all the way to No-konoshima Island and Shikanoshima Island, even appeared in his dreams. Further away from the two islands, all the inhabitants on Iki Island had all been massacred or kidnapped as slaves. He was not going to let that happen a second time. Tokimune was prepared to do whatever it took to ensure this.

"Make haste! Yuan will attack soon," Tokimune said vehemently.

"But there have been a large number of complaints, my lord."

"Are they still complaining about their rewards? They would do well to properly understand the situation we are in."

"Many of the gokenin vassals are dissatisfied with their lack of income. Many have only been given war expenditures and no rewards."

Tokimune pondered for several seconds. *Not everyone fought to protect this country of Nippon. A great many fought only for the compensation he would receive. Yet they all put their lives on the line in the fight against Yuan. Reward and Service. These values shape the bond between the Kamakura shogun and the gokenin. If that bond were to break, then no one would come the next time they are called to battle. The lord of Kamakura must be fair to all samurai. Even I could not rush to Kyushu the last time. My hands were full with governing the samurai in Kamakura. When Yuan attacks again, I must go to Kyushu and take command. Until then I will make the government here as sturdy as a rock and prevail in the power struggles within the family and the Imperial Court.*

"What about that Buddhist priest, Nichiren?" Yasumori asked, interrupting Tokimune's thoughts and changing the subject.

"Is he still circulating that nonsense?"

"The foreign invaders arrived, as he predicted, but not the end of Nippon. Nichiren's following has grown," Yasumori said.

"It is unwise to let him be. He is a danger to our government."

Nichiren is not wrong, however. The Mongolian invasion was a national crisis. I need the samurai and citizens of Nippon to band together and fight against the invaders. They must completely defeat Yuan this next time.

"Is it advisable to leave it in the hands of Lord Yoritsuna once again?" Commander Tairano Yoritsuna was the head of Tokimune's inner circle. He had suppressed Nichiren's disciples and banished Nichiren to Sado Island for attacking other denominations and criticizing the shogun.

"And what about the foreign warriors and sailors who washed up on our shores?" Tokimune asked, ignoring Yasumori's question.

"They have left Hakata and should be here in ten days. I am surprised to hear that they hail from a country farther west than Yuan."

"Does this mean our land is vulnerable to even more foreign threats?"

"As soon as they arrive in Kamakura, they should be beheaded. No matter where they drifted from, it is obvious they came to spy on our nation."

"Let us meet them first. We can always make that decision later," Tokimune said.

At first, Tokimune had written a letter to Morimune ordering the foreigners to be beheaded. However, he tore it up when he received a second letter from Morimune with only one sentence written on it: *They saved my life.* It would not be too late to decide their fate after he met with them.

"So, their homeland is farther west than India. The world stretches out that far, huh?" Tokimune murmured as if to himself.

"They could have heard about our war with Yuan. That the nation Yuan attacked was in the East. And so they sent out men to find out how vulnerable and easy to conquer our country would be."

"The Yuan Dynasty . . . and foreigners from lands far away in the West . . . It seems Nichiren's ramblings were not altogether lies."

"Do not talk foolishness," Yasumori admonished.

"The presence of these foreigners might reopen the debate on sending our men overseas on military campaigns."

"As soon as they arrive in Kamakura they should be decapitated immediately."

"No, bringing them here could help strengthen our defenses," Tokimune said cutting off Yasumori. "You have to bear in mind that there are countless barbarians who have their eyes on our land. We need more power than we have now for Kyushu's defense."

The world is vast. One day, I want to see these foreign nations for myself. But before that, I must be the foundation for the world of the samurai here in Kamakura. This was the mission my father entrusted to me. To do so, I killed my own brother, Tokisuke. I have become both the demon and the snake. I am prepared to be as coldhearted as I must be to accomplish this. Tokimune sighed softly while contemplating the stream in his garden.

TOKIMUNE

CHAPTER

30

As the ship left the channel in Naniwa, the river-like Seto Inland Sea gave way to the open ocean. Edward, Zafir, and WangSheng stood portside, looking out at the expanse of land before them.

"Have you been to Kamakura, WangSheng?" Edward asked.

"I have been several times with Lord Morimune for about a month each time."

"Then you must know it well."

"Kamakura is the samurai capital. Two hundred thousand people live there. As far as I can tell, it is one of the most prosperous cities in the world," WangSheng said.

A mountain with gentle sloping sides loomed in the distance. It was unlike any mountain that Edward had ever seen.

"That is Mount Fuji," Zafir told Edward. "I have heard it is the tallest peak in Nippon. And a volcano. Some of the elders say that it was still smoking several decades ago. But I'm not sure if there is any truth in what they say."

"It's beautiful. There is elegance and refinement within its magnificence."

"I agree. I think the people of this country have a spirit akin to that mountain."

"Which direction is Kamakura?"

WangSheng pointed north.

"At first, Morimune and I would take an overland route. Starting from Kyushu, we would head along the Seto Inland Sea to Naniwa and the imperial capital, Kyoto. Then we would head out to the coast along the lake in Omi. From there, we would go north the same as we are proceeding now. Eventually, we would reach Kamakura fourteen days after traveling along the Omi, Mino, Owari, Mikawa, Totomi, and Suruga roads."

"Then traveling by ship is faster?"

"It is if there are no storms at sea," WangSheng nodded in agreement.

"Kamakura is a natural fortress whose front faces the ocean while mountains enclose its other three sides. They cleared away parts of the mountains and created narrow passes, called kiridoshi, through the hilly terrain as entrances to Kamakura. They call them Kamakura's Seven Entrances. The roads are named Gokuraku-ji, Daibutsuzaka, Kewaizaka, Kamegayatsu, Kobukurozaka, Asahina, and Nagoe."

"So, they act as checkpoints into the city?"

"That is correct. The Inamuragasaki Road once ran along the steep coast and acted as the front door when one arrived from Kyoto. However, the path has become very dangerous. Rough waves have eroded and cracked the cliffs. It is rarely used now."

"It seems the best way to travel is by boat from Kyushu. Yet, there are still many people who enter Kamakura from inland, no?" Edward indirectly asked. He wanted to know all the routes to Kamakura in case Yuan attempted to attack Honshu from Kyushu.

"Before Inamuragasaki, the safest route was along the valley from Shichirigahama Beach through the Gokuraku-ji kiridoshi, which lands you in front of Yuigahama Beach. From there, you would pass through Yuigahama and head north to Wakamiya Oji Street and enter the center of the city."

"Does Kamakura have a harbor?"

"Hundreds of ships are connected to the beach at Yuigahama, which overlooks the ocean. Kamakura's port is similar to Otsu City's in the Omi province. The harbor is bustling with throngs of ships and traders in the southeast corner of the city. The city itself is lined with thousands of houses that seemingly stretch as far the Oyodo River in the capital. Despite not being built on a vast plot of land, the town is formed by the numerous roads that lead in all directions. All the gokenin residences are collected around the ministry. You'll find that Kamakura is equally as flourishing as Hakata," WangSh-eng said plainly in a tone of voice that greatly resembled Zafir's.

Edward nodded as he listened. He understood that this country had a rich culture and was prosperous. However, he had yet to fully understand its people. They were outwardly calm, serene even, but he sensed that there was something unfathomable concealed within them. The thought created an uneasiness in Edward that stuck in the back of his mind.

The night before they docked in Kamakura, Edward met with Morimune.

"There's something I'd like to ask you," he said in opening the conversation.

"Please ask me anything."

Morimune's expression stiffened at Edward's formal demeanor.

"Is the rumor true? Was a Yuan envoy beheaded after being brought from Dazaifu to Kamakura?"

"If you mean Du Shizhong, then it is true. Once before, a Yuan emissary came to spy on our land, and that apparently led to the Mongolians' first invasion. We decided that Du Shizhong had come to our country for the same reason, and so he was beheaded, Morimune said candidly.

"You should be well aware that we have no such intentions. Our ship ran aground, and we happened upon this land by chance. We are not spies."

"I am aware of this," Morimune said, frowning slightly. "But final judgment will be left to Lord Tokimune and the Hyojoshu."

"The Hyojyoshu?"

"As the regent of the shogunate, Lord Tokimune is the head of the Hyojyoshu in Kamakura. The Hyojoshu is a group of prominent gokenin vassals who advise the regent. The details of you drifting ashore to our country will be discussed at one of their meetings."

"After that, they will help us return to our home country?"

"I hope that will be the case," Morimune said, choosing his words carefully. Edward tried, but he could pry no more information out of Morimune.

When they arrived in Kamakura, they disembarked on the western edge of Yuigahama and proceeded into the city. On the bustling main street, Edward noticed a number of samurai wearing splendid kimonos with long swords hanging from their hips. The merchants here, Edward observed, did not seem as prosperous as those in Hakata, Yet there was a sense of significance and gravitas about this political center. Just as WangSheng had described, the city was enclosed by three large mountains. The town was formidably built against enemy attack.

"Authorities in Kamakura rectify injustices, issue directives to punish wickedness, and govern the whole country. Even though the people here are proud, they are also righteous, knowing that the eyes of the regent of the shogunate are ever present. The residents of Kamakura keep the entrances of their homes unlocked," Morimune proudly explained. WangSheng nodded fervently as he translated for Edward and Zafir.

"Where the hell is this country he's talking about? I can't see it at all here," Alan said, his voice laced with sarcasm.

Just as in Hakata the streets were lined with shops. However, there were far more beggars, as well as what appeared to be abandoned dead people littering the streets. Edward thought it was likely because Kamakura was a more populated city, but the cause went beyond that.

"Unfortunately, the last several years of civil war have swollen the number of poor. Many have lost all their family and have resorted to begging in order to survive," Morimune explained.

Edward was reminded of the villages that had turned into battlefields during the Crusades. The annihilated villages overflowed with people with lost limbs and women and children forced into beggary. Sadness and hatred permeated those villages. The knights and soldiers brought about such misfortune, and it was always the people who were trampled down and left to mourn and weep.

A deep voice rang out from the public square and interrupted Edward's reverie. Impoverished-looking merchants, farmers, and laborers gathered around the speaker.

"Who is that?" Edward asked Morimune.

"He is a bonze, an agitator who leads the populace astray."

"A bonze?"

"Bonzes convey the word of god. In that, they are very similar to Catholic priests," WangSheng told Zafir to tell Edward.

"I would say they are closer to monks, actually," Zafir added.

"They teach the Buddhist doctrine. But they do not interpret it heedlessly," Morimune chimed in.

"Jesus also walked among the poor and preached the word of God," Edward said and pushed aside a soldier who tried to prevent him from getting closer to the monk. Morimune watched silently.

"What is he saying?" Edward asked once he realized that Zafir and WangSheng were standing next to him.

"Let's go. It's just Buddhist nonsense," WangSheng scoffed. But as he turned to leave, Edward grabbed his arm. The man shouting out in his sand-colored vestment and the earnest faces of the listening crowd had captivated Edward.

"That is the monk Nichiren. He is preaching the Lotus Sutra," Zafir told him.

"What's that?"

"A type of religion."

"Similar to Islam?"

"It is a sect of the teachings of Buddha. It is pagan, to put it simply."

"Nenbutsu Mugen Zen Tenma, Shingon Bokoku, Ritsu Kokuzoku," the filthy, yet strangely intimidating, monk shouted out to the crowd. Many cheered in agreement, while others mocked him and frowned in disagreement.

"Listen! Those who recite the prayers of Nenbutsu Buddhism will fall into the hell of uninterrupted suffering. Zen Buddhism is the extension of demons of the sixth heaven in the realm of desire who prevent you from doing good. Shingon Buddhism will lead to the destruction of our nation. And those who believe in Ritsu Buddhism are traitors," Nichiren's oddly pleasant voice echoed throughout the square and resounded deep within Edward.

What was this? It was if he had heard it before on his travels in England, Jerusalem, and other sacred places. The masses would delight in that voice, and occasionally raise their own voices in anger.

"He is self-indulgently slandering other sects. It would be best not to commit that to memory," someone said next to Edward. He turned around and saw that Morimune had come unnoticed and stood beside him.

"Does he also criticize the king?"

"That is why he is a problem."

"Why don't you kill him then?"

"Killing, or the destruction of any living thing, is a heinous act in Buddhist doctrine. And he is a monk. Though I may not be perfect, I still follow the teachings of Buddha. I cannot kill as I please."

"It is the same in my country," Edward said while feeling a strong sense of contradiction. *How many people have I killed in the name of God, and how much more of God's forgiveness do I therefore need?*

"The Lotus Sutra is the only true teachings of Buddha. True Buddhism is only contained in the eight volumes, twenty-eight chapters, sixty-nine thousand three hundred eighty-four characters of the Lotus Sutra. This is the only absolute truth." Nichiren's voice grew in intensity and power the more he spoke.

"All you have to do is believe in it. This is the only way to save this nation from unprecedented national disaster! Earthquakes, windstorms, floods, plagues, and famine. Why are we assaulted by such calamities? It is because so many of our people have put their faith in the wrong teachings. What are these incorrect teachings? They are Nenbutsu and Zen Buddhism. Cast out their evil design! And recite Nam-myoho-renge-kyo."

"Why do you attain the merit of Gautama Buddha by chanting Nam-myoho-renge-kyo?" a heckler called out.

As Nichiren scowled in the direction of the voice, a man who seemed to be an adherent stepped before the heckler.

"Listen up. Seventeen years ago, the holy superior predicted the national crisis we now find ourselves in. Civil unrest, invasion by foreign nations, and the destruction of Nippon. These calamities will come again to our world. It will not be long now. Your homes will be destroyed, your villages burned, and your families murdered. Everything will fall into hell."

"I have not heard of such a prediction," the heckler told him.

"Read the Risshō Ankoku. All is written there," the disciple countered.

"I can't read!"

"Then chant Nam-myoho-renge-kyo. Reciting it is enough. In doing this, the country and everyone in it shall be saved."

"That is all we have to do to be saved? Chant?" The heckler's tone had changed.

"That is all you have to do. As long as you believe in the Lotus Sutra, natural disasters will end, and foreign countries will cease to invade."

From somewhere in the crowd several people began chanting Nam-myoho-renge-kyo. The scattered voices gradually increased, and the disconnected echo merged into a large chorus. Even though he didn't understand it, the powerful melody penetrated Edward's soul.

"Is this the power of faith?" he murmured almost without thinking.

Edward had often seen spectacles similar to this on his journey to Jerusalem. But it did not take long before the populace, who once held wild enthusiasm for Christ's Army, to turn fear-filled gazes at their approach.

"Let's go," Morimune prompted Edward who had been listening intently.

Before long, they arrived at a mansion, surrounded by white plaster walls and enclosed by a moat. One of the samurai who had accompanied them from Hakata opened the gate and escorted them in.

"Well, this is no castle. A place like this could easily be destroyed," Alan sneered as he ridiculed their surroundings.

"Don't be stupid. Trying to bring down this house isn't going to help us leave Nippon," Edward snapped.

"I know, I know. I just had to say it."

"Where is Tokimune?" Edward asked.

"Lord Tokimune does not reside here. This is one of my relative's estates, Morimune told him with a smile. "You will meet Lord Tokimune later on."

"When?"

"I will tell you as soon as I find out."

"Let it be as soon as possible. My soldiers and sailors are desperate to go home."

"We've prepared an evening meal for you. For tonight, make yourselves comfortable." Morimune bowed and left.

The food was similar to what they had eaten in Hakata. As usual, the dishes contained no meat, but there was more variety, including roasted chestnuts and soybeans. The men, exhausted from their travels, retired to the four rooms assigned to them immediately after dinner.

Restless and unable to settle, Edward quietly slipped into the garden. Next to a large tree was a well with a wooden bucket attached to a rope and pulley. He drew water and poured it over his head. The cold water felt refreshing on his skin. He relaxed and became drowsy.

CHAPTER
31

Later that night, a loud noise woke Edward from a sound dreamless sleep. He sprang to his feet and put himself on guard. He saw dozens of soldiers brandishing spears lined up in the garden. Behind them were soldiers with bows and arrows.

"I knew it would come to this!" Alan spat out as he burst into Edward's room. "We should have stolen a ship and escaped when we had the chance. If these pagan bastards are planning to chop off our heads, then I'm going to fight back. Even if I have to rip a throat out with my teeth, I'm taking someone down with me," he growled before pulling out his dagger.

"Don't be foolish. If you make a racket one of those arrows is going to find its way straight to your heart. And all of our men will die with you."

"Shit." Alan realized too well the situation they were in.

"Get Morimune! He will tell you that we are not your enemies!" Edward shouted out in the samurai's native tongue.

The man who seemed to be the commander hesitated for a moment when he heard Morimune's name, but he nonetheless hauled Edward and his men away.

"Where are you taking us?" Edward repeatedly asked him.

"Tatsunokuchi, the Dragon's Mouth," he said, after finally giving in to Edward's frantic pleas. It was the execution site where Du Shizhong and four other envoys from Yuan had been beheaded.

Edward was held fast by both arms. The samurai were a lot stronger than he expected. The commander faced Edward, pulled a letter from his pocket, and read it out loud.

"What is he saying?" Alan asked Edward.

"I'm not sure, but I think they are going to behead us."

"Are they really going to kill us? This is your fault! You are soldiers, but we're just sailors. No matter how cruel they are, they wouldn't kill sailors, would they?" Enrico said as his eyes welled up with tears.

"Be quiet!" Thomas berated Enrico, but his face was ashen and his lips quivered as he spoke. "We must show them the true spirit of sailors from Genoa." A throng of people began to crowd around them.

A samurai brandishing an unsheathed longsword broke through the crowd and approached.

"I'm going to throw myself at the bastard with the sword, and while he's trying to cut me, wrest the blade from him," Alan whispered to Edward.

"I can't! My hands are bound."

"Then find a way out!"

Edward desperately tried to free his hands, but the rope bit deeper into his wrists. Just then Enrico screamed out as the samurai grabbed him by the arm and dragged him away.

"Take me!" Edward shouted as he hurriedly stood up.

Alan lunged at the commander, who drew his blade and bashed Alan across the head with the handle, knocking him out. The commander yelled, and two samurai came and yanked Edward toward a samurai with his katana raised overhead. Edward lifted his head and glared at his executioner.

"Wait! Lower your sword!" Morimune's voice thundered.

Morimune pushed his way through the crowd on horseback, jumped down, and rushed to Alan's side.

"This is an order from the regent of the Kamakura shogunate! Untie these men and take them to their estate at once!" he shouted.

All were completely shaken and exhausted. Enrico, unable to walk properly, had to be supported by two other sailors. Back in the safety of the estate's garden, Edward stopped at the sight that greeted him. All of their weapons and armor were laid out on top of a woven mat.

"I return these to you," Morimune announced.

Alan found his sword among the pile and unsheathed it, thrusting it toward Morimune's throat.

"Returning your weapons is my apology for the misconduct you have received. And to earn everyone's trust. But I do so with conditions. I ask that you do not leave the estate with them," Morimune said bluntly, not the least bit unsettled by Alan's hostile gesture.

"Why? Are we scary?" Alan scoffed.

"It is to avoid unnecessary quarrels. You have my word that we will protect you all," Morimune asserted, speaking directly to Alan.

Once they were alone, Morimune bowed deeply to Edward.

"The wrong against you today was at my father Adachi Yasumori's direction. Lord Tokimune has firmly reprimanded him."

"I was preparing for that to be my end. I am embarrassed to admit I showed an unsightly side of myself to my comrades," Edward admitted.

"To ensure such a mistake doesn't happen again, Lord To-kimune wishes to meet with you tomorrow. I ask that you properly prepare yourself," Morimune said, before once again bowing his head.

CHAPTER
32

Hours before Morimune was to come and fetch him the next morning, Edward washed himself with water from the well in the garden. He then dressed himself in chainmail, armor, and helmet; fastened his sword to his side; and held a shield in his left hand.

Morimune stared in disbelief when he saw Edward.

"What is this guise?" he asked.

"I am going to meet the man who governs this nation, am I not?"

"But—"

"I am a knight of England. I want to meet your king as a proper knight."

"At least leave your sword behind."

Edward's eyes dropped to Morimune's hip.

"You always have your katana on you."

"But we never carry our longswords in the presence of the regent of the shogunate."

"Is that so? A sword is a tool that cuts down enemies *and* protects God's land."

Zafir shook his head, signaling that Edward was not to press the matter and that he should go along with everything Morimune asked of them.

"I trust the samurai have the same spirit as knights," Edward said, removing his sword and putting down his shield. However, he kept his dagger on him.

Edward was about to enter Tokimune's residence, when one of the samurai standing guard at the door stopped him and tried to seize his dagger. Edward grabbed his wrist and twisted it. Seething with anger, the other samurai drew their swords. Morimune raised his hand and ordered them to put away their weapons.

"His blade is the same as our katana. It is not just a tool to wound others. It also protects our spirit," Morimune said. He looked to Edward for confirmation. Edward nodded and entered the hall with his dagger.

Lined up at attention were more than thirty samurai wearing black-lacquered headgear, known as eboshi. The atmosphere was dignified but more intimidating than anything Edward had ever experienced before. All eyes were fixed on Edward and Zafir. The stares were mostly inquisitive, but some tried to feign indifference. Morimune urged them to continue walking.

"Before you is Lord Tokimune," Morimune whispered in Edward's ear. Edward inhaled sharply. The man was in his late twenties. *We are the same age. Yet he governs Nippon?*

Tokimune stared at Edward. Before him sat WangSheng as interpreter.

"Follow me," Morimune urged and walked to the center of the room.

The closer Edward came to Tokimune the more surprised he became. He was even younger than Edward.

Edward and Zafir followed Morimune's lead and sat down.

"I have brought Lord Edward Gawain to you."

"So, they have come from a country called Europa that lies farther to the west than India?" one of the samurai said to WangSheng, who translated for Zafir, who did the same for Edward.

"We came from England."

"I hear you are a nobleman there," Tokimune prompted.

"My father was lord of a manor. I became a knight at his behest and joined the Army of Christ."

"Yours is an army that fights for a god?"

"The army was created to take back the Holy Land of Jerusalem from the pagans who occupy it."

"Then you lost your lands to another country? We find ourselves in a similar dangerous circumstance."

"Pagans are like Mongolians," one of the samurai called out. "We simply wish to defend the Nippon nation without foreign interference."

"Morimune tells me you can speak our language," Tokimune said, ignoring the interruption.

"Only a small amount," Edward replied.

Edward had responded in the Nippon tongue before WangSheng and Zafir had a chance to translate. A flicker of surprise crossed Tokimune's face, while the samurai let out faint gasps of shock.

"Who taught you?" Tokimune asked.

"It has been more than a month since we drifted to this land. I learned to survive. If I can't communicate, I can't live."

"Still, it's not easily done. Morimune thinks highly of you."

"Lord Morimune?"

"He has praised you the most, saying you possess much wisdom. According to Lord Morimune, you have much to share about the Mongolians. And for that reason, you should be treated with care."

Edward proceeded to tell them what the merchant from Song had told Zafir. That before long Yuan would invade again. That warships and soldiers would be greater in number than the last time. When he had finished, Tokimune eyed Edward for some time in silence.

"Now tell us about yourselves," he finally said.

"We come from a land farther west than continental Asia."

"Farther west than Goryeo? Farther west than Yuan and India?"

"Yes. On the western edge of Europe are Germany and France. My country is farther north, across a channel."

"It is an island country?"

"Yes. The King of England governs it."

"Why did you leave England and cross a sea to fight pagans?" Tokimune already knew about Edward and his men. But ever vigilant he still asked.

Edward gave his reason for joining the Army of Christ and why the army fought Muslims. He spoke in Japanese, only occasionally relying on WangSheng and Zafir to interpret his story for Tokimune.

"Then your people believe in just one god? And you live for the sake of gaining forgiveness from that god?"

"I fought for that forgiveness."

"In Buddhist teachings, the destruction of life is wickedness. Yet humans kill fellow humans. The teachings are very contradictory, wouldn't you say?"

"Do you have nothing you believe in?"

"I believe in Buddhism. Humans are born from humans; and when we die, we return to the soil. Outside of that, nothing else is certain. How a person conducts his life determines whether he reaches nirvana or descends into hell. It's quite like your teachings."

"Those who believe in Christ and those who follow Allah's teachings both kill each other for the sake of going to heaven in the afterlife."

Edward shocked himself. He had never articulated what just passed his lips.

"We're the same. We believe in paradise, believe in being freed from the suffering of reincarnation, and pray to the gods and Buddha," Tokimune said, letting out a light sigh.

The assembled gokenin listened in silence as the two continued their conversation for two hours.

CHAPTER

33

"Lord Tokimune has taken a liking to you," Morimune enthused when they returned to their estate.

"How do you know? He didn't look particularly entertained. I'd say he looked rather bored," Edward said.

"I've never seen him speak with someone for that long. Samurai do not show emotion."

"That is a strange custom."

"Do you forget the last thing he said to you?"

Edward didn't respond, but he remembered Tokimune's exact departing words. "Please, tell me more at our next meeting," he had said.

"How old is Lord Tokimune?"

"He's twenty-seven. He had his coming-of-age ceremony and entered the Lower Board of Retainers at seven. He learned politics from Lord Hojo Sanetoki and became regent of the shogunate at eighteen."

What had I accomplished when I was eighteen? Edward thought.
I didn't think much and devoted myself to my knight's training.

"From the day he was born, Tokimune's destiny was to unite
the samurai world in Nippon. His father, Lord Tokiyori, determined
this and raised Tokimune to live up to his destiny."

"That is a heavy burden to bear," Edward said, thinking of his
older brother.

They had been raised together. However, once Edward turned
ten, he was aware of the growing difference between his and his
brother's positions. Edward was sent to become a knight, while his
brother stayed at home. After that, they only met one, maybe two
times. That may have been for the best. Edward believed it was in
his nature to be a knight. There was no other life for him. It was his
destiny to join the Army of Christ.

CHAPTER
34

"Come with me," Morimune whispered.

"Where?"

"Trust me."

"This country truly wants to keep everything a secret," Edward grumbled as he put aside his pen and got up. He had been practicing writing Nippon characters.

Edward followed Morimune to a moonlit lake where a man stood at the edge. It was Tokimune.

"I trust you and your men are feeling no discomfort during your stay here. If you lack anything, please let me know."

"We are plenty content. But . . . our true hope is to return to our homeland. Many of the men have families waiting for their return."

"I ask you to spare me a bit more of your time. You are now well aware of our nation's state of affairs. We know little of foreign lands. I hope to learn more about them through you. When we find a solution to this difficult problem, I shall definitely—" Tokimune suddenly fell silent.

No one spoke for a long while. Edward was hesitant to ask for anything more than he already had.

"And how are your companions managing?" Tokimune finally asked, changing the subject.

"My soldiers and sailors tell me that at this rate their bodies will grow fat and their reflexes will dull."

"Your knights are like our samurai. They make an oath of loyalty to a ruler and exist to fight."

"There are many knights who have lived without fighting and died of old age. Those men who simply swear their loyalty are also excellent knights. However, we live in a time of war. The fight to recapture the Holy Land has lasted over a hundred years."

"It is the same for the samurai. We, too, are in a bad era. We had countless civil wars among ourselves, and just when we came together as one, the Mongolians invaded us. All of us were born to fight for the reigning emperor."

"That is also the will of God."

"The general belief is that a great wind came during the night, sank all the Yuan ships, and the sea swallowed their soldiers. Even if there were survivors, only a few could find their way back to their homeland. Would you also say that this is the will of God?"

"Everything operates through God's will. That is what I was taught."

"You hail from far away in the West and yet managed to come to our nation of Nippon. So, this is also God's will?"

Edward couldn't respond. *God's whim was more like it,* he thought. On occasion, God tended to act in ways beyond human comprehension.

Tokimune studied Edward in silence before speaking.

"You know, having arrived in Kamakura from Kyushu, that our country is surrounded by ocean. You have come from crossing an ocean even farther away than Yuan. I haven't even been to Kyushu yet. Will you tell me what the nations beyond the sea are like?"

Edward was stunned. He wasn't sure what would be best to talk about. *Did Tokimune simply want to hear about Europe? Or did he have something else in mind?*

Tokimune looked long and hard at Edward. It seemed as if his eyes glittered with curiosity. *This man truly wishes to learn,* Edward realized.

"Europe is divided into a vast number of countries. As I told you, I was born and raised in a country in northern Europe called England."

"Do all the people of England look like you? With gold hair and blue eyes?"

"There are people with red and brown hair, as well as black like yours. And people with green and dark eyes. Diverse people come and go throughout England."

Tokimune wanted to know about England's villages and their way of life. He asked about the country's systems and politics. Edward told as much as he knew about each subject.

CHAPTER

35

From then on, Edward was regularly called to Tokimune's manor. Tokimune showed an extreme interest in the weapons and tools that Edward and his men had brought with them to Nippon. Particularly, the chainmail, armor, and helmet that Edward had worn when they first met.

"So, you swing this heavy longsword when you fight? Those swords are too big for us."

"And yet you use longbows. They're difficult to handle, but your arrows have great power to them."

"You said your enemies were the Saracens. This past war was the first time we had ever fought a foreign adversary. All of us were shocked and baffled by Yuan's grotesque weapons. It wasn't just their weapons that made sport of us, but their unfamiliar battle tactics as well. Do you also get surprised and confused in battles with other nations?"

"Neighboring countries in Europe have been battling each other over territory for a very long time. Depending on their culture and traditions, weapons and battle tactics differ greatly from country to country. But this is the same for enemies and allies alike. Destroy the advantages of the enemy and make the best of the advantages of the allies. I think that is the best way to fight."

"Can you tell me more about that?" Tokimune asked leaning forward. "I want to know more about you joining the Army of Christ and the war in Europa."

He spoke calmly, but deep within his eyes a strong determination burned. And deeper within that was—

"Lord Tokimune, Lord Adachi Yasumori is waiting for you," an attendant interrupted.

"Let him wait."

"I am afraid not, my lord."

"Then, Edward, can you further regale me in front of the others? It will be useful for the upcoming war with Yuan."

Being young, Tokimune said what he thought. However, having a foreigner teach samurai the basics of war was difficult for older soldiers to accept.

Once again Edward found himself speaking in front of the Hyojyoshu council assembly. As before, the decision-making body of the shogunate lined up on either side of him. More than twenty of Tokimune's close associates sat behind them. As he spoke, more people entered the room.

"When we were fighting in the city of Elba, the Saracen troops were at least three thousand strong, while my army was just short of three hundred. Nonetheless we took cover behind the rocks above a valley and waited for the enemy. We lay down on the rocky ground under the blazing sun. It felt like iron plates scorched by fire. Several soldiers died from dehydration, and those who tried to flee were cut down by their commanding officers. We lay next to corpses and held our breaths, still waiting. Finally, on the third day, the Saracen army appeared at the entrance of the valley. They halted, evidently to decide whether they should pass through the valley or make a detour.

"Half a day passed. The air around us became more and more putrid from the rotting corpses. Just when I thought I couldn't take much more of it, the army began to advance. They had waited that long to ensure that the valley offered safe passage."

The samurai gulped and listened intently as Edward continued.

"Once the main body of soldiers had marched into the valley, we attacked. First, we blocked the valley's entrance and exit with boulders to cut off the Saracens' retreat. Then we fired a rainstorm of arrows. The three thousand men panicked, and chaos ensued. We filled bottles with oil, inserted cloth wicks, lit the wicks, and threw them as far and as fast as we could. Screams echoed throughout the valley as it was engulfed in flames and a hail of cliff stones fell on the enemy. After several hours, the valley was strewn with charred and broken Saracen corpses."

"How cowardly!" a voice rang out.

"Samurai know that single combat is the only way to fight in a battle."

"Exactly! We have always fought fair. Hiding oneself to ambush and slay your enemy with stone and fire is not an honorable fight."

"It was three hundred against three thousand. How do you fight those odds?" another samurai ventured.

"Whatever the numbers you should always find a path forward. That is the way of the samurai."

"So, you're saying it is better to lose a battle you know you can win?"

"Yes, I would choose an honorable defeat over a cowardly victory."

"To throw away your beliefs and be beaten in a battle that could be won is cowardice."

Dissenting voices of the council continued to flutter out.

"Do you know what comes after defeat?" Edward's voice silenced the bickering.

"Villages are burned, men are slaughtered, and the elderly, women, and children are beheaded. All that's left on the battlefield are dead bodies and heaps of severed heads. Young women are raped and those who survive are carried off to foreign lands as slaves, never to return to their homeland. That is the reality of war," Edward said solemnly, remembering the battles he once fought. Almost every battle was a massacre. Kill or be killed. Edward had desperately swung his sword driven by that thought. All he could recall was the color and scent of blood, and the piercing sound of screams. God was not there.

"There is no cowardice or lack of cowardice in war. You seize any means necessary to ensure victory," he declared strongly.

At that moment, a samurai stood up and mimed shooting an arrow at Edward's chest.

"I am a match for a thousand warriors. My bow shall strike down every Mongolian invader," he shouted, before storming out of the room.

"Who was that?" Edward asked Morimune.

"Lord Hojo Akisada, the top archery master in Kamakura."

"Just archery?"

"He is also the top samurai in horsemanship and longswords."

Edward was questioned further about Western military strategies, and in response he told the samurai how to arrange the cavalry to pierce an enemy army's flank. He told them about night attacks.

He revealed tactics on how to lure enemies into valleys or down narrow roads and assault them with arrow fire.

CHAPTER
36

After the Hyojoshu left, Edward and Tokimune were alone in the silent room.

"You surely haven't always been victorious. You must have also lost a battle."

"The Saracens were brave. They believed that if they died in battle, they would go to heaven where seven virgins and other pleasures awaited them. They fought with no fear of death."

Tokimune grimaced but said nothing.

"The battle of Damietta was disastrous. The enemy's cavalry was two thousand strong, and their infantry four thousand. Our numbers were evenly matched. But we lost our courage. They charged at us with swords upraised, screaming Allah's name. We frantically fired arrows at them, but they used their own comrades as shields and continued to advance. They pulled arrows out of the dead and fired them back at us. The smell of blood and dead flesh was overpowering. Heads and rotting torsos were scattered everywhere. There was even more death and destruction in the villages as we retreated until we finally escaped their pursuit," Edward's voice shook as he spoke.

Although several years had passed since Damietta, it still haunted Edward. He had been wounded by arrows, and when a light cavalry brandishing swords rushed them, a sword slashed through his shoulder, leaving a scar diagonally across his back. Alan caught Edward when he fell, and carried him through the night to their camp.

"So, you praise God's name and yet fear death?" Tokimune sighed. He knew that fear, and that religion created it. Yet religion also relieved the fear of death.

"Are you not afraid of death?" Tokimune suddenly asked Edward.

"I—" Edward stopped himself. He couldn't get the next words out. He wasn't afraid. All sins were forgiven in death and he would go to heaven and meet God. Yet, in that moment, Edward could not say it. He had slaughtered too many.

Edward shook his head and the memories away with it.

"Death is the unknown. I am indeed afraid of it," he eventually said.

These were words he had never thought before. Words he blurted out in a foreign land, and in front of a pagan, no less.

Tokimune nodded. He, too, feared death.

"When the Yuan invaders make their next assault, will only the Kyushu gokenin fight?" Edward asked.

"There is a strong bond of lord and retainer between the Kamakura shogun and the gokenin. If I summon them, samurai from all over the country will come."

"So, it is a connection between master and servant?"

"It is a connection between reward and service. That is what it means to be a samurai," Tokimune said standing up. He scanned the room, as if looking for something.

"The night grows late. It would be best to get some rest," he said, politely bowing before taking his leave.

CHAPTER
37

On another visit, Tokimune took Edward into the garden.

"What is this?" Tokimune said, indicating what remained of the severely damaged catapult brought from Hakata. Exposed to rain and salty sea air, the wood had decayed and the metal fittings were covered in rust.

"A catapult. It's a machine that throws stones far distances."

"What kind of stones?"

"It can launch a stone the size of a head. Larger catapults can even throw rocks the size of a person."

"What does throwing these stones accomplish that bows, which are smaller and easier to handle, cannot?"

"Large stones can bring down castle walls, and drive back an enemy army, creating chaos and weakening their resolve."

Tokimune must have known this already. Morimune had told Edward of the Mongolian army using a similar contraption that had caused great damage and fear in the Nippon army.

"Can it only throw stones?" Tokimune asked.

"On the ocean, you can hurl flaming oil jars that create a sea of flames atop the water's surface. On land, it—" Edward said stopping mid-sentence.

"What can you fire on land?"

"A catapult can throw the innards of diseased animals or human corpses that have perished of plague. It can spread illness inside enemy castle walls or throughout an enemy camp."

"The heads of enemies also—"

"Yes."

Tokimune knew all of this beforehand. Why then had he asked Edward about it?

"Can you repair this device?"

"I would need a skilled carpenter and materials. Given enough time, it could be fixed. But it would be better to build a new one," Edward said in a low voice.

Tokimune grew silent, lost in his own thoughts. He eventually told Edward that he had a meeting with the Hyojyoshu and excused himself.

The following day, Edward was once again fetched by a messenger and brought to Tokimune's estate. Edward looked into the garden as he walked down the manor's hallway. Suddenly, he stopped. A faint smell of smoke was in the air. In a corner of the garden, he saw the burnt remains of lumber with a plume of smoke still rising.

"That's—"

"The catapult that was transported from Dazaifu. Lord Tokimune ordered it to be burned this morning," the messenger said.

"You destroyed it?!"

Edward recalled Tokimune's demeanor the day before. He had been full of curiosity about the catapult. *What the hell was that all about?*

When Edward and Tokimune met, they continued their talk about the war in Europe. Neither brought up the catapult. Tokimune must have known Edward had seen its smoldering remains in the garden, but Edward had no wish to bring up the subject.

Once Edward returned to his own estate, he told Alan and Zafir about Tokimune burning the catapult.

"I thought you said he was going to fix it or build another. That a catapult would be a huge military advantage over Yuan," Alan said.

"I thought the same. He even asked me what skills and materials would be needed to build one."

"In the end, he's just an idiot. I bet he never even threw rocks when he was a lad."

Zafir pondered quietly while the others vented.

"That man clearly doesn't know the true power of catapults. That's why he burned it," Alan barked.

"Then why did they bother bringing it all the way here and hold onto it until now? I don't think he simply burned it after he listened to what I told him."

"Is it not similar to their unwillingness to use poison arrows?" Zafir chimed in. "Before Yuan invaded, this nation had only engaged in civil wars, where enemies can be friends or even relatives. Which is why before battle warriors would exchange names with each other and respect their opponents' honor. These people even follow the custom of burying their enemies. No matter how many wars they fight, their hearts have shown great restraint so as not to resort to barbaric acts or use weapons designed for mass slaughter."

"But they beheaded that messenger from Yuan!" Alan countered, but it was clear from his expression that he agreed with Zafir.

"That is different from war."

"Do you think these people have the will to win against Yuan? The enemy that's coming for them is the same giant empire that has found its way to Europe. If they really want to fight and win, they need a catapult."

"I believe Lord Tokimune is thinking about what would happen after that. If they win against Yuan, but the use of catapults spreads domestically, then those weapons could also be used in civil wars that would become even bloodier. Not to have such weapons would be in their best interest," Zafir said, considering each word carefully.

Did that gentle-looking young man's thinking truly extend that far into the future? Edward wondered. *But if they were to lose against Yuan, then Nippon would have no future.*

CHAPTER

38

"Alan has been taken into custody by the samurai!" Thomas said, angrily bursting into Edward's room.

A year had passed since their arrival in Kamakura, during which Edward and his men were treated as honored guests from a faraway foreign land. For the first time since leaving the Crusades, they were guaranteed food and shelter, without having to do anything to earn it. They put on weight, and some had grown too fond of sake and stayed out late. To minimize trouble, Edward had endorsed Morimune's order that no one was to be armed when venturing outside the estate.

"What did he do?" Edward asked.

"He got into a fight."

"That idiot. Did he kill anyone?"

"He broke the other man's arm."

"If he just broke his arm, why did the samurai arrest him?"

"His opponent was someone of high rank."

"Kamakura is in an uproar!" Morimune called out. The sound of his footsteps coming down the hall preceded his arrival in Edward's room. "Let's go!" he said brusquely.

They found Alan sitting on the floor of a gloomy cell in the samurai commission office. His eyes were closed as if he were asleep. At Edward's voice, Alan wearily opened his eyes.

"The bastard tried to kill one of the townsfolk. All I did was try to save him," he said before Edward could get a word out.

In England, Alan would often get drunk, fight, and Edward would clean up his mess, apologizing to the people Alan had injured, and reimbursing them for damages.

"Then why did you end up in here?"

"Because that dirty bastard had ten men with him, and they all charged at me at once. They're just like the damn Mongolians. I thought the samurai of Nippon only fight one-on-one."

"Your foe was at fault. He is the second grade of fifth rank, Lord Fujihara Toshihide. I'm shocked that you quarreled with Lord Toshihide." Morimune was greatly perplexed when he returned from talking to the jailer.

"Who is he?"

"He is a member of the Imperial Court. And a relative of the emperor in Kyoto."

"My father used to say if you look far enough down our family tree, you'll find William the Conqueror's blood there. He was a king. Yet my father was a poverty-stricken knight without even a castle to his name," Alan mocked.

"Oh will you shut up!" Edward raged. "I'm always telling you not to get into trouble. What happens if we can't go home because of your stupidity? Think about that. We're only alive because of the kindness of the Nippon samurai." Then Edward noticed Alan's side.

There was blood.

"How bad was the fight?" Edward whispered.

"Well, my opponent swung a longsword. Whereas I pulled a support pole from a street stand and fought back with that."

Edward asked the jailer for a lamp. Alan's face was alarmingly pale, and he was lying down now.

"The bastard stabbed me in the gut. So, I smashed the hell out of his arm with the pole. It would have been better if I smashed his head."

"Open this door right now. If you don't, I'll open it myself!" Edward threatened, as he rattled the cell-door bars.

"Let me handle this," Morimune quickly interjected. Edward's outburst had clearly alarmed him.

Morimune spoke to the jailer, who hastily unlocked the cell door. Edward entered and helped Alan sit up. His weakened body hung limply in Edward's arms, a pool of blood spreading underneath him.

"Zafir can treat wounds. We need to send for him."

"Don't do anything rash until I get back," Morimune admonished Edward before he left the cell.

Morimune returned soon after with a brawny man, a fisherman Edward and Alan had seen several times in town. Children would throw stones at him, teasing him for his smell. One day, Alan drove away the children, and the fisherman reached into his large bucket and gave Alan a fish in thanks.

"He was in front of the prison. This is the fisherman whose life Alan saved," Morimune said, not knowing what to do in this situation.

The fisherman curled his body like a shrimp and repeatedly muttered something. He was very scared.

"What about Zafir?"

"I've summoned him. He should be here soon."

"If the inner part of his stomach isn't wounded, that's good," the fisherman said as he examined Alan's injury. The gash was about three fingers away from his navel.

"Press firmly down on the wound. When we have these types of injuries in my village, the first thing we do is stop the blood. That's what my grandmother would do."

Edward quickly put his hands on the wound before the fisherman could touch it with his hands reeking of fish.

At long last, Zafir, with his surgery tools in hand, rushed in. Thomas followed behind him. Zafir looked grave as he examined Alan's wound.

"If the intestines have been injured, then internal bleeding puts his life in danger. This will be difficult, but I need to examine further. Get as many lamps as you can find. Can someone please boil water? I need to sterilize my tools."

They made a temporary bed by placing a crate underneath a detached sliding door and carefully laid Alan on top of it.

"Bite down on this," Zafir insisted as he brought out a small stick with innumerable bite marks on it. It was the same one Edward had bitten on in the past.

"I don't need it. You won't hear a peep out of me."

"If you bite through your tongue, you will not be doing yourself any favors."

Alan gave in and bit down on the stick as he endured the pain. Zafir pushed a hot towel into Alan's stomach. The fisherman grimaced next to him but looked on with intense concentration.

Zafir pulled out the cloth. It was soaked in blood.

"Is it bad?" Alan asked tentatively.

"The blood is not from the intestines. A kick did the damage. I've drained the abdomen. The wound is from a slash, rather than a stab. If I stitch it, he should be fine. That is, if the wound does not fester," Zafir said as he threaded a needle. Alan had lost consciousness.

"Smear the cut with this. It's what we use when we get injured out at sea," the fisherman said, offering a small jar without a lid. Inside was a thick black substance.

"I used this when a shark sank its teeth into my leg. I slept it off and recovered easily."

Everyone looked down at the man's leg and saw the scar where a chunk of flesh had been chewed.

"It is most likely a mixture of medicinal herbs," Zafir observed. He hesitated and looked at the smelly fisherman. But what other option did he have? He spread the herbal paste over Alan's wound before wrapping it in a cloth.

"Am I dead?" Alan asked weakly as he came to.

"There's no way in hell you're dead. How many times have we evaded death before now? Do you think you would die in a place like this?" Edward said, though he wasn't fully confident in his own words. The man laid out before him was deathly pale.

Zafir could read Edward's mind. "It's because he's lost a lot of blood," Zafir said to ease the other man's anxiety. "But the bleeding has been stopped. If you had not pressed on the wound, he would have lost a lot more."

"I'll tend to him tonight. But if Alan dies, I won't let Toshihide live," Edward told Morimune.

The fisherman crouching by Alan's side rose.

"Please tell Lord Alan that I owe him my life. He has my deepest gratitude." He bowed his head multiple times and left.

"Well, well, when I saw his big body and head, I thought him to be lacking in intellect. How does he know so much about curing wounds?" Morimune commented.

"It's the wisdom that ordinary folk live by," Edward replied.

"You should not have tangled with Lord Toshihide," Morimune reprimanded Alan.

That night, as Edward sat in a corner of the cell watching over
Alan, his mind wandered.

The day had been typically gloomy and cloudy for early winter. It
was on a day like that his father summoned twelve-year-old Edward. Next to him stood a young, muscular man. His father gave
Edward his grandfather's sword, a sword too heavy and long for
such a young boy, fastened a dagger to his hip and hung a cross
around the boy's neck. It was the same cross his mother always wore.

"Hold onto this sword and dagger and follow this man. He
will bring you closer to God," his father said, resting his hand on
Edward's head.

As Edward rode away, he looked back at his home. He
thought he saw two shadows nestled against one of the fortress win-
dows, watching him depart. *Was it mother and father?* When Edward paused to check, his companion grabbed the reins of Edward's
horse, and they broke into a gallop.

After riding for two days, they arrived at a stone castle at the
top of a hill. A small figure, wielding a sword, waited for them in the
center of the courtyard. No sooner had Edward dismounted than
the figure jumped at Edward before he could ready himself. That
diminutive figure was Alan, who now was a fist taller than Edward
despite being two years his junior. From the moment they met, Edward's training as a knight had begun.

A faint noise woke Edward from his reverie. The cell was dark, the
only source of light coming from the eerie flickering of a torch. A
shadow was crouching next to Alan. Edward instinctively shot up.
His heart pounded in his chest, and he began to sweat.

"Is he dead?"

"He is sleeping. His breathing is more at ease now," Zafir said, emerging from the darkness.

The tension in Edward's body eased, and he crawled closer to Alan. His friend's face, contorted in pain just a few hours ago, was now at peace.

Morimune came before sunrise. When he saw Alan and was told that he had come through the night, he sighed in relief. He pulled from his pocket a cylinder of water and a bamboo-wrapped parcel containing grilled rice balls and salt. Only then did Edward realize how hungry he was. He hadn't eaten anything since the previous afternoon.

"This will alleviate one of your burdens," Morimune sympathized.

"When can Alan leave? He can't stay here. We need to care for him properly," Edward implored.

Morimune massaged the bridge of his nose as he thought.

"He broke Lord Toshihide's arm. That will not be resolved easily," Morimune told him, melancholy spread across his face.

"Alan was stabbed in the stomach, kicked by multiple people, and came close to dying. His foe only has a broken arm! It's not as if he killed him!"

"That is not the problem. Even in your country, if you injure someone of high rank, no matter the reason, it is not easily forgiven."

Edward could not find the words to retaliate. Such absurdities over rank and title were a part of everyday life in Europe as well. It never came down to what was right and what was wrong. Edward had even once accepted this to be an unchangeable reality of the world.

"I'll do whatever it takes to save Alan."

Unnoticed, Alan had opened his eyes and was staring at Edward and Morimune.

"Let me challenge Toshihide to a duel. This time one-on-one. The samurai way. If he's afraid, I'll accept one-on-five. Provided that I also get to have a sword," Alan suddenly spoke out in a fevered state. Three days had passed since his capture. Edward could see that as his wound healed, his spirit worsened. Edward had requested a meeting with Tokimune several times, but received no response.

CHAPTER

39

For the first time in three days, Edward returned to the estate. "What pains you so?" Morimune asked.

"Alan detests more than anything his freedom being stolen from him. Or rather, he fears it," Edward sighed.

Alan was afraid of tight dark spaces. Edward first realized this when Alan was twelve, and they had gone to a cave close to the castle. It wasn't a deep cave, and light faintly spilled in from the entrance. But the always adventurous Alan drew back.

"What's wrong?"

"Nothing."

"You're shaking."

"It's cold."

"But you're sweating."

Alan then told Edward about the time he had been locked in a dungeon when he was seven.

"It was a damp and dark hole. The only light came from the torches at the dungeon's entrance. Other than that, it was black as pitch. When the wind blew the torches out, the darkness was unending. The only things I could smell were piss and shit. The guards brought me bits of moldy bread and foul-tasting water once a day. I went in at first snowfall and left when flowers were in bloom."

"Why were you there?"

"My old man lost a wager, and I was taken to ensure he would pay back the money. It took him three months to get the money before I was let out."

Edward didn't know what to say.

"What happened to your father?" he eventually asked.

"He traded me for a horse, and I joined the Army of Christ. That way I could 'earn salvation from God.' I haven't seen him since," Alan answered boldly.

"Isn't Alan your servant?" Morimune asked after listening to Edward's story.

"We grew up together like siblings. No matter what it takes, I want to get him out of prison as quickly as possible."

Morimune furrowed his brow and sighed a few times. Alan was in more trouble than Edward knew.

Just then Zafir breathlessly joined them.

"Alan attacked the jailor and escaped!"

"What of the jailor?" Morimune asked.

"He is fine. But where on earth would Alan flee in Kamakura?"

Edward groaned. *I should have stayed by his side.*

"With a wound like his, he should not have run away," Morimune reasoned.

"He ran away knowing the risk."

"So, rather than die in jail, he chose freedom?"

"Even after he turned twenty, he told me he still fears small dark spaces more than he does death. Desperation helps him overcome most of his fear. But if left alone in a small room, he says he imagines everything around him crumbling into dust."

The next day Edward learned that Alan had been recaptured. He had been hiding in a ship at the port. One of the sailors found him asleep and reported him to the magistrate. Edward asked Zafir to contact Morimune and rushed off to rejoin his friend.

He arrived to see two samurai haul Alan out of the prison. Alan's hands were bound behind his back, his feet dragged beneath him, and he was in pain. *Where are they taking him? If his wound reopens, it would be fatal.*

"You bastards, get your filthy hands off me!" Alan cursed. But the two men on either side of him rebuffed his attempts to shake them off. Their bodies were strong, despite their small frames. A third samurai behind Alan bashed him on the head. Edward flew at them in a rage. He kicked down the two samurai holding Alan and, while pushing away the third, drew the man's katana from his waist.

"I'll protect you, Alan, even if it costs me my life!" Edward shouted. He brandished the katana and quickly cut Alan free. Alan collapsed with a low moan.

Drawing their swords, the other samurai surrounded Edward and Alan.

"If Alan dies, I will kill you all!" Edward screamed with a murderous glint in his eyes.

At that moment, sounds of a struggle came from the front of the jail. Edward's knights and Thomas' sailors rushed toward him with swords in hand. They created a protective wall between Edward, Alan, and the samurai. The air was tense.

While Edward struggled to get Alan on his feet, several more men ran in, led by Morimune.

"Cease this madness at once by order of the regent!" Morimune demanded.

An out-of-breath Zafir staggered in behind Morimune.
There was slight bleeding, but Alan's wound had not reopened.

CHAPTER
40

"You met with Lord Tokimune last night? What did you say? Did you promise him anything?" Zafir asked Edward after they had brought Alan back to the estate.

"I told him this nation's weapons and battle tactics are a hundred years behind ours. If they want to drive away the Yuan army, they need to learn how we fight. That's why they are letting Alan live," Edward said.

"You are quite the tactician. You will become a good general."

"I merely told them the truth."

Zafir beamed.

"However, I do not think that Lord Tokimune would have agreed to spare Alan's life for that reason alone. What did you say to the others?"

"That Alan is the son of one of the king of England's mistresses. And that keeping him alive could be beneficial for them in the future."

"So, a good story for a desperate situation. But did they believe it?"

"Lord Tokimune didn't. But his subordinates did."

"Then he was looking for an excuse to pardon Alan," Zafir said, giving a knowing nod. "Clearly the story of Alan's background is compelling. But it was not just that, correct? When I went with Lord Morimune to appeal for Alan's clemency, Lord Tokimune looked pleased."

"I have nothing more to say."

"It is but simple curiosity. Will you tell me about it someday?"

"It's boring."

"Now I'm even more curious!"

"I'll let you know when the time is right," Edward said before leaving to check on Alan.

CHAPTER

41

While Alan daily regained his strength—and haughty and overconfident manner—Edward and Tokimune continued to meet. They began to trust each other and gradually let down their guard. Alike in age and demeanor, they were opposites in upbringing and destiny. Tokimune inherited the position of regent of the shogunate from his father and was raised his entire life to lead Nippon. Edward, on the other hand, was the youngest of three brothers. His elder brother would inherit the family estate and title; the middle brother served as the spare in case the firstborn died. So as not to be a burden to his brothers, Edward was apprenticed to a knight.

Which of us is happier? Edward wondered. *Tokimune must be lonely. Many of his close aides are elders, who can be helpful to a young man in such a position of power. But what do they have in common?*

At a meeting with the Hyojyoshu council, Edward sat amid eighteen samurai in ceremonial silk robes and black-lacquered headgear.

"Yuan's second assault on Nippon is fast approaching," he argued. "The Yuan Dynasty has invaded Europe in the West and claimed dominion over the Southern Song Dynasty. The next target is Nippon."

"The gods and Buddha protect Nippon. We have nothing to fear from something as insignificant as the Mongolian army," Yasumori asserted in a strong voice.

Edward sensed that if Yasumori were to have his way, he would be killed.

"What you experienced in the last attack was not a true Mongolian assault but a test of Nippon's military strength and strategy. As we speak, huge numbers are gathering in Goryeo, the core of them being shipbuilders. You need to prepare for an invasion force that could annihilate all of Nippon."

"Thousands of Mongol corpses littered the battlefield in the last war, and the cowards who survived ran for their lives. This time no matter how they attack I—"

"What do you think is best for us to do?" Tokimune interrupted Yasumori and turned to Edward.

"Strengthen Kyushu's defenses at once."

"We are already preparing that."

"I wouldn't call that preparation."

"Do you mock the people of Dazaifu? They are doing their best to build stone walls on the coast of Hakata—"

"You already know the power of Yuan's weapons and the strength of its cavalry. You know how useful that stone wall will be," Edward scoffed.

"You are dissatisfied with the progress of the wall's construction. So am I and everyone else in this room. But ours is an island nation. The coastlines facing Goryeo and Song are long. It would be impossible to build defenses everywhere. But we have to do so," Tokimune said, his words strong with intention.

"For now, we will mainly focus on Hakata, Nagato, Hizen, and the surrounding areas as the places where Yuan will disembark. We will dispatch our troops there to start," Tokimune continued.

"In the last war, they landed in Hakata. It would be logical for them to think the city has greatly increased its defenses since then and therefore avoid it. It is important for us to fortify other places," Yasumori spoke directly to Tokimune.

"The Mongolian army's true strength is cavalry warfare, a group tactic focused on force of arms. I think they will unleash a large army on us the moment they land their fleet. They'll likely aim for a port the shortest distance from Goryeo and Song, where they can quickly and safely unload their soldiers. Given that, Hakata has a gentle coastline and a tranquil bay, making it the most ideal location to disembark troops," Edward reasoned.

"Bringing down Dazaifu, which is known to be the right arm of the Imperial Court, would be a huge morale boost for their soldiers. Advancing on Kamakura from such a place would be of great significance to Yuan," Yasumori countered.

Edward was reminded of the Yuan soldiers who had attacked Morimune on the coast of Kyushu. They had clearly come to spy on Hakata and the surrounding area, with the intention of capturing one of the Nippon army's commanding officers as a prisoner of war, and torturing him for information. All of this pointed to Hakata being where they would land next. Edward was convinced of it. However, if he wanted to persuade the Hyojyoshu, he would need more evidence.

"What do you think is the most important thing in war? Soldiers, weapons, armor, or tactics?" Tokimune suddenly asked Edward.

Edward thought for a moment before replying, "A great cause. Without a great cause, there is no meaning to war. Otherwise it is simply murder."

"Is God your great cause? You fought the pagans to take back the sacred land where Jesus was executed."

"At one time—" Edward began, but the words stuck in his throat. He intended to say that he would have once sacrificed himself for God. But his resolve had weakened. He still sought God, but he could neither see nor feel Him. Instead, he had slaughtered men and women, and witnessed great suffering all in God's name.

"Over many long years, civil war ravaged our land, bringing much killing and strife to the Imperial Court, among the samurai, and in families. Just as order has at long last been established, we now face war with Yuan. My destiny is to bring peace to Nippon and establish a world with the samurai at its center," Tokimune said matter-of-factly and devoid of enthusiasm. He then spoke directly to Edward.

"I would like to put you in charge of training our military. I also ask that you become an advisor to help devise countermeasures against the second onslaught from Yuan."

Tokimune's statement caused a stir throughout the room.

"You should have consulted us before deciding to place a foreigner in charge of our men. We cannot accept this!" a voice rang out, followed by a chorus of similar dissent.

"Then would you say there is a person among you who has the confidence to create a band of warriors to defeat Yuan? If there is, let him come forward," Tokimune challenged the Hyojyoshu council.

Not a single man came forward.

CHAPTER

42

"Do you think this country truly has the disposition to fight against Yuan?" Edward asked Zafir and Alan later that night.

"Lord Tokimune has strengthened his resolve since the end of the last war," Zafir said.

"Like when he decapitated the messenger from Yuan?" Alan chimed in.

"Du Shizhong was not simply a messenger, but a high official of Yuan. He, his deputy delegate, official interpreter, and five others were beheaded at the Dragon's Mouth in Kamakura."

"Did you accept Lord Tokimune's offer, Lord Edward?" Zafir wanted to know.

"I told him I needed to think about it."

"So you accepted it?"

"I haven't given him my answer yet."

"But you are going to accept it?"

Edward nodded.

Alan spread his arms and shrugged. But he looked pleased.

After spending a few days in Hakata, WangSheng returned to Kamakura with news.

"Up until recently, debate raged in Kamakura on whether Nippon should go on the offense or defense against Yuan," he reported to Edward, Alan, and Zafir. "Kanazawa Sanetoki argued for offense, Adachi Yasumori advocated defense. In the end, an offensive strategy has been adopted."

"They mean to cross the ocean and attack Yuan? That's mad!" Zafir exploded.

"Indeed. It is madness," WangSheng agreed with a light sigh. "The reasoning is that Yuan did not have the guts to complete their attack on Nippon in the last war. Some of those in the Hyojyoshu no longer fear Yuan."

"Those who make light of Yuan's power will lead to Nippon's destruction," Edward observed.

"Lord Tokimune is well aware of this. In addition, a faction was forming to find ways to make peace with Yuan. Tokimune beheaded the envoy to put Nippon in a position they could not turn back from."

"If that's the case, then not only Hakata, but Kamakura's defense is lacking," Alan said.

"All this time Tokimune has not only been engrossed in affairs of domestic unrest. He has been steadily preparing for the impending Yuan invasion."

WangSheng closed his eyes for a while as he recalled what he could.

"First, he has ordered the regions of Sanin, Sanyo, and Nankaido —the west and south provinces in Nippon—to immediately mobilize their navies. Then Lord Tokimori is to be dispatched to the capital."

"Tokimori?"

"A senior member of the Hojo clan. At seventy-nine, he exercises great influence in the Imperial Court in Kyoto. He turned opposition to the expeditionary campaign into acceptance."

"Does Tokimune plan to send soldiers to Yuan?" Alan asked.

"He cannot rule out any possibility. Lord Tokimune changed the shugo—the military governors of the provinces where Yuan is expected to land in the coming battle."

WangSheng paused, as he brought out paper and a small inkstone from his pocket. He ground the dry ink, mixed it with water, dampened the tip of a brush, and drew a map from Kyushu to Honshu.

"The Hizen and Buzen provinces were confiscated from Lord Shoni Sukeyoshi. Protection of Buzen was left to Hojo Sanemasa. Chikugo province was confiscated from Lord Otomo Yoriyasu. One of Lord Tokimune's younger brothers, Lord Munemasa, protects it now. Suo province was seized from Lord Nagai Yasushige and Nagato province from Lord Nikaido Yukitada. Lord Tokimune's other younger brother, Muneyori, has assumed responsibility for both of those provinces. There is the possibility Yuan may sail farther east. Harima and Bitchu provinces belong to Lord Tokimune himself. Echizen, Hoki, and Iwami provinces also belong to the Hojo family."

WangSheng marked many areas on the map with the Hojo clan symbol.

"So, these regions were distributed to the Hojo clan in the wake of the Mongolian invasion?"

"Exactly. However, it is true that the defense system has become stronger,"

WangSheng pointed to spots on the map.

"Lord Muneyori, as the new commissioner for Nagato, has been reporting on the military force in the other regions. The gokenin who are likely to fight, as well as the number of subordinates and horses they have and the size of their territories."

Edward and Alan listened intently as WangSheng spoke.

"This was something I also directly encountered in Hakata. Each of the gokenin were given orders from Kamakura as they prepared to depart to Yuan. The number of boats and oars in the territory. The names, ages, and number of sailors and mariners. The weapons they can carry. They were to prepare the above articles and report them." WangSheng quickly read out the decree.

"Who is Xie WangSheng?" Edward asked Zafir after WangSheng had left.

"There are many people from Song in Hakata. While traveling to Nippon for trade, many of the merchants' homes were destroyed by the Mongolians, so they immigrated to this country. One of those merchants is a major dealer named Xie Guoming, who has shops in both Hakata and Kamakura. He and Xie WangSheng are related."

"And Morimune used WangSheng as an interpreter."

"I think it was easier for Morimune to make such a request, since the two already had a close friendship. It seems WangSheng thought he was going to enjoy a leisurely trip wandering the outskirts of Hakata, while accompanying government officials of the shogunate. But then—"

"He ran into us."

"Indeed."

"He is an enviable man," Edward muttered. "He can freely spread his wings. But a knight without a sword is useless. We can only do one thing: kill others."

"Yet those acts can lead to others being saved," Zafir consoled him.

CHAPTER

43

Edward had been in Kamakura for two years. Tokimune called upon him every day, and they would talk of battles in Europe and Nippon's defensive preparations. Occasionally, Edward would participate in Hyojyoshu council meetings. Edward's soldiers and sailors frequented the town even more now. After the incident with Alan, some of Morimune's samurai accompanied them, but eventually they were allowed to go out without escorts as they became more accustomed to the country and its ways.

One day, there was a commotion at the front gate of their estate. Two samurai were dragging Michael, one of Edward's knights, into the compound. Michael's wrists were bound behind his back.

"What happened?" Edward asked Zafir.

"He got drunk and broke into a house. He raped and killed the young woman who lived there. And then he killed her parents when they returned home."

"What the hell was he thinking?" Edward spat out.

Edward knew something like this would happen. But it was far more disastrous than he thought it would be. He stared at Michael, a twenty-six-year-old soldier who had been with him since they left England. He was usually law-abiding, but he was too fond of alcohol and would get into fights when drunk.

"I . . . I don't remember anything," Michael murmured.

"Lord Tokimune requests that his punishment be left to his commanding officer, you," one of the samurai told Edward.

His meaning was clear.

"I see."

The samurai released Michael and stepped back, but made no attempt to leave.

"Please spare my life! I don't remember anything! I just want to go home! I want to see my parents and siblings again!" Michael screamed as he fell to his knees before Edward sobbing.

"You won't be killing anyone, right? Michael was drunk."

"Give him twenty lashes, and that'll teach him. He'll never touch a drop again."

"It was only pagans that died. I've done the same thing, but no one complained about me."

The various voices of Edward's soldiers rang out.

"You saved my life. Save Michael's too," Alan implored.

"What you did was honorable."

"What about it! Michael is our comrade," Alan said raising his voice.

Edward pushed Alan aside.

"Don't be afraid. God is watching over you. I'll make it quick and painless," he whispered in Michael's ear.

"You're going to kill your comrade? A friend who fought alongside you in battle?"

"He only killed someone. God will forgive him!"

"They were pagans. It's what God would have wanted!"

As Edward unsheathed his sword and took one step back, Alan rushed between Edward and Michael. In a second Michael's head was separated from his body, and Alan held aloft his blood-covered dagger.

Edward looked down at Michael.

"That was my duty to carry out," Edward admonished Alan.

"If you had killed him, you would have lost the trust of your men. He felt no pain." Alan wiped the dagger on his sleeve.

The two samurai, who had been waiting in a corner of the garden, approached Michael, confirmed that he was dead, bowed to Edward, and left.

"Those two stayed behind to make sure that you did the right thing. If you had set Michael free, they would have immediately reported it to Lord Tokimune," Zafir told Edward. "Lord Tokimune was testing you."

"Take a good look at what happened to Michael," Edward warned his soldiers. "We are in a foreign territory. We have been accepted as guests of this nation. If any of us forget that and fail to abide by the laws of this land, the only thing waiting for him is death. This is the same no matter who the person is or what rank he holds."

"I had no choice but to do it," Alan told Edward when they were alone.

"I am grateful."

"I should be the one thanking you."

This was the first time Alan had ever spoken to him so seriously. "I was afraid when I was sent by myself to become a knight apprentice. I thought I was going to starve and be beaten even more than I had been. But soon I was happy that my old man had sold me off. I wasn't hungry anymore, and I didn't have to worry about finding a place to sleep. All I had to do was train with a sword. I was worried about what kind of master you would be, but it was a huge relief you ended up being weaker than me. If I didn't like you, I could always beat you up."

Edward was silent as his listened to his friend. The moment they met, Alan recklessly hurled himself toward Edward with a wooden sword, and struck him without giving him a chance to ready himself. From then on, Edward's body was covered in bruises.

"So that's why you were always hitting me."

"All part of your training. No matter how rich or powerful a knight your father was, we are equal at the end of a blade."

"It's thanks to you I can take a beating now."

"I think of you as my older brother. There's nothing I won't do for you."

"And you are my little brother."

CHAPTER
44

"The men are acting strange," Edward confided in Zafir a few days after Michael's execution. "I think they're avoiding me. They hardly speak to me."

"It is your responsibility as their superior to read and understand the hearts of your subordinates," Zafir said in a tone that made Edward understand.

"Michael's loss pains me. But there was no other way."

"I am sure the others know of your suffering, Lord Edward. However, the human heart is not one-dimensional. Not everyone is like you and I. Each person has different desires and goals."

Alan alternated looks between the two by his side.

"The discontent building at present will eventually erupt," Zafir continued.

"Discontent? If you think of what we have gone through up until now, what is there to be discontented about? We have a roof over our heads and food in our bellies," Edward replied.

"A person's heart cannot be satisfied with only that. That's a life without purpose. What's to become of us? Will there come a day when we are suddenly brought before the execution block? Everyone has grown impatient and afraid. At this rate, most of the men will drown themselves in wine and women. What happened to the goal to return to our homelands?" Zafir reasoned.

"This nation is on the verge of a crisis. Once that is settled, I am sure they will send us home."

"Edward, are you sure you're not putting too much trust in Tokimune?" Alan asked.

"That man, as you call him, holds our lives in his hand. Right now we are alive. No, we are being kept alive. A single word from Tokimune saved your life."

"I've heard he killed his brother! He's a cruel bastard. Relatives, even parents and children, kill each other without batting an eye in this country. You have no idea when he could change his mind!"

Edward had no response. Maybe what Alan said was true, but his words pierced his heart nonetheless. Everything was justified for the sake of protecting one's country.

CHAPTER
45

Eager to show off Nippon's weaponry, Morimune invited Edward, Alan, and Zafir to a yagura armory on his estate. As their eyes adjusted to the dim light, they saw a flat pedestal in the middle of the room and a variety of weapons arranged on it. Naginata pole arms and bows were hung on the walls, and boxes filled with hundreds of arrows were placed around the room.

"It looks like it wasn't just the storm that killed Mongolian soldiers," Alan said pointing out a full suit of Nippon armor to Edward. A kabuto helmet sat atop the breastplate, and the armor was assembled as if its wearer was sitting. It was similar to the armor Morimune wore the first time Edward met him. Made with iron, raw ox hide, deer suede, silk thread, and plaited cord, the individual pieces protected most of the exposed parts of the body. Together, they offered solid defense, but were also elastic, allowing for dynamic movement.

"Even if you've been hit with a few arrows, you can still fight while wearing this," Morimune boasted.

"It's a splendid suit of armor. But it looks heavy. Do you wear this into battle?"

The kabuto helmet with its long ornaments is beautiful, but not suitable for combat, Edward thought.

"The crest recognizes distinguished service by hikitsuke officers on the battlefield," Morimune explained, as if he could read Edward's mind. "Each man designs his own crest, based on the rewards he receives after a war."

"If you stand out too much, you're a walking target for the enemy," Alan quipped.

"The crest is a source of pride and honor."

"Doesn't make much sense to me," Alan said, arching his eyebrows and shrugging his shoulders.

"With its strong cavalry brandishing heavy longbows and wearing this armor, the Nippon army would be formidable," Edward observed, as he stepped closer to the armor and touched its fine details. "What are these little iron slabs fastened like scales on the iron plate?"

"They are called kozane. Each rectangle is as long as a finger. Lacquer is applied on top of the black iron rectangles, and thousands are tightly laced together in layers to make the armor impenetrable to arrows," Morimune responded much pleased at Edward's interest.

"Over here you can see examples of Yuan's armor and weapons," Morimune said as he walked to another part of the room.

Morimune picked up a Yuan helmet and handed it to Zafir. The helmet was made of leather held together by iron studs.

"Yuan helmets don't have any unnecessary decorations," Zafir observed. "It is as if they turned a pot inside out and attached a small visor to it. It is thoroughly functional, making it completely different from Nippon's helmets."

He looked further.

"In terms of protection, Nippon's armor is superior. But in terms of mobility, I would say Yuan's is more successful. It's the same with the bows. Nippon's bows are long and difficult to handle, but the arrows fired are unbelievably powerful. You can shoot rapid-fire arrows long distances with a short bow, but it's difficult to fire an arrow that maintains a lot of power."

Morimune removed a naginata, a bladed weapon with a long shaft, from the wall and showed it to Edward.

"Typically our country favors longswords. Since the battle of the Genji and Heike clans, there has generally been more of a preference for sturdier blades. As well as the nagamaki, which is an even longer nodachi sword. Many warriors prefer it because its exceedingly elongated handle is excellent for keeping your enemies at a distance while in battle."

Alan flourished a naginata.

"But, in the end, I believe the most powerful weapon is the bow and arrow." Morimune took one of the longbows and pulled back its string.

"The Yuan armor is only glued to wood. It would not put up much resistance if hit by a Nippon arrow. But the Nippon armor is the opposite. It would be hard to fight with soldiers wearing Nippon armor," Zafir said before he stabbed one of the Nippon arrows into the Yuan armor.

"I guess it wasn't a lie that the samurai fought with Yuan soldiers while their armor had been hit with several arrows," Alan added.

"Even if an arrow strikes the armor, so long as the flesh isn't pierced there is no need to worry about the poison. The samurai weren't just bragging, they were telling the truth," Edward said, strumming his fingers on the torso pad.

CHAPTER

46

When alone together, walking in Tokimune's garden, Edward and Tokimune would invariably talk of warfare and spirituality.

"You have said you fought the pagans to reclaim your Holy Land. Correct?"

Edward's response stuck in his throat. He had been thinking about this for a long time. No, it wasn't to reclaim. The crowned prince who had left England with them fled the war early, abandoning Edward and his men in a hostile foreign land. It had been over seven years since he left home. He couldn't say the journey he had been on was very fitting for the Army of Christ. They pillaged and slaughtered everywhere they went. Every battle created more hatred of pagans. And that hatred provoked more fighting and gave rise to even more barbarous acts. This cycle was centuries old. And it would repeat itself in the future.

Who is God, and what is the purpose of a knight? The thought was constantly on Edward's mind.

"In Buddhism, we learn the concept of nothingness. That this world is only temporary and everything within it will eventually return to nothingness," Tokimune offered.

"I wish to live for something tangible. Whether that is God or not, I'm not sure."

"Is that not contradictory to your God and your Christ's teachings?" Tokimune said, and looked at Edward with an amused expression.

"Even so . . . there should be a way of life that God wishes for," Edward responded in a low voice.

"You've told me that you have been fighting for God, but have you ever been rewarded?"

"I don't fight to be rewarded. I fight for the salvation of my soul."

"So, you kill people for your soul's salvation?"

"Some things can't be protected unless you kill for them. You of all people should understand that."

Tokimune sighed. "You say that you fought these pagans, and that God will forgive you for killing them."

Edward could not respond.

"What kind of deity is your God? Are you not your own person outside of your God? You are aware some people can attain salvation through their actions without actively seeking it out."

"Then what is Buddha? You say he is the figure of a man who became enlightened after death, yet you stay living."

Edward and Tokimune starred at each other for some time.

"Both God and Buddha promise happiness after death, but people must find happiness while they are alive," Edward eventually said.

That was truly what he believed.

Thus far his eyes had witnessed too many brutal deaths. He wondered if any of the dead souls had attained salvation and made it to Heaven.

"In truth, I think the same. However, humans are weak. They can't live unless they have something to cling to," Tokimune murmured.

The two men were silent for a long while. In due course, they smiled and laughed together for some time after.

CHAPTER

47

Edward, Alan, and Zafir had been cooped up in their manor for several days, so when Morimune enticed them to join him in Kamakura, they eagerly accepted.

Many samurai residences and temples flanked the main street leading to the Yuigahama Beach and Tsurugaoka Hachiman-gu Shrine in the center of town.

"That's my father's residence," Morimune told them.

"Who's that?" Alan pointed to a samurai sitting in the formal seiza position in front of the mansion.

"He is probably one of the men from Kyushu who has come to petition the courts for his rewards. My father is the magistrate in charge of administering the rewards from the previous war," Morimune explained in a somewhat bored tone of voice. "But in spite of his distinguished service in previous battles, he may not receive enough. He must be here to negotiate. The samurai system consists of service and rewards. The gokenin risk their lives for the Lord of

Kamakura, and land is given to them in return. But no new territories were procured in the last war. So, the regent of the shogunate has a problem."

"They don't like working for free, huh?" Alan scoffed.

"It would be the same for anyone," Edward responded.

"It's been three years since the war. They should be preparing for the next war that's on their doorstep."

"I would also complain if I risked my life to fight and received nothing for it."

"When we fought for God, what exactly did we get out of it?"

"The path to heaven." Edward had said this many times before.

"After Lord Takezaki Suenaga traveled all the way from Kyushu to Kamakura and was rewarded his sakigake after making an appeal, countless other samurai have been visiting Kamakura," Morimune interrupted.

"What's sakigake?"

"It means the man who leads the attack in battle and is the first to cross blades with the enemy before all other warriors."

"And here I was expecting it to be a reward for the number of his countrymen's lives he saved," Alan jeered.

"Does your country reward such achievements?"

"It was just a sudden thought I had," Alan pouted.

Edward was reminded of the scene they had witnessed in Kyushu. The mountain of skeletal corpses. They said it wasn't only Mongolian soldiers, but Kyushu citizens mixed in with the bones. Many people had lost their families. Some even said the only reason they were alive was to get revenge on the Mongolian soldiers.

"Aren't the samurai the ones who protect the people? I'd also give up my life to do so," Edward said.

"Go home!" a furious voice behind them shouted out. "Hurry your ass home! Yuan's going to attack sooner or later. Protect your people this time around. Then you'll get your reward!"

As Edward turned, he saw Alan berating the samurai sitting in front of the gate. Morimune, clearly embarrassed, looked between Edward and Alan.

CHAPTER

48

"Who's there?" Edward called out as he entered his room that night.

He sensed that someone was in the back of the room, where the moonlight was barely shining in, and instinctively gripped his sword's handle. As his eyes adjusted to the darkness, he saw a woman with long hair wearing a white kimono.

"Who are you?"

The woman said nothing.

"These are my quarters. What are you doing here?"

"I am doing as Lord Morimune ordered," she answered quietly.

"What did Morimune tell you?"

"To come here."

Her voice was barely audilble.

Edward remembered the suggestive look Morimune gave him when they parted earlier that day.

"Get out."

Edward was about to put his hand on her shoulder, but pulled it away. Her shoulders were shaking. He could see that she was crying. Edward didn't know what to do. He sat down and looked at the woman.

"What's your name?"

"Haruno."

"I'm—"

"Lord Edward."

Edward could just see Haruno's oval face in the pale light. She had delicate features, but her lips were painted a deep red.

"You are a warrior from a land farther west than Yuan. You drifted ashore in Kyushu and saved Lord Morimune's life."

Edward wanted to say something, but could not.

Eventually, Haruno stood up. She let her kimono fall from her body, and her thin white form shimmered in the darkness. She humbly knelt before him. Edward lifted her up and embraced her. Her body was softer and more supple than any he had touched before. Her skin gave off an exotic fragrance that filled his being and intoxicated his soul.

Later when she shook her shoulders to free herself of his embrace, he gently removed his hands and stepped back.

"I must go," she murmured against her will.

"Will I see you again?"

"Please ask Lord Morimune," she said in a low voice as she gathered her kimono and quickly left.

Edward lay down, but he could not sleep. Restless, he turned this way and that in his bed. It had been a long time since he had been with a woman. They had exchanged only a few words, yet Haruno's voice echoed deep within him. Her scent lingered, and no matter how tightly he screwed his eyes shut, her face and body appeared, promising a future he dared not imagine.

As soon as the sun rose in the sky, Morimune came to visit.

"Why did you send me a woman?"

"Did you not like her? I thought she was a good choice."

"It's not that."

"You're a man. You've been away from your homeland for several years. I simply thought you must be lonely. It's important to have a little companionship now and again. If it made you feel awkward, I won't do it again."

"No, please, I want to meet her again," Edward blurted out.

That night when he stepped into the darkness of his room, he found Haruno sitting within. His arms enfolded her, and she entrusted her body to him. Edward desired her with a fierce passion, and Haruno accepted it. But she was silent, as if breath itself could not escape her lips.

"Do you hate me?"

"No. I only—" Haruno paused.

"I want to know more about you."

"What will you do when you know more about me?"

"To know about you is to know this country. No, that's not right. I want to know only about you. And . . . I want you to know about me," Edward fumbled for words. This was the first time he had ever felt this way. After another silence, Haruno nodded.

They began to meet every few days. Haruno would tell him about daily life in Nippon, entertaining him with stories about the common people, the samurai, and the nobility. She brought him books and taught him the basics of reading Japanese. Edward's heart soared.

CHAPTER

49

Every day was filled with new experiences for Edward, and rarely was he bored. Zafir was the same. They were no longer inconvenienced by an inability to communicate in the Nippon language. However, Alan, Thomas, and the others were less able to learn the intricacies of the language. Frustrated, they grew restless and resentful, and quarreled over the smallest matter. Morimune visited them during one of those moments of dissension.

"If your men continue like this, they will be miserable," Morimune observed to Edward. "Why don't you and they hunt with me tomorrow?"

"What are you hunting?"

"Wild boars and deer. I'm sure Lord Tokimune would like to demonstrate his skill with a bow."

"We would be happy to accompany you."

"There is no easy way to say this, but only twenty of your men may accompany you. I also ask that you please refrain from bringing your weapons."

"I'd like us to bring our bows."

"Lord Tokimune has great interest in your crossbow. You may bring one of those."

He wants to see how we use our weapons in combat, Edward thought.

"Can you grant permission for at least five?"

"I shall allow three. That is all."

"Can we bring our swords?"

"Swords are unnecessary when hunting. However, I shall ask Lord Tokimune."

A knowing smile slowly crept over Morimune's face and he leaned in.

"I see you have been meeting with Haruno."

"She's teaching me the Nippon language. Her reading and writing skills are superb."

"Is that all?" Morimune chuckled, before saying his goodbyes. Both Alan and Zafir shot Edward mysterious looks as he left.

The next day, their swords, spears, shields, and chainmail were lined up in the garden.

"Lord Tokimune has given his permission. You are free to use these today," Morimune said.

Alan looked at Edward and shrugged.

"He really puts on airs over every single thing."

"Please give him our thanks," Edward said to Morimune.

"This shows how much faith Lord Tokimune has in you. Please don't betray his expectations."

Edward had last worn his armor two years ago, when he first met Tokimune. Wearing it on a hunt was completely impractical, he knew that, but it was nonetheless sobering to wear it once again. Alan and the other knights were in high spirits as they dressed. They felt as Edward did.

"Is this the resurrection of Lord Edward's elite troops of twenty-three knights?" Zafir asked as he looked at Edward, wonderment spreading across his face.

"Lord Tokimune will be bringing thirty samurai on horseback and another thirty underlings," Morimune said as he, too, watched Edward and the others put on their armor.

"Tokimune trusts Edward more than we thought. But what shall you be hunting in such gear?" Zafir asked sarcastically.

"People!" Alan jested, though it felt like there might be more than a little truth in his words.

Morimune took Edward and his men to the rear of the estate, where a herd of horses awaited them.

"Please ride whichever horse you want. Lord Tokimune has arranged them for you."

Alan whistled.

An hour later, Edward's twenty-three riders joined Tokimune's thirty-man cavalry and his thirty foot soldiers.

CHAPTER
50

Tokimune's subordinates were dressed in hunting attire; only the samurai escorts wore helmets and armor. Edward's cavalry, fully armed with shields and clad in chainmail, was the first Western army they had ever seen.

Morimune led the way with twenty of his men, followed by Edward and his knights, and ten samurai on horseback behind them. The infantry brought up the rear. As they left Kamakura, people stopped and stared at the strangely attired band of Englishmen.

Tokimune rode in the center of Morimune's group. Outwardly, he showed little interest in Edward and his men, but he was tracking every movement they made.

"Is that bastard Tokimune really that stupid or is he just that daring of a man?" Alan said in a jovial tone, standing up in his stirrups to view the formation in front of him. "If we wanted to, we could take him as our hostage and finally get a ship home."

"True, but don't even think about it," Edward warned. He reminded himself of the trust Tokimune had put in them. "Tokimune intends to test our capabilities. That's why he returned our weapons."

"He also wishes to see the depths of your spirit," Zafir added. Alan frowned disapprovingly at Zafir.

After several hours, they came to a gently sloping hill surrounded by a forest dazzling in the sunlight. *The sky in England is overcast and cloudy most of the year,* Edward thought, *but here it is clearer than I could ever have imagined.* He breathed deeply, and the forest scents spread throughout his body. *What a beautiful country.*

"What happened to the beaters?" Morimune asked a subordinate. "I don't see or hear them."

"On our hunt the neighboring peasants will drive the beasts toward us, and we can kill them as well. It's Lord Tokimune's favorite pastime and also good for military training," Morimune had informed them the day before.

Morimune rode up to Edward and surveyed the surrounding area.

The ominous stillness was suddenly broken by the bellowing of animals and the pounding of horses' hooves in pursuit. The sounds became louder. The samurai on horseback tensed and spread out, ready to shoot the game.

"Be careful. The horses are on edge." But before Edward could finish his sentence, the ground beneath them shook.

Twenty yards ahead, three boars charged out of the tall grass. Tokimune had his bow ready. In that moment, Edward thought the samurai's horse next to him must have violently reared and the rider fallen. But he saw an arrow protruding from the man's chest as he lay on the ground.

"Enemy attack!" he yelled, drawing his blade.

Alan had already unsheathed his sword and held his body low to his horse.

"The enemy is over by the thicket!" he yelled.

"How many?"

"I can't tell. A dozen . . . or more!"

As if on signal, scores of arrows came flying toward them. Tokimune's close aides, including Morimune, quickly crowded around him to protect him from the onslaught. The mass of arrows converged, and more than ten samurai were struck and tumbled from their horses.

"Everyone dismount! Keep low and avoid the arrows!" Edward ordered in English as he leaped from his horse. The others did as he commanded.

Holding his horse's reins in his left hand, Edward used his other to raise his shield against the oncoming rain of arrows. Arrows pounded into his shield from every direction. They were surrounded.

"Testudo formation! Tokimune in the center!" Edward shouted at the top of his voice.

Edward's men encircled Tokimune. Some formed a wall on all sides with their shields, while others lifted their shields up and overhead. But they were too few in number, leaving chinks between the shields. Edward wasn't sure how long they would be able to hold out.

"Here they come," Alan alerted, as more than fifty warriors on horseback and a similar number of infantrymen came charging out of the forest.

"Ready the bows!"

Three soldiers with crossbows stood up, and the samurai steadied their longbows.

"Aim for the horses!"

At Edward's signal, the arrows were released at the same time. The enemy in the lead bent backward as he was struck, but kept charging as he clung to his horse.

"We don't have enough arrows! If all of us had bloody bows, we could easily drive back these bastards," Alan spat out.

"Here comes the advance!"

"Bring out the spears!"

At Edward's command, Morimune's men thrust their spears through the openings in the shields and steeled themselves.

"Crusaders, I want to hear you roar!"

Edward's men let out a blood-curdling war cry. Although clearly taken aback, their samurai companions imitated the deafening cry.

The enemy brought their horses to a stop in front of Edward's battle formation. They were clearly bewildered and unsure of what to do. Some charged the shield wall, but the protruding spears stabbed the riders and cut their steeds. Others swung down their longswords with great force.

"Aim for the throat and armpit! Their armor is weakest there!" Edward shouted as he grabbed one of the crossbows and tried with all his might to protect himself against the swords' blows.

"Don't let them break through! Close ranks!" he shouted at the top of his lungs.

In the middle of the formation, Tokimune sat on a folding stool, his demeanor unchanging amid the chaos. He made no attempt to take command and remained calm as he watched Edward and the others fight. *Is it because he has faith in his men and me?* Edward wondered. *Or is this what the leader of Nippon is supposed to do?*

After half an hour, the enemy retreated into the forest.

"Is it over?" Alan panted.

"They're watching us from the trees. Our tactics took them by surprise. They'll attack again and soon. Can't we call for reinforcements?" Edward asked Morimune.

"We have another force at the foot of the mountain. If anything strange was to occur, they were to immediately rush here."

"Another unit? You didn't tell us anything about that!" Alan exclaimed as he reset his crossbow.

"They were to transport the bag at the end of the hunt," Morimune said, although it was clear they were to serve a very different purpose. "Fire flaming arrows into the sky and blow the conch horn. We need them here now," Morimune ordered.

At that moment, an army of horsemen emerged from all four directions and unleashed a torrent of arrows. Some of the arrows made it through the shield wall and killed several samurai.

"The formation's breaking! Steady up! Steady up!"

Two of the enemy horsemen jumped from above and smashed into the Testudo.

"Protect Tokimune!"

Alan grabbed a longsword and plunged it into one of the riders' chest. Edward aimed a crossbow at the other man's neck. The two fell in an instant. But the number of arrows flying toward them increased more and more. Already half the samurai were injured, and the other half were dead. Several of Edward's men had been hit.

"There must be over a hundred of them," Alan grunted.

Edward turned to find Tokimune standing in the middle of the formation with his eyes closed.

"Are you out of your mind! Crouch down!" Edward bellowed, as an arrow whizzed past his ear. Tokimune did as he was told.

"Shit! I've no more arrows," Edward said, throwing down the crossbow and unsheathing his sword. "While I cut my way into the enemy and distract them, the rest of you head to the mountain and bring back the reinforcements. Let's go, Alan. May God protect us."

The front of the Testudo formation opened, and Edward jumped out, Alan following. On the run, Edward evaded the swing of a naginata sword from an enemy rider and rammed his sword into the man's back. The man tumbled off his horse. Seeing a discarded naginata on the ground, he used its pole to prop himself up and angrily faced Edward. He swung the naginata down over Edward's head. The impact made Edward's arms go numb. He had never felt a blow like it. The naginata swung at him again and again, and Edward could barely parry the blows. Suddenly the warrior swung the naginata to the side. The pole swept under Edward's legs, and he fell to the ground. The warrior thrust the blade toward Edward's chest. Edward quickly rolled over, just missing the blade's edge. As he rolled, he swept his own blade to the side and cut off the warrior's leg. Edward quickly jumped up and stabbed his sword through the fallen warrior's throat.

"We can't go on like this!" Alan shouted.

Edward turned to Alan and saw more than fifty fully armed riders charging toward the shield wall from the forest.

"Run!" Alan yelled, still wielding his sword.

Just as Edward was about to give up hope, the horsemen attacked the enemy. *Odd,* Edward thought.

Morimune stood up. "It's the reinforcements! We're saved!"

The enemy rushed toward Edward, the reinforcements in pursuit.

"Strengthen the lines! Don't let the shields fall!" Edward yelled as he ran over to Tokimune. An arrow flew over his helmet.

The horseman who had loosed the arrow raced toward them. Edward tackled Tokimune to the ground. An arrow penetrated Edward's chest and knocked him onto his back. He sat up but couldn't stand.

"Edward, what's wrong?" He heard Alan's voice in the distance.

I can't breathe. The arrow . . . I can't feel anything . . . my chest.

As he tried to inhale, he choked, and lukewarm blood flowed from his throat.

"Don't move! You'll lose too much blood. Your ribs are broken. I'll have to operate here. Someone build me a fire! And hot water! I need hot water!"

Edward heard only fragments of Zafir's orders, and saw nothing but whiteness. He had a vague awareness of blood draining from his body. A black void opened up, and he lost consciousness.

CHAPTER

51

Lost in a dreamlike state, Edward swiveled and swung his sword. He could feel the dull sensation of the blade ripping through an abdomen. A man whose face was concealed by a black cloth toppled to the ground, clasping a dagger. Edward turned the man over with his foot. With the tip of his blade, he removed the face covering. There was a youth in his teens. Edward bent to take the necklace he saw peeking out of the boy's collar but stopped himself. He had killed a woman not yet twenty. *If you kill a heathen, God will save you. What lies*, Edward murmured.

His chest ached, with a dull but strong pain as if a horse were kicking him, again and again. His body felt as if it had been buried deep in the ground. *Am I dead? That may be for the best. If that is what God wishes.* He opened his eyes but saw nothing. He heard nothing. He tried to lift his arm, but he trembled all over. Had all his senses gone numb, or had they completely stopped working? *Where am I?* He desperately tried to scream, but he had no voice.

"He still hasn't come to?" Alan's words echoed deep within his mind.

I'm . . . I'm fine, he meant to call out, but didn't.

"I have done everything I could." This time it was Zafir who spoke. But rather than hear his voice, Edward sensed the air reverberate as he faded out of consciousness once more.

Is the one that guides us God . . . or the Devil? No, that's not right. The one I seek is . . .

"Don't go. Come back," a voice resounded in Edward's soul. The voice was small, but powerful, as it pulled Edward out of the darkness. A ray of light enveloped him and guided him through the darkness. It felt as soft and warm as a mother's love.

Haruno . . .

CHAPTER

52

Edward opened his eyes, then quickly closed them. The sunlight blinded him and dazzled his brain. His body felt like it was submerged in water. He doubted he could move it.

"You've come to."

The voice was familiar. Edward forced his eyes open and saw Alan before a bearded face pushed his countryman aside.

"Zafir," Edward said in a hoarse voice. His mouth felt sticky, like it was filled with oil. Words could not come out.

"Edward's alive!" he heard Thomas shout out, followed by a cheer from his men.

He tried to get up, but an agonizing pain radiated throughout his body from his shoulder and chest.

"Your wounds have not closed yet. You should not strain yourself," Zafir said, as his hand gently pressed Edward to lie down.

"Where are we?" he struggled to ask.

"I want you to follow my finger," Zafir ignored his question and moved his index finger in front of Edward's eyes, which followed the finger.

"Next, grip my hand."

Edward squeezed Zafir's hand, but his strength was no more than that of a child.

"You will be fine. But you need to rest. We are still at the hunting grounds."

"The hunting grounds?"

He tried to remember. *That's right.* They were hunting with Tokimune when they were attacked. They fought desperately, but the enemy outnumbered them, and it was only a matter of time before they would be defeated. But reinforcements arrived. And the arrow meant for Tokimune pierced his chest instead. The memories fell into place.

"Where's Lord Tokimune?"

"Back at his estate. It was too dangerous for him to remain here."

"What about me?"

"Lord Tokimune had this hut built for your recovery. You can't be moved yet."

Alan, Thomas, and several samurai crowded around him.

"You were struck by an enemy arrow when you protected Lord Tokimune," Zafir continued. "The arrow broke a few ribs but stopped there. It was a miracle your chainmail stopped the arrow from penetrating further. But had it been off in the slightest, it would have pierced your lungs and you would be dead."

"Our men?"

"None are dead, but several are injured and are being treated. You suffered the most serious injury. You have been unconscious for three days."

"Three days, huh."

Edward sighed. *Yet again I have escaped death. Is this God's will? Is there something God still wants of me?*

"Who's that?" Edward said, indicating a monk behind Zafir.

"Wuxue Zuyuan, a monk from Song with a knowledge of herbs and alchemy. Lord Tokimune sent him. He's made a salve to keep your wounds from festering and to help them heal faster. It is similar to the salve the fisherman applied to Alan's injury. He has also prepared a medicine to nourish you and build back your strength."

"Please give him my thanks. And Morimune?"

"He and thirty of his men are protecting the perimeter. We don't know if the enemy is still lurking about."

"Was Morimune injured?"

"He is fine. He is most grateful that you saved Lord Tokimune's life."

"Who were the enemies?"

"It is likely they were Lord Tokimune's—" but Zafir didn't finished his sentence.

"Relatives?"

"We can move you in a few days," Zafir said, avoiding Edward's question.

Edward closed his eyes, saying he understood. There weren't many people who could send a military force that size. That was why Tokimune returned and left Edward behind.

Two days later, with Zafir's aid, Edward rode in a palanquin Tokimune had sent for him, and returned to Kamakura protected by an escort of samurai. As they re-entered Kamakura, the townspeople stared at Edward. News of the foreign knight who had saved Hojo Tokimune's life had spread throughout the town.

CHAPTER
53

Once Edward was able to walk on his own, a messenger summoned him to Tokimune.

"How are you feeling?" the regent of the Kamakura shogunate asked.

"As you can see."

Edward stretched his back and straightened up. A dull pain spread throughout his body.

Tokimune kneeled.

"You sacrificed yourself for me."

"I'm glad you weren't hurt."

Tokimune stood, nodded, and Morimune approached, holding a katana.

"This is a sword handed down in the Hojo clan. It is called the Demon Slayer."

Tokimune drew out the blade. Beautiful ripples floated up the gently curved blade. As Edward looked at it, it felt as if its cold wave could permeate his soul. He had heard that Nippon katanas cut through flesh and bone by pulling, whereas European swords smash rather than cut. Using a heavy force to bring down the blade, one could tear through flesh and shatter bones.

"I think our swords have differing spirits," Edward commented. *The cold tranquility of the katana may have nurtured the souls of this nation's samurai,* he thought.

Tokimune sheathed the katana.

"I'd like you to have it. You saved my life," Tokimune said. Edward saw gratitude in the depths of Tokimune's eyes. He accepted the sword and felt its weight.

"Please follow me."

Tokimune led the way at a fast clip. With every step Edward took, he felt pain, but he kept pace with Tokimune.

"Where are we going?"

"The stables. There's someone I want you to meet."

Once inside, Tokimune stopped in front of a stall.

"This is Hayate—Swift Wind. My horse," he said. "He is a good horse. And lean. The horses of this country are small, but they are strong and powerful."

As Edward went to pet his muzzle, Hayate pulled his head back and snorted. The horse glowered at Edward and pawed the ground.

"He doesn't like you, huh? He has a fear of strangers," Tokimune laughed. "He's a hard horse to please, with a fierce temper. But warhorses must be like that. The more violent the temper, the stronger the horse."

"But horses like that don't always obey their riders."

"The responsibility for that lies with the rider. In battle, man and horse must be one, body and soul."

Edward studied Hayate.

"Do you not remove the balls?"

"Remove the balls?" The idea shocked Torimune.

"Male horses in Europe are castrated unless they are kept for breeding."

For warriors in this land to not do this and still manage to maneuver their horses in battle showed they possessed considerable skill and bravery, Edward thought. He was reminded of the first time he had met Morimune in the Kyushu territory. He would have sworn Morimune was a knight the moment he appeared in armor atop his horse.

Determined, Edward once again approached the agitated chestnut stallion. While stroking Hayate's cheek to calm him, Edward slowly brought his lips to his ear and whispered something. Hayate began to lick Edward's hand.

"What did you say to him? Can you speak horse?" Tokimune asked him, a grin spreading across his face.

"I told him he needed to settle down."

"Truly?"

"And that if he acted up any more, I was going to eat him."

"You mean cut off his balls," Tokimune said as he burst out laughing. "Have you taken a liking to him?"

"A strong and resilient horse is a good companion for a knight and doubles his power."

"Then I give him to you."

Edward looked at Tokimune in surprise.

"And Hayate has taken a liking to you," Tokimune said, before his expression stiffened. "If you and your men hadn't been there, I would have been killed. In truth, I was prepared to die."

"Was the enemy disposed of?"

"It is a matter of great importance to this country that the root of an evil not be left behind," Tokimune stated definitively, before shifting his gaze to Hayate. Edward could tell that he had no intention of answering any more questions.

"You are very knowledgeable about horses. And also liked by the beasts. Hayate has attained an excellent rider. However, he is quite wild," Tokimune warned, suppressing a smile.

"If I were to ride into battle now, I wonder if I would have enough strength."

"You won't know until you do."

CHAPTER
54

That evening, Edward brought Hayate to the estate.

"This is an excellent horse. Tokimune is a generous man. He may look like a coward, but he has more guts than I thought. He didn't look at all scared during the battle," Alan said, unusually complimentary of Tokimune.

Edward expressed Tokimune's gratitude to his men.

"You saved Lord Tokimune's life, so it is only natural you received the katana and horse. Besides, let's say you saved our lives as well," Morimune said suggestively.

"Tell me so I can understand," Edward said. "Your words and phrasing are sometimes strangely incomprehensible."

Morimune pretended to think for a moment.

"The mastermind behind that attack was Ujiakira of the Hojo Clan. Just thinking of Lord Tokimune being murdered and Ujiakira becoming regent of the shogunate makes my stomach turn."

"So, the country is still not unified?"

"That's not the case," Morimune hurriedly denied. "All Kamakura samurai willingly obey the head of the Hojo Clan as their leader."

"What happened to Ujiakira?"

Morimune fell silent.

"Did you kill him? He was probably Tokimune's uncle," Alan, who had been quietly listening, interrupted.

"If the country is in chaos, we won't be able to fight against Yuan. The samurai leadership must be secure. That is Lord Tokimune's first concern."

"So, you killed them all?"

Morimune was silent.

"That Lord Tokimune is a dubious man," Zafir said once Morimune had gone. "He was so calm during the attack because he knew reinforcements would rush in."

"You must be jesting. He was simply so scared he couldn't even move," Alan mocked.

"Those extra troops Tokimune had stationed ahead were conveniently armed to the teeth. He had them lying in wait in case we betrayed him on the hunt. Luckily their presence ended up being incredibly helpful to us in the unforeseen circumstances of the attack."

Alan listened to Zafir with his mouth half open. Edward recalled what Tokimune had told him that afternoon. He certainly knew how to read and understand men's hearts.

CHAPTER
55

One day, Edward, Alan, and Zafir were in Kamakura when they came upon Nichiren preaching to a crowd.

"Don't you think he looks familiar?" Edward asked Alan.

"Well, do you want me to say he looks like our Lord, Jesus Christ?"

"So, you thought the same?"

"It's not only the way he looks. Jesus preached to the masses about God, which the rulers didn't like, so they crucified him. It's probably going to be the same for our monk friend here. But I don't understand what the hell he's talking about. And I don't intend to find out."

"No matter what rulers demand, the will to preach without compromising his views is similar. He is merely an eccentric man. It is best to pay him no mind," Zafir said, though out of the three men he seemed the most interested in Nichiren. As usual, he had his notebook out.

"Are you saying that Christ was also an eccentric?" Edward asked.

"It is a metaphor," Zafir said, focusing his attention on Nichiren. "He has been exiled by Lord Tokimune and was almost killed several times."

"But he's just a monk," Edward said.

"He wrote a book called the *Rissho Ankoku Ron*, predicting the Mongolian invasion and blatantly criticizing another sect of his own religion. He deserves to be hated."

"Is he a prophet?"

"He is similar to one."

"We already know the only prophet in the world. Yet I have seen many a prophet in this country. Do you not think there are too many gods?"

Zafir responded to Edward's sarcasm-filled words with a bitter smile. Zafir believed in the teachings preached by Muhammad, who was also worshiped as a prophet.

The next time Edward and Tokimune met was in the regent of the shogunate's private temple. Edward was shown to a shadowy room where Tokimune sat alone, contemplating several Buddhist mortuary tablets inscribed with his ancestors' names. Though they were contemporaries, Tokimune appeared in that instant far older than Edward. *This man carries the weight of an entire nation on his back during a time of great crisis,* Edward thought. *He lives with death every day.* And then he remembered Tokimune's words after the attack on the hunting grounds. "I was prepared to die," Tokimune had said. *Could he have been lying?*

"This is where my forefathers rest," Tokimune said quietly. "I grew up knowing that it was my mission to protect this country and inherit what my ancestors had built."

"I know nothing of the god of this country," Edward said.

"We have gods, but we also have Buddha. We are taught that the gods and Buddha live within us. Having discipline over oneself ultimately brings one to a closer connection with them."

"People seek salvation in God. He is an existence that transcends human beings. Humanity is full of sin and weakness."

"People have the ability to overcome those sins by borrowing strength from Buddha. We call this achievement Zen."

"Do you intend to kill the monk Nichiren?"

"He torments my mind. I tried to kill him once, but was unable to do so. I thought it would be difficult to attempt to kill someone who has already cheated death."

"It was good of you to let him be."

"Yet, because of that, a rumor has spread that he wasn't beheaded because the executioner was frightened when a bolt of lightning struck close by."

"It is said the dead tell more tales than the living. They settle into people's hearts. By sacrificing himself, Nichiren will become like a god, and his teachings will spread throughout the populace."

"Is it the same for your god? You said he attained eternal life by hanging on the cross."

No that wasn't it, Edward told himself. *Jesus attained eternal life through resurrection. He was recognized as a being beyond human. God is God and is nothing else. That is faith.*

When Tokimune and Edward eventually left the temple, sunlight washed over them after the darkness within. Edward instinctively shielded his eyes with his hand, and the cloud that had shadowed Tokimune's mood vanished.

"How is Hayate?"

"As his name suggests. He is as fast as the wind."

"Let's have a race sometime. My Demon Tokige won't lose to your Hayate," Tokimune said cheerfully. He had reverted to being a young man in his twenties.

CHAPTER
56

Edward and Haruno climbed together up Mount Tendai, just northeast of Kamakura. The sea stretched out before them.

"That sea flows to my homeland, England," Edward murmured without thinking.

"I have never left Kamakura. Do you like this country, Lord Edward?"

"I don't know. But I don't hate it."

His feelings for Nippon were changing. He often thought he would be content if time continued to pass by as it had been.

"I was worried about you. Lord Morimune told me of your wound," Haruno said hesitantly, her expression suddenly serious. "I called at your estate many times, but I was not allowed to enter."

"I had even worse wounds in Jerusalem, yet I miraculously survived. Zafir says God still has work for me to do."

"You are protected by your God."

With her finger, Haruno gently tracked the scar on Edward's chest.

"I've heard that knights are the same as samurai. Is it true?"

"I don't know much about samurai."

"Then what of knights?"

"I was taught that knights carry out justice for the weak."

But have I really done that? he thought. *I've only swung my sword in the name of God. Looking back at the horrors of the Jerusalem expedition, the life I am living now seems like a dream.*

"I've never felt this at ease in my entire life," he said. He had been fighting since he was twelve years old and began his training as a knight. His sword never left his side. When he was awake, when he was sleeping, his sword was always within reach. "For me, living was a battle."

"I wonder how long it has been since I also have experienced such ease?" Haruno said, as her eyes looked out over the sea. Edward had never known such a woman before. All he had known were dressed-up noblewomen and the whores who followed the army.

He gently touched her hair.

"I hear some of the women in your country have golden hair," Haruno teased in a soft voice.

"You are my first woman with black hair *and* black eyes," he lied. Islamic women had the same coloring. But Haruno was different from any other woman Edward had ever been with.

"You truly are skilled at our language," Haruno said.

"That's because I've been studying like mad, so I can understand everything about you," Edward said, not taking his eyes off her. Haruno returned his gaze. *This woman.* When the arrow that pierced his chest left him hovering between life and death, the one who brought him back from darkness was this woman.

"You are the one who pulled me up from the pit of despair and saved me. Not just my body, but my soul as well. You gave me

new life," Edward said, believing every word to the core of his being. He had caught a glimpse of what he should protect and what
he should believe.

Edward grasped her hand and pulled her closer to him. He
could feel her heart beat as they embraced. Opening his eyes, he
saw the mountain range spread out in the distance. *What a beautiful
country*. Yet, this country was soon to be assaulted by foreign armed
forces. Edward longed to protect it and Haruno.

CHAPTER

57

Tokimune was sitting in the corridor facing the garden. Yasumori waited beside him.

"Why do you put so much trust in the foreign man?" Yasumori suddenly asked. "At this time of national crisis, keeping a suspicious person next to you is not an action fit for the regent of the shogunate."

"Is that an opinion shared by the rest of the council?"

"Yes. Many are not pleased that you gave Hayate and the Demon Slayer to him."

"What do you think?"

"If you let the foreigners stay here, it may lead to conflict. On the other hand, if you send them back to Hakata and give them a ship, they will return to their land knowing too much about our nation."

"Are you saying I should kill them?"

Yasumori was silent.

"That man saved my life and the life of your son Morimune."

"I had prepared myself for my son to join the dead once he was sent to Hakata. Many people lost their children and parents in the war against Yuan. However, only a few have received sufficient rewards for their sacrifice."

"You mean even now there are those who wish to complain?"

"It is as you say."

"It was a war to protect all of Nippon. Even though we were victorious, we gained no new territories. Everyone, including those here in Kamakura, made sacrifices."

"In preparation for the next war, we have demanded much labor and great funds for the stone wall construction. There is growing discontent among the gokenin servants. I believe you also fully understand this, my Lord. What is most important for our country is to come together as one nation. To accomplish this, we must do everything in our power," Yasumori continued.

Tokimune silently listened before speaking.

"Don't you think I also greatly doubt these foreigners?"

"Then why do you keep them so close?"

"Because I want to know. The continent to the West is called Ajia and farther west than that is Europa, as well as a giant continent called Afurika. I'd like to see them for myself one day."

"No matter how small a nation we may be, we should still hold true to who we are and have been as a people."

"I think the same, which is why it is necessary to know what lies beyond us."

"I cannot guess what that man is planning."

"Edward is too kindhearted," Tokimune muttered.

Tokimune had never met a man like Edward, and it wasn't just his appearance or the foreign language that he spoke. Maybe it was because the things they believed in were different? No, he didn't think that was it.

"Have you changed your mind about the Mongolians?"

"No. Our nation will never belong to another."

"Soon Kublai Khan will know that we have slain his emissaries. If we do not prepare ourselves properly this time, the Mongolian army will march all the way to Kamakura."

"I'm aware of that. That's why I'm—" but Tokimune stopped. *That's why I'm trying to learn new knowledge from Edward and his men. If we don't fight against Yuan with new battle tactics, we will be defeated and that would be the downfall of Nippon.*

"What has Nichiren been up to?" Tokimune asked, suddenly changing the subject.

"As usual, he does and says as he pleases. He continues to mislead people. A rumor is also spreading that the Lord of Kamakura is too weak to defend against the Mongolian invasion."

"No capable person wouldn't believe in the Lotus Sutra, I suppose. Edward also believes in a god called Jesus Christ. He did not hesitate to kill his enemies because they were all heathens."

"That religion of his is truly blasphemous. It is not suitable for our nation."

"Religious affiliation does not fit in this nation. When people die, they go to the Pure Land. That's why they endure suffering in this world. That is faith."

"You are too naive, my lord. And that naivety may prove to be deadly."

"Do you think I will bring this country to ruin?"

Yasumori couldn't respond.

"It would be good if that weren't so," Tokimune said under his breath.

KAMAKURA

CHAPTER
58

E dward rode Hayate daily. He had exchanged the Nippon saddle and reins with those he had brought from England, finding it easier to control the horse that way.

As Edward returned to the stables one day, Zafir was waiting for him.

"How is he? Your new steed?"

"He has speed, stamina, a wild temperament, and beauty. He is magnificent."

"Castration may not be necessary then."

Edward laughed.

"He seems a little small though."

"It is just that I am too big."

"It appears your Hayate has long been admired by Lord Tokimune's subordinates."

"So I have heard."

"As well as your katana." Zafir glanced at Edward's belt.

Since the attack at the hunting grounds and his recovery, Edward wore traditional suō samurai garb with a hakama divided skirt, eboshi hat, and katana. It was truly a splendid sword. The hilt and sheath were beautifully decorated in silver and gold. The blade had a cold brilliance. Morimune described the katana as the soul of a samurai, but it was not until Edward began to carry it on his person that he understood what he meant.

"It is a famous sword passed down from generation to generation in the Hojo Clan," Zafir emphasized.

"Then it is too much for me."

"Many people think the same, though in a different way from you, Lord Edward," Zafir said with a meaningful smile.

"Among the samurai?"

"Their opinion of you has changed."

Edward was aware of this shift. What was open hostility before had changed into something more complex.

"Why?"

"They are envious. A foreign castaway is called to Kamakura and warmly welcomed by the regent of the shogunate? As one would expect, his close associates cannot accept that."

"Then what should I do?"

"There is nothing you can do. Just remember that we are foreign residents and different from the people of this country."

Edward was going to ask how they were different but stopped himself. He knew the answer. The difference was something he could not bridge.

"I shouldn't carry around this sword then," Edward admitted.

"Your own sword suits you better, Lord Edward," Zafir said earnestly.

CHAPTER

59

Later that day, Edward and Morimune sat under the shade of a tree in the garden.

"Kagirinaki kumoinoyosoni wakarutomo hito-o-kokoroni okurasamuyawa," Edward recited.

"Did Lady Haruno teach you that?" Morimune asked after a moment of silence. Edward nodded.

"What does it mean? She wrote it out for me when we last met."

Morimune fell silent, a troubled look on his face.

"Is it something bad?"

"I would not say that, but it is not good either."

"Can you not be a bit clearer? This is such a bad custom this country has."

"Lady Haruno is falling in love with you."

"Falling in love?"

"She yearns for you. She reveals her feelings in the poem."

"Where?" Edward recited the poem again.

"'Even if I am separated from you beyond eternally distant clouds, my heart will never part from you.' That is what it means."

This time Edward fell silent.

"You should forget about Lady Haruno."

"I cannot."

"Her full name is Takakura Haruno. She is a distant relative of mine. Her father worked for the Adachi house and died long before I sent her to you. Well, since his death, many things have happened, and now she accepts offers like this."

"What do you mean by 'offers'?"

"Exactly as it sounds. Now she cannot even maintain the pride of a samurai family. She was once the most beautiful and talented woman in Kamakura. Many men courted her. I, too, desired her, but she rejected us all. No one was good enough for her. At least that was the impression she gave. And so a rumor spread, likely by the men she declined. By then, she was twenty-seven and far too old to marry respectably. For a time, she was indentured to the Mori Clan, but she left because of the poor treatment she received there."

Edward was at a loss for words.

"She ended up having no choice but to sell her body. That is who Lady Haruno is. It is inexcusable that I introduced such a woman to you, and for that I apologize." Morimune deeply bowed his head.

"I do not want to hear such talk ever again," Edward said furiously and walked away, Haruno's saddened face floating before him.

CHAPTER
60

The longer Alan lived in Kamakura—it was now three years— the more proficient he became in the Nippon language. Although not as fluent as Edward and Zafir, he understood what was being said. But true to his obstinate nature, he refrained from speaking the language on purpose, unless a situation warranted it, as it did when he once again encountered Nichiren preaching to the masses.

"It's that monk again. The one Morimune says is misleading the people," Alan grumbled.

"He may be leading the people," Zafir offered.

"Are you implying that filthy priest is the same as Jesus?"

"I don't know," Zafir said to defuse the argument.

As Alan approached, the crowd listening to Nichiren moved out of his way and made a path for him.

"He is filthy for someone preaching the word of a god."

"Jesus also wore tattered clothing, and his feet were covered in mud and sand," Edward joined in.

Nichiren interrupted his sermon and looked toward Edward, Alan, and Zafir.

"You over there, who is your god for? For the nobles? For the samurai? For you? Buddha is for all who are oppressed in this world. Only those who wear rags and wander hungry need peace in the world beyond. Only the one who saves them is the true god, the true Buddha," Nichiren said fiercely.

"Have you met that 'true god'? Why should you be the preacher for that god?"

Edward and Zafir were astonished. Alan had spoken in the Nippon language.

"Through my ascetic practices I have come to know the true teachings of Buddha. I learned Buddhism on my own."

"So, you became a god?"

"Not a god. I heard the voice of Buddha."

Alan drew his dagger and pointed it at Nichiren's throat. Many in the crowd screamed.

"What is Buddha telling you now?" he threatened.

Zafir moved to stop Alan, but Edward held him back.

"He might get into trouble as before," Zafir pleaded.

"Last time was a noble. This time a rebellious monk. Alan learned it the hard way."

Nichiren looked at Alan without fear.

"If you want to kill me, do it. A human life is as valueless as a stone at the end of the world. However, your God and my Buddha will both witness the fact that you killed me. Judgment Day will come."

"You are a fraud," Alan sneered and lowered his dagger. Edward led him away but not before Alan spat on the ground.

"Nichiren was exiled and almost beheaded. A mere dagger will not frighten him," Edward said.

"I should have killed him! He is a pagan. God would approve."

"But you cannot ignore his message. God is for the oppressed in this world."

Edward thought of Nichiren's followers. To them, Nichiren's words were like Christ's.

"The samurai of this nation kill their enemies to acquire rewards and land. We kill our enemies to seek salvation from God. I wonder how much difference there is between us?" Edward mused.

"This is blasphemy. We simply need to believe in god, and entrust ourselves to his will," Zafir interjected.

"Was it God's will that we drifted ashore to this land? I resent God. I would rather be fighting Saracens," Alan said, his voice full of sarcasm.

"God is for the weak," Edward murmured. *The strong can survive on their own. But is there such a thing as a strong person? Even those with power and influence cower in the face of death.*

"Are you calling us weaklings?" Alan fumed.

"Humans are fragile. With the mere cut of a sword, in battle or in peace, we hang in the balance between life and death. I know this to be true, as do you."

Alan turned his head away in indignation.

"You, who believe in Jesus, and I, who believe in Allah, have come to trust each other," Zafir, ever the peacemaker, said. "There lies salvation. Differences in gods have nothing to do with the true nature of people's hearts."

"I believe the same," Edward agreed.

CHAPTER
61

From where he stood in Morimune's manor, Zafir could see the reddish glow of bonfires burning in the gardens of Tokimune's estate.

"What is happening?" he asked his host.

"An envoy from Yuan has arrived in Hakata. The council is meeting."

"Should you not be there, Lord Morimune?"

"I attended the meeting last night. It seems Tokimune's mind is already made up," Morimune responded as he looked toward the estate.

"A messenger from Yuan?" Edward recalled the fate of the last envoy from Yuan.

"He carries a letter from the emperor of Yuan. Likely advising Nippon to surrender."

"Why don't you just kill him? It is obvious what the motive for coming is. He is a spy," Alan said and smirked at the thought.

"You think so?"

"Ask the messenger. Not that he will give you an answer. If you want, I can ask him for you."

Morimune quickly shook his head.

"He is a diplomat. We will not treat him the way you treated the two Mongolian soldiers you captured in Kyushu."

"Diplomat, soldier. People are the same. Torture them a little, and they will talk.

"That was 'a little'? The soldier was covered in blood."

"It's better than if you see your ally's blood," Alan responded coolly.

Morimune hurriedly entered Edward's room the next morning.

"Lord Tokimune wants to see you at once."

Escorted by Morimune, Edward and Zafir hastened to Tokimune's manor, where the regent of the shogunate and eighteen of the Hyojyoshu council awaited them. Everyone looked grave.

"We have been discussing what to do with Zhou Fu, the messenger from Yuan," Tokimune said by way of opening the discussion.

Several of the Hyojyoshu glared at Edward and Zafir with malicious intent.

"Have you reached a decision?"

"We have squandered countless hours, which is why I have called for you," Tokimune said calmly.

He has already made up his mind, Edward thought. *But the majority of the men here must not agree with him.* Edward had heard that Tokimune's views were different from those of the Imperial Court, and that his method was not to impose his opinions. Publicly, at least. Rather, under the guise of listening to other people, he resolutely held his own counsel.

"What does Kublai Khan say?" Edward asked.

"He says we should come to a peaceful resolution. That Nippon and Yuan should trade with one another, and that we should visit each other's countries to deepen our understanding of each other. He proposed sending Yuan merchants and farmers to Kyushu," answered Tokimune.

"The idea is to fill Kyushu with citizens from Yuan, Goryeo, and Song," Edward said.

A chorus of voices rang out in response.

"Kublai Khan is trying to handle things peacefully this time."

"Quite so. The previous war simply gave a taste of Yuan's military strength. How much would we have to sacrifice if we truly competed with Yuan?"

"If it was only a matter of making sacrifices, that would be fine. But Nippon could be destroyed," Edward responded.

Edward could not believe that many among them had once argued in favor of sending Nippon's army to the mainland.

"Kublai Khan will send an even larger army next time," continued Edward and voices from the council stopped.

"In Goreyo and Song, construction of warships has already begun on orders from Kublai Khan."

"We do not know whether that is true or false," Tokimune said.

"Zafir has obtained information from the merchants and pirates in Hakata," Edward offered, motioning Zafir to speak.

"At present, it appears there are nine hundred ships being built in the Jeolla and Gyeongsang provinces in Goryeo," Zafir began. "But the main force in the next battle will be the Southern Song Dynasty, which Yuan has newly acquired. That navy far surpasses the one in Goryeo."

Deep sighs could be heard from within the Hyojyoshu. In the last war, three hundred ships and thirty-two thousand soldiers invaded Nippon. But those unfathomable numbers would be eclipsed in the next conflict.

"Who told you this?"

"A Goryeo merchant."

"Someone from an enemy nation!"

"Goryeo was responsible for the main war expenditures and military forces in the last war and in this one. Their people are greatly oppressed under the present control of the Yuan Dynasty."

"And if what he says is false, what then?"

"The Matsura pirates have also been to Goryeo and Southern Song, and they have brought back the same foreboding news," Zafir said matter-of-factly. Tokimune and the Hyojyoshu listened quietly. When Zafir had finished, the air in the chamber could be cut with a knife.

"Are we in agreement then?" Tokimune said as he surveyed each of the council members.

"Let us send Zhou Fu's head and those of his entourage to Kublai Khan at once."

"What did Zhou Fu say exactly?" Edward asked.

"He wants to come to Kamakura to meet Lord Tokimune."

"Does he not know the emissary before him, Du Shizhong, was beheaded in Kamakura?"

"If he knew, he would not have asked to be brought to Kamakura. It is likely Kublai Khan also does not know Du Shizhong's fate. That's why he sent another messenger."

"He may be simply stalling for time while he prepares to go into battle."

Once again, a cacophony of opinions flew around the room.

"Maybe they are trying to slow down our defensive preparations in Hakata."

"Their intention could be not only to disrupt Hakata's defense, but also to throw Kamakura's leaders into confusion," Edward added cynically. "What you need is to toughen your resolve and be decisive."

"Do you mean we should kill Zhou Fu?"

"I simply said that a strong conviction is necessary if you are to succeed."

The Hyojyoshu members were once again silenced. They thought that if any one of them spoke, then responsibility would fall on him. And so they sat in silence.

That day was the turning point. Yasumori and the others who had insisted on the appeasement of Yuan never spoke of it again.

CHAPTER

62

"Last night, I sent my order to Hakata," Tokimune confided to Edward when they were alone.

"Then the next battle is inevitable."

Tokimune nodded.

"You look dejected."

"To be honest, as of this moment, we have no chance of winning. As Zafir mentioned yesterday, Yuan is sending a massive and unparalleled army this way."

"Then Nippon will be defeated," Edward said.

"I agree . . . But we will not lose." Something like a smile slowly spread across Tokimune's face. "We must win no matter what. And to do so, I need your advice." He fixed his gaze on Edward.

"The enemy will be exhausted and perhaps even ill after crossing the sea to get here. Our army should engage them on the shore," Edward said without hesitation.

Our army—how easily the words slide off my tongue. Does this mean the soldiers of Christ under my command will fight for this country?

"We have the advantage of being on land. The enemy will unleash the large army first, and at the same time build a bridgehead close to the coast. That must be prevented by any means necessary."

"Stone and mud walls are being constructed along the coast."

"They must be solid piles of stones, not just piles of mud. The walls must withstand catapult fire."

"Catapult fire, you say?"

"It can break down ramparts, destroy towers, and terrorize people."

"Go on."

"Castles in Europe are made of stone. Their walls are ten times taller than a man. All castles have a water source within their walls, and there are secret passageways for escape. Archers high up on the castle ramparts fire arrows on approaching enemies. When enemies attempt to climb the castle walls, they can be brought down by either dropping heavy stones or pouring blazing oil on them."

"Such a castle is impregnable."

"When it comes to attacking a castle, you can loose flaming arrows and use catapults to launch not only rocks into its walls, but also jars of flaming oil. If you use a large enough catapult, the walls can be breached, and soldiers can enter the castle."

Tokimune listened attentively to Edward.

That night, Edward stopped in front of a temple, attracted by a blazing fire burning in the center of its grounds. Dozens of monks encircled the pillar of flames. Their voices blended together as they chanted the nembutsu and reverberated as one enormous hum rumbling through the earth.

"Can we go in?" he asked Morimune.

"The monks are praying to Buddha," Morimune said as they stepped inside.

"What are they praying for?"

"For Yuan not to attack. Or in case of attack that we be guided to victory the same as in the last war."

"Will Buddha listen to their plea?"

"They pray so intensely because they believe he will listen. Is that not right?" Alan answered Edward, but looked at Morimune for confirmation.

"You are a soldier in the Army of Christ. Does your god not listen to your prayers?" Morimune asked.

"We can't test the Lord, whether he listens to our plea or not. He always watches over us. You go to either heaven or hell when you die. Even I have a chance to get into heaven," Alan said.

"I heard if you kill pagans, you will go to paradise," Morimune said.

"That's why we have fought up till now," Alan said.

"To the people of Nippon, we are pagans. Yet, rather than kill us, they help us," Zafir remarked seriously.

The roar-like echo from the nembutsu chant penetrated their bodies, while the flames from the Homa ritual bonfire colored their faces red.

"What do you fight for?" Zafir turned to Edward. "I have always meant to ask."

"For God . . . that's what I believed," Edward said, remembering the battles fought for Jerusalem. In his mind's eye he saw thousands of corpses endlessly laid out before him. Soldiers, villagers. Saracen and Christian armies slaughtered each other and all who got in their way, while calling out their god's name. *Is this what God wanted? Is this the duty of a knight?* He had asked himself over and over again, never finding an answer. *I have killed too many. I will not enter the Kingdom of God. Believing I will is a deception.*

"And do you feel differently now?"

"I'm not sure."

"You've changed since you have come to this country."

"How so?"

"In Jerusalem, you were a young and headstrong knight, filled with ambition. You were reckless and lacked discretion, forcing your way forward. You acted before you thought. Now, you think before you act."

"Perhaps. But I am still the man I was."

"No, I believe this is the true version of you, Lord Edward," Zafir said, his words charged with emotion.

The rising flames wrapped around the monks' nembutsu like a scarlet dragon dancing in the night sky.

CHAPTER

63

"Is this—" Tokimune stood dumbstruck at the entrance of the room.

"A replica of Hakata Bay," Edward said.

The rough-hewn model of Hakata Bay, made of dirt, sand, and wooden planks, filled the room from one end to the other. The coastline had been laid out with sand, and dozens of small-scale wooden ships resembling Yuan warships were placed on top of the planks that represented the sea. Thomas' sailors, under his guidance, had even recreated Iki, Tsushima, Shikanoshima, and Nokonoshima islands and Mount Bishamon.

"This is the route Yuan forces took when they invaded," Edward said as he moved the ships and re-enacted the last invasion.

"Once Yuan took control of Iki and Tsushima, they gathered in Hakata Bay. They burned the town after disembarking and then returned to their ships later the same day. Why didn't they press on and march on Dazaifu?"

It was a subject that had been debated time and time again, with neither a definitive nor reasonable conclusion.

"Since we put up such a fierce resistance, they must have thought it wise to pull back," Tokimune offered by way of explanation.

"I wonder if that was the real reason," Edward said. "It is true that Nippon best shows its strength and prowess in one-on-one, hand-to-hand combat. However, in a battle of numbers, the Mongolian army dominates with their rapid-fire short bows. I have heard they startled your horses with thunder crash bombs, and ceaselessly beat drums and gongs to create chaos among the samurai. Ultimately, everything was overwhelmingly in Yuan's favor."

Tokimune listened in silence as he stared at the Hakata model. The samurai who had accompanied him glared at the model, too. *Are they thinking about the last battle?*

"The Mongolian army will land in Hakata," Edward stated definitively.

"Are you certain?"

"I am. Your troops stationed in Yamaguchi and Nagasaki should be deployed to Hakata."

"That is too risky. If Yuan does not land in Hakata, but in another province, we would allow them to land too easily," Tokimune argued.

"Can you afford to disperse your soldiers throughout the country?" Edward answered, with just a hint of sarcasm in his voice. "Hakata's defenses are weak. The Mongolians will easily disembark when they land there. You should be concentrating your forces on Hakata."

Tokimune thought for a moment.

"Yuan must know that we have been bolstering our defenses in Hakata. That is why they sent the emissary to spy. When they attack, they will choose a more undermanned location."

"The Mongolian army is an army of a size that you and I have never seen before. It is to their advantage to choose a coast they have already waged battle on, rather than an unknown location. Moreover, they probably assume that they can break down any line of defense with the size of the army at their command."

"Then we know the location of the attack," Tokimune relented without objection. "But when?"

"We are looking into that. I'll notify you once I have more information."

"And how should we defend ourselves?"

"Yuan did not build an outpost on the coast in the last war because your samurai were so formidable and prevented them from doing so. No, they simply wanted to assert their presence and flaunt their military might."

"You mean to say that Yuan did not fight in earnest?"

"Their objective was most likely to investigate the state of the Nippon defense system. In order to march all the way to Kamakura, they would have had to muster a sufficient number of troops, weapons, and provisions. Invasions that involve crossing the sea can fail if there are not enough supplies and if there are problems with logistics. Hence Kublai Khan is still preparing for a full-scale attack."

"Then it is good we are building stone walls along the coast."

"That is no defense," Edward said, again just barely holding sarcasm in check. "I saw those ramparts, and any large army could easily break through them."

Tokimune frowned in displeasure.

"Strengthen the rampart walls with stones so catapult fire will not destroy them. The top part of the rampart should be six feet thick and the base should be around nine to ten feet thick. The height must be over ten feet. The side facing the coast should be steep while the inland side should gently slope, so we can ride up it on horseback. If you aim a bow down from the top of the rampart, the arrow travels faster and its power doubles. By building ramparts like these on top of the sand dunes that continue out from the sea, they appear more intimidating when viewed from a ship than they actually are," Edward said in one stretch.

"The number of ramparts should be increased. You should build a rampart from Imazu to Kashii with Hakata Bay at its center as soon as possible. The enemy will launch their assault starting with Shikanoshima Island and Nokonoshima Island. Their garrisons should be strengthened along with their rampart defenses to buy time before the enemy lays siege to Hakata."

Tokimune listened silently.

"The Yuan cavalry is formidable and dauntless. Ramparts are indispensable in impeding horses."

"A rampart from Imazu to Kashii would be twelve miles long. How do you suggest we build something so massive?"

"Use all the samurai in Kyushu."

"I see. The work can be divided between Kyushu's nine provinces. Send a message at once to those in charge in Chikuzen, Chikugo, Hizen, Higo, Buzen, Bungo, Hyuga, Osumi, and Satsuma," Tokimune ordered the secretary who had been taking down notes.

"And tell them to make haste. The method of construction and the stone materials used need not be the same from region to region. However, each region will be responsible for the protection of the rampart it makes. That way they will not do careless work," Edward stated, before letting out a strained laugh. He realized that, before he knew it, he had put himself in the middle of a foreign nation's war.

"Is there anything else?" Tokimune asked.

"Watchtowers should be built on Shikanoshima and Nokonoshima to keep an eye out for enemy fleets the moment they appear. Smoke signals from one tower to the other are the best way to sound the alarm," Edward continued, before he paused and stared at Tokimune.

"You need to reform your system."

"Reform?"

"You need a unified army under one commander."

"Do you think that our samurai are not unified?"

"If we fought one-on-one, we would be victorious over Yuan. But war is not a duel between individuals."

Tokimune was silent. He knew Edward was right.

"What should I do?"

"Place several commanders under one supreme commander and divide them into multiple units. The commanding officers must act under the orders of the supreme commander."

"My army is not capable of that."

"Why? Because each commander answers only to himself? Yuan's army shares one goal, and one goal only: the conquest of Nippon. That's why they acted in unison when they heard the drum and gong signals in the last war."

"So, my army is disconnected and disorganized. That is indeed true."

"It is important for the soldiers in your army to know that their goal is to fight to protect their country, its people, and their families."

"I understand. But let us continue this conversation at another time and go outside. The air is suffocating in here," Tokimune suddenly said. He indicated that Edward should follow him into the garden. The sun had already begun to set.

"How would you define your country?" Tokimune abruptly asked.

Edward was taken aback at first and could think of no suitable answer.

"It is a group of people who live under God," he eventually said. *But that is not what I want to say or even mean when I think of England.*

"For me Kamakura is Nippon," Tokimune said, choosing every word carefully. "It is the world of the samurai that took ninety years to establish. My mission is to protect Kamakura and the Hojo Clan, which in turn means my mission is to protect Nippon." These were without a doubt Tokimune's true feelings.

"Nippon faces its greatest crisis since it was founded in ancient times. If we allow this crisis to overcome us, Nippon will be destroyed. Please lend me your power, your war strategies, tactics, and methods." Tokimune turned to Edward and bowed his head deeply.

CHAPTER

64

After dinner that night, Edward gathered his men and the sailors to discuss their future. There was much dissension and drinking.

"Phrases like 'for God' and 'for country' don't apply to this nation's military commanders," Alan declared angrily between gulps of sake.

"Then what are they fighting for?"

"Fucking rewards! They fight to score more land and property."

"Aren't we the same? We set out to destroy the Islamic army and reclaim Jerusalem so that our reward would be entry into God's kingdom. And is fighting for that celestial territory so wrong?"

"But the samurai's lust for merit and earthly rewards is too obvious. Greedy bastards! Only God should know one's deeds and the motive for them."

"They cannot hope for new territories and other spoils of war in the next conflict with Yuan. They cannot get what is not there to get."

"But there's respect, honor, and virtue to get. The same rewards a knight seeks," Edward murmured after hearing his men argue back and forth.

"Anyway, this is Nippon's problem. It has nothing to do with us."

"Edward, have you told Lord Tokimune that we want to go home?"

"Sorry, Tokimune and his associates are preoccupied with Yuan's upcoming attack. Now is not the right time to talk about returning home."

"But we have been here three years. Will the 'right time' ever come? Do you have any idea how worried my wife must be?"

"Ha ha, mate. Your wife has remarried and is too busy taking care of her new husband and kids to worry about you."

"I don't have a family, but I have a house. Someone else is probably living there now. They probably think I'm dead. I'll take back my home when I return."

"Ah, I wanna drink wine and eat lamb—"

"I could bury my bones here," Enrico, the sailor from Genoa, spoke out.

"What? You're always going on about your wife and kids in Genoa."

"We shouldn't just cast this country aside. The sake is good, and the food isn't bad."

"And the women are good!" Alan laughed loudly.

CHAPTER

65

Edward's proposal to reorganize the gokenin under a single supreme commander was hotly debated at the next Hyojyoshu council meeting.

"The Mongolian army is a collection of common soldiers, whose movement is regulated and controlled. Collective adversaries like these are more powerful than individual adversaries. I think it is imperative we adopt this method of fighting for the upcoming battle," Edward argued.

"Are we inferior to Mongolian soldiers?"

"I don't want to go into battle with such strict rules and regulations."

"If we follow the strategy you propose, it is difficult to know which of us will achieve distinctions of great merit. I will continue to fight in the way I always have."

The various opinions of the council rang out.

"Do you only think about what is best for you? Now is the time to fight for the survival of Nippon," Yasumori, who had been listening silently, barked out suddenly. He glared at the other samurai, infuriated by the selfishness of the gokenin vassals. Until now Yasumori had opposed Edward.

"I want to see how you carry yourself in battle," Tokimune said to Edward.

Edward dressed himself in full regalia. He had not worn his chainmail since the hunt. It was heavy, and his helmet limited his vision. The armor dug into his body and was awkward to walk in. Every nerve tensed and his body tightened. But holding his sword put him at ease. Something deep within him welled up. *This is my mission. I am a knight. I will not fear. God and this armor protect me.* As he mounted Hayate, he gently whispered in his ear, quieting the horse's agitation.

"What are you thinking? I cannot condone you getting into any trouble," Zafir said as he looked up at Edward astride Hayate.

"Men, it is time to become again the knights we were when we first marched to Jerusalem," Edward addressed his soldiers. His helmet and chainmail shone brightly in the brilliant sunlight. "We are about to present ourselves as knights of Christ's Army before the samurai of this nation. Let them see what warriors of God are made of!"

CHAPTER

66

Edward looked up at the sky. A single black kite flew across the blue expanse. Hills lush with fresh greenery stretched out far into the distance. Next to him, Tokimune was at the center of his close aides, backed by fifty gokenin, their subordinates, and soldier escorts.

At the foot of a hill, all twenty-three of Edward's men were lined up in a row. They were on horseback and armed to the teeth as they awaited Edward's command. When he unsheathed his sword and gave the signal, Alan moved his horse from the right end of the formation to its front.

"Forward march!" Alan ordered, as the others slowly advanced behind him.

Edward lowered his sword to the right. The formation turned ninety degrees and formed a fan. Each time Edward moved his sword his army of knights changed formation and direction in accordance with his commands.

As the formation advanced, it split into two, then three, and finally four ranks.

The samurai behind Tokimune wordlessly watched the geometric patterns unfold.

At Edward's final visual command, the horsemen regrouped into a single line.

"Unsheathe! Charge!" Alan's voice bellowed across the hills.

The knights drew and extended their swords. As they picked up speed, the ground shook.

"For God!" they roared in unison.

At Edward's orders, the formation changed from a horizontal row to a V shape with Alan leading the charge at its head.

"We use the wedge formation to break through enemy lines," Edward explained.

"It is beautiful," Tokimune muttered in awe.

When Edward next thrust his sword into the air, the formation made a sweeping arc and galloped toward Edward and the samurai. Five hundred yards, four hundred yards. The beating of the horses' hooves rumbled the earth as they approached. The samurai began to fidget.

"You are in the presence of Lord Tokimune. What are you doing?"

"Cease this at once! Stop!"

More than ten samurai rushed in front of Tokimune and threw out their arms to shield him. Tokimune himself looked bewildered. Edward's men were two hundred yards away, and they were not slowing down.

"Please draw back, my Lord," Yasumori called out, but Tokimune did not move.

When the men were a hundred yards out, Edward stepped in front of the samurai and lowered his sword. The knights came to an abrupt halt fifty yards in front of him.

"Swords away!" Alan ordered.

The wedge's wings moved to the front and once again lined up in a row, before slowly approaching Tokimune and the others.

"This is how our army wages battle," Edward said. "A disciplined corps working as a unit is more successful than numbers and produces several times the power of the individual soldier."

"Who gets the reward for leading the attack?" one of the gokenin asked.

"Our knights are all men of valor. For the sake of victory, we become one body," Edward answered, but he felt a sense of emptiness in saying so.

For the sake of victory, that is why we fight. Yet in Jerusalem, the enemy was victorious over us again and again. It is likely the Mongolian army is even more powerful than the Saracens. How capable can our little army be?

"Can our army be trained to fight like this?" Tokimune asked as he faced Edward.

"If your samurai have the mind to do so."

"Then I want you to train them."

A huge commotion broke out, but Yasumori quickly quelled the stir.

"I will do everything I can," Edward responded in a calm voice.

Akisada, the archery master, looked at him with displeasure, but said nothing.

CHAPTER

67

Training began immediately. Edward built fencing on the shore-line and instructed the samurai in how to defend against a cavalry attack from the beach, using longbow arrow fire and spears to drive back the enemy. But Edward could not be sure that they truly understood these new tactics. Changing from an individual battle strategy to a group mentality was more difficult than he had imagined.

"This country's cavalry excels in martial arts," Zafir told. Edward upon returning to the manor after a day of training. "They are archers and lance wielders. The infantry also uses bows and katanas. They are much more versatile as individuals compared to the Mongolian army, where cavalry is cavalry, infantry is infantry, and archers are archers. The warriors of Nippon are not restrict-ed to one role. Though they lost the battle on the beach in the first war, they were equal to the enemy in hand-to-hand com-bat. That may have been one of the reasons why the Mongolian army retreated to their ships, rather than immediately push on to Dazaifu."

"So, the Kamakura samurai can fight close combat in their cavalry and infantry."

"Depending on the way it is used, the naginata pole arm is a powerful weapon in battle. It is both a katana and a spear."

"If attacked, the Kamakura samurai would not be easily defeated."

"True."

"There should be a chance of victory—"

"No country can gather more than a hundred thousand troops in a short period of time. Nippon possesses great military power," Zafir said matter-of-factly.

One month into training, fifty samurai, arranged in five rows of ten men each, assembled in front of Edward, Tokimune, and the others.

"Bows at the ready!" Alan commanded. It was rare to hear Alan speak the native tongue in public.

As one, the soldiers fixed arrows to their bows.

"Aim!"

The soldiers drew back their strings and aimed midway between sky and ground.

"Release!"

Fifty arrows created a parabola as they flew.

"Where on earth are you aiming? Do you not know where your arrows are heading?" Akisada, who stood next to Tokimune, shouted to the samurai before glaring at Edward.

Edward maintained his composure. "If you aim them in that direction, they fly farther," he said to Akisada.

"If you looked you would understand," Akisada fumed. "Arrows are not things you want to fly far off. They should be aiming at the enemy, no?"

"So long as the enemy is where the arrows will reach. Depending on wind conditions, you estimate where the enemy will be when the arrows fall to earth and then shoot the arrows all at once."

"During the last war, Yuan launched a barrage of arrows out of nowhere. They could use the same tactic," Akisada muttered to himself.

"Bows are meant to be aimed and fired. There is no meaning in this sort of play," another samurai objected.

Soon other voices joined the discussion.

"It is imperative to weaken as much of the enemy's military strength as you can before engaging in close combat."

"Then it would be best to send a group of samurai horsemen to the enemy front line and have them fire their arrows there."

"The enemy would not just watch that happen. They would attack those cavalrymen."

"We could ask for nothing better. We would then fight with a vengeance, one-on-one."

"This lot is useless!" Alan spat out in frustration. "These lads only care about beheading the enemy, particularly enemy generals. Shooting arrows from the rear is a concept they cannot grasp."

On the way home after the day's training, Alan posed the question they had been debating since agreeing to help Nippon. "Do you really think Nippon can win against the Mongolians?"

"There is no battle you can win if you think you will lose," Edward replied.

"No matter how much I think it over, I don't think they can win. The Mongolian cavalry defeated the Saracen army and invaded Jerusalem. Their army is invincible."

"But how can the Mongolian cavalry fight here? On one side of Hakata there is ocean. Even if they were to make it inland, there are mountains and a web of rice paddies. The Yuan cavalry is unmatched on a grassy plain, where they can maneuver freely. But the terrain of this country hinders mobility. On top of that, they have to cross a great distance over the sea to get here. They won't have a sufficient number of horses, and both men and horses will be exhausted from living on shipboard. This country has the advantage."

"That may be, but I don't believe these samurai can make the most of their advantage."

"We just have to teach them how to make use of that advantage. The samurai are greatly skilled in battle. They can accurately fire arrows on horseback, and are properly trained in wielding a sword."

Alan acknowledged that much.

"If they can be taught group battle strategies, then their combat abilities will surpass those of Yuan."

"Group tactics, that is the most difficult thing for them."

Edward agreed.

But we don't have much time. We need to hurry, he thought as he gripped the reins of his horse.

CHAPTER
68

Early in the afternoon on a fall day, Edward's soldiers and Thomas' sailors were making a row.

"Are they gambling again? Let's give them a good walloping and take them for all their money," Alan said and rolled up his sleeves.

The soldiers and sailors cleared a path for Edward and Alan. In the center of the group was a surprised-looking plump woman with a baby in her arms and a two-year-old girl by her side.

"This is chief navigator Enrico's wife and children," Zafir said in a low voice.

Enrico stood behind the woman and children. He was wearing a kimono, had his hair done up in an odd manner, and looked like a bearded Nippon man.

"The bastard—" Alan began. "Don't you have a wife and three kids back home?"

"I have four. One more will have been born by now."

"Then what of this woman and her two kids?"

"T-three."

Edward and Alan saw the swell in the woman's stomach.

"It's been over five years since I left home. I don't know what's become of my family. And we still don't have any idea when we'll be able to return."

"And what of it? What about your family?"

"I will work to support them. I'll live happily working as a carpenter and—"

"You idiot! I meant your family in Genoa!"

"She's a strong woman. And as a sailor's wife she accepts that her husband might not return from the sea. She has the kids to help her. They have a good mother. My kids told me that even if I didn't come back, they would take good care of their mama and live happily."

"You can't go on like this," Alan said and hit Enrico over the head. The woman and little girl glared at him.

"You were the one who was the most desperate to learn this country's language. Now I know why. Look at you! You look like one of this country's praiseworthy fathers."

"I like this country," Enrico muttered.

"You like this country's women. You love women. It doesn't matter the country."

"Nippon reminds me of Genoa. The sea and mountains, and the way the sun shines. Besides, don't you think this land's people are kind?" Enrico said as he placed a hand on the woman's shoulder. She shyly attempted to pull away, but Enrico held her fast. The little girl tried to clamber onto Enrico's back, before he scooped her up and nuzzled her cheek.

"Do whatever you want," Alan said as he turned to leave.

"Don't make your woman cry," was the best that Edward could tell him. He was thinking of Haruno.

"What is going on here?"

Edward turned and saw Morimune staring at Enrico and his new family.

"We were just talking about what a good country Nippon is."

"I don't know about other countries. I have no desire to go to them, unlike Lord Tokimune."

"Tokimune wants to go abroad?"

"My father has warned him against travel. Now is not the time to even be thinking of such things. Not when we have to deal with Yuan."

Morimune took Edward and Alan aside.

"People have seen you and Lady Haruno holding hands when walking in Myogetsu-in Temple."

"Is that so bad?" Edward said without shame. Alan rolled his eyes as he listened. "Haruno hated my doing so because the visitors could see, but I took her hand anyway."

"You two should live together. As man and woman. Even if she is a pagan, if you follow your heart, I am sure your God will forgive you," Morimune laughed.

"I cannot justify it to my men. They dream of returning to their hometowns. As do I," Edward said. Morimune's expression changed.

"What will happen to Haruno when I go? I want her to be happy," Edward said.

"I'm in trouble. I don't know what you and Lady Haruno should do now."

"You are always in trouble. There is no way you will live a long life."

"I am prepared to die at any time. This is the samurai way."

"Are you married?"

"Yes. And I have children."

"Then do not die. Don't make your wife sad."

Edward thought of Haruno. He did not think it strange for him to want to stay in this country and continue living as he was. He had no woman and children waiting for him in England.

"Do not trouble Lady Haruno too much."

Edward meant to say, "Of course," but he was not sure what Haruno was troubled with.

CHAPTER

69

One day, Edward persuaded Tokimune to come with him to the Namekawa River, much to the disapproval of Morimune. Several samurai escorts and servants, including Akisada, accompanied them. On the vast dry riverbed were two torso armors fifty yards away. One was from Nippon, the other from Yuan.

"Can you hit one from here?" Edward asked Tokimune.

Without saying a word, Tokimune snatched his longbow from his attendant and drew back the string. The arrow hit the Yuan armor in its center.

"And the other one?"

Hesitating for only a moment, Tokimune removed an arrow from the quiver on his waist, nocked and fired it. The second arrow also found its target.

Edward drew back one of the short bows the Mongolian army had used and proceeded to fire his arrows at the two torso armors. They were also direct hits, landing close to Tokimune's arrows.

Edward and Tokimune walked in silence to the torso armors. Tokimune's arrows had skillfully pierced through both torso pieces. However, Edward's first arrow had pierced through the Mongolian armor, while his second arrow stuck in the Nippon armor without breaking into the armor's interior.

"You should be proud of the strength of Nippon bows. But—"

"Say it, Edward."

"Shoot an arrow as far as you can."

Tokimune drew back his bow and loosed an arrow. Edward did the same with his Mongolian short bow. They walked a hundred yards forward, and found the Nippon arrow stuck in the ground. Thirty yards ahead was the Mongolian arrow.

"Our bows excel in power, but are inferior to Yuan's in distance, it would seem."

"That is because the Mongolian army's arrows are lighter. But the Mongolian arrows were coated in poison in the last war. So, power isn't that necessary for a Yuan arrow to succeed. Just having the poisoned arrow scrape the body would be enough to bring down an enemy. It may not cause instant death but it would wound severely. If the arrow hits a truly vulnerable spot, it would bring about an agonizing death. It is a convenient form of destruction in warfare. The enemy would have to find and use more manpower to compensate for the injured and dead soldiers."

"What is your point?" Akisada raised his voice as he stepped forward from behind Tokimune.

"In the upcoming battle, the Mongolian army will likely send their army to Hakata and try to construct a beachhead, where they will transport goods from their ships to the mainland. I have heard they are bringing seeds, farming tools, and even farmers with them. If they capture Hakata, the farmers will settle there, and they will be able to provide their own food and other resources as they march to Kamakura. That is something we must defend against."

"Are you saying we should use Yuan's bows to do so?"

"I mean that you should use short bows, not the bows from the Mongolian army. When the Mongolians land in Hakata, you can expect hand-to-hand combat. In that kind of fight, a short bow that can fire rapidly is to your advantage rather than the longbows you use now."

Scornful laughter could be heard among the attendants, though none of them were smiling.

"We have battle tactics that suit us. We will not fight pretending to be something we are not," Akisada said solemnly.

Edward looked to Tokimune, but Tokimune did not respond.

"At least let the infantry have short bows to use in close combat," Edward reasoned.

Tokimune still remained silent, so Edward continued.

"We have a hundred thousand arrows that we can fire from behind the ramparts as the enemy comes ashore."

"What? A hundred thousand!" one of the samurai escorts exclaimed in disbelief.

"The more arrows we have, the better," Edward insisted. "And the more we avoid close combat, the fewer casualties we will have. Yuan will also likely rain arrows down upon us from their warships before coming ashore."

"Even in close combat we have plenty of opportunities for victory," a samurai asserted.

"The enemy is probably also saying the same thing," Edward countered. "In the past war, they thoroughly studied the Nippon army's battle tactics. They already know your strong and weak points. The Yuan Dynasty has been able to advance its influence this far because it has studied its enemies."

"We have also studied our enemies. That's why we are building the stone walls in Hakata."

"Do you really want to win this war?" Edward said loudly and with barely concealed frustration and anger. "If you lose this war, your country will be destroyed."

"We are well aware of that!"

"Then why won't you consider adopting new battle strategies?"

"For countless years, we have fought and trained in the bow our way. It is not something we can suddenly change," Morimune, whom Edward had not noticed, spoke up.

"Even you agree with the others?"

"This is the Nippon samurai way."

Edward had no response.

CHAPTER

70

The next day, Akisada marched up to Edward at Tokimune's estate.

"I challenge you to a duel," Akisada said, staring fixedly at the Englishman.

This is not the time to be thinking of that, Edward thought. "I have not used my sword in years," he said in response.

"You are a knight, no? Knights and samurai are alike. Neither knight nor samurai runs from a fight."

"Don't do this," Zafir implored. "It would be ally killing ally."

"We will use arrows without heads and swords without sharp blades," Akisada announced decisively.

"Does Tokimune condone this match?"

"He is against it if we end up holding a grudge and resenting each other. But if we both merely wish to test our martial arts skills, then it is of great interest to him." Akisada ended the conversation and left.

"What a selfish bastard!" Alan said as he shook a raised fist at Akisada's retreating figure. "Let me fight him. I'll wager my honor as a knight of England and soldier in Christ's Army."

"Akisada would never agree to that. He challenged me. If I refuse, everything I have done up till now will have been pointless. He is testing my courage."

Alan thought for a moment.

"Then fight him in a month. If you fought him now, you would lose."

"At the most we can meet in a week. I doubt he can even wait that long." Edward recalled the bitter expression on Akisada's harsh face. He could not suppress his indignation. *What did I do to him?* Edward muttered to himself.

"Leave it be. This country does not have time for such things at present," Zafir said. But in spite of his words, he knew that the duel was inevitable.

CHAPTER
71

What has happened to the resolve I once had? Edward thought. His armor weighed heavy on his body and on his soul. He shook his shoulders as if that simple action would ease his anxiety.

"Get your head out of the clouds," Alan admonished him.

Edward swung his sword a few times, feeling a familiar sensation return. Suddenly, Alan charged at him with his sword drawn. Edward countered the oncoming blade, but barely.

"Come on. We have to get your old self back," Alan said and jumped into the garden, with Edward following. The soldiers nearby stopped what they were doing and stared at the two men.

"Your countering is weak. If I wanted to, I could have rammed my sword right through your stomach," Alan boasted, launching into a flurry of slashes and thrusts of his blade. Edward frantically blocked the attacks. Even as he tried to counterattack, the best he could do was parry Alan's blade.

"What's wrong? You're only taking the hits, you have to fight back," Alan taunted and swung his blade again and again. "A Saracen brat could do you in! Are you that weak?"

Edward closed the gap between them in an instant, slipping past Alan's blade and ending up behind him. Alan quickly spun around and, catching the oncoming blade with his own, rebuffed Edward.

"Fighting isn't thinking. Only when you fight like a soldier can you command other troops. It is the same with women. You lose your nerve if you get too absorbed in them."

At those words, Edward charged at Alan. But as their swords met, Edward wobbled and fell backward. Alan thrust the tip of his sword at Edward's throat.

"And this is the end of my master, Edward Gawain," he said triumphantly before lowering his sword.

"It is not bad to use your head, but don't forget that you are a knight," Alan said imitating Edward's usual tone.

Edward stood up, but he was breathing so hard he could not speak.

"You have only five days until the duel."

Alan shoved Edward, who stumbled and grabbed Alan's arm before he could fall.

"We have to build up your strength."

From that day on, Edward's intensive training began. While wearing his armor he ran around the garden or raced Hayate up hills. Using the wooden swords the sailors made for them, Edward practiced with his fellow soldiers as opponents. Alan watched each bout and threw out advice. By the third day, Edward's endurance had improved. He could run at full speed with his armor and weapons, and not be out of breath. After the fourth day, he could beat his soldiers, with the exception of Alan.

The day before the duel, Edward and Alan had their final training session. In one exercise, Edward swung his wooden sword to the side, intending to cut into Alan's stomach. Alan quickly ducked out of the way and aimed his sword at Edward's head. Edward blocked the blow, but the impact made his arms go numb. While holding his stance, he smashed his body into Alan, but was pushed back. Alan's strength still outmatched Edward's. The moment Alan swung his wooden sword, Edward's sword struck Alan in the right shoulder. Alan's retaliatory swing from above Edward's head hit the crown of Edward's helmet.

"My loss," Edward ceded.

"No, my loss. Your sword was a second faster than mine. If we had used real blades, yours would have torn my arm off. That is why your brain is good and safe," Alan said, unusually out of breath and touching Edward's helmet with his gloved hand. "Your instincts have returned. But Akisada will be more difficult than you think. He intends to kill you."

"I know."

"No, I don't think you do. If you did, you would not be fighting this foolhardy duel."

Alan's right. This duel makes no sense. If I win, the samurai will hate me more than they do already. If I lose . . . I don't want to think about that. I just have to survive.

"Will you use a bow?" Alan asked, interrupting Edward's train of thought.

"No, a sword."

"Good. With your armor you would only be able to aim a bow at his horse. And you do not have the nerve to hit the horse, or any horse, do you? Akisada will fire his bow first. Don't avoid it. Protect your vitals with your shield. He'll be using arrows without heads. They'll bounce off your chainmail. Even if one manages to pierce the chainmail, the wound will not be serious because the arrows will not be coated with poison. Keep charging at him and use your shield to throw him off his horse. If he wears the same armor as before, you can easily throw him off-balance and knock him down. Then just kick him off his horse. You won't even have to use your sword," Alan instructed.

You make it sound easy, but you know, as do I, it is easier said than done. The first thing is to keep calm when Akisada aims his bow directly at me.

CHAPTER

72

The sky was cloudless on the day of the match. At Akisada's request, they met at the hill where Edward had given his cavalry training demonstration. Edward was the first to enter the list. Hayate walked them forward in a dignified gait and then stopped. With his armor covering his face, chest, torso, and legs, Edward appeared bigger, bulkier, and more imposing than before. His shield hung on his back.

Surveying the gathered crowd, Edward saw Tokimune among the gokenin. The regent of the shogunate feigned indifference, but he could not completely hide his interest in the spectacle that was about to unfold. Among the spectators from Kamakura, those with animosity toward Edward had also come to watch the performance.

Akisada rode in next, wearing full armor and holding a longbow in his right hand. Edward adjusted his helmet and took the shield from his back and gripped it in his left hand.

Yasumori gave the signal for the match to begin. Edward readied his shield and squeezed his legs as a sign for Hayate to gallop forward. The distance between the two warriors closed. Akisada drew his bow. Edward brought up his shield to protect the upper part of his body, while holding tight to Hayate's reins. Hayate changed course to the right. Akisada swiftly turned his body to face Edward and fired. Edward blocked the oncoming arrow aimed for his face with his shield. As the two passed each other, Edward bashed his shield over Akisada's helmet. Akisada lost his balance and tumbled from his horse, just as Alan said he would. After racing ahead, Edward stopped Hayate and turned around. Akisada was struggling to get to his feet.

"Kick him down, Edward!" Alan called out.

Edward jumped down from Hayate and unsheathed his sword.

Akisada, now standing, readied his sword while fiercely glaring at his opponent. Edward brandished his sword and slashed it down over Akisada's head. As Akisada's sword bounced backward from the clash with Edward's blow, it struck Akisada's helmet. Akisada staggered. Edward aimed for his torso and swung.

"The legs! Aim for his knees! One blow and he won't be able to stand. Or aim for his elbows that aren't guarded! Blow off his arms!" Alan screamed.

Edward continued to swing down his sword. Each time he struck Akisada's armor, a high-pitched tone reverberated. Akisada staggered repeatedly. Whenever Edward struck unprotected places on Akisada's body, he would subtly turn his blade to avoid hitting Akisada with the edge.

"Are you playing, Edward? Your blade is asleep! Raise your sword properly and cut him!" Alan hollered louder than before.

Akisada fell back unable to parry Edward's blade. He was outclassed.

"Dodge his sword and fight back!" Akisada's fellow samurai called out.

Edward swung his sword again. Akisada hastily blocked it, but the impact sent his sword flying out of his hand. Edward raised his sword high and brought it to a stop above Akisada's head.

"Do it, Edward! Smash his head open!" Alan yelled. But Edward ignored him and lowered his blade.

"This is good enough," Edward spoke in the Nippon tongue.

The color drained from Akisada's face, and he bit his lip. Edward looked for Tokimune, but he was nowhere to be found.

CHAPTER

73

That night, they held a celebratory feast at the manor. Alan, the soldiers, and sailors drank late into the night, but Edward and Zafir withdrew early to Edward's room.

"Lord Tokimune is a dangerous man," Zafir said in a hushed voice.

"Why do you say that? He is asking for our help."

"Anyone who seeks aid from heretics is an extremely dangerous man. Sooner or later divine punishment will be delivered."

Edward could not help but laugh. He had never expected Zafir of all people to speak in such a way.

"I ask you, a Muslim, for advice all the time. I trust and rely on you more than anyone else. Do you think that is a mistake?"

"It is said that god supports the spirit and friends support everything else. However, can we say that Tokimune is a friend? I think he is using you."

"Why should I object? We are being treated fairly, and we may even be given the chance to return home one day."

"The Yuan Dynasty is going to attack, and this nation will lose. You would do well to think of what comes after that and make a plan."

"Are you saying we should come to a secret understanding with Yuan?"

"That may lead to another path of survival. You rely too much on Tokimune. I have no idea what is going through his mind."

"And I have no idea what is going through the minds of any of the people in this country. They listen too closely to what monks like Nichiren tell them."

"Do you know why Tokimune left immediately after the match started today? The moment he saw you in full armor with sword and shield, he knew you would be victorious. As the leader of the samurai, he did not want to see his own warrior lose to a foreign knight."

"How did he foresee that I would win?"

"I too would like to know that. Tokimune likely concealed himself and watched the match."

They sank into silence as the voices of the drunk soldiers and sailors filtered into the darkness.

CHAPTER
74

"Is it not too dangerous to entrust the training of our samurai to such a man?" Yasumori said.

"Not if there are results," Tokimune answered.

"Exposing our country to foreigners and asking them to train our men . . . I am not in favor of that."

"They are familiar with the Mongolian army's battle tactics."

"If they end up becoming close to Kublai Khan, or if they have an agreement with him, then the enemy will know all about our internal affairs."

"That is not the case. It is far better to use the foreigners as an ally than reject them as an enemy."

"I think we should put someone we can trust in charge of training the gokenin."

"Who in Nippon do you think can teach our army new battle strategies? The only person capable of doing that is the Englishman."

"You place too much faith in him, my lord."

"I am doing what I think is best for our country."

Yasumori argued no more and changed the subject.

"In the match against Lord Akisada, he disgraced our warrior way by not using a bow and attacking with his shield."

"It was Edward's win. If that had been true combat, Akisada would have lost his life."

"There is an etiquette in battle."

"The Mongolian soldiers know nothing about etiquette. They do not give out their name before partaking in single combat as we do. In the last war, many of them swarmed and attacked a single man. I have heard they laughed when they heard the sound of the kabura-ya whistling arrow signaling the start of battle. It is all the same to them if they act cowardly."

"That is true, but—" Yasumori stopped mid-sentence.

"Edward defeated Akisada," Tokimune insisted. "That means his weapons and tactics are superior to ours. We have to admit this. This approaching war puts the very existence of Nippon in jeopardy. We have to do whatever we can to ensure victory," he asserted, his voice expressing his unmistakable determination. "We need those knights to win."

"You think our own men are not strong enough?"

"New enemies require new methods to fight against them."

"Be that as it may, a rumor is going around that Edward has been meeting with Nichiren."

"It is not a rumor. It is true."

"You knew that, my lord, and yet—"

"Those who share a peculiar temperament tend to want to talk with one another," Tokimune said with a half-laugh.

Edward and Nichiren's opinions directly conflict with each other, Tokimune thought. *Edward believes in Jesus, and Nichiren preaches that reciting the Lotus Sutra can save people. The two of them can't accept heathenism. The two of them wouldn't consort with each other. Re-*

ligion truly is an odd thing. While having the purpose of giving people salvation, it also drives them to hell. It shows how weak people are. Even I, myself, cannot live without being obsessed with something.

"Kublai Khan will not hold back. He is ready to completely conquer Nippon," Tokimune said with a light sigh.

"The gods protect our country."

"Do you truly believe that?"

"Protecting Nippon means protecting Kamakura, the world of the samurai, and the Hojo Clan."

"Is that really for the good of Nippon?" Tokimune said under his breath.

PREPARATIONS

Edward's eyes opened wide as he entered the room. A bearded man wearing Song clothes stood next to Zafir and quietly bowed to him.

"Xie WangSheng?"

"I am not Xie WangSheng. My name is Zhang Xin. I am a merchant from the Southern Song Dynasty. I come bringing important news," WangSheng said before he could bear it no more and burst out laughing. "I went to Southern Song and had some interesting days there."

"And here I was worrying that you had crossed all the way over to Europe," Edward said.

"It has finally begun," WangSheng said, the smile disappearing from his face as he fixed his gaze on Edward. "Kublai Khan has finally learned that Du Shizhong was beheaded in Kamakura."

"I see . . . So, as we expected, Kublai Khan did not know that Du Shizhong had been executed when he sent Zhou Fu and the other messengers to Nippon. Lord Tokimune has beheaded Zhou Fu in Hakata. Kublai Khan should be furious."

"He is, and he intends to attack Nippon without delay."

"How strong are his forces?"

"On New Year's Day, four years ago, the Southern Song Dynasty collapsed with the bloodless surrender of its capital city, Lin'an. As a result, all of Song's riches and its naval power are now under Kublai Khan's control."

"So, by surrendering and not putting up a fight, Southern Song's military remained unharmed."

"It is as you say. Yuan typically attacks a new country using the riches and soldiers of the countries it has previously invaded. The one hundred and thirty thousand men in Southern Song's navy will sail against Nippon."

Edward sighed.

"An enemy force of a hundred and fifty thousand will be difficult to hold off," Zafir, who had been quietly listening, spoke out.

"Do you think we won't be able to block them?"

Am I not to blame for Kublai Khan's anger? Edward thought. *I could have persuaded Tokimune not to behead Khan's messenger in Hakata.*

"You are not to blame," Zafir calmly told him, as if reading his thoughts. "We knew it would come to this. We have given this country a chance. Whether the samurai effectively make use of it or not is up to their ruler."

"You were the one who said the enemy was just a jumble of troops."

"If we want to be victorious, we will have to take advantage of that."

"How?" Edward implored.

"That is something for you to determine, not me," Zafir said with a faint smile.

When showing WangSheng out, Edward brushed past Haruno in the corridor. She wordlessly bowed and continued in the opposite direction.

"She is truly beautiful," WangSheng said, looking at the retreating figure. "Is she someone special to you, Lord Edward?"

"She is. I love her."

"Well, well, well. Just as I would expect from a foreigner. You go straight to the point. Then you should live together."

"I have been told that before."

"If you need your own residence, I am sure you could ask Lord Morimune."

"The day will come when I will return to England."

"Take her with you then."

"What if she says no?"

"If she says no, kidnap her," WangSheng said frankly.

"That might be a good idea," Edward responded in spite of himself.

"I have only seen her this once, but in spite of her delicate appearance, I can tell that she has a strong will. And the way she looks at you Lord Edward is deeply meaningful. She would most likely adapt well to living in a foreign land."

"My country is completely different from Nippon."

"The roots of the human heart are all the same. The only differences are habits. And new habits can be learned. Look at me. I have completely become a citizen of Nippon!"

"Then if we decide to live in Nippon, can Haruno and I work for you? I would feel closer to my country since you deal with many foreigners."

"I would be delighted. I hope to see the two of you at my estate one day." WangSheng laughed and bowed deeply to Edward.

CHAPTER
76

The following day, Edward met with Tokimune, who immediately sensed something in Edward's expression.

"Any news?" Tokimune asked.

"My friend has just returned from Hakata. I have good news and bad news."

Tokimune's eyes twitched slightly.

"Tell me the good news first. Bad news is always better after the good."

Tokimune flashed his usual pleasant smile.

"Two-thirds of the stone ramparts have been built on the coast. The soldiers' morale is high."

"Thanks to your advice. We alone could not have made this much progress."

"The ramparts will be finished in a few months."

"And the bad news?"

Edward proceeded to tell him about WangSheng's report. Tokimune listened intently, but he did not look as discouraged as Edward expected. *The people of this land really do not express their emotions,* he thought. *Or perhaps Tokimune does not grasp the severity of the situation.*

"From now on, will get weekly reports from Hakata. Zafir has made the arrangements."

Tokimune's spies in Goryeo and Song were also tracking Yuan's movements, but no one around him could properly evaluate the information and tell him what it meant for Nippon.

"Before the approaching battle commences, I have a suggestion," Edward proceeded cautiously.

"Tell me."

"It is that you review and correct how you distribute rewards at the end of a war."

"What would you do?"

"The rewards should firstly go to the families of fallen soldiers. Secondly, to the injured. Thirdly, to those who exhibited meritorious war service. The first two should be given equally to whoever participated in the battle. If you don't do that, then the soldiers won't be able to fight with peace of mind."

"I will think it over. What do you mean by 'meritorious war service'?"

"A person who has influenced the victory or defeat of the battle."

"Up until now, we have given many rewards to those who have led the first charge into battle, have brought me the heads of enemy generals, and have been the last to retreat so as to protect their comrades. They all fought hard to earn their rewards."

"If rewards alone are what soldiers strive for, then there is no military discipline. Only chaos. This system of yours may have worked up until now, but to fight and win against a strong foreign invader, you must cast aside self-interest and fight as one."

"So, you think that we only fight for our own selfish desires?" Yasumori said sidling up to Edward with a furious face.

"I understand 'service and rewards' is the basic rule of the master–servant relationship in the samurai world. The gokenin fight for the shogun to get land as a reward at the end of a war."

Yasumori could not dispute him.

"But there will not be any new territory to claim in this war. The prospect of receiving land as the reward for going to war must no longer apply."

Edward stole a glance at Tokimune, who though he showed no reaction, likely believed the same.

"What do you fight for? We need a cause for the next war," Edward asked.

"Let's discuss this another time," Tokimune said and walked away.

"Lord Tokimune understands the problem, but he cannot solve it. At least not yet. That is why he left," Morimune said to Edward.

"He has to sort it out soon. Individually, each samurai is strong and capable. But as a group, they are useless in war. On the battlefield, it's every man for himself in pursuit of rewards."

"The gokenin are the masters of their own clans. They hate being under someone else's command."

"Then we can't win this battle," Edward said.

"We have to win. For the people of this nation," Zafir intervened as he looked from one to the other.

"Is there any way to make the gokenin really serious about winning the war without a reward?" Morimune observed.

Zafir gave a meaningful smile.

CHAPTER

77

After that day, rumors about Mongolian atrocities spread through the streets of Kamakura.

"Mongolian soldiers eat the hearts of the enemy commanders they capture."

"They hang, draw, and quarter captured soldiers by tying their hands and feet to horses and cows."

"Mongolian soldiers play kemari football with enemy commander heads."

Alan told Edward about the cruel and savage deeds of the Mongolian soldiers, and that the townspeople would ask him if they were true or not.

"What do you tell them?"

"That I don't know. I remind them that I fought Saracens, not Mongolians. They all turn green when I tell them those Saracen bastards would peel the skin off their prisoners and then sprinkle them with salt."

"Was that true?"

"I only heard of it. I never saw it for myself. An old geezer by the name of Old Braggart told me. He hated the Saracens. That's why I fight so desperately."

Alan looked serious, but Zafir pulled a face.

"I heard from someone I know that when Mongolians capture high-ranking officials they stuff them into a leather bag and have a horse kick it until the men inside die," Morimune added with the utmost composure.

CHAPTER

78

At the next meeting of the Hyojyoshu council, Tokimune abruptly confronted Edward.

"What kind of army do you think is the strongest?" he asked.

All eyes focused on Edward.

"An armed force with command and control is unrivaled," he replied after taking some time to gather his thoughts. "I heard that in the last war Mongolian soldiers would march and advance to signals from gongs and drums. I also heard that they fired hundreds of arrows simultaneously. It is next to impossible to have arrows pour down like the rain itself. Yet the Mongolian soldiers all fired their arrows at the very moment their commander ordered. An army that can act in perfect unison is a powerful force to be feared."

Edward had already spoken of this many times before, and the men gathered in the council chamber had heard him do so many times before. Nippon's weakness, and also its strength, was that it did not seek new ways of fighting.

Edward continued.

"As I said before, the samurai's individual battle ability is very impressive. But as a group, the samurai cannot display their real power in battle."

"What do you think would be best?"

"It is necessary to make a major change in the organization of your forces, and further clarify and document the rewards system."

No one voiced an objection. The desire to gain victory no matter the personal sacrifice had finally won acceptance. Like others in Kamakura, the Hyojyoshu council shrank before the rumors of Mongolian brutality.

Edward then turned to Tokimune.

"There is something even more important."

Tokimune looked at Edward more seriously than ever before.

"In war, the most important thing is to have a great cause, a cause that is worth giving your life for."

"What is your great cause?"

"I—" Edward stopped as he had once before. He could not say the words then, and he still hesitated to say them. But now he felt as if something new had been born inside his heart.

"It is different for each person it seems," Tokimune muttered and turned away from Edward and back to the council.

CHAPTER
79

Six years had passed since Yuan's first attack, and over four years since Edward and the others had come to Kamakura. Countless reports came in that Yuan was preparing for the next invasion, but when it was to occur was anybody's guess. To pass the time during the stalemate, and with Alan and Zafir to help him, Edward continued his study of the Mongolian weapons that had been left behind. He fired Nippon arrows at Yuan defensive gear many times over. And did the same with Yuan arrows and Nippon armor.

"Sure enough, this country's bows have a great deal of power, which is best exhibited in one-on-one fights between men on horseback," Edward said.

"But outside of that, they are good for nothing. I'll rely on my sword every time, thank you very much," Alan said.

"How many times do you say the same things?" Morimune said with a laugh.

The Hyojyoshu council met on a daily basis now that the situation was growing more desperate. Edward was always in attendance.

"The enemy will rain down thousands of arrows as they did before," Edward reiterated. "Arrows laced with poison. Our army should be planning similar strategies."

"You want us to imitate those lowly Mongolians?" one of the samurai reacted.

Edward met the eyes of each of the Hyojyoshu as he spoke.

"Each group of samurai must be under the leadership of one man. And those groups in turn must be unified under a supreme commander. Meaningless acts of misguided heroism in search of personal glory and reward, such as charging ahead of others in battle, must be abolished," he once again lectured the council.

"And you don't need to exchange introductions on the battlefield," Edward said.

Tokimune hesitated before he said, "The way of the bow was a reward for those who would take the first charge against the enemy. Samurai give their names to allies, not enemies. It is a way of introducing themselves to those around them who witness their heroism and help them claim rewards. Young gokenin in particular will engage in foolhardy one-on-one fights for the sake of rewards."

"If you lose there will be neither honor nor rewards," Edward admonished the council. "Your head will be severed from your body and added to the pile of your comrades' skulls. And that will lead to the slaughter of your families. The rumors fluttering through the streets have reached your ears, no? In the approaching battle the only thing that should be on your mind is victory."

The Hyojyoshu nodded in agreement.

"I propose that all individual acts in battle be strictly prohibited and considered a violation of military rules," Edward said.

"And the punishment for such a violation?" Tokimune asked.

"Death or the seizure of the offender's land and property."

Tokimune took a moment to think, then nodded.

Edward turned to the Hyojyoshu and made his final case.

"I implore all of you to change your past ways of thinking. This fight will not be for the sake of an individual's great achievements and rewards. No, it will be a fight to protect this nation and its people. This is a war you cannot afford to lose. Try with all your valor to stop and defeat Yuan's invasion of your home, rather than rush toward individual fame and honors."

The Hyojyoshu listened in silence.

CHAPTER
80

Edward and Tokimune met nearly every day to discuss the approaching war. While they argued in public in front of the Hyojyoshu, they talked amicably as comrades in arms when they walked together in Tokimune's garden.

"So, what do you think the Mongolian army will do?" Tokimune asked.

"The soldiers will most likely secure the bridgehead immediately after landing, so as not to make the same mistake as last time. As for us, it will take a considerable amount of sacrifice on our part to overcome the sheer number of troops once they spread out along the coast."

"Then we have to push them back while they are at sea, before they get the chance to build their encampment on the shore."

"I agree. But six years have passed since the last invasion. Do you think Kublai Khan has been sitting idly by all this time? He will mobilize his army and attack having spent the last six years studying and learning about Nippon's terrain, its defense systems, the size of its army, its physical and mental strengths—and its weaknesses."

"But we have also prepared for battle. We know Yuan's strategies from the previous war. And our solid stone wall defense system is well under way. Just as you advised."

"Then who is to be the supreme commander of all the samurai?"

"Kanazawa Akitoki, a member of the Kanazawa Hojo Clan."

"I think you should reconsider and choose someone who is close to you and in your bloodline. When King Richard the Lionheart of England joined the ranks of the Army of Christ, his presence alone raised the morale of all the troops."

"Perhaps."

"You have not made an official announcement, have you? The gokenin from Kyushu were at the heart of the last war. But this time around, because Yuan will increase its forces several times over, Nippon will have to collect armies from all over Nippon and unite them into a single force. The supreme commander as the cornerstone of such an army must be someone of status, good lineage, and prodigious feats of arms. Someone who can lead the samurai troops in every way."

Tokimune silently listened.

"I would like you to take command in the upcoming battle."

Tokimune sighed.

"I have thought of doing so, but I cannot."

"Because of the circumstances here in Kamakura?"

"The Kamakura shogunate and Hojo Clan are not established solidly enough yet. Even in this national crisis, a rebellion could occur if I leave Kamakura. It's a damn shame!"

"Then we must find someone who can take your place," Edward said. "What about Lord Munemasa?"

Tokimune pondered for a moment. Munemasa was Tokimune's younger brother. Edward had learned that their father, Tokiyori, the former regent, had favored Tokimune and Munemasa out of all his children.

"Agreed. I will send Munemasa as the acting regent to Kyushu. However, I have a request of you. Can I ask you to go with him to Kyushu and help him?" Tokimune bowed his head deeply to Edward.

"I will do my best to be of service."

"Thank you for granting such a request."

The nighttime silence of Kamakura enveloped the two men. The faintest sounds of the monks' nembutsu chant whisked through the air.

CHAPTER

81

One day in January, Zafir burst into Edward's room. "The Yuan invasion will be in June," he said, panting and out of breath with excitement.

"You are sure?"

"One of WangSheng's messengers brought the news from Hakata."

"Then it is happening quicker than I expected," Edward said. His body tensed, but he was not surprised. He knew the Mongolians would come, the question was when. Considering the time it would take to build such a vast armada, he had estimated the invaders would sail in late summer or early fall. Now they would arrive earlier than anticipated, but not by that much. War was imminent.

"I was told the combined forces from Yuan, Song, and Goryeo come to a hundred and fifty thousand men. Their forces have already begun to gather in the ports of Song and Goryeo."

Can I ask you to go with my younger brother to Kyushu and help him? Tokimune's words flashed across Edward's mind. *Is it right of me to ask my own men to throw their lives away for Nippon?* he thought.

"Is something wrong?" Zafir seemed troubled as he peered into Edward's face.

"It is nothing. I must speak with Lord Tokimune," Edward said. They had less than half a year left. There was no time to lose.

CHAPTER

82

That night, Edward gathered his knights and Thomas' sailors. He told them of the fast-approaching invasion and that Tokimune had asked him to go to Kyushu to fight.

"Why do we have to fight in a foreigner's battle?" one of the men demanded.

"That's right! This pagan war has nothing to do with us," another agreed.

Voices protested from every corner of the room.

"The Mongolian army is known for its strength and savagery. I want no part in a battle against them."

"Let's go back to Hakata, steal a ship, and finally go home!"

Thomas, who often kept his opinion to himself, raised his arms to silence the crowd.

"The people of this land saved us and have treated us with kindness," he said.

Edward, after listening to Thomas and the others, calmly rose to his feet.

"I understand your concerns. Pagan quarrels are not something that we should drag ourselves into. That is not God's wish."

"What are you trying to say?" Alan interrupted, his voice filled with irritation.

"First, face your foes without fear. Second, be courageous. Third, fear not death and speak truth. Fourth, protect the weak and live righteously. That is what you have all vowed as knights," Edward's voice resounded throughout the room. "I was twelve when I left my home to train as a knight. As I departed, my father said to me, 'Whenever you feel lost remember these four oaths of knighthood.' And with that he struck my cheek sharply. Through the pain, and in spite of it, I knew then that I would never forget my vows for as long as I lived."

The room was silent.

"There is time before I return to Hakata. I want all of you to think about what I have said before coming to your decision."

"Why are you not telling us to fight with you?" Alan's voice rose up.

"This fight will be more painful and difficult than anything we have experienced before. Surviving will be a challenge. I cannot decide your destiny for you."

"It is God who decides that."

"I want you to decide of your own free will. Whatever choice you make, I know God will support you."

Every time God's name slipped past his lips, Edward's heart ached. *Is there truly a God? Is He still watching over us?* He gripped his sword and shook the thoughts away.

CHAPTER
83

The following day, Edward informed Tokimune of the planned invasion in June. Afterward, Morimune, with a large number of attendants in tow, visited Edward's estate.

"I bring gifts from Lord Tokimune to thank you for the training you have been providing." Morimune signaled and his attendants carried in twenty wicker baskets. "He gives these to you and your retainers."

In one of the baskets was a complete vermillion lacquered armor set.

"It is beautiful," Edward said.

"Please put it on."

"Why, do all of us have to put this thing on?" Alan spluttered. "Do you want us to become like this country's samurai?"

"It is a present from Lord Tokimune. You should gratefully accept," Zafir said to pacify Alan. But there was a deeper meaning to the gesture, which Zafir discerned but chose not to pursue at this time. Contrary to Alan's reaction, the rest of the men were curious and gathered around the gifts.

"These are clearly very valuable," Thomas said as he examined one of the helmets.

"There is one for each of you. Later, someone will adjust them for you. It is because of Lord Tokimune's great trust in you and gratitude for all that you have done that you receive such treasures."

"Can I put it on?" one of the sailors asked excitedly.

"By all means."

Within an hour the men were in their new armor. Even Alan wore a helmet with its hoe-shaped crest and matching red chest armor.

"This armor must weigh well over sixty pounds," Alan said, as he took a step forward and staggered. "Chainmail is heavy, but not like this. Samurai get on their horses and fight with this on?"

The others stiffly moved about.

Determined, Alan began to take larger strides as he grew in confidence. "Do not let this armor hold you back, men," he shouted. "We are God's soldiers!"

"Do you intend to fight in that?" Zafir asked after silently watching all the men parade in their armor.

"They have yet to decide if they will fight," Edward said.

"Alan and Thomas intend to. Several of the sailors, too."

"Is that what they have been saying?"

"They do not have to. Just look at them. Lord Tokimune is truly a talented schemer."

Edward nodded.

"What do you think of this armor, Zafir?"

"It is magnificent, but too bulky. And it stands out too much. It is not suited for real battle. Well, perhaps in the civil wars and skirmishes fought here. But it is significantly different from the Mongolian army's combat armor which is nothing if not practical."

"Did Lord Tokimune say he wants us to fight the enemy in this armor?"

"Why else would he send it to you? It is the samurai of this country who will repel the Mongolian forces. It cannot be anyone else."

"Then he will make us fight like Nippon samurai."

Edward and Zafir went out to the garden. The sun had set, and stars shone against the jet-black night sky.

"You are not a knight, Zafir. You are a merchant. Come with us as far as Hakata and then return to your home."

"I shall think about it once we get to Hakata," Zafir said in his customary calm tone.

"You have family back in your homeland, do you not? I should have asked before now."

"I have never had a wife. I lived with my mother, father, and three sisters. But I would be traveling for most of the year." Zafir fell silent and looked up at the sky, lost in thought and remembrance.

"When did they die?"

"A year before I met you, when the Christian army invaded Baghdad," Zafir replied without hesitation. "Our house was burned to the ground. My parents and sisters were trapped inside."

"Do you not hate the Christian army for murdering your family?"

"I hate them. Once, I wanted nothing more than to kill them."

"Do you think the same of me?"

"You are not the one who killed my family."

"But I am a soldier in the Army of Christ."

A light swept across the darkness. It was a shooting star. *Haruno.* Suddenly, the figure of a woman standing in a grassy field shimmered and filled Edward's mind.

CHAPTER
84

"It is true you are going to Hakata?" Haruno asked Edward when they met the next evening.

"So, you have heard."

"I would know even if I had not heard it. Kamakura talks of nothing but the Yuan raid. And you have been training the samurai. Will you fight against Yuan, Lord Edward?"

"Tokimune has asked me to. He says it is to protect Kamakura. I do not know how much I can do, but I want to do all that I can."

"You are teaching the samurai your country's methods of war, no?"

"The battle tactics of my land greatly increase our chances of victory in a war against Yuan."

"I hate war. No matter who wins or loses, there is suffering and death."

"You are right. But this war with Yuan is one we must win no matter the cost. If we lose, then the nation will be destroyed and many of its people will die. I am entrusting you to Morimune and WangSheng when I am gone."

Haruno did not reply. Edward gently wrapped his arms around her shoulders and pulled her closer to him. Her body felt soft against him.

Haruno was different that night. She took him into her as if it was a challenge.

"Though the god you and I believe in is different, our hearts are one."

For Haruno's sake, I will win this war, Edward swore.

CHAPTER
85

The day of departure finally arrived. Early that morning, Edward, Alan, and Zafir left the manor but stopped as soon as they exited the front gates. There, Edward's knights and Thomas' sailors had gathered to meet them. They were wearing the armor that Tokimune had given them.

"You are all coming?"

"Almost all. Let us bring down the Mongolians and then go back to our homes!"

"Almost?"

"We haven't seen Enrico. He took his armor, but we haven't heard from him."

"I think he has made up his mind then. Let us wish him good fortune."

And with that Edward led the party out. As the sun began to rise, they merged with Morimune's cavalry of a hundred men. Troops under the command of the acting regent, Hojo Munemasa, had already departed and were traveling to Hakata by land. As Edward and his men reached the port, a man wearing blue armor and helmet greeted them.

"You are late!" Enrico yelled out, taking in Edward and his comrades.

"You stay behind," Alan said to him.

"Please let me join you," Enrico pleaded. "If the Mongolians defeat this nation, my wife and children won't survive. I want to win this fight whatever the cost. I have to protect my family."

"I won't let you be killed. I'll protect you no matter what," Thomas told Enrico and patted him on the shoulder.

"You overslept didn't you! That's why you came straight to the harbor," one of the sailors teased.

"It was hard to leave my kids."

"Your wife too, I bet!"

"I said my goodbyes to my wife last night. I told my kids to help their mother and take care of their new sibling about to be born."

"You are a good father, in spite of being irresponsible!"

"With Enrico we have the whole unit," Alan told Edward.

Just as they were about to weigh anchor, Morimune approached Edward. His face was more earnest than it had ever been before.

"I received a message from my father," he told Edward.

"I saw Lord Yasumori on the dock. He is worried about you, as one would expect of a father."

"He apologized for the many inconveniences and wanted to thank you for your devoted guidance. He asks that you assist Lord Munemasa in Hakata. This was the message Adachi Yasumori came to give," Morimune quickly said before letting out a great sigh. "My father came to see you off. He may be stubborn, but he is not a fool.

He recognizes what you have done. But he is old and stuck in his ways. It is not easy for him to accept a foreigner. Please excuse him."

"My father was the same."

Edward and Morimune stood in silence for a time and looked toward Kamakura.

"What of Hayate?" Morimune suddenly asked.

"I left him in WangSheng's care. I told him he is a good horse and that he should be cherished."

"The same as Lady Haruno?"

"Do not compare her to a horse," Edward said, gently scolding Morimune. "I just want her to be happy."

"We will make it back alive without fail," Morimune reassured Edward.

As the ships drifted away from the pier and sailed into the open sea, they could see the entirety of the Kamakura townscape stretching east and west. Gradually it became smaller and smaller before disappearing entirely.

"We lived there for over four years," Thomas said and squinted his eyes toward the shore. He might have been crying. "It is the longest I have ever lived on land."

"If you want to go back, you can. There will be plenty of chances to do so," Edward said to comfort the sailor. But whenever he thought of what awaited them in Hakata, a void opened up before him. There was no certainty they would survive.

CHAPTER

86

An emissary from Dazaifu waited for them at the dock in Hakata.

"A letter has been received from Lord Tokimune," he announced, looking at Edward suspiciously. "While the general commander of the gokenin from Kyushu and the surrounding regions is the governor of Dazaifu, all are to follow the council of the acting regent, Lord Munemasa, and his advisor Lord Edward."

Without delay, they gathered the gokenin who had amassed in Hakata and held a meeting to discuss the approaching Mongolian invasion. The gokenin had come from all over the country, with the majority from Kyushu and its surrounding areas, as well as Kanto. Many of them were there to perform individual meritorious deeds in the upcoming war and subsequently acquire rewards. Most were likely unaware of the Lord of Kamakura's decisions, and if they were, they did not pay them any attention. Edward once again explained the importance of group battle strategies. From that evening on, their training began.

Suddenly, gongs and drums struck without warning. The startled horses reared, and several samurai fell off their mounts.

"Hold formation!" Morimune shouted as he clung to his bucking horse. "Immediately capture those making that racket."

"I gave the orders," Edward called out while barely managing to stay atop his horse as he attempted to soothe it. "Nippon horses are not used to loud noises. I have heard that in the last war many samurai were killed when the sounds of gongs and canon fire frightened their horses. We must train both horses and samurai to deal with such disturbances."

"The horses and soldiers here are the same. They both jump at the slightest noise. Even though they still have their balls they have no nerves," Alan said loudly while he cleaned out his ear with his finger.

"Deafen the horses' ears."

"What? Have you lost your mind?" Alan rebuked Edward.

"If the horses cannot get used to the sounds, that is the only option. Or do you think that the riders should cover the horses' ears with their own hands?"

"All right. I'll figure something out," Alan said unusually obediently. He sensed the resolve in Edward's tone.

"Where's Hayate?" a voice called out. Edward turned and saw Akisada approach on horseback.

"I left him in Kamakura."

"A fine horse lives for the battlefield."

"The sea voyage would not have been wise for a strong-tempered horse like Hayate."

Akisada signaled and one of his men brought over a chestnut-colored horse.

"This is the second strongest horse I own. I think it will suit you well. It is several times better than the horse you are currently riding. It will stay calm in spite of the gongs," he told Edward and laughed as he rode off.

CHAPTER
87

Later that day, as they returned to their encampment, Zafir entered Edward's tent.

"I have found out the route the Mongolians and their allies will be taking," he said as he sat and spread out a map of Goryeo, Southern Song, and Nippon.

"The main force of fifty thousand from the east will depart from Gatsupo, and the hundred thousand from Southern Song will later depart from Mingshu. It is likely they plan to join up on Iki Island. From there they will make their assault."

"Then we will intercept them in Hakata."

"The stone walls in Kyushu are now complete, and the gokenin from Kamakura have been sent to guard them. The enemy will not be able to disembark as easily as they did last time. If they manage to make it ashore and invade inland, then there is no chance of winning. Once Yuan gains control over Kyushu, it will inevitably become the stepping-stone for them to invade Nippon's main island, Honshu. We must block them at the coast by any means necessary," Zafir said before continuing.

"There are rumors that the commander in chief of the Gangnam army has fallen ill. We are spreading rumors of plague to our advantage. Originally, Yuan and Southern Song were not allies. If the transfer of control falls into chaos, then the merging with Song's hundred thousand men could be delayed more than a month. During that time, we can do as much as we can to damage the spearhead from the east."

This fight is going to be more than challenging for Nippon. Might it be wise to avoid becoming involved in the war and surrender to Yuan? Maybe then we could get home. Edward thought of all of the acts of barbarity he had seen and heard since he landed in this country. *But if Yuan manages to advance to Kamakura, then ten times, no, a hundred times as many tragedies will occur.* Edward brought his attention back to the map in front of him.

CHAPTER

88

Edward, Morimune, and Alan walked along the beach, the stone rampart stretching endlessly before them. Above them, heavily armed samurai were on alert. But none of this eased Edward's apprehension. In front of them, Edward could see the beautiful sand beach and the two islands, Nokonoshima and Shikanoshima, beyond that. Shikanoshima and the Kyushu mainland were connected by a narrow spit of sand that separated Hakata Bay from the Genkai Sea. The Yuan warships would enter and anchor in Hakata Bay seeking shelter from the Genkai Sea's rough waves.

"The beach looks wider than when I last saw it," Edward observed.

"It is low tide right now," Morimune told him.

Edward squinted his eyes toward the sea, then turned back to the coast. Twenty horsemen were approaching.

"Which cavalry is that?"

"That is Lord Takebe's regiment."

"Aren't they supposed to be protecting Odahama?"

"That is true."

"Then why have they left their station without permission?"

"In the previous war, the enemy came ashore in Imazu. They probably thought it was meaningless to defend Odahama." Odahama was a beach west of Imazu. It was farther from where they expected the Mongolian army to land, but it would not hold out long if it was left defenseless and then attacked.

"Yuan draws nearer to us with five times the forces they attacked with before. The whole region must be protected. Not simply Hakata and Imazu bays. This should have been decided by the war council."

"Do the samurai truly not want to win?" Alan questioned full of rage. "Even now they still want to take the lead in battle. They just want to rush in blind!"

"It is evidence of their bravery," Morimune claimed.

"Bravery and recklessness are as different as up and down! Recklessness can put your allies in danger. Their little ploy could lead to the end of us all!"

Morimune had no reply. He was well aware of everything Alan had said.

CHAPTER

89

Morimune showed Edward, Alan, and Zafir around the armory, where all the bows, arrows, and katanas were safely stored.

"I have said it again and again. We don't have enough arrows. What we have here is enough for one battle only," Edward complained.

"As expected, no one in this country listens to a single thing we say. Let's just leave them to their fate," Alan said, turning on his heel.

"Tell me how many more arrows are necessary," Morimune said. Edward learned later that Morimune's father, Yasumori, had told him to fully cooperate. Even though Yasumori hated Edward and his foreign knights, he still could recognize that they had their uses and talents.

"We need around five hundred bows and a hundred thousand arrows. The bows should be short, like those used by the Mongolians."

Morimune swung his head round. It was an outrageous number.

"I can get the bows, but getting even half that number of arrows will be difficult."

"Then we won't win this war," Edward asserted.

Yuan was approaching with an army of a hundred and fifty thousand men. Compared to that, Nippon had less than fifty thousand. Nippon could not afford to fight fairly if they were to win. Yuan's weakness was that its army had a great distance to cross over the sea. While Nippon was prepared for a drawn-out war on its home turf, the enemy would grow impatient if the fighting dragged on. Nippon therefore had to prevent the enemy from making camp on the beach. They had to shower arrows down on their foes and drive away their ships. That was the conclusion that Edward, Alan, and Zafir had come to. Victory would not be theirs if they tried to directly engage an army that far exceeded their own in numbers.

"Understood. I will make every effort to do as much as possible."

"We can't win by effort alone. If you want to win, you have to do as I say," Edward insisted.

"Five hundred bows and a hundred thousand arrows. I will ready them in five days without fail."

"Make it three days. I want to start training the men with them."

"Four days. The bows and arrows will be delivered in the order they are produced."

Edward glared at Morimune and nodded.

"It seems there is little understanding of how a supply of arrows is quickly depleted. Though Nippon surely has many different types of them," Zafir said as he admired the arrows lined up in the armory.

"Arrows are meant to rob people of their lives. Not something to be decorated and enjoyed. A fact this country clearly does not understand," Edward said.

"Don't just stand there lamenting. Let's do something about it. Tokimune asked you to protect this country, didn't he?" Alan said as he hit Edward's shoulder, cheering him up even though he had suggested leaving Nippon to its fate just a few minutes before.

Edward, Alan, and Zafir, accompanied by several of the knights, went to the watermill on the outskirts of town, where they had hidden the other catapult before leaving Hakata. The catapult, covered with a woven mat and placed in the corner of the room, was just as they had left it four years ago. On top of the mat was a thick pile of grit that crumbled when touched.

"Will we even be able to use this?" Alan huffed as he pulled out the catapult.

It was damaged when they left it, but the past four years had not been kind to it. Rust covered the metal fixtures, and bugs had eaten through parts of the wood.

"Give up. This thing couldn't even fling a stone the size of a fist," Zafir said.

"Can't we fix it?" Edward said.

"Impossible," Alan scoffed.

"Let's just fire it once. We don't even have to aim it at anything," Edward insisted.

"You do it. I'll watch from over there," Alan said and turned away.

"For now, let's bring it to the beach."

Ever hopeful, Edward, helped by the others, carried out the catapult and took it to the end of the cape, where they repaired the damaged parts as best they could.

"Now then, let's get her ready," Edward said signaling to the soldiers to rotate the pulley. But just as the arm of the catapult began to bend, a cracking sound came from the wood.

"This is good enough. Load the stone."

Suddenly, the wood split, and the catapult's arm flew off. A piece of wood the size of a human body grazed Alan's head before smashing into a nearby rock and shattering.

CHAPTER
90

The following day, Edward and Alan, accompanied by Zafir, visited the outskirts of Hakata. They informed the villagers of the impending Yuan attack and asked for their help.

"We're different from the samurai. Using katanas and bows is too much for us," the elderly village head said while looking between Edward, Alan, and Zafir.

"We will teach you. Just like you, the samurai did not know how to handle a katana and bow when they started. If you practice, you will manage."

"You want us to learn how to kill people?"

"It is so that both you and your families will survive."

"I refuse," the village head said quietly. "Our duty is to work the land and raise crops. Even if they are our foes, we cannot take their lives."

"In the end, farmers are farmers. Instead of fleeing from their enemies, they just tremble and cry before them," Alan said unsympathetically as he turned to leave the village. He always had a cold look in his eyes when he was among farmers and townspeople. Unlike Edward, he had lived close to the peasantry when he was a boy, so his experience and knowledge of them was different.

"Nevertheless, their words have a weight all their own. Such farmers keep us alive. It is our duty to protect them," Edward responded.

Zafir silently listened as Edward spoke.

"They willingly offer up their necks," Alan raised his voice. "Those who are defeated without fighting back are nothing but cowards."

Several children innocently played in a corner of the village square, where fifty to sixty men and women had gathered. Half of them were townsfolk, the others were vagabonds who had lost everything in the last battle with Yuan. What they had in common was that some, if not all, of their family had been killed.

"In several months, Yuan will once again attack these lands," Edward's voice boomed out. "Will you wait to be killed? Or will you protect yourself with your own two hands?"

The crowd stirred.

"If you so desire, we will teach you how to fight back."

"Will I be able to use a katana?" a voice from the middle of the crowd asked.

All heads turned toward the owner of the voice.

"You will. But I cannot say that you will have enough time to properly learn it."

"Even if we carry katanas, isn't it the same as just waiting to lose our heads?"

"That is right. But if the Mongolians capture you, you might be killed by a more violent means of torture. That is something all of you should be aware of."

"Wouldn't it be better to flee?"

The commotion gradually grew louder.

"Edward, you are wasting your time trying to get these people to fight. It is pointless to give cowards weapons," Alan said.

"No one is going to protect you!" Edward shouted out, ignoring Alan. "Remember what happened in the last war. If you don't want to lose your heads or become slaves in a foreign land, then learn to protect yourselves! Protect your family!"

"The samurai protect us!"

"The samurai will do everything in their power," Edward argued. "But the Mongolians are sending an army of a hundred and fifty thousand men. We need everyone to fight together!"

The commotion died down.

"Your weapons will be bows. With a bow there is no need to be close to the enemy or cross blades with him. Even from a great distance you will be able to slay your foes."

"Can I join?"

"Of course. Anyone who has the desire to do so may."

"I'll do it!" A shout rose out from the corner of the square and quickly spread throughout the crowd.

"Those who wish to fight, stay here. You will be given a weapon and taught how to fight."

No one left the square. Edward raised up the bow and arrow in his right hand high in the air.

From the next day on, they trained the village people in archery. They divided them into groups of ten and had them practice firing arrows. At the end of the first day, the groups competed against each other for the number of arrows that would hit the mark.

"You don't need to hit the middle of the target," Alan shouted out. "If the arrow flies in the direction you aim at, that's good enough. Ultimately you should be able to fire long distances!"

"It's easy enough to learn, but how useful is it actually going to be in combat?" Alan confided to Edward.

"They don't need to hit anything."

"They won't be any use at all in close combat. They'll just hinder their allies."

"We won't let them fight head on. It will be our job to protect them then," Edward said, his words filled with intention.

Later that evening, several warriors on horseback approached Edward on the beach. At the party's head was Munemasa.

"Is it true you have been training the local townsfolk and peasants in archery?" he asked without ceremony after dismounting.

"As soon as their bows and arrows are ready, we will start full-scale training."

"It is not necessary for citizens to use weapons. It is the job of the samurai to protect the people."

"Is that what you truly think? If there is any falsehood in your words, it will lead to the slaughter of your own people."

"I would like you to collect all the weapons and disband the peasants and townsfolk."

"Your people have a right to protect themselves. I want to help them do so."

"A weapon is not something a person will let go of easily once they have it in their hands. When you have power, you want to use it."

"That is something you can think about after you win this war. But if Nippon falls to Yuan, then you will not have to worry about such things ever again."

"I would like you to consider my words the same as you would those of my brother, Tokimune."

"As you wish. But they still do not have enough weapons."

"Heed my words."

"When you return to camp, Lord Munemasa, please tell Lord Morimune that tomorrow is the day he promised."

Munemasa shot him a puzzled look and left without saying anything else.

"That bastard sure has a lot of time on his hands. It is best he only trains the samurai," Alan said as he glared at Munemasa riding into the distance.

The farmers and townspeople resented Alan shouting at them, and they rebelled against his orders. They also lacked concentration.

"It is a waste of time teaching them how to use a bow and arrow," Alan said and sighed in frustration. "Their bodies aren't suitable for fighting. Their torsos and limbs are too long and too short to handle the large Nippon bow and arrows. They're strong, but slow. The samurai have been training, like the knights, since they were young. These are and always will be farmers."

Edward fixed an arrow to his short bow, drew it back, and fired at the target. The peasants' eyes followed the arrow's course as it pierced through the center of the target.

"This is one of the short bows the Mongolians used," Edward told them. "It is easy to use, and the arrowheads are dipped in poison. Your parents, siblings, relatives, and friends lost their lives to these bows and arrows. The next will be you. If one of these arrows penetrates your chest or stomach, or even scratches a limb, you will die in agony. What do you think? Should you shoot at them with the very same weapons they once used against you?"

All around them voices raged and fists were raised.

"My father died after eight arrows ran through his body. This time it's my turn to give it back to them!"

"An arrow only grazed my right leg, but it had to be cut off. I was a carpenter. I can't climb roofs now."

"Have you still not acquired more short bows and arrows?" Thomas asked, a longbow in his hand.

"Zafir should be here any minute—" Edward started to say, but before he could finish Zafir came through the gates with several men leading five packhorses loaded with boxes. Zafir unveiled the boxes, revealing Mongolian bows and arrows tightly packed inside.

"Aren't these the ones that should have been buried four years ago?" Alan said as he picked up a bow with a cut string. "Where did you hide them? I thought it was strange when you said the poison would have spread if they were burned."

Upon closer inspection, they could see that more than half of the arrows were rotten and infested with insects. They were unusable.

"Have the farmers make a large quantity of the same type," Edward ordered optimistically. "They should be easier to produce than the Nippon bow and arrow. Pay them accordingly."

"We're going to pay them?" Alan questioned. "Even though it's to protect their own lives? I see, even money can save lives. They are far from their trade or agriculture in this war."

Alan taught the farmers and townspeople in and around Hakata how to make short bows and arrows. Groups of five people were required to make ten arrows a day and one bow in three. With five hundred people working together, a hundred bows were made in three days and a thousand arrows were made daily.

CHAPTER
91

Edward squinted his eyes as he rode on the beach, where fifty farmers with bows were lined up. Alan and several knights stood in front. Edward turned his horse away from the dazzlingly shining sea and trotted over to Alan.

"What's the matter?" Edward asked.

"I finally understand that there are some things people are born with and some things that they are not."

"Oh, so you finally understand that. Took long enough."

"Half of their arms are bent," Alan said looking at the farmers with frustration. "Their arrows either don't make it into the air, or they fly off in different directions. If they're unlucky, they will end up hitting their own allies in battle."

"It can't be helped. They're farmers. We can't grow potatoes, but they can use a hoe."

"You can learn to use a hoe in a day. But aim an arrow properly? They couldn't learn that in a hundred years!"

"And even if you could use a hoe, that doesn't mean you could grow potatoes. They never touched a bow and arrow in their lives up until now."

Alan gave the farmers the order to fire their arrows. The arrows scattered, as he said they would. And as he said, some arms were bent.

"The enemy will fill up the beach. Just firing the arrows will be enough to hit some of them. It will be fine if they can at least fire in the general direction they aim," Edward said to give some encouragement.

"Then it isn't necessary for them to work hard at aiming?"

"It is enough to train them in proper bearing and how to fire in swift succession. That's not too difficult, is it?"

"It's going to be a pain in the ass, because it will be difficult for them."

"Divide in two groups!" Edward ordered the fifty farmers. "Those who are skilled in aiming their arrows stand over here, and those who aren't stand over there. Those who can hit the target will receive further training. Those who cannot, will be trained in shooting arrows as far out as possible."

After a few days, close to half of them almost never missed the target fifty yards away. The other half could fly arrows a distance of a hundred yards.

"Do you think you can fight?" Edward asked a middle-aged man, who had pulled back his bow with a steady and strong arm.

"Perhaps. Though I don't know if I'd be able to fire my bow with an armed Mongolian charging at me," he said in an unconfident voice.

"You won't be directly fighting the Mongolians. We'll have you on alert behind the samurai, and all you'll have to do is fire your arrows at the Mongolians when signaled. You won't even see the enemies' faces."

"Then I can fight," the man replied, relief spreading across his face.

Edward proceeded to teach them two-stage firing, a battle tactic where two groups would release their arrows at intervals. One group fired arrows, while the other readied theirs and then fired when the first group reloaded.

CHAPTER

92

"This little devil snuck in," Alan said as he dragged a young boy by the collar toward Edward. The boy cursed as he struggled against Alan's grip.

"What is your name?" Edward asked.

"Taro."

"This is no place for children, Taro. Hurry back to your family." At the word 'family,' the boy fell silent.

"Is your father one of the archers?"

"The Mongolians killed my father and mother. I haven't seen my older sister since then either. I want to take my revenge," Taro told them, his eyes close to tears.

"There are plenty of people out for revenge here. Compared to that lot of brainless samurai who are only in it to compete for rewards, these people will be more useful."

Many women and children in the area had approached Alan asking to learn to fight.

"Give them bows and train them," Edward ordered Alan.

"We don't have enough bows and arrows for them," he complained to Edward.

"Then they can throw stones. Stones are everywhere."

Edward taught those without bows how to throw stones using a rock sling. While it could not hurl great boulders, it was a hand-sized weapon with a leather pouch at the end of two long straps. A stone, no bigger than a fist, would be placed in the pouch, and, by swinging round the straps several times, the stone would be propelled far into the distance, injuring and perhaps killing a foe.

"Don't be concerned if it will hit or not," Edward instructed. "There is no way of telling where your stones will fall, but they will still impede the enemy. We can use that as an opportunity to send down our arrows like rain."

The women in particular were zealous in their training. The fate of the women in the last war lived in their flesh and bones.

"What is that?" Zafir asked.

Three horses, each with a pair of baskets hung across its back, drew near. One of the children frolicking around the horses pulled a mat from a basket and revealed fist-sized stones piled to the top.

"We took them from the dry riverbed in the mountains," he said, triumphantly flourishing the mat. "There are lots of rocks like these. We'll bring more tomorrow!"

"One's life must be protected by oneself, would you not agree?" Zafir laughed and pointedly looked at Edward.

CHAPTER

93

Within the week, the farmers and townsfolk had in one way or another mastered the use of short bows and slings.

"They are becoming an armed force, aren't they? Finally, they can send their arrows and rocks forward," Zafir chuckled.

"Now I'll have them commit command executions to memory. Whistling arrows will be used to signal the start of an offense. Then I'll teach them to change direction as a unit," Edward said.

The children were faster learners than the adults. After several days, they were able to march together in formation.

"Teach me how to use a katana," Taro exclaimed. "I want to slit the throat of a Mongolian."

"Later," Alan, the disciplinarian, answered back. "For now, concentrate on bows, arrows, and slings."

Later that afternoon, Morimune paid them a visit for the first time in a long while. He had been in Dazaifu.

"Lord Munemasa is greatly troubled that you are teaching the farmers and townsfolk how to fight."

"We are also 'greatly troubled,'" Alan joked. "Christ, I'd teach a monkey to wield a sword if it would help."

"Lord Munemasa is an honest man. He knows when a thing is good. But he is also the representative of the regent of the shogunate. You should not trouble him so," Morimune said discreetly as he stood next to Edward and looked out to sea.

"What of those farmers? I thought the head of their village refused your offer?"

"They changed their mind. At any rate, they won't get in your way," Alan said in Edward's stead.

"They will only be a hinderance once war is upon us."

"We have no intention of teaching the peasants and children how to wield a sword."

Alan furrowed his brows at Edward's statement.

"They won't be on the front lines. We'll keep them in the rear, where they will fire arrows and throw rocks," Edward asserted plainly, earning a resigned expression from Morimune, who decided not to press the matter further.

"The defense guard on the stone walls is shorthanded. The samurai have abandoned their stations," Thomas said irritably as he returned from making his rounds on the coast. He and his sailors were dressed in the armor Tokimune had given them.

"Gather all the pikes you can find," Edward ordered. "They should be close to sixteen feet in length. They will be an extremely effective defense against enemies advancing on the ramparts."

"Sixteen feet?"

"About the length of three Nippon adult men. Anything longer would also do. We'll thrust them out from the ramparts to make it difficult for foes to climb over."

"There is no one in Nippon who could use such a long spear. I can't even say that we have such weapons,"Morimune said.

"Then make some as quickly as possible."

"How many?"

"The more the better. For now, five hundred should suffice. Line them up in the infantry every three feet. We'll make a line of spears held at the ready. The Mongolian army won't be so eager to attack with sixteen-foot spear tips staring them in the face."

"Hakata can't produce that many spears like that."

"Then make bamboo spears, and embed them in areas of the wall where there are no soldiers."

"Make arrangements to produce them right away!" Morimune ordered his subordinates.

CHAPTER
94

With time, the farmers and townsfolk evolved from a disorderly mob into a regiment ready to go to war. Edward even thought their combined power excelled that of the samurai.

"All of you are weak, so avoid engaging directly with the enemy," Alan cautioned them again and again. But contrary to what he said, he ended up teaching them sword fighting—more as a means to increase their confidence, and less as a way to slay enemies.

"Keep your distance from the enemy. Don't even think of crossing blades with them. Find an opening and run," Alan told them every time.

"What do we do when we can't flee?"

"Dive for their chest. Don't hesitate to stab there. Kill with a thrust. Then, if luck is on your side, you will be able to flee," Alan instructed and demonstrated by hitting his left fist on his chest. Alan's expression and attitude had changed. The darkness that Edward had sensed in him was vanishing. Now he had someone to protect. He and the people had grown closer. The same was true for the people of Hakata.

CHAPTER
95

Ragged thin beggars rounded up from the streets of Hakata formed a new band of archers being trained by Alan.

"How are they fairing? Any improvement?" Edward asked Alan, who was yelling orders at them.

"They just stand around. Although they have finally stopped firing arrows at each other," he replied with a hint of humor beneath his frustration.

The young boy, Taro, stood next to Alan, with a bow in his hand. For the past several days, Edward had often seen Taro's small form trailing behind Alan.

"Even after a hundred years of training, this lot wouldn't be able to hit a target a hundred feet away," Alan said in an irritated tone, though it looked like he was enjoying himself. He was not as menacing as he once was.

"Since coming here, I feel like I have finally realized why I fight," he confessed.

"Did you not fight for God?"

"At one point, I did. But then the Saracens chased us, and we escaped on the *Bel Oceano*. After that I believed in nothing. But now, from the bottom of my heart, I truly want to protect Taro and the others. Rather than fighting to slay enemies on the battlefield, I want to fight to protect the innocent. Even if it costs me my life."

Edward listened to his friend in silence. He felt the same. He would rather fight to protect the people of this land than fight for God.

"Is that why you're teaching Taro to use a sword? I've seen you two practicing with wooden swords."

"When I heard Taro's story, I didn't feel like a stranger."

"He reminds you of you when you were young?"

Alan had been raised no different from an orphan after his father sold him to the Christian army in exchange for a horse.

"I think of the children of the people I killed. No matter where I go, there are those who seek revenge on me. Perhaps one day the blade of a child like Taro will kill me."

"Throw those thoughts at the enemy!"

"That is what I intend to do," Alan enthusiastically said and stood up as if shaking off the memories he had just revisited.

The hut looked like it could collapse at any moment. An old man opened the rickety door. The inside was brighter and more spacious than expected. Several men were working among scattered wood chips.

"I heard we could find a skilled carpenter here. A man by the name of Sosuke," Edward said upon entering.

The oldest man in the group slowly stood up and shuffled forward. At first glance, it seemed like his mind was perhaps not entirely there.

"I'm not sure about a skilled carpenter, but you can find Sosuke here," he muttered.

"Where?" Edward and Alan scanned the room, but the other
men continued their work without so much as glancing up.

"In front of you."

"It is impossible for this old dotard to build a catapult," Alan
whispered in Edward's ear.

"I have heard he is the best carpenter in Hakata," Edward
countered.

"Sixty years ago more like it! We'll find someone else."

Ignoring Alan, Edward showed the old man the broken remains of the catapult his men had dragged in. Edward could not
fail to notice the faint movement of Sosuke's eyes when he saw the
catapult. Sosuke stooped down, and examined the broken neck and
insect-eaten fragments.

"Can you make something like this?"

Sosuke knelt in front of the catapult and examined the joints.

"Do you plan to use this against the Mongolians?"

"Yes."

"It throws rocks."

"Then you know what it is?"

"Mongolians shot out stones covered in fire from their ships
in the last war. I imagined they must have used a device with this
kind of shape and structure to do so."

"You know then how it works."

"When do you need it completed?"

"As quickly as you can. If the first one goes well, I would like
you to make many more. And can you can make it several times
larger than this one?"

"Several times, you say?"

"As large as you can make it, so large boulders can fly great
distances through the air."

Sosuke lifted his face.

"I understand. Now leave at once," he said while pointing to the door.

"What the hell is wrong with that graybeard. He's an unfriendly bastard," Alan vented once they were outside.

"He's not as old as you think," the man who had guided them to the hut said. "He's only thirty-six. He became like that in a day. The Mongolians kidnapped his wife and daughter in the last war. His daughter was only nine. He was shot by an arrow here and fainted. It somehow saved his life."

The old man grabbed his crotch and squeezed.

CHAPTER
96

Three days later, Edward and Alan visited Sosuke again. A brand-new, five-foot-tall catapult was waiting for them.

"It's quite the beast!" Edward said. "Even though you had the sample model to work from, making this was not easy."

"You are truly an excellent craftsman," Alan, who was never one for compliments, praised the carpenter.

Edward looked and saw three more catapults lined up in the corner of the hut.

"I'll have two more finished by tomorrow," Sosuke promised. "If it is to fight against the Mongolians, I will do whatever is in my power."

Sosuke had even reenforced with metal fixtures what Edward thought was the pivot.

"I have tweaked it a little. It should shoot farther than the Mongolian ones."

"Have you tested it yet?" Alan asked.

"I don't need to," Sosuke said, giving Alan a sideways glance.

"I would like a total of seven catapults," Edward said as he walked around the weapon. "We'll keep three behind the ramparts and arrange the remaining on the seashore. I want to do some test fires today. Will you come with us?"

"I'll stay here and focus on making more. I already know how they will fly."

On Edward's orders, the catapult was transported to the end of the cape.

"I brought Genji," Thomas told Edward when he arrived for the test. Genji was the fisherman with one leg they had met when they washed ashore.

"Do you remember me?" Edward asked. Genji nodded wordlessly.

"You said, 'I will kill them all. Not a single Mongolian soul will leave here alive.' Do you remember that?"

Genji looked surprised, but nodded again.

"We will help you avenge what the Mongolians did to you and your family. But first we need you to help us."

Genji's expression changed, and he looked at Edward as if his eyeballs were about to pop out.

"Do you still fish in these waters?"

"I cannot live if I leave here," he said. His voice was as coarse as the sound of sand crunching underfoot.

"Look carefully at the sea," Edward instructed Genji, then turned and signaled. A sharp whistle of wind cut past their ears, and a dark mass hurtled above before disappearing with a small splash in the center of the bay.

"Now remember where you saw the splash," Edward told Genji.

The sun shone as red as fresh blood, and its rays bathed Hakata Bay.

"Fire!" Edward ordered. The same whistle of wind resonated above their heads, and a spray of water rose up in the bay for the second time.

"Did it fall in the same place as the first?"

"It was about six feet to the right."

"Are you sure?"

"If you doubt me, don't ask."

"I'll leave it to this man to decide."

Edward turned to Zafir, who said to Genji, "You truly have a good eye."

"That is to be expected of a Hakata fisherman."

"Do you think your fellow fishermen could distinguish between those positions?" Edward enquired further.

"They wouldn't be fishermen, if they couldn't."

"Gather as many fishermen as you can," Edward commanded loudly.

The next morning, before sunrise, Edward was awakened by one of Morimune's men.

"A message has arrived from the carpenter. He needs to see you at once."

Edward and Alan hastened to Sosuke's hut.

"We may fire your head, instead of rocks—" Alan began before stopping, his mouth agape as he stared ahead. An enormous catapult had been constructed in the middle of Sosuke's work area. It stood ten feet tall, and its arm looked to be fifteen feet in length. Edward gasped. *The Mongolian army will not have prepared themselves for such a weapon*, he thought.

"When did you make this?"

"I finished all the parts yesterday, and we put it together this morning. We have yet to test-fire it."

"It has been a long time since I have seen a catapult this large. Is it easy to handle?"

"Try it. Three people should be able to operate it."

They partially disassembled the catapult and brought it to the cape, where they reassembled it according to Sosuke's instructions and loaded a rock about fifteen and a half inches in diameter. On Sosuke's signal, they detached the pin and, with a groan, the rock was launched into the sky. They saw a splash of water rise up far out to sea. The rock had soared one and a half times farther than it would have if it had been fired from a smaller catapult.

"We plan to construct another in a week's time," Sosuke told them.

"Make as many as you can!" Edward ordered.

"The smaller catapults will be positioned behind the stone ramparts, and the larger ones at the tip of each cape. Bring a fisherman to each of the catapults and have him locate precisely where the rocks make impact in Hakata Bay," Edward said to Morimune's soldiers charged with operating the catapults.

Since returning to Hakata, preparations were steadily progressing for the arrival of the Yuan army in two months. When Edward returned from his reconnaissance of the beach, the townspeople had collected in front of the lookout huts behind the walls. A fire burned in the center of the group, and the sounds of young men and women laughing, together with the smells of food cooking over the fire, carried in the air.

"What do you think this is?" Alan's voice rose up and admonished the gathering. "This is a battlefield! Not some pleasure ground!" One of the women held out a wooden plate heaped with food and muttered something.

"They want us to eat, Alan," Edward said. "They want to show their gratitude. Let them entertain us tonight."

They sat around the fire as the children and elderly watched them.

"They're feeding us in spite of being hungry themselves," Alan grumbled in a low voice, but he began to eat.

"All of you, come! We can't eat with you watching us like that." Enrico beckoned the children and elderly to come closer.

Soon merry sounds from around the bonfire melted into the early evening air. As the coastline darkened, the singing voices of the village people, knights, and sailors resounded throughout the long and peaceful night.

CHAPTER
97

Tokimune and Yasumori sat facing each other in a dimly lit room. Since Edward and the others had departed Kamakura for Hakata, the Hyojyoshu met less frequently. A messenger was instructed to bring news from Hakata to Kamakura every day, but the reports were of little interest until shocking news arrived a week later.

"The Mongolian army has attacked Iki Island. Iki's garrison and its residents have been annihilated."

Tokimune had braced himself for news like this, but hearing it from Yasumori made his blood run cold. *Should we have been more prepared? Should all the inhabitants have taken refuge in Hakata?* he thought. *But we couldn't do that. Iki Island was Nippon's territory. Although it would have been a temporary evacuation, to withdraw the residents and garrison to Hakata would have been to abandon the sovereignty of Iki out of fear of Yuan.*

"How are the preparations in Hakata faring?" Tokimune asked.

"Lord Edward has been training the Kyushu gokenin army."

"Those who follow one supreme commander mobilize in perfect order. It will surely be worth the effort."

The gokenin have been instructed to follow through on Edward's strategies, Tokimune thought, *but they are too proud of the way they drove Yuan away in the last war. It will be difficult for them to act in unison under the one commander I have sent from Kamakura.*

"They are using a new weapon. One that can throw large rocks."

"A catapult."

"You know of it?"

"It was a weapon Yuan used in the previous war. It caused us a great deal of damage, and even robbed many of our men of their fighting spirits."

"I distinctly remember it."

"I burned the one Edward brought with him to Kamakura. Yet they have built a new one in Kyushu."

"They were able to do so because they concealed the second one from their ship in a watermill. I was told in a letter that they recreated it through the help of a carpenter in Hakata."

"What should I do?" Tokimune said under his breath.

Yasumori stopped what he was about to say and took a moment to think before speaking again.

"There is something that I am worried about."

"What is it?"

"The townspeople and farmers are being trained to use weaponry in battle. Will they also stand on the battlefield as soldiers?"

"The people have been given weapons?"

"It has been reported that they are training in archery. There are seemingly hundreds of people, including women and children, who are participating."

"What has Munemasa been doing? I warned him not to let Edward take things too far. That was his role there," Tokimune said, his voice full of irritation.

Yasumori looked slightly taken aback. Such behavior was unusual for Tokimune, who rarely showed his emotions.

"It seems that Lord Munemasa is struggling under the pressure of regulating all the Kanto, Kyushu, and Chugoku gokenin," Yasumori concluded.

"Then how successful has he been training the people with weapons?" Tokimune's voice had already returned to his usual calm tone.

"The peasants have considerably improved their skill in archery, I am told. Eventually, they may no longer be inferior to the gokenin. They have also been training in the spear."

"The spear?"

"Yes."

Tokimune brooded. From what he had experienced of Edward's speech and conduct, his behavior in Hakata was neither surprising nor out of character.

"He says the people's will to survive is even stronger than that of the gokenin."

"And are the results encouraging?"

"I cannot be certain of that."

"This war will decide survival or death. Anyone would want the opportunity to protect themselves and their families."

"Do you think they cannot rely on the samurai?"

"Look at what became of that reliance in Iki."

"That was—" but Yasumori stopped before he could say more.

"I guess we will just have to wait and see," Tokimune said resignedly, before slowly getting to his feet.

THE BATTLE

CHAPTER
98

Heavy footsteps ran up and down the hallway outside Edward's room.

"Lord Edward," Morimune's voice called from the other side of the sliding door. Just as Edward went to open it, Morimune entered in full armor.

"Are they here?" Edward asked. Morimune nodded.

The sun had not yet risen when Edward, his men, and the samurai climbed to the top of the hill that overlooked Hakata Bay. Yuan warships were heading toward them, sailing between Shikanoshima Island and Nokonoshima Island. At first, in the semidarkness, only a few ships appeared. But as the sky lightened and turned pink, they watched in silence as an armada of several hundred filled the bay.

"Do you remember the last battle we fought in Jerusalem? Before we boarded the *Bel Oceano* to escape the Saracens?" Alan asked hoarsely. "Back then, the enemy greatly outnumbered us. But we didn't pull back, not one step," he continued vigorously, though it sounded like he was trying to reassure himself.

"How strong is the enemy?"

"Close to twenty thousand? But we had less than half that—"

"There are close to a thousand ships down there, carrying thirty thousand soldiers," Zafir interrupted Alan. "And more are on the way."

"How many men do we have?" Edward asked as he watched the Yuan warships blanket the bay.

"Nineteen thousand? No, over twenty thousand? At any rate, the samurai from Kyushu, Chugoku, and Kanto will be here shortly," Morimune answered.

Just as Zafir had warned, Yuan warships entered the bay seemingly without end.

"What do you think?" Edward asked Zafir.

"They will not attack immediately. It will take time to ready an army of that size."

"Which ship holds their commander in chief?"

"It should be somewhere in the center. But it is hard to tell from this distance. The ship will look the same as the others so as to ward off attack."

"Will the attack begin tomorrow then?"

"Most likely. The enemy does not fear Nippon. Yet I do not believe they think us weak. They will attack our front once their forces are properly readied. They also want to assess how much we have prepared in the last four years."

Munemasa, accompanied by fifty samurai on horseback, slid to a stop next to Edward. Momentarily at a loss for words, he surveyed the Yuan ships covering Hakata Bay.

"It will still take several days for the samurai from Kanto to arrive," he said, his voice shaking. "Do you think we can hold out until then?"

"That is your duty, Lord Munemasa, as Lord Tokimune's proxy," Edward said and once again shifted his gaze to the warships entering the bay. He took a deep breath before exhaling and nodding in Alan's direction.

"All men prepare for battle!" Alan shouted to the samurai.

The soldiers, who had been motionless as if paralyzed, quickly returned to their stations. Edward and the others went to command headquarters behind the ramparts. From the top of the stone wall, they could see the whole of Hakata Bay. The soldiers became restless as they watched the ever-expanding armada of Yuan warships.

"Don't panic. Just do as you have been instructed," Edward told them as he did his best to maintain a calm composure.

Piles of timber lined up and down the beach were lit. As the oil-doused wood burned, great plumes of black smoke rose in the air and spread over the beach, cutting off the ships' field of vision. All at once, several thousand military flags were erected on the beaches of Kashii, Hakata, and Momochi. It looked like tens of thousands of soldiers lined the coast, but close to half those numbers were farmers and townsfolk.

"Let them hear your war cry!" Alan ordered.

In unison, the soldiers on the beach and the samurai and townsfolk stationed on the stone wall screamed out. The bay rumbled with the sound, and for a moment, the ships seemed to stop moving as if the reverberation of the voices blocked their advance.

"Light bonfires tonight and for two more nights throughout the region," Edward commanded Munemasa. "Let the people take refuge behind them."

Now that he had seen the Mongolian threat in Hakata with his own eyes, Munemasa became more pragmatic and obediently accepted and cooperated with Edward. He was an honest man, just as Morimune had said.

"From now on there should be three times the number of guards keeping watch."

"The Mongolians can see how heavily defended we are. They would not attack easily."

"I am not only worried about the enemy. I am worried about the rashness of some of our allies," Edward muttered.

"Look!" a voice called out from the coast.

Out in the open sea, two rowboats were paddling toward the Yuan warships. The early summer sun bounced off the vermillion-colored armor of the samurai in the boats.

"Who's that?"

"Judging from the insignia it is Lord Kusakabe of Amakusa."

"How many times have I told them!" Edward fumed.

As one of the rowboats neared a warship, a rain of arrows poured down on it. An arrow shot through a samurai's face, and he fell backward and sank into the sea. The warship then pelted the rowboat with rocks. The samurai panicked and stood up, causing the boat to tilt to one side before capsizing. Zafir watched as the men disappeared into the water, never to surface. *Wearing armor as heavy as theirs is like trying to swim while tied to a rock*, he thought.

The other rowboat, seeing what had happened, turned and fled back to land. At the same time, a Yuan ship lowered a rowboat of its own with ten oarsmen onboard. The boats drew close as the enemy rowed with a fierce vigor.

"They won't be able to outrun them. Where is Akisada?"

"I am here", Akisada responded, as he pushed past Morimune and moved to the front with his bow in hand.

"How many samurai are in that boat?" Edward demanded.

"From what I can see, three."

"Can your arrows reach that far?"

"If they can make another fifty yards."

"Shoot them."

"What?" Akisada looked at Edward in surprise.

"The enemy will capture them, and they will reveal our plans."

"They won't talk."

"They will under torture. Your comrades being harmed would be unbearable for you. Shooting them will be a quick death without agony."

Akisada wordlessly fixed an arrow to his bow. He closed his eyes for a moment and then fired. The arrow pierced through the throat of the samurai in the prow; he fell over the side, and the waves swallowed him. Akisada fired the next arrows in rapid succession till there was no one left alive in the samurai's boat. After circling the rowboat, the Yuan soldiers withdrew. On the lookout in the stern of their boat, a Yuan soldier brandished the Yuan banner. Akisada pulled back his bow one more time. The arrow struck the soldier in the chest, and he plunged into the water below, dragging the Yuan banner down with him.

"Let what occurred just now be a lesson to you," Edward shouted. "Sear it into your minds that anyone who acts against our rules for the sake of glory will never be forgiven. Never!"

That night, a war council met in the command station. Hojo Sanemasa, the governor of Kyushu, and Shoni Tsunesuke, the foreign defense minister, sat in front with Munemasa, the proxy regent. By Munemasa's side sat Edward, his advisor.

The gokenin around them stopped talking as soon as Munemasa rose to address them.

"At last, Yuan warships have come to our waters. There are roughly nine hundred ships, carrying over forty thousand soldiers. We will meet them with our own military force of sixty thousand men. We have been preparing for this day for a long while. The prospect of victory is in our favor. I ask all of you to drive back these invaders with all the strength you have."

What Munemasa knew, but did not say, was that half of that sixty thousand had yet to arrive. He also failed to mention the hundred thousand troops coming from Southern Song that would join up with the Yuan armada. While well aware of this, he did not want to cause any unnecessary anxiety. It would be better to focus only on the enemies that were before them now.

"The samurai who acted of their own accord today could have endangered all of us. Therefore, from here on in, if anyone else attempts such a scheme and defies our rules, he will be severely punished. And no matter what he accomplishes, all his rewards will be revoked. Make sure all the men in your charge understand this fully," Munemasa said as looked down at the gokenin. He had delivered the speech that Edward had written and taught him before the war council convened.

It was Edward's turn next.

"Tomorrow, the Mongolian army will try to make landfall. We must not allow a single enemy to step foot over Hakata's stone wall defense. We will keep them on the coastline. For what other reason did we build the ramparts?" Edward looked at each man in the room to ensure he understood.

"But the enemy must be tired from the voyage from Gimpo to Iki to Hakata. They may attack after tomorrow" Shoni Tsunesuke said, unleashing a storm of viewpoints from others in the room.

"They would have attacked today, but they saw the wall and the troops atop them, and are now most likely improving their battle strategy. Delaying their attack allows us more time to prepare."

"Seven years have passed since the last war. Both sides have finished their preparations for battle. Perhaps Yuan is waiting for us to make the first move?"

"Yuan has expended their barbarity with their attacks on Iki Island and Tsushima Island. It would be rash for them to jump into an all-out attack as exhausted as they are now. Tonight, they will allow themselves to rest."

For the most part, the samurai from Kyushu agreed with Edward. But the samurai from Kanto, in particular, were naive in their opinions about Yuan. Very few of them had any experience in fighting a foreign foe.

Edward looked around the room. "At this moment, the enemy is finalizing its preparations for a full-scale attack tomorrow when they will disembark on the beach with the rising sun and advance all the way to Dazaifu."

The gokenin stirred.

Edward nudged Munemasa, prompting him to stand up.

"What do you intend to do?" Munemasa asked the gathering. "We also have not been needlessly wasting our time these past seven years. We have constructed stone wall defenses, studied the enemy's combat methods, and planned our countermeasures. Forces not only from Kyushu but also from Kanto and the neighboring regions have answered the call to meet the Yuan army in battle. Let's fight! What do you say?"

"We have no objections. Lord Munemasa's word is the word of Lord Tokimune."

The gokenin nodded deeply in agreement.

"Expect tomorrow's attack to be relentless." Munemasa spoke to the men just as Edward had instructed him. "Those keeping watch must increase threefold. Now go and ready yourselves for tomorrow."

Munemasa's words lack impact, Edward thought. *Is it because I am comparing him to Tokimune?* Not far off, a thousand warships waited on the open sea. Edward grew anxious.

CHAPTER

99

After the meeting, Edward and Alan sat atop a hill. The breeze from the ocean felt good on their skin, while countless lights from the Yuan warships illuminated the darkness and reminded them of what was to come.

"I have always been envious of you, Edward. You are from a wealthy noble family. Whereas I am the son of an impoverished knight who wandered from place to place. I don't even know what my mother looked like. When I was little, I was told that she had died of a sickness. But she ran away. She didn't want to live a homeless life wandering from castle to castle. I became a knight's squire and your servant because my father's horse died and he sold me in exchange for a new one. But you treated me like your younger brother. Even though I was the stronger one."

"It is hard for an older brother to look after a younger brother who is stronger than himself and still maintain his honor," Edward replied in kind to Alan's gentle, brotherly taunt about being stronger.

"You are the person dearest to my heart," Alan said, his voice full of emotion. "Treating me as your brother made me feel I had a family for the first time."

"It was always my dream to have a younger brother. Although it would have been better to have a younger brother weaker than I," Edward jested. "But in all honesty, I ended up with an excellent, if brash, younger brother."

"And I with an excellent older brother."

The lights on the ships became brighter, and there was hurried movement on the decks. The attack was imminent. Edward and Alan returned together to the camp.

CHAPTER

100

The sun had yet to rise. Thick clouds covered the sky, and it looked as if it could rain at any moment. Edward, accompanied by Alan and Zafir, rode the horse Akisada had given him to look over Hakata Bay. The number of ships anchored in the bay had increased.

"Yuan's going to try and land the moment the sun rises," Alan grumbled.

Soldiers could be seen moving about the decks in the front row of warships. Soon rowboats were lowered and headed for the shore. As the sun rose, everything rapidly became brighter.

"It's starting," Edward told Munemasa when he returned to troop headquarters behind the ramparts. "Signal the army."

On Munemasa's command, signal fires were lit, and thin smoke rose into the glow of the morning sky. Before long, Yuan rowboats packed with soldiers closed the distance between warships and beach.

"Let's release the arrows," Munemasa said turning to Edward for confirmation.

"We will once they make it ashore and draw near the wall."

The first rowboats hit land, and the soldiers jumped out and pulled the boats onto the sandy beach. Wary of the eerily quiet beach, they looked toward the stone wall, but did not notice the ranks of archers lying in wait behind the rampart.

When half the beach was flooded with Mongolian soldiers, a war cry echoed out from the western coast. Edward spun around and saw ten samurai on horseback galloping toward the enemy. Behind the horsemen, more than ten foot soldiers charged. The Mongolians aimed and fired their bows in unison.

"Who the hell are those fools?!"

"That's Lord Yanagida's insignia. He is trying to lead the attack."

"Start the attack! At this rate Lord Yanagida and his men will be annihilated."

The horsemen were quickly surrounded by enemy forces. Half of them were pulled from their horses and relentlessly stabbed with spears from all sides. Several arrows flew out from behind the stone wall. Edward watched as the enemy soldiers surrounding the samurai crashed to the ground as the arrows met their target. An enemy soldier pointed toward the stone wall and let out a great cry. The sound of gongs began to resound, and all the soldiers on the beach simultaneously turned their shields toward the stone wall and stood at alert. Other soldiers hid themselves and watched from the landing boats. Eventually, they fired their own arrows toward the wall.

"Blast it, they've found us out! Begin the attack!" Edward shouted.

From behind the ramparts a powerful meteor shower of arrows hurtled toward the Mongolian soldiers, penetrating the gaps between shields. Yuan soldiers fell in succession.

"Fire the stones!"

Catapults set up behind the wall propelled large stones aimed at the rowboats coming ashore. Boats crashed and sank, but the Mongolian army was dauntless. Soldiers stomped over the bodies of their fallen comrades and advanced toward the rampart. Several soldiers carrying ladders made it to the wall's edge.

"Don't let them climb up! Bring out the spears!" Edward shouted at the top of his lungs.

Enemy soldiers toppled off the wall as the sharp metal penetrated their skulls. In spite of the onslaught, some managed to climb over and cut their way into the Nippon ranks. The samurai protecting the ramparts began to crumble from the endless Mongolian arrows fired their way.

"The western wall's defenses are breaking! They need more men!" a messenger ran to tell Edward. The western wall was Yanagida's to defend.

"With me!" Edward yelled as he unsheathed his sword and rushed on horseback to the shore. He hacked a path through the Mongolians with his sword.

"Watch out for the arrows! They're poisoned!" Edward warned Alan and the knights following him. "If they graze you, withdraw to camp and suck out the poison!"

Blood sprayed as he relentlessly swung his sword down, avoiding enemy spears thrust at him. Alan protected Edward's rear as he too wielded his longsword. With Edward and Alan leading the charge, the cavalry of knights stormed the length of the coast.

"After them!" Akisada's voice suddenly resounded.

Leading a cavalry of Nippon samurai, Akisada jumped over the rampart and began cutting his way into the Mongolian soldiers.

The battle raged to midday. Eventually, the rhythmic beat of drums resounded from the Yuan warships offshore. The Mongolian soldiers fighting on the beach turned back. Explosions rang out all over and smoke covered the beach. Horses bucked and bolted. The Kanto gokenin's horses, in particular, were greatly startled by the explosions, and their riders were unable to get them under control.

"Don't let them get back to the ships! Kill them all on the beach!" Edward heard Alan's voice yell out, but the Mongolian soldiers were quick and withdrew to the boats. Despite aiming the stones from the catapults toward the boats, they were only able to destroy half. *Had they fired all the stones they had?* Edward wondered.

By evening, corpses littered the sandy shore. Most were Mongolian soldiers, but some Nippon samurai were also among the dead. Edward and the others stood frozen amid the carnage.

"This was a great victory! My men and I led the charge. The rewards will—" Yanagida began before Alan's fist crashed into his face and cut him off.

"What the hell, you think this is a great victory?! Thanks to you bastards, half of the rowboats got away! We could have completely annihilated them. And the part of the wall you were assigned to protect almost fell! Never forget how many of your friends died because of you!"

"Calm yourself, Alan," Edward said, grabbing Alan's arm before he could land another punch. Yanagida looked up at them dumbstruck. He had no idea what was going on.

"Looking at the stupid look on that bastard's face makes me want to spew," Alan said and spat on the ground.

"You are not wrong," Zafir said agreeing with Alan. "But no matter what you say to them, they will not understand. It is best to stop expecting anything more of them."

"Don't disturb us," Edward told Munemasa, who looked at him with a troubled expression.

"They just want rewards. We can't win like this," Alan said.

"That cannot be the case. All of them have families too. They are fighting for the sake of those families," Morimune, who had been quietly listening, suddenly added.

"If that were so, they wouldn't act so selfishly," Alan said.

"Even I wish I could have struck Yanagida and his men. If I had the chance."

"Listen!" Edward thundered. "Collecting enemy heads is not what matters. What matters is not letting the enemy make camp on the beach!"

The samurai looked at Edward as if he was out of his mind.

"Then how can we procure our rewards?" one of them demanded.

"Gokenin and knights are much the same. Isn't it your duty to lay down your lives to protect your shogun and your people?" Alan shouted out as he raised his sword overhead. The samurai looked at him as if he, too, was raving like a mad man.

"It will be some time before they attack again, no?" Zafir said, as he studied the Yuan warships anchored out at sea.

"They should be in a panic about now, seeing as they took on more damage than expected. But, if it weren't for Yanagida and his fucking bastards, we could have completely crushed the Mongolian army when they came ashore," Alan said, his voice still boiling with irritation and anger.

"We've earned two days. But when they attempt to land again, they will be more cautious. I pray the main force from Kanto arrives by then," Edward said to no one in particular. But Morimune listened and heard.

"An enemy!" a samurai suddenly yelled. A lone Mongolian soldier had broken cover and was running down the hill.

"Don't let him escape! He's a scout!" Edward shouted.

All at once arrows were fixed and fired in his direction, but the soldier evaded the barrage from the short bows. One arrow did find its target, but it lacked the force to penetrate his armor. Then Akisada slowly drew back his longbow. His arrow pierced the Mongolian's back. After running a few more steps, he collapsed. Alan gave a short whistle.

"Was he a survivor from today's battle? Or has a new scouting party landed? Increase the defenses on the beach immediately!" Edward hollered.

CHAPTER
101

Another war council convened that night. Pumped up by that day's unexpected and overwhelming victory, the gokenin were in a good mood and boisterously expressed it.

"If everything continues like this, we will purge the Mongolian army in a month. Then Kublai Khan will never dare attempt to invade Nippon again."

"Let us take advantage of this victory and commence our attack on the Mongolian ships tomorrow! I and my men will be in the vanguard."

"The Mongolian army isn't so fearsome. We should reconsider attacking them on their mainland."

"We were lucky," Edward cautioned the gokenin.

"Lucky?"

"Yes, lucky. One, the enemy underestimated us. Two, they landed their army without first sending an advance scouting party. Three, our catapults threw their army into chaos and destroyed many of their rowboats as they escaped back to sea. However—"

"Do you make light of our army's victory? It is a fact that the Mongolian army scurried back to the safety of their ships," one of the samurai said, interrupting Edward.

"Lord Kusakabe of Amakusa must have been mortified, being killed by his allies," another cried out.

"That was going too far. When we could have defeated the Mongolian army and secured our victory—"

"Shut up! Lord Edward is speaking, and the word of Lord Edward is the word of the Lord of Kamakura himself," Munemasa yelled as he shot to his feet.

The gokenin were silenced in an instant, and Edward once again held their attention.

"From now on the Mongolian army will be much more vigilant. They won't put themselves in range of our catapults, and they may even resort to using the catapults on their own ships when they next attack us. The main body of the Mongolian army is the Gangnam army of a hundred thousand strong from Southern Song. There have been reports of them arriving unscathed in Hirado and its surrounding islands. Our best option is to trap the Mongolian army on the sea and wait for them to exhaust their resources. Believe me when I say the enemy has already hatched a plan for when they next attempt to disembark on our shores."

CHAPTER

102

"As expected, the power of thunder crash bombs is immense," Zafir said on the way back from the war council.

Edward nodded silently. The enemy's retreat was truly admirable. The deafening reverberations, explosions, flames, and smoke of the thunder crash bombs threw everything into confusion, yet allowed more than half of the enemy soldiers to withdraw from the battlefield. And even though Nippon horses had been trained to withstand the sound and fury of battle, they were still frightened. *They used thunder crash bombs more as a means to retreat than as a weapon of attack*, Edward marveled.

"I should have studied more seriously how to make such things," Zafir said as he looked through his notebook. Five years ago, on their way to Hakata after washing ashore in Kyushu, they had found many discarded bombs.

"Zafir, you have done enough. It was only natural that the horses would have been frightened. Even human stomachs churn hearing such a sound. It is something called 'gun powder,' no?" Edward said.

"If only we had such a weapon—"

"We can't always get what we wish for. I was taught to do the best I can whatever situation I am in," Edward said.

When Edward, Alan, and Zafir returned from the war council late that night, a sailor was waiting for them with a message from Thomas. They were to follow him along the coastline to a rocky stretch at the end of the rampart.

"Tread carefully," he warned. "It's quite steep."

Two figures appeared in the moonlight. One of them was Thomas.

"I have the rowboat," he said. "We should be able to reach a Yuan warship in twenty minutes."

"Was this Alan's idea?" Edward asked.

"It was mine," Zafir admitted. "I asked Thomas to get the rowboat."

"Don't be a fool. I won't allow such recklessness."

"It is essential that we know what the enemy is up to."

"Then you should stay behind. You would only be a hindrance."

"This is my idea. I wish to go by all means."

Edward could not make out Zafir's expression, but his tone was stronger and more determined than usual.

"So, you are after their thunder crash bombs? You truly are a troublesome fellow," Edward said.

"Let's go, let's go!" Alan's voice cut through the darkness as he gave Edward's shoulder a shove. "I, for one, am not a great swimmer, but once we are on the ship's deck it will be like being on land."

The six men climbed into the rowboat and pushed off from the rocky wall. The sea was calm. Thomas and two sailors soundlessly rowed the boat on the water's black surface. Ahead, they could see a light coming from a Mongolian ship.

"If they discover us, they'll throw stones to sink the boat," Alan cautioned in a muffled voice that was nonetheless full of excitement. "Are we just to steal bombs? We should burn down a few ships as long as we're here," he said and pulled out flints and a candle from his pocket.

"Turn back the moment you sense danger. A much more important battle awaits us tomorrow," Edward added.

The single ray of light split into hundreds of lights the closer they approached the armada.

"Now that's a sight," Alan said in a low voice. "The warships are as thick as a forest." *If we lose our way in this forest, we won't be able to easily find our way out again,* he thought to himself.

Edward looked up to the sky and memorized the position of the stars.

"All you have to do is investigate the state of the ship. I want us to return without the enemy noticing us, if possible."

"It would be just the same if we killed them all," Alan said.

"Including the sailors, there are more than a hundred men onboard. There are only six of us."

"So, seventeen or thereabouts for each of us? We could kill them off," Alan boasted.

As they neared one of the ships and saw it up close, Edward realized for the first time just how massive it was. Sounds of drunken men carried down from the deck. Thomas skillfully maneuvered the rowboat, found a handhold, gripped it, and started to climb up the ship's side. After a few minutes, he tossed a rope down for the rest of them. Leaving a sailor to keep watch on the rowboat, Edward and the others climbed up the rope and onto the deck, where half-naked Yuan soldiers were asleep. The deck was still hot from the heat it had absorbed during the day.

Drunken voices came from below, but the jolly singing lacked any hint of tragic heroism. Obviously the Mongolians believed they had won the battle. They were celebrating.

"Looks like they think they can afford to get drunk," Alan commented.

"Find and search the armory," Edward whispered.

A sailor stayed on deck to keep watch, while the other four men descended below. The room in the back looked like it could be an armory, but there were no guards stationed there. The defenses onboard were too relaxed.

They sneaked into the armory. Bows, arrows, swords, and other weapons were piled up. The number of arrows was overwhelming.

"To think these bows and arrows are spares. There are well over ten thousand arrows here. If you match these with the number of ships, that is an enormous number. They are certainly serious this time."

"I found the bombs," Zafir whispered. Five thunder crash bombs lay nestled in a wooden box filled with sawdust. Scores of similar boxes surrounded it.

"Let's bring them with us," Alan said.

"The most we can bring is two. The rest—" Edward began.

"What do you think? We explode the rest?" Thomas said.

"If we douse them with oil from the lamps, they would blow up when lit," Alan said.

"Who would light them?" Thomas asked.

No one answered.

"At any rate, carry them out." Edward motioned for Alan and Thomas to lift two boxes.

"Go back to the boat and wait there," Edward told Zafir, who looked like he was about to object until Edward pushed him on his way.

Edward stood in front of the remaining boxes. Once he lit them, he would hurry to the deck and jump into the ocean. But how could he make enough time for his escape? He took a candle from the pouch at his hip, cut it down, nestled it in the sawdust around the thunder crash bombs, and lit the wick. The wick quickly burned, and flames spread throughout the sawdust.

Edward ran out of the armory. Just as he was at the top of the stairs leading to the deck, his eyes met the eyes of a Yuan soldier sitting against the side of the ship. The soldier was about to raise his voice when Edward flung a dagger toward the man, but the soldier's call was faster. Suddenly, an uproar of angry shouting, footsteps, and metal fittings clanging together filled the air. Edward sprinted toward the side of the ship while driving past Mongolian soldiers aroused from their drunken revelry. It was opposite to where Zafir and the others had left the rowboat, but there was no time to turn around. As he plunged into the dark waters below, he felt a sharp pain in his left arm. An arrow had grazed him. Mongolian soldiers were shooting arrows in the direction of where he had dived. Holding his breath, he swam under the ship and came up the other side, where Zafir and the others were waiting for him.

"Pull away from the ship! The bombs are going to blow!" Edward screamed as he held on to the edge of the rowboat.

"Get him up! They'll notice us any minute now!" Alan said as he took his crossbow and aimed it upward, where a Mongolian soldier was peeking over the ship's side. Alan's arrow connected with the man's skull. More faces appeared and more arrows were fired. Zafir and Thomas brought out the shields to protect them from the onslaught. Rocks began to fall down on them. One scraped the side of the boat before splashing into the sea.

"This isn't good. Do you think if we dive in, we can get away?" one of the sailors shouted as he cowered and covered his body.

At that moment, a thunderous roar was heard, and the Yuan ship began to shake.

"Hurry!" Alan yelled, stretching out his arm to grab Edward by the nape of the neck and drag him into the boat.

When Edward turned around, he saw the deck of the warship erupting in flames and smoke. The nighttime sky was as bright as day. Another explosion, and fragments of the hull pelted the rowboat. Thomas and the other sailors sped up their rowing. Eventually, there were no more explosions, and a quiet darkness spread around them. They could hear occasional pops as they left the burning ship far behind. Edward leaned against the gunwale exhausted.

"Your arm is bleeding," Alan said.

"An arrow grazed me when I dived in."

"A poisoned arrow?"

"I don't know."

Alan brought his mouth to the wound and sucked. Zafir took a cloth and tightly bound it around Edward's shoulder.

"Good thing you were wounded in the water. The poison must have flowed out and been washed away," Zafir said encouragingly.

CHAPTER
103

E arly the next morning, Zafir visited Edward's tent. "How are you feeling?" he asked.

"Neither good nor bad. I didn't sleep well," Edward said, getting himself out of bed. *Is it because I slept on a hard board that all my joints are creaking?*

"The arrow wasn't poisoned. It seems for safety reasons they only apply poison right before battle," Zafir said with a sigh of relief. He took his notebook from his pocket and flipped through it until he found the page he wanted.

"Yuan will commence their attack at ebb tide."

"How do you know?"

"They did so in the last war. It is well recorded. But it is something I also would do. When the tide pulls out, the beach becomes larger, and they can land more of their soldiers. With a massive number of soldiers like that, they could break though the wall in an instant and invade the city."

Edward silently listened.

"First, they will attack the soldiers hiding behind the stone wall with a rain of arrows and stones from their shipboard catapults during high tide. After that, they will take advantage of the ebb tide and send their infantry in all at once."

"But to do that they will have to bring their warships closer to the shore."

"Exactly. We cannot let ourselves miss that opportunity."

That afternoon, the warships began to move with the high tide, just as Zafir had predicted.

"They've stopped. They will attack from that position. But their arrows can't possibly reach us from there," Alan said.

"They'll use their catapults. What of our own?" Edward asked.

"Our largest can barely reach them where they are now," Alan answered.

"Begin the preparations," Edward informed one of his men, who galloped in haste to the capes where the catapults were waiting.

"Here they come!" Alan yelled.

But before he could finish, dozens of rocks from the warships soared through the sky aimed for the beach. Several of them collided with the wall and smashed through the stones. Others flew behind the wall and hurtled down on the samurai hidden below.

"What of our catapults?" Edward yelled.

Several splashes of water rose up in front of the warships, but none of the projectiles hit the ships.

"Switch to the oil jars! They're light and will travel farther," Edward hurriedly ordered.

Before long, they heard the beating of drums coming from the warships. It was the signal to attack.

From behind the warships countless landing boats rowed into sight. *Do they intend to go ashore before ebb tide?* Edward wondered.

But the boats stopped halfway to the shore. In unison, each craft unleashed a storm of arrows. Several hundred to several thousand arrows barreled toward the rampart. The enemy knew that samurai with bows waited behind the wall from yesterday's attack.

"Counterattack with stones and arrows!" Alan shouted.

"We are!" Morimune confirmed.

But no projectile hit its target.

"Hold fire! They'll be ashore soon."

Just then a flame rose up from one of the warships. An oil jar had struck. But the rising flames were quickly extinguished.

The landing boats began to move again. The moment they landed on the beach, Mongolian soldiers jumped out. A group holding a ladder sprinted toward the wall.

"Fire!" Edward ordered, and a flurry of arrows was unleashed.

The Mongolian soldiers struggled at first to defend themselves against the arrows that showered down on them. But they quickly reformed and, using their shields to block the arrows, advanced on the wall.

"How many are there?"

"About twenty-seven thousand. Twenty thousand are already on the beach."

"It's the Battle of Cannae. Raise the signal beacons!" Edward roared.

Edward had grown up hearing his father tell the tale of the historic military battle between the Roman and Carthaginian armies. If he heard it once, he heard it over and over again until he could repeat every detail. The Carthaginian army, led by Hannibal and greatly outnumbered by the Romans, encircled and annihilated their foe. Hannibal's tactic was to attack from both flanks, while drawing the main force of the enemy army to the center. Following Hannibal's lead, Edward hid two hundred horsemen and four hundred infantrymen on each end of the beach. At the beacon's signal, they began their assault.

Taken by surprise, the Mongolian army tried to fight back but could not hold out against the energy and passion of the Nippon cavalry. The horsemen pushed their way through, herding the enemy to the center of the formation, cramming their bodies together, and making it impossible for them to move.

As a second wave of Mongolians made their way ashore, another surge of arrows shot out from behind the stone wall. Once again, the Mongolians attempted to protect themselves by raising their shields, but they could not hold them steady while being jostled by the entrapped soldiers. At Edward's command, the catapults behind the ramparts sent out a hail of rocks, throwing the Mongolian army into complete chaos. In minutes, corpses and the injured overwhelmed the beach.

Warships moved closer to the center of the beach, positioning themselves to disembark more soldiers.

"It seems the Mongolians are willing to commit all of their forces to breaking through the central part of the rampart," Zafir observed.

"Even if it means abandoning both flanks?"

"Those are Goryeo soldiers. They see them as expendable," Zafir said.

"Then they will breach the center."

"Let's go!" Edward said as he took his sword and raced toward the center of the rampart, where there were as many casualties from poisoned arrows as on the beach.

"Archers forward! Strike down the enemies crossing the wall! Defend the wall to your last breath!" Edward shouted.

At the top of the rampart, hand-to-hand combat broke out. The Mongolians climbed over the corpses of their own countrymen only to be pushed back by Nippon spears.

"Come at me!" a samurai yelled and jumped from the wall, slashing into the Mongolian horde.

Edward followed him, frantically flourishing his blade and blindly blocking, cutting, and stabbing the enemy. Mongolian blood sprayed his body red.

"Ring the bell! Sound the alarm!" Edward shouted. Bombs detonated with a fury. Alan had set off the thunder crash bombs stolen from the warship the previous night, blowing away the Mongolian army with their own weapons. Escaping soldiers collided with those still coming ashore, and havoc erupted within the Mongolian ranks.

The beating of drums grew louder from the warships. It was the signal to retreat, and those landing boats that could headed back to the warships, chased away by Nippon's unexpected counterattack.

When he became aware of the retreat, Edward stood still, using his sword for support. So many corpses littered the ground, he could not get a proper foothold.

"Are you all right?" a familiar voice called out.

"I can feel nothing in my left arm," Edward told Zafir.

"You were stabbed with a sword. Did you not notice?"

Edward remembered nothing except repelling enemy blades and giving the same back to his opponents.

"Bleeding has stopped, but it is best if I stitch it."

"Wait," Edward said and walked to the beach, stepping over corpses. Alan was sitting on one of the Yuan landing boats.

"Is this what God wants?" Alan called out. He who had witnessed countless bloodbaths could not bear looking at the carnage before him.

"Most died from either arrow or sword wounds, others were crushed to death," Morimune came and told them. "Our side of the wall also overflows with casualties from arrows and stones. Many men with bodies swollen from the poisoned arrows are now simply waiting for death."

"The battle was a draw," Edward said.

"But there are more Mongolian corpses. This is our win!" a samurai triumphantly exclaimed.

"You fool, look at how many of your comrades are dead! This was no victory!" Alan berated him.

CHAPTER

104

"The warships are on the move!" Edward awoke to the angry voice of a samurai watchman calling out.

It was early morning on the third day of battle. One of the warships, moored to the side of another ship, stirred.

"Look," Thomas said to Edward and pointed to a small boat approaching the warship. Alan suddenly rose to his feet.

"That's Sosuke! What the hell is the carpenter doing? Is he insane?" Alan fumed.

No sooner did Sosuke's boat reach the warship than the Mongolians threw rocks overboard and into his boat.

"Run, you dullard!" Alan screamed from atop the rampart, but to no avail. It wasn't until all the samurai climbed to the top of the rampart and began yelling that Sosuke turned around, seized the opportunity, and started to row back to land, pursued by the warship.

"They're going to smash into Sosuke and capture him!"

As if to taunt the samurai frantically calling out, the warship edged closer and closer to Sosuke.

"Prepare the catapults!" Edward ordered.

Sosuke rowed as fast as he could, but he was no match for the warship. The enemy was gaining.

"It's all good, carpenter," Alan called out, sending whatever encouragement he could.

"Hold on! Don't fire! He's still a hundred yards offshore," Genji, the fisherman, spoke out.

"He's already beyond the point where he's in range," Alan insisted.

"He needs thirty more yards," the fisherman said, ignoring Alan.

"All right! Get ready, men! Just a little more."

"We're ready!"

"Fire!" Edward signaled, and a lit jar of oil shot into the air. Every eye on the wall followed the fireball as it soared through the sky.

"Hit it, you bastard!" Alan screamed.

The jar smashed onto the deck, and flames engulfed the ship. A second jar also hit its mark. As they cheered on land, Mongolian soldiers, their skin torn and melted by flames, desperately leapt into the sea.

The burning ship crashed into Sosuke, and he went down.

"Do you think Sosuke rowed out there to lure one of the ships within range of the catapults?" Edward questioned.

"How the hell would I know?" Alan barked before softening his tone. "The enemy ships burn easily, don't they? Could we not set small boats on fire and crash them into the warships?"

While Edward listened to Alan, he was reminded of what the old man who had led them to Sosuke's workshop had told them, *The Mongolians kidnapped his wife and daughter in the last war. His daughter was only nine. He was shot by an arrow in the groin.*

"Don't forget what happened to Lord Kusakabe of Amakusa," Edward warned. "If the enemy discovers us before we can ram their ship, they'll sink us any way they can. Arrows, stones, boulders. The only way to get close is under the cover of darkness. And we have to set the boat on fire before it collides with the warship." Edward turned to Thomas for approval.

"It's possible if you drift with the tide. Fishermen will know about the tidal currents inside the bay," Thomas said after thinking for a moment.

"Get Genji," Edward ordered. "He taught us the catapult's landing range. He'll know."

"What is the drift of the tide inside the bay?" Edward asked once Genji had been brought to him.

Genji narrowed his eyes and looked out to the open sea. The Yuan warships hid the horizon clustered as they were side by side.

"The current is strong in the center of the bay, so ships tend to be carried away by it," he said, as if talking to himself. "That's why they are lined up like that. Swaying is also severe."

"Can you show me?" Edward asked, as he brought the fisherman to the command station, where Genji drew a bold line on the chart of Hakata Bay spread out on the table before him. The line cut across the center of the bay and continued out to the open sea.

"Around the time when the sun sets, the line where the two currents meet changes. The speed of the current heading toward the open sea is the stronger and will stay that way till morning. At that time, no matter how many able-bodied young men are at the oars, they cannot break free of it. But, if you ride it, you would drift out to sea at amazing speed. The Mongolians have connected each of their ships together to prevent that."

"Would a small boat be able to ride that tide if it left from the beach?"

"You would first have to row halfway out before the current would catch you."

"We need rowers who can get us out far enough to ride the current," Edward gulped. "But if the tide is that strong, how will they return?"

"Rather than thinking about it and talking it into the ground, someone needs to do it," Genji said bluntly, looking at the collected samurai before leaving.

"I'll do it," Alan volunteered courageously, if recklessly. "All we have to do is sneak up close enough, set the enemy warship on fire, jump into the sea, and make our escape. The distance from ship to shore is nothing to worry about."

But Alan and Edward both knew that Alan was not a good swimmer. *How many times did I save Alan from drowning when we were children?* Edward remembered.

As the sun began to set, one of the fishermen came up to Edward.

"Genji will try it, so watch carefully," was all he said before running off.

When the light that had dyed Hakata Bay scarlet faded into a thin darkness, Edward, Zafir, and the others, climbed to the top of the stone wall.

Thomas was the first to exclaim.

"Look!"

Edward strained his eyes and could just see the dark shape of a rowboat heading from the western rocky wall to the open sea.

"It's Genji. How on earth will he make it back with that body of his?"

"He doesn't intend on returning," Alan said. "He's going to join his family."

The village folks clasped their hands together, faced the open sea, and prayed. Genji's boat disappeared as it melted into the darkness. After half an hour a mass of flames rose up and sped toward a dark shape, a Yuan warship. Enemy soldiers crowded on the deck and shouted as the inferno drew nearer. They aimed their catapults, but they were too late. The stones arched over the flames before descending useless into the water.

Just as the burning boat made contact with the enemy fleet, Edward saw a figure standing proudly in the flames. Genji. The jars of oil he had loaded onto the boat burst open, and the ball of fire spread first to one warship, then the next in line and then the next. Blazing ships lit up the black sky as if it were day.

"Only Genji could have done this." Edward praised the fisherman's bravado and then warned his men. "Don't even think of copying him."

"We should board the warships," Alan said.

"You would be signing your own death warrant. Unless that's what you want."

"The way we're going we'll never make an effective attack. It would be better than waiting for them to come to us. I—"

"Let us use a fuse," Zafir interrupted. "Before rowing out to the ocean current, we can soak a rope in oil. The rope will be as long as the time it takes for the fuse to reach the jars of oil onboard. We light the fuse, escape, and wait for the fiery rowboat to hit a warship. Genji said this current would continue till morning."

"Those Yuan bastards won't expect another attack tonight. Let's do it. For Genji," Alan said.

The first boat, with Thomas and Enrico onboard and packed with oil jars, slowly drifted before gradually picking up speed and vanishing into the darkness. Thirty minutes later, Thomas and Enrico pulled themselves out of the water and onto the beach. They had lit the fuse and jumped into the sea to swim to shore. Edward and the others clenched their jaws in anticipation. But there was no change in the darkness.

"It's a failure. The fuse must have gone out."

At that moment, a flame burst through the inky black night. The massive silhouette of a Yuan warship glowed as if it had inhaled the mass of flames crashing into it.

"It hit!" a voice rose from among the samurai.

"Ready another boat!" Edward commanded.

They hurriedly prepared five boats. This time, several samurai stripped off layer after layer of armor and nimbly rowed the boats. Three boats hit warships that night. With every strike, the village folks were moved to tears. Were they tears of sadness for the loss of Genji? Or were they tears of joy for the revenge?

Edward stood alone on the beach and watched as flames consumed the darkness and thought of the next battle.

CHAPTER

105

The battle in Hakata Bay was at a stalemate. The Mongolian fleet had made no conspicuous movements since its second attack. Edward had the uncanny feeling of a beast lying motionless, hidden in a thicket, waiting to pounce and ensnare its prey. Groups of ten or so samurai and oarsmen would occasionally take the initiative, man a boat, and launch sneak attacks on the Yuan ships. Some succeeded, but most were repelled with arrows and rocks as before. Both armies continued to glare at each other for several more days.

"What the hell are they doing on the ships?" Alan said, venting his irritation and frustration.

"Yuan soldiers have been seen on a nearby beach," Morimune reported to Edward. The enemy must have been sneaking onto shore in the dead of night.

"Scouting for a new site to disembark?"

"Probably looking for water."

"Right enough. They most likely didn't bring enough water to sustain a military force that size. So, let's cut off their water supply!" Edward said with a gleam in his eye. "Where are the best sources?"

Morimune indicated several places on the map. Some were close to the coast, where defenses were limited. Another area was around the river that flowed into Hakata Bay.

"It's best to deploy soldiers at these five sites and attack where the enemy has already visited."

"We've just been thinking the same," Morimune said.

At that moment, Edward pointed to one of the ponds on the map.

"We'll defend this pond," he said.

"But you have much more important things to do," Morimune said.

"No, cutting off the enemy's supply route is crucial in warfare," Edward responded decisively. "Collect as many enemy corpses as you can."

On Edward's orders, some of the men piled the dead on the backs of horses and took them to the pond. The bodies were swollen, they stank, and the heat of the summer sun had quickened their putrefaction. Flies and other insects buzzed and followed in their wake.

"Take off their clothes and tie them down with rocks. Tie the rocks tight enough, so the bodies don't rise to the surface. Their stomachs will break down and poison the water."

They threw the corpses into the pond.

"I can see them at the bottom," Alan panicked.

"The enemy will collect water at night. They won't notice," Edward reassured him. "The rest we leave to God. Or the Devil more like it."

"This water is no longer drinkable," Zafir warned everyone as he scowled at the pond's surface. "If we drink, it will cause great sickness in the body."

"We fell for this trap when we fought in Rusafa," Edward said. "Of our hundred and fifty comrades, only half were able to fight properly. Of the other half, half died of fever and the others, unable to move, were slaughtered by our adversaries."

Morimune's face paled as he listened.

"This is war. If you lose, even more hell waits for you."

Edward focused his eyes in the silence. He could just make out the pale forms of the dead bodies lying inert at the bottom of the pond.

On the second night of sitting watch over the pond. Edward looked up at the sky. Stars glittered all over its expanse. *Could they see the same stars back in England? Were his parents, brothers, and younger sister looking up at the same moon and stars? And Haruno . . .* The image of Haruno on his last night in Kamakura rose above all others.

"Something's here," Alan whispered, bringing Edward back to reality. Moonlight shone on the black surface of the pond twenty yards away. There was movement nearby.

"A wild boar?"

"There's more than one. In fact, I'd say there's quite a lot of them," Alan said, his eyes fixed ahead of him.

A small light emerged from the blackness. Ten people pulling carts followed. When they came to the pond's edge, they lowered barrels to the water.

"Don't attack. We'll let them go back," Edward instructed as he and his men concealed themselves among the trees and darkness.

After filling their barrels, the Mongolian soldiers paused to drink from the pond before turning back the way they had come.

"Let's get out of here."

"Are we going to leave the corpses?" Morimune asked.

"If you want to fish them out, feel free to do so," Edward replied. "But none of my men will help you." The corpses stayed where they were.

The war council met the next morning.

"We killed twelve enemy soldiers who came to the Muromi River watering hole. Enemies were also driven back from three other ponds and rivers," a samurai bragged.

"Let the enemy drink freely from the pond by Odahama. Once they realize it isn't being guarded, the whole army will go there to fetch water," Edward informed the council. Several voices protested.

"You want to win by using such foul methods?"

"We cannot agree to such a plan. Battle is the only dignified way to win a war."

"After Yuan retreats, what will become of the polluted pond?"

"You can talk about all that after we win!" Alan exploded, fed up with the endless chatter and indecision. "Remember, if you lose, your heads won't be on your shoulders, your families will be strung up for public display, and anyone who survives will be a slave. As the horrors unfold around you, think well and hard on what you should have done right now."

Groups of samurai gathered as they left the council, talking among themselves and furtively glancing at Edward and the others. Alan scowled back, and they quickly looked the other way.

CHAPTER
106

Other than a small skirmish in Hakata Bay, Yuan's army made no further attempt to land.

"We don't have enough arrows," Alan complained when he returned from making his rounds among the farmers. "We mowed down the enemy with arrow fire the first time around, but it's all over for us if we don't have more arrows."

"Have we collected enemy arrows from the beach?" Edward asked.

"The tide's carried them off."

"How far did arrows fly when fired from Yuan ships?"

"Around fifty, sixty yards," Alan said.

Edward turned his gaze to the bay, where the anchored enemy warships seemingly filled the distance between Shikanoshima Island and Nokonoshima Island. Eventually, he stopped thinking and gave instructions in rapid succession.

That night, Edward, Alan, and close to a hundred farmers crossed the sandbank to Shikanoshima Island. There, on a hundred-yard stretch of the island's Hakata-facing coast, they silently lined up hundreds of straw figures dressed in kimonos and built bonfires in front. The Yuan warships were less than sixty yards away, just barely in range of their bows.

"Raise your voices and light the fires!"

On Edward's signal, the roar of the farmers shattered the night air. Simultaneously, the bonfires were lit and red flames burst out up and down the sandbank. As seen from onboard the warships, it must have looked as if a massive army was lying in wait behind the bonfires.

"Fire!" Edward ordered.

Flaming arrows arched high in the sky and rocketed toward the enemy warships, setting fire wherever they landed. Soldiers frantically ran about to extinguish the fires. Now aiming at the figures on the ship, the archers unleashed yet more arrows. Soldiers tumbled into the ocean from atop the decks, while others, joining the commotion, launched a storm of arrows toward the straw soldiers on the sandbank.

"Grab a torch and run!" Edward commanded.

Hearing this, the farmers grabbed torches in both hands and screamed as they scurried this way and that behind the straw figures. The Mongolians must have thought thousands of soldiers were attacking them. They released an even more violent onslaught of arrow fire. But after an hour, they must have suspected that something was amiss. The fires in the area dimmed and went out. Innumerable arrows pierced the straw men and were scattered on the sandy beach.

"Collect all the arrows before daybreak. Be wary of the arrowheads. They're covered in poison," Edward warned.

By sunrise, not a single arrow was left on the beach on Shikanoshima Island or on the sandbank. More than thirty thousand had been collected.

CHAPTER
107

A dozen cavalrymen barged into the stronghold. "The Mongolian army attacked Tachibana village in Kashii. They came ashore from the sandbank," one of the samurai reported as he jumped down from his horse.

"What about the villagers?" Edward asked. "Forty people should have still been there." What he knew, but did not say, was that the forty were the elderly, women, and children. Men who could fight had joined the archery regiment in Hakata.

The samurai was silent.

"You lot didn't stay and fight to protect the villagers?" Alan spat out.

"The enemy was over two hundred strong. We only had thirteen men. How could we fight?"

"Prepare for battle at once! We're going to rescue the people of Tachibana," Edward shouted as he ran out.

"It's too late! By now all of them should—" Morimune began, but Alan and the others disregarded what he said and followed Edward. Morimune reluctantly got to his feet with his sword in hand.

Over thirty horsemen raced toward Kashii, east of Hakata. As they passed through the forest, they saw billows of black smoke rising from the valley. Edward remembered what Zafir had told him not so long ago.

Mongolians use a village they attack and overpower as their base for when they attack the next village, and so on. Unlike the Saracen and Christian armies, they rarely burn down an entire village. The longer the expedition they are on is, and the more extensive the regions they conquer become, the supplies they brought from their homeland eventually run out. Naturally, they need food. That is why they raid villages. However, rather than using the farmers to work the fields, they kill them. They can't go into the next battle encumbered with prisoners of war.

"Dismount. The enemy is close by. Not a sound," Edward directed.

As they proceeded on foot, the village came into sight. Just as Edward thought, only three sheds were burning as a warning to nearby villages. If they didn't surrender and give over the village, they'd turn out the same way. As they drew closer, they saw soldiers, who looked to be about twenty years old, setting up an encampment. Carts rolled in, one after another, carrying supplies. More troops were obviously expected.

"So, that's over two hundred? Christ. Let's attack them now," Alan urged. "We're in trouble if they continue to attack the villages surrounding Hakata. We should strike now while we can."

"We're outnumbered. If we charge now, we'd be overwhelmed," Edward reasoned.

"Then we just sit on our hands and watch?"

"We have no choice but to wait till dark. They haven't killed the village folks."

"How do you know?"

"I can't see any bodies anywhere. Can you? They're likely imprisoned in a shed somewhere at the center of the village."

As the sun began to set, and the valley around the village quickly grew dark, Edward shouted with all his might.

"Charge!"

The Mongolian army who had been relaxing or preparing their evening meal looked on as the cavalry galloped toward them, not realizing at first if the horsemen were friend or foe.

"Kill them all!" Alan shouted as he raised his sword.

A Mongolian head whirled up into the sky. Within an hour, half of the enemy soldiers had fallen.

In the center of the village was a small mound with a mat over it. Morimune let out a loud shout as the mat was removed. It was a pile of headless torsos. Opposite it was a smaller pile also covered with a woven mat. Severed heads. The dead were all elderly and children. Twenty women, naked and covered in lacerations and bruises, were locked in a nearby hut.

"This bastard is still alive. Is there anyone who can tell me what the hell he is saying?" Alan said, dragging a Mongolian soldier with a gash across his stomach. His intestines were peeking out. One of Morimune's men could speak the Yuan language.

"If he wants an easy passing to the next life, he'll tell me everything he knows. If he doesn't talk, I'll hand him over to the women his lot stripped naked and tortured," Alan said, and pointed to the women whose eyes burned with pure malice.

"He said tomorrow at dawn a new regiment will be arriving. The plan is to set up a supply base here and get behind us while we deploy most of our forces for a frontal assault."

"Well, then, we should quickly withdraw," Alan said before kicking the soldier toward the women.

"Burn down the village and collect anything of importance," Edward instructed the men and surviving women.

"We don't have enough horses," Morimune said. "I'll send a messenger to headquarters, so we'll have to wait."

"We don't have time. We'll use the Yuan soldier's carts. Burn all the food we can't carry, the houses, barns, storehouses, everything!"

"You can't burn their homes. Where will they live once this war is over?" Morimune argued.

"If we leave the buildings, they will only be of help to the enemy. We don't have time. Make haste!"

"But it's the villagers' fortune."

"Their lives are the greater fortune. Tell them to take care of it."

Morimune looked displeased but said nothing more. The women began to load supplies into the carts.

"Don't forget the seed rice. You will need it when you return here." Morimune's voice resounded.

"Take refuge in Dazaifu. Bring along any villagers you meet along the way. Burn down every single village," Edward instructed Morimune.

When preparations for departure were complete, Edward gave his final order.

"Light the village and burn it to the ground!"

"You are the same as the Mongolians," a woman in her thirties said as she faced Edward, her eyes brimming with hatred. "If you burn our homes, what have we to return to? It's the same as killing us."

Alan raised a torch.

"Stop!" a woman threatened as she readied a Mongolian bow.

Alan slowly lowered the torch. At that moment a young woman jumped out. It was the woman who had stabbed a sickle in the forehead of a Mongolian soldier. She pried the torch from Alan's hand and threw it on the house. The thatch roof instantly burst into flames. As if on signal, the other women each began throwing torches, destroying their own homes.

"Take a good look," Alan said as he took in the scene of destruction before him. "Aim the hatred you feel at your enemies."

The women stared wide-eyed at their village engulfed in flames, searing the image forever in their memories.

The line of carts and women led by Morimune departed for Dazaifu, while Edward and his men headed toward the beach.

CHAPTER

108

Edward stopped his horse once they had returned to the coast and silently surveyed the area.

"The rampart was twice able to hold back the enemy," Alan said. "But it's no use now. If we're lucky, it will last half a day in the next all-out attack."

"The wall will fall," Edward said and looked behind him. Gentle hills stretched out before turning into dense forests.

"We can't let them into Hakata," Edward swore as he rode in front of the wall.

"Dig two parallel trenches here," he hastily instructed. "Each one arm deep and five hundred steps long. The distance between the trenches should be forty steps. Place small branches and twigs inside each."

"Why here?"

"This is where the wall is weakest, something the enemy has surely noticed."

In the dead of night, Edward, accompanied by a hundred farmers and townsfolk, returned to the beach with spades and hoes.

"We don't have enough time to set up booby traps. Not to mention, the enemy could easily jump over a trench this size," Alan grumbled.

"All it has to do is stop their momentum. That's when we attack," Edward said and stared into the darkness. He could faintly hear the sound of waves in the blackness. Out there, the monstrous Mongolian armada lay at anchor ready to spring.

The trenches were completed before dawn.

"Drench the branches and twigs in oil, and then we're ready," Edward told Alan.

CHAPTER

109

Several hundred warships, intent on making land, sailed toward the beach as soon as the sun rose.

"I've had enough of these stubborn bastards. They're like a horde of ants. They just pop up out of the ocean," Alan whined. "They're going to build a beachhead no matter the cost."

"Don't do anything yet. Let's entice them farther inland," Edward ordered.

Close to five thousand enemy soldiers crouched motionless on the beach. They had learned their lesson. They knew Nippon archers lay in wait behind the stone wall. Ultimately, the vanguard infantry slowly inched forward as if recovering from a paralysis.

"Those fools are acting on their own again," Alan spat out in disgust when he saw a regiment of thirty samurai cavalry and close to a hundred foot soldiers advancing on the enemy infantry.

"Just what the Mongolians want. A frontal charge they can completely decimate," Edward moaned. "Now we're the bastards who haven't learned their lesson." To ease the situation, he yelled, "Fire!"

A bombardment of arrows hit the front row of enemy soldiers, and they dropped like flies. Quickly recovering, they raised their shields and created a protective wall. When gongs sounded, the wall of shields, which looked like an enormous tortoise shell, advanced.

"Units one and two, ready your bows!" Edward ordered, and behind the rampart the farmer and townsfolk archers lined up at the ready.

"Aim for the openings between the shields. You can do it. It's the same as we practiced."

The first unit fired, then the second unit released its arrows. Exactly as they had trained. Arrows continuously battered the enemy formation, and it began to crumble. The gaps between the shields expanded making it easier for Nippon arrows to penetrate. But the Mongolian army's superior numbers allowed them to replace dead or wounded soldiers with new ones who advanced the formation one step at a time.

"They're about to reach the first ditch!"

Those at the head of the formation noticed the ditch and tried to stop, but they were shoved and hemmed in by the soldiers marching behind them.

Edward lowered his arm.

Flaming arrows ignited the oil-soaked clothes and twigs in the ditches. Black smoke and screams filled the air. The inferno spread, breaking the shield wall, and trapping the Mongolian army between the two ditches. Defenseless burning bodies rolled around in horror. There was no escape.

"Fire!" Edward yelled, and another round of arrows rained down upon the exposed soldiers who had abandoned their shields to strip off their burning clothes. Heavy black smoke enshrouded the area. Visibility was next to zero, and all Edward could hear were screams, coughs, and cries for help. Climbing over the charred bodies of their fallen comrades in the ditches, the Mongolian army boldly remade its formation. Reinforcements relentlessly disembarked from the warships.

"Shit, this isn't good. The wall will break at any moment!" Alan said.

"If we can only hold for a little longer, I'll send a messenger requesting reinforcements," Morimune, who had returned from Dazaifu, said.

The Mongolian soldiers who had made it to the bottom of the rampart were hoisting ladders and even climbing up with their bare hands.

"Kick them down!" Alan shouted and unsheathed his sword.

No sooner did a soldier scale the stone wall than his head was sliced off. Soldiers were pushed off the wall as the samurai thrust the blades of their long spears into flesh and bone. The dance between offense and defense lasted for thirty minutes before one part of the wall fell, and Edward watched as the enemy, having heaped their comrade's corpses one on top of the other to climb up more easily, overran the top of the rampart.

"Fall back! Retreat to the hills!" Edward ordered. "Escape into the woods!" he yelled as he sprinted with the rest of his men.

The Mongolian army regrouped once it had made its way to the top of the rampart, and gushed out from where the wall had been breached, its numbers swelling from several dozen to several hundred in the blink of an eye.

Edward looked from the hills to the forest behind him. In front of the forest were close to fifty lumps of dry grass tightly bound into spheres. Peasants carrying lit torches stood by.

"Light the fires!" Edward shouted.

As the grass balls were lit, wind fanned the flames, engulfing the spheres in an instant. Flames twice the size of a man twisted into the air.

"Roll them down!"

The balls of fire tumbled down the hill, scattering sparks as they picked up momentum. The Mongolian soldiers who had been cheering as they raced up the hill, stopped in their tracks, and looked up dumbfounded at the balls of flames careening toward them. The soldiers turned around and hastily ran away. One of the fireballs struck a Mongolian soldier, and continued to gain momentum as it swallowed up more soldiers. The hills were flooded with those fleeing from the spinning masses and those who had been lit on fire as they fell. An uproar of screams and cries for help echoed across the landscape. Those who managed to slip through the spaces between the fireballs continued to climb the hill.

"What is he saying?" Edward asked Zafir, indicating the loud voice coming from a Mongolian soldier.

"That anyone who tries to retreat will be killed," Zafir replied.

"Release the logs!" On Edward's signal, a row of logs were cut from their bonds.

Dozens of logs rolled across the width of the hill, sending soldiers flying. Screams carried on the wind as men darted about consumed by flames or blindly collided with the logs, frantically trying to hold together their cracked-open skulls. Many crashed onto their backs as they spiraled down the hill.

"Attack! With me!" Edward said and remounted his horse.

He drew his sword and roared as he charged into the plumes of black smoke. Every time he swung down his sword, a bloodied Mongolian soldier fell to the ground. Arrows were shot directly at him, but he continued to swing down his blade, protecting his face with his shield. Edward's cavalry charged into the center of the enemy, leaving behind a slew of corpses and their discombobulated comrades.

The battle continued until sunset. The Mongolian army continued to pour more and more new soldiers onto the battlefield. The ditches, already filled with corpses, rising flames, and black smoke, gave off a putrid odor. The Mongolians heaped together the corpses and used them as shields against Nippon attacks.

"How many arrows remain?" Edward asked.

"Only a few more rounds," Alan responded.

"Once the arrows run out, have the peasants fall back. Retreat to Dazaifu. We'll make our assault and buy them time to evacuate."

"We should also fall back and regain our position! Already a third of our soldiers are dead or injured. We should give the peasants swords and let them fight!" one of the samurai violently disagreed. He had a cut across his forehead that was so deep it showed bone.

"The farmers' duty is to till the land and raise crops. They cannot brandish a sword and fight! That is our duty!"

"We also want to fight!" a thin man said to Edward. It was the same elderly village head who had once refused to fight in battle. "We are all people of Nippon and want to protect our nation."

"The sword is not for you. The spade and hoe are more essential. Don't forget that."

"You'll slow us down. Leave the fighting to us," Alan said as he tested the balance of the man's sword and swung it around. Nicks and chips marred the blade.

"Hold fire!" Edward said. "You will retreat to Dazaifu. Gather all the remaining arrows." A stir spread among the farmers.

"There are plenty of arrows left. We can fight! Do you think us peasants are fools?"

"I truly admire your spirit. However, our foe is an army seasoned in battle. If you were to meet them head-on, you would be massacred. And that would be a waste of life. Look—" Edward pointed to the hill and sea. Corpses of Mongolian soldiers blanketed the hill, and warships filled Hakata Bay. Throngs of enemy soldiers stepped onto the beach with each new landing boat. The Nippon samurai holding them at bay seemed insignificant in comparison.

"You've all done more than enough. Which is why you must retreat for now and prepare yourselves for the next battle. Your families should be waiting for you at Dazaifu."

Edward didn't have the heart to tell them about the slaughter in the village. Though there was some solace in the women having escaped to safety.

"What should we do with the remaining arrows?" a farmer asked.

"They'll aid you in your retreat."

"Those who have skill with the bow, come forward!" Alan demanded, and one quarter of the farmers stepped up. There were over fifty of them. Alan chose ten.

"Give all the remaining arrows to them. They'll cover your retreat," he said. Despite the order, there were only enough to supply each man with five or six arrows.

"Make your retreat through the forest. Those covering should climb up the trees along the path. After everyone has pulled back, we'll lure the enemy to the path. Once we get them in position, we'll attack them all at once," Edward said.

"You heard him! Start the retreat!" Alan ordered.

CHAPTER
110

The peasants began their retreat and headed toward Dazaifu. About two hundred proceeded down the forest path. To protect themselves, or rather give themselves the illusion of protection to bolster their courage, they clung onto their bows, even though they had no arrows, and the damaged swords they had stolen from dead Mongolian soldiers in the previous war.

"Make haste or you will be slaughtered!"

Although the Mongolian army on the coast had lost much of its power, there were still seven thousand soldiers remaining. And those soldiers were on the move, heading inland, in response to Nippon's change of direction. The Mongolians may have realized that their foe had run out of arrows.

"They're launching their pursuit. The bastards have noticed our movements," a knight reported as he returned from scouting.

The Mongolian army drew near to the top of the hill.

"The farmers need another hour before they reach safety," Edward said.

"I'll make sure they get that hour," Alan offered as he drew his sword. "Go and lead them."

"I'll return as soon as they are safe."

"I'll go with you, Edward," Morimune announced. Behind him were over ten horsemen and thirty infantrymen.

"Let's go!" Alan roared. "And may God protect you!" he shouted, his eyes locked on Edward. A smile spread across his face, and Edward reciprocated. They held their brotherly gaze for a moment, then Edward turned and galloped toward the farmers on the forest path.

"The men covering the farmers have at best five to six rounds each," Edward told Morimune who rode beside him. "Once they run out, order them to quickly make their escape. The moment we get the peasants to safety, we'll rejoin Alan and the others."

A war cry echoed from the coast. Edward could hear the blasts of thunder crash bombs. Another all-out attack had begun.

"Hurry!" Edward commanded. "The enemy has breached the wall." *They have to be stopped from building an encampment at all costs.*

CHAPTER
111

Trees grew thickly on both sides of the thin forest path leading to Dazaifu. As the farmers walked forward, Edward and the others concealed themselves in the dense growth. Suddenly, the ominous sound of footsteps came nearer. It sounded like a hundred people. *If only we had a little more time. What has happened to Alan and the others?*

At that moment, Edward spied the head of the Mongolian army, proceeding at a fast pace without their shields on guard. Edward gave a short whistle. Arrows shot out in unison from between the trees. Taken by surprise, the enemy soldiers in front were shot down one by one. Falling into chaos, the regiment could not pinpoint where the arrows were coming from. One of the Mongolian commanders shouted out. It seemed as if he was ordering his men to keep moving, but they looked ready to flee. They only moved forward because the soldiers behind them kept pushing them on.

Edward whistled again, and the second salvo of arrows was discharged. This time it wasn't only the front ranks that the arrows poured into; the center of the regiment was hit as well. The soldiers screamed and scrambled to counterattack, but they still could not tell from which direction the arrows were coming. The narrow path impeded their movement, and they were being shoved from behind. After several more rounds of arrows were loosed, close to half of the enemy soldiers had fallen. By then Edward and his men had run out of arrows.

"Prepare to attack," Edward directed, breaking cover and re-mounting his horse. "Charge!" he yelled and galloped forward.

Edward, Morimune, and their men slashed and scattered the enemy while sprinting through the woods. After ten minutes of striking down the enemy, they came out of the forest to a clearing on a hill overlooking the coast. They looked down at the battle unfolding below.

"They can't hold out much longer! Our army is being destroyed," Morimune exclaimed.

"That is also God's will," Edward replied and crossed himself.

The Nippon army of five thousand had been reduced to half, while the steady stream of enemy soldiers disembarking from the warships anchored offshore only increased.

"We're too late. We should head to Dazaifu, too," Morimune said and glared at Edward.

"I'm going to save my friends," Edward asserted, and he and the cavalry descended the hill.

Mongolian tactics had not changed since the last war. In one such stratagem, several soldiers would single out a military commander, surround him, and attack him with spears and swords. The samurai's bravado made him vulnerable to such an ensnarement, and he knew it. A fall from his horse, and in a whirlwind of activity, the enemy would encircle him and he would be at their mercy.

"Wedge formation!" Edward yelled.

The twenty horsemen at his command pushed into the heart of the enemy, who closed in on them. Edward swung his sword left and right as he hacked his way through them. His sword was slippery. Sticky clots of blood slicked the blade and slid down to the hilt. He instinctively bent down, and an arrow skimmed his cheek.

At that moment he saw Alan ahead of him.

Several arrows had punctured Alan's armor. He no longer held his usual longsword, but a sword he had picked up from a fallen comrade. Spurts of blood splashed out each time he swung at an enemy. Edward thought their eyes met, but was he hallucinating? Alan's eyes were jovial as Edward looked into them.

Edward missed a spear thrust at him, and as he pivoted to engage his sword with the spear, his horse's knees buckled, sending him hurtling to the ground. As Edward looked back, he saw his horse collapse, convulsing with an arrow sticking out of its neck. Edward stabbed his sword through the horse's chest, putting the beast out of its misery.

Acting on impulse, Edward jumped to his feet and swung his sword to the side, his blade tearing through the chest of an oncoming Mongolian soldier. What happened after that was a blur. He desperately avoided arrows, slipped past blades, and blindly swung his sword, up, down, diagonally, any way that he could. His movements became more sluggish as exhaustion spread throughout his body. *What of my comrades?* he thought. But he soon lost the ability to think clearly and simply moved his limbs on reflex. *This must be my end. I wasn't able to see God, after all. But I shall meet him soon.*

Edward felt a pain in his leg. A spear was lodged in his thigh. Turning around, he saw the grim face of the Mongolian soldier who had wounded him. Without hesitation, he lashed out at the man's neck with his sword and hit.

Suddenly, the sound of a gong echoed out. The Mongolian army stopped and fell back to the beach. Edward could hear the explosive sounds of thunder crash bombs in the distance. The soldiers crowded into the landing boats, but their movements were slower than before. They were just as exhausted as Edward and the others from this drawn-out battle. They would row back to the ships, properly replenish themselves, and reassemble.

Edward kneeled on the beach among the vast number of dead bodies and looked at the retreating Mongolians in blank amazement. Morimune walked up to Edward. His armor was covered with arrows and blood trickled down his forehead.

"It looks like they're calling it a day. The sun will be setting soon," Edward said.

"Did we win?" Morimune asked.

"For the moment. But they'll attack again tomorrow," Edward said and pulled out the spear.

Zafir came running up. His face was pale and sorrowful. Blood also dripped down his forehead. He wordlessly beckoned Edward to follow him.

Not far off, seven of Edward's knights lay on the beach in full Nippon armor.

"Alan," Edward choked as he stumbled to his motionless friend.

Close to ten arrows had pierced Alan's body. Slowly, Edward pulled out each one. The arrow lodged in his neck dealt the fatal blow. A deep gash ran the length of Alan's cheek, but the blood had already hardened. Edward scraped away the blood with his fingertip, carefully and lovingly.

"Alan fought like a demon," Thomas told Edward as he, too, kneeled next to Alan. "When we were surrounded by enemies several times our own, he kept on fighting, even when a poisoned arrow shot through his throat. At the end, he charged into enemy lines, broke their battle formation, and created an opening for us to break through . . . all by himself."

"I want him buried on the hill . . . that hill," Edward said as he pointed to Mount Iimori. It was where Alan had once looked up at the dazzling western sky.

"After we clean Alan and the other knights' bodies, dress them in their proper Christian armor," Edward ordered Thomas and then left the beach.

CHAPTER
112

"The death of a close friend is always sorrowful," Zafir said to Edward after Alan's burial.

"He was like a brother to me. No, he was by my side longer than my real brothers."

"Death comes for all of us in the end. There comes a time when we must accept this."

"But there is an order to things. Alan was still young. Younger than me in fact."

"He has lived his life. And now he shall be watching over you with your God."

"Do you truly believe that?"

"Your God and my god may be different, but our beliefs are the same. We believe that the human heart is fragile. That life is fleeting. That we leave troubles behind us. That there are no troubles after death. That we feel more at ease in life if we have something to believe in."

"Your words have stirred my heart and comforted me more than any priest has ever done."

"Lord Edward," a man suddenly appeared. He was a large man dressed in Nippon travel clothes that Edward knew he had seen somewhere before. He quickly recalled that he worked for WangSheng in Kamakura.

"I have a message from my master."

The watermill shone in the dim light of the moon. A horse was hitched to the front of the hut. It was Hayate. When he noticed Edward, he eagerly shook his head. As Edward stepped inside the mill, he could see the outline of someone standing in the darkness. Just as he gripped the handle of his sword, a sweet scent tickled his nose. The familiar aroma of flowers.

"Haruno?"

"How I have longed to see you again," her soft voice responded as they embraced.

"Why are you here?"

"Lord WangSheng charged me with bringing Hayate to you."

As Edward's eyes adjusted to the darkness, Haruno emerged in the moonlight flowing through the window. Her white skin and beautiful features. But her face looked gaunt as she stared at him.

"Are you injured?"

"I am fine. Didn't I tell you that I am protected by God?" Edward pointed upward.

"You, my lord, are a human being made of flesh and blood the same as me."

"It's dangerous coming here. Didn't WangSheng tell you that?"

"Lord WangSheng greatly opposed me coming here. But I was persistent. I told him I would go by myself if no one was to accompany me."

"The battle with the Mongolians is on. Even where we are now is not safe."

"Lord WangSheng also told me that."

"Then why did you come?"

"I told you. Because I miss you."

"Where are you staying?"

"We've just arrived in Dazaifu from an overland route."

"Dazaifu is too dangerous. The force of the Mongolians is greater than you can imagine."

"Lord WangSheng intends to leave soon. He says he wants to take you with him. He will cross over to the main continent, and from there he says he can send you home."

Edward gave a weak laugh.

"He told me you would refuse. Which is why he sent me." Haruno's voice trembled. Edward grabbed her hands. They were shaking and cold to the touch.

"This place will likely—" but Haruno cut off his words and brought her lips to his. Her dainty and shivering body pressed firmly into his as he pulled her into a tight embrace. They clung to each other.

"Promise me something." Edward pulled back slightly and looked into her eyes. "That you will live strong and be happy even if I don't return."

Thick tears began to well up in her eyes and fall down her cheeks.

"I will always be watching over you," Edward said.

Haruno nodded her head silently.

CHAPTER

113

"We may have caused great damage to the enemy, but our own forces took heavy losses as well. It's best to withdraw to Dazaifu and restore our strength to fight once again."

The war council was in chaos.

"At this point, we'd have to lure them farther inland to fight. Even in the previous battle we were one step ahead on land. Not to mention we have thorough knowledge of this region which the enemy does not. I also approve of pulling back to Dazaifu for now."

"As do I. If the Mongolian army is on land, then they are cut off from their supply chain. The advantage of knowing the area allows us to make surprise attacks."

"All of the citizens in Hakata have already taken refuge in Dazaifu. It would be a good plan to lure the enemy into a surprise assault."

The majority opinion among the gokenin was to withdraw to Dazaifu. Munemasa, who had cooperated with Edward up to then, was indecisive. He feared the extensive force of the Mongolian army.

"If we allow them to disembark, they will build a stronghold and bring ashore their entire army. Which is why we must fight them on the coastline no matter what it takes. We must continue to prevent them from making a frontline base," Edward argued. He explained in detail the horrors that would befall them if the Mongolians were to establish a beachhead, but the gokenin were against him.

After the council, Edward met privately with Zafir.

"It seems there was much dispute. Don't tell me anything. I can see the answer on your face," Zafir said laughing. "No matter what the decision, I will be at your side."

"It's odd. To think you and I were once enemies."

"God and man are different. Though man may be cleverer and more adaptable," Zafir said and gave out another amused laugh. "Humans are ridiculous and contradictory beings. God must be astounded, yet also forgiving."

Zafir looked up to the sky, and tweaked his nose as if sniffing something.

"The air is damp, and the wind blows toward the sea this time of the year. The seawater is also unusually warm. A large storm might be coming this way."

"A storm?"

"By tomorrow the Mongolian army will make another attempt to land," Zafir said and looked out over the Yuan warships floating in Hakata Bay.

"Shouldn't the Mongolian army avoid trying to advance day after day?"

"They have likely concluded that circumstances have changed following today's attack. They see the Nippon army preparing to flee, and they would not miss such an opportunity. So, it would be best to prepare their army's descent on the beach throughout the night."

They could see more activity than usual onboard the warships. Crowds of soldiers gathered on the routinely lightless decks, loading up the landing boats they had lowered down.

"It looks like it won't just be a simple attack this time."

"They are intent on making a beachhead by whatever means. Also, they may have noticed the approaching storm. If so, they shall desperately want to launch their attack. This battle is the key to victory or defeat."

"It will be fierce."

"No matter what, you must push the enemy army back to their ships. If you can do that, then we have a chance of victory. Even so, the Nippon side is being careless. They are simply holding councils and tending to their armor."

Edward staggered for a moment.

"How is the wound on your leg?"

"There isn't any pain, but I can't put my full weight on it."

"It is likely because you are exhausted. You should rest a little. If you can."

"Tell Morimune that a full-out assault is tomorrow," Edward requested before returning to the encampment.

CHAPTER
114

"Lord Edward," a low voice called out causing Edward to jerk upright and half-draw his sword.

When did I fall asleep?

Since he had buried Alan, Edward wondered if his grief would ever let him sleep again. But in the end, he could not overcome his exhaustion. He had slept so deeply he had not even dreamed.

Thomas was staring at him as he stood at his side.

"Please follow me," Thomas said and led Edward outside the encampment where three sailors were waiting.

"What is this?"

Thomas brought his finger to his lips, signaling Edward to be silent. The five walked through the starless darkness with only Thomas' torch to guide them. When they came to the coast, Thomas and the sailors stopped, faced Edward, and pointed to a black hulk in the sea.

"It's a Yuan warship that has run aground," Thomas whispered. "One of my sailors found it after returning from taking the last of the peasants to Dazaifu. Food, water. There is plenty still onboard. The soldiers and crew must have rushed to escape, seeing as they came too close to shore. They thought Nippon soldiers would attack them if they were discovered."

"If the ship's run aground and cannot move, then it's useless," Edward said.

"If we all push together at high tide, we can get it away from the reef. Let's climb onboard and find our way home. We won't be able to hold out against the next attack. We should leave now. We have no intention of dying for the sake of this nation's samurai."

"It's not for the samurai. It's for the people," Edward blurted out. Though he spoke without thinking, the declaration did not feel odd or out of place.

The lights on the open sea grew stronger. The Yuan warships were relentlessly preparing to force their way onto the shore. It was clear that their next attempt would be different from before. They had lowered the majority of their landing boats and filled them with supplies.

"Take this ship and return to your homes. If any of my knights wish to go home, let them join you."

"And you?" Thomas asked.

"I will stay here."

"Why?"

"To protect the people," Edward said, and the moment after he spoke he had a strange thought. *Never once have I thought of such words. Yet here I am honestly accepting them as my own.*

"They're foreigners. What's the point?"

Edward stayed silent and faced the sea.

CHAPTER

115

"That armor suits you well," Zafir said admiringly, as Edward left his tent.

Edward had taken off the Nippon armor and helmet, and replaced it with his chainmail. Over the chainmail he wore a white tunic with a red cross emblazoned on the chest. It was the dress of a knight. Zafir took a step away from where he stood next to Morimune, and appraised Edward approvingly.

"I've thought of giving this to you," Edward said to Morimune as he held out a katana. The Demon Slayer.

"But this is the sword Lord Tokimune gave to you. I—"

"Which is why it is mine to give now. I want you to have it."

Edward slid the sword into Morimune's hand, before resting his own on the sword fastened to his hip.

"This is the only blade for me."

———

Thick, threatening clouds blanketed the sky, and a tepid wind blew. Just as Zafir had predicted, a storm was brewing.

The sea was already covered with incoming Yuan landing boats.

"Why will the samurai not move? If that army makes it ashore, there will be nobody left to protect Hakata."

"The main force of our army has already left for Dazaifu. All that remains are two hundred cavalrymen and three hundred infantrymen to cover the main force's retreat," Zafir told Edward.

"And you?" Edward said turning to Morimune.

"Lord Tokimune instructed me to help you—"

"Will you help me?"

"And to protect Nippon."

"How many horsemen do you have?"

"Fifty."

"Good enough!"

Yuan soldiers began to make landfall, engulfing the coast. They even pitched several tents on the sandy beach.

"Let's get on with it," Edward said as he grabbed Hayate's reins.

At that moment, around thirty horsemen came riding into view.

"Thomas, you—" Edward exclaimed.

Thomas, his crew, and Edward's knights sat upon their horses wearing chainmail and clutching shields.

"We talked till dawn, and decided we all want to eat the food here one more time," Thomas began before he was joined by a chorus of sailors.

"I want to sing with the townsfolk and teach them how to dance. I promised young girls in this country I would."

"The wine isn't bad here either! If we don't protect the people, then what will become of that?"

"The people here treated us with the best food they could offer, even when they themselves were hungry."

Smiles spread across their faces, then vanished as Thomas spoke next.

"Those days on our voyage and the time we spent in Kamakura were adventurous and exciting. We've decided we want to see this battle to the end."

"We'll fight together to the end!" knights and sailors swore together.

There were more than eighty horsemen in Edward and Morimune's combined forces, plus the two hundred Kanto cavalry left behind to cover the main army's escape. Altogether, two hundred and eighty cavalry and three hundred infantry were amassed at the base of the hill behind the stone wall.

"The enemy has commenced landing. We'll throw ourselves in front of them and prevent them from disembarking," Edward ordered.

He held his sword in one hand and gripped his shield in the other. On his right, Zafir waited, holding his Islamic saber. When all were ready, Edward squeezed Hayate's ribcage with his calves, and he raced down the hill at the head of the cavalry. They cut their way through the thousand or so enemy soldiers on the beach while roaring their battle cry.

"Set the tents ablaze!" Edward shouted out, and one by one his men lit the tents, leaving them to burn.

Despite being outnumbered, they overwhelmed and agitated the enemy, chasing them in every direction. At one point, the Nippon army had the strength to push them back to the sea, but then the pendulum swung and the Mongolians regained their advantage. The battle seesawed until the sun began to set, and darkness fell.

The Mongolian army halted its advance and stood by on the beach and in the landing boats. Were they waiting for the signal to retreat? Or perhaps they were closely watching the Nippon army's movement? An ominous silence hung over the beach.

"At this rate they'll be able to easily break through the wall. Gather the samurai together. We must regroup our forces." Edward signaled to Morimune. "What happened to the Kanto go-kenin's cavalry of two hundred?"

"They left for Dazaifu."

"So they fled!" Thomas seethed.

"It was their duty to hold off the enemy until the main body of the army could retreat to Dazaifu. They've fulfilled their duty," Morimune reasoned to cover for the other soldiers.

"Line up the torches on the top of the stone wall. Position the entire army next to them and wait for my command," Edward quickly instructed.

The sound of a gong rang out from the sea. As Edward turned his eyes to the water, black shadows floated on the dark sea. Once again, the Yuan landing boats were attempting to come ashore. Just as Zafir had said, the enemy would stop at nothing to take Hakata.

"If that many come ashore, we won't last long."

The gong beat faster. The Mongolian army, which had been awaiting orders on the beach, advanced on the wall.

"They've begun their attack."

"Shall we let out our battle cry?"

"There is no need. We'd only give the enemy more motivation."

The Yuan warships moved as one into position and faced the beach.

"Light the fires!"

Each of the torches lined up and down the top of the rampart was lit. Suddenly, the wind shifted and blew inland. Half of Hakata Bay was dyed red as the wind fanned the flames, giving the illusion of thousands of soldiers lurking behind the stone wall.

"Wait until the first boat reaches the beach. Begin the attack once the first wave of soldiers lands ashore," Edward ordered, his voice rising through the wind.

CHAPTER
116

One by one the landing boats were brought up onto the sandy beach.

"They look like ants," Enrico remarked as they all watched the enemy soldiers carpet the beach.

This was Yuan's largest attack yet. The entirety of their army had been sent out. The odds were against Nippon being able to push this enormous force back.

"Shall we go?" Edward said as he looked to his comrades and unsheathed his sword.

Suddenly, a battle cry echoed from behind them. They turned their heads and witnessed arrows pouring down upon the Mongolian army. Again, the battle cry rang out. The voices were powerful enough to push back the wind blowing in from the sea and rumbled throughout the bay.

"Have reinforcements arrived?" Edward questioned.

As he looked toward the hill, torches were spread all around it, and drums and gongs were blaring. Another war cry and even more arrows were unleashed. Soaring through the sky with the arrows were fist-sized rocks. The rocks painted the Mongolian soldiers' heads and faces red with blood as they crashed into them.

"It must be hundreds, no, thousands of reinforcements."

"Whose insignia do they bear?"

"There is no insignia."

"It can't be."

From behind the rampart to the hill, farmers and townsfolk brandished bows and long spears.

"It is the people you trained. They escaped to Dazaifu, but have returned with more of their kin," Zafir said.

"Let me hear your battle cries!" Edward roared to his new mass of fighters. On his command, a thunderclap of cries bellowed throughout the bay.

For a moment, the Yuan soldiers spread out on the beach stopped moving. But the continuous push of soldiers behind them prevented them from retreating.

"Fire the arrows!" Edward commanded.

The archers standing ready behind the wall unleashed in unison. Their arrows made a gentle arc in the sky before descending on the Mongolian army. They launched the catapults which smashed several landing boat to pieces and massacred Mongolian soldiers attempting to advance on the wall. The enemy's landing slowed.

The same citizens we were trying to protect are now protecting us. Is this also God's will? Edward muttered to himself.

The ebb and flow of the battle continued throughout the night. As the eastern sky began to lighten, the coastline and surface of the sea faintly emerged. But thick, low-lying clouds blocked out the shape of the rising sun.

"This isn't good. Once it gets brighter, the enemy will come to see exactly the state of our forces and descend upon us all at once," Edward said.

The majority of the Mongolian army had landed. While such a mighty force should have already cleared the wall and rushed into the city, it remained on the shore avoiding the assault of Nippon arrows as best it could.

"Why won't they launch an all-out attack?"

"They're taking in the situation. They have a plan," Zafir replied knowingly.

"Then let's seize this opportunity to rebuild our formation."

"Even if we do, what more can we hope to accomplish?" Thomas asked.

About twenty horsemen, including Edward's knights and Thomas and his crew, were all that remained of their cavalry. And Edward couldn't see ten of the riders, though he didn't have the time to confirm if they were dead or alive. Half of his remaining knights were injured elsewhere.

"How is your leg?" Zafir asked.

"It's starting to hurt."

"Good. It is a sign you are alive."

The two armies glared at each other for a long time. The Nippon forces continuously rained down arrows on the Mongolian army which, seemingly stuck, was unable to judge the situation. Eventually, the intervals between arrow fire became longer.

"The citizens who came to support us should escape by whatever means they can."

Edward turned his head back to the stone wall. Behind it were over five hundred farmers and townsfolk with their bows at the ready. But their supply of arrows was running out.

"We should escape to Dazaifu with them. Our military forces are reorganizing there and have the means to confront Yuan,"

Morimune said, but he knew that once the Mongolian army invaded Hakata, it would be difficult, if not impossible to stop their momentum.

"Lead the people back and protect them. We'll stay here and keep the Mongolians at bay."

"Will do!" Morimune told him strongly.

Prompted by Edward, Morimune and his men set off for Dazaifu, protecting the farmers and townsfolk.

Raging winds and crashing waves shook the beach as Edward's troops gathered on the hill behind the wall. Edward found a spot and sat on the grass next to Zafir. Until a short while ago, this didn't seem like a place where thousands of men would be slaughtered. Though the dimness concealed them, countless corpses, both friend and foe, lay on the beach below, exposed to the elements. Some were still alive among the piles of the dead. Yet Edward strangely did not feel anything for them. His would be the same fate.

"It is not so bad to die in foreign lands. Many legends are likely to be born this way," Zafir remarked.

"How can people attain peace when the fire of their life goes out? They have no land, no status, no fortune. And God doesn't offer them salvation. All that's left is a story of how they lived," Edward said almost as a whisper.

"Are you denying God? That is not very like you."

"I accept him. Only God knows my life."

Zafir gave him an understanding look.

"The enemy has become nervous. They've stationed lookouts all around us. We won't be able to launch a surprise attack," Edward muttered.

"Do you still intend to gain victory?"

"We are God's Army. I have no intention of losing," he responded, but his words were blown away by the wind and disappeared.

No, we have already won. We repelled each of the Yuan assaults. Together with the farmers and townsfolk, we forced back an advancing enemy far greater in number and prevented them from constructing a beachhead. The rest I leave to God.

Boisterous sounds stirred Edward from his reverie. Men shouting, objects crashing together, the roar of wind and waves. Several hundred landing boats and more enemy soldiers were heading toward the coast in the darkness.

"The main force is finally making their way ashore."

"What we experienced until now wasn't the main force? Just how many Mongolian soldiers are making landfall?" one of the soldiers questioned.

"Let's charge and finish this," Edward heard Thomas mutter.

"The enemy already knows we are few in numbers. They will put all their power into this next attack. We must do whatever is necessary to prevent them from constructing an outpost on the coast. Once the next attack commences it will be the decisive battle that holds our very lives in the balance. I will blame no man who wishes to leave now. You have all done more than enough. I am proud of every one of you."

When Edward had finished, all the soldiers fell completely silent.

"We have been of one mind since we left Kamakura. We will stay with you," a voice was heard.

"It would be an honor to fight by your side."

"Beside God!" several soldiers cried out. Their will became one and grew stronger as it coursed through their hearts.

Edward rode Hayate over to Enrico. Enrico's back was straight as he held his spear.

"I have a favor to ask of you," Edward said. He took the dagger fastened to his hip and gave it to Enrico. Then he removed the cross from his neck and gripped it tightly.

"This dagger and cross have been in my family for generations. I'd like you to bring them to the woman who is waiting by the watermill."

"But I also—" Enrico began.

"We make our assault before noon. You should be able to return by then."

Enrico carefully put the dagger and cross into his pocket and mounted his horse.

"Can I count on you?"

"You can."

Edward watched Enrico disappear into the forest.

"You stay behind too," Edward said, turning to Zafir. "It is your duty to tell the tale of what happened here."

"What is the matter? I have always enjoyed watching your next achievements. I will stay with you," Zafir responded with a smile. "I asked you to tell me one day what you promised Lord Tokimune for sparing Alan's life. Is now the right time?"

"I promised Tokimune that I would take him with me when I went back to my country after this war ended," Edward revealed.

Zafir let out a laugh.

"That is truly a dream-like tale. Now I understand Lord Tokimune's true feelings. He wants to see the world!" Zafir's voice shook as it was carried off by the wind.

"Gather the men. We'll arrange our battle formation and charge," Edward told him.

Zafir silently nodded and put his notebook back in his pocket.

All the torches stuck into the beach's sand were lit at once. The whole area became as bright as day. As the wind picked up, the crackling sounds of flames rose. Edward unsheathed his sword and raised it high in the air.

"We, as soldiers of Christ, left our motherland of England and crossed a continent. From Jerusalem through the Indian Ocean, we have traveled around Asia and now find ourselves in this island country. Think on what we have done. Thanks to the people of this land, we have never suffered a day of hunger. It is our duty to protect these people. God is still with us, even in these eastern lands. God's divine protection blesses us still!"

"For the people!"

"By the grace of God!" the knights shouted out.

Zafir looked up to the sky. The wind was gusting, and rain began to mix with it. Lights on the warships on the open sea swayed as if they were dancing.

Edward took hold of Hayate's reins. *With this horse, I could fight a hundred times more enemies than those I will fight today.*

As the sun began to break through the thick clouds, Edward saw nothing but the Mongolian army's soldiers who covered the sandy beach ahead of him. They easily exceeded five thousand. And those numbers were growing moment by moment. But, once more, they would push the Mongolian horde back to their ships.

Yet, as Edward looked at the scene of enemy soldiers overflowing on the coast and sea, his confidence and determination momentarily faltered. It already seemed too late to attack. *No, that's not right*, he cleared his mind. Behind them were farmers and townsfolk desperate to live. *I will fight with them and for them.* A warrior wearing red armor dashed by on a horse. It was Alan, followed by the knights and sailors who had lost their lives on the beach. Pulled by the vision, Edward moved Hayate forward and rallied his knights.

"Charge!"

The mix of rain and wind grew fiercer. Within the raging tempest, the band in shining silver silently rode, gradually increasing their speed.

CHAPTER
117

The sky was crystal clear, and waves gently broke on the shore. Corpses of Mongolian soldiers covered the sand. Some had died in the battle, others had drowned and washed up on the shore. The Yuan warships that once crowded the bay were gone. Only the sun glittered off the water.

Enrico and Haruno had come to the coast after the tempest had passed to search for the bodies of Edward and his men. But they could not find a single one of them.

They met a young boy on the beach and asked if he had seen Edward and the others, but he shook his head. The boy held a broken sword, Edward's sword. They asked where he had found it, and he said it was stuck in the sand below the stone wall. When Haruno asked if she could buy the sword from him, the boy silently handed it to her and ran off. Enrico looked at the small retreating figure and realized it was Taro, who had often tagged behind Alan. Enrico called out to him, but he had already disappeared into the thicket of the forest.

Enrico and Haruno stood together on top of the stone wall. The wall Edward and others had laid down their lives to protect. Enrico placed the broken sword inside the hole he had dug and covered it with soil.

"I will be returning to my family in Kamakura. What are you going to do?" he asked.

"I will stay here . . . in Hakata, where Edward died. Lord Xie Wangsheng says he will need help with his business."

Haruno put a hand on her stomach and stared at the sea. To the right was Shikanoshima Island and to the left was Nokonoshima Island. As Enrico stretched his hand out to the sky, he paused. Between the two islands, Alan, Zafir, Thomas, and the rest of the knights and sailors galloped on the surface of the sea, with Edward at their head.

CHAPTER

118

Tokimune stopped in front of his garden pond. As he turned around, he saw Yasumori looking at him.

"Is it good news?" he asked.

"The Mongolian army has been destroyed."

"Is it true?"

"The majority met a watery grave in a tempest overnight and disappeared."

"The Yuan forces have been completely destroyed?" Tokimune repeated, just to be certain.

"Almost all were annihilated. Only a few ships remained, and they were either sunk or captured by the Kyushu gokenin. This will be a huge blow for Kublai Khan. He won't attempt to invade again for quite some time."

Perhaps this is the end of it? According to reports from Zafir's spies, Yuan is dealing with a new enemy on the main continent. They won't have the time to be concerned with Nippon any longer. However, we have to keep up with our defenses. I think I'll hide that fact for the time being.

"And what of Edward and the Christ's Army knights?" Tokimune continued.

"Their achievements were remarkable. They prevented the enemy from coming ashore and protected Nippon."

"I see," Tokimune murmured. "Are they well?"

"They've disappeared."

"Disappeared?" Tokimune said and stared at the water for a short while with a quizzical look.

"Without their efforts, the enemy would have made camp and instantly had Hakata in their clutches, before eventually marching on Dazaifu—" Yasumori began.

"They saved our nation, you say?"

"They used catapults to launch stones and fire, which caused great damage to the Yuan warships and threw their soldiers onshore into chaos. They kept the Mongolian army trapped in the bay and then the storm came which—"

"Where is the messenger from Hakata?"

"He's still here."

"I want to hear it from him directly."

The messenger was brought before Tokimune. He was a tanned and fearless-looking young man, but he could barely stand from exhaustion. Tokimune told him to sit and recognized the man for his services.

"Tell us what happened in the battle," he asked.

"The Christian knights fought in the vanguard and all were killed."

"All of them—" Tokimune was at a loss for words.

"It was a tremendous achievement. The next messenger will be able to report more of the details."

"Tell me as much as you know."

The messenger took a moment to think before speaking.

"On the morning of the last day, Edward and his knights came out wearing foreign armor."

"Was it the knight's garb?"

"They wore armor made of knitted chains, with helmets, and a red cross painted on their chests. The same cross was dyed on the banner they carried. The people called them Crusaders. Accompanying them was Lord Morimune, leading a cavalry only fifty strong. Sir Edward and the others were backed by a volley of arrows and stones released from behind the stone wall and the use of spears close to sixteen feet long."

"Our spears were truly that long?"

"They were carved out of bamboo on Sir Edward's orders."

Tokimune sighed several times.

"They said the battle lasted from early morning until the evening. It was a fierce fight."

"And what was the damage to our army?"

"Our army had withdrawn to Dazaifu. It was the intention of Lord Munemasa and the other leaders to hold Dazaifu and fight the enemy there."

"Then who was it that fought with the bows, stones, and long spears?"

"The people of Hakata."

Tokimune took a moment to think.

"So, you are saying those responsible for defeating Yuan were Edward, his Crusaders, and the people of Hakata?"

"T–that is not what I meant," the messenger denied in a fluster. "Nevertheless, I heard a magnificent tale about their feats in battle," he added as if he could not help himself.

"What did Edward say?"

"That a knight is someone who devotes himself to the people."

"Did he mean that the gokenin vassals should do the same?" Tokimune muttered.

"Did you ask something?"

"It is nothing. Thank you for your hard work. You may take your rest."

After making sure the messenger had withdrawn, Tokimune let out a deep sigh. *That man found his great cause.*

"What should we do about the Crusader's achievements?" Yasumori asked.

"Edward said that he fought for the sake of the people, no?"

"That is what I heard."

'What do you fight for?' Did Edward find the answer to his question? But that is an answer not befitting my nation.

"Burn all of the Crusaders' swords, armor, and anything else they used."

"For what purpose?"

"To erase any traces of them. Their existence was noble, but dangerous for our country."

Yasumori listened to Tokimune silently.

"If the gokenin were to fight for the sake of the people, then what would become of Nippon's structure? If we rid ourselves of the lord-and-retainer concept grounded in rewards and service, then the very foundation of Kamakura will become unstable. Not to mention, if it was the people who saved our Nippon, then the world of the samurai we have only just barely established will collapse," Tokimune said quietly, though his words were strong with meaning.

"The victory must have been achieved by the gokenin, who served and fought for rewards, and by the monks, who desperately prayed for our nation to win the war. Revealing anything about the Crusaders' existence is forbidden. Tell Morimune."

"As you wish," Yasumori nodded. "But can we truly prevent the people from speaking about them?"

Tokimune stared at Yasumori.

"Humans are ruthless creatures. The dead are in the past. The people will look for the next living person to follow."

From outside the wall, they could hear the voice of a monk giving a sermon.

"We will erase Edward and his companions from our history. Our country would be thrown into chaos if it was known that a foreign god's army saved our nation. We must tell them that our lands were saved by the gokenin who have sworn loyalty to the shogun and by the squall of divine wind that monks and Shinto priests prayed into existence," Tokimune repeated in a resolute tone, before he murmured lowly, "I guess he couldn't carry out his promise to me."

"What?"

"It is nothing. Never mention those men again. And burn all the catapults and long spears. Tell all those having to do with the Crusaders that they must also adhere to this without fail."

But—" Tokimune hesitated and cast his gaze up to the sky.

"Find out more about Edward and his men's deaths, and report anything new to me."

He then turned back to look at his pond. Floating on the water's surface was Edward Gawain, sitting atop Hayate, dressed in his chainmail armor, and carrying a shield engraved with a cross.

EPILOGUE

Professor Shun Gaue looked across the lecture hall as he gripped the mic. More than a hundred students sat in the circular room. The room had a four-hundred-person capacity, so three-quarters of the seats were empty. He had hoped for a smaller classroom, but this was the only one available.

"Crusaders. The name for soldiers in the Christian army dates back to the sixteenth century," he began.

There was no reaction from the students.

"But it is generally agreed that the Crusades themselves started around 1096 and lasted for two hundred years, during which various Christian countries in Western Europe dispatched expeditionary forces to the Middle East to reclaim the Holy Land of Jerusalem from Muslim control."

Shun was aware of whispering in different parts of the room. Usually he would stop and reprimand the offenders. But today he ignored the chatter and continued. He was thinking about the excavated objects lying on his office desk.

"The populace enthusiastically supported the Crusaders' ideals. To fight against the Muslim enemy was to fight a Holy War decreed by God. Those who died would be martyrs, and the sins of the living would be forgiven. In the beginning, commonly known as the People's Crusade, twenty thousand ordinary people from Constantinople invaded Anatolia, only to be annihilated by the Islamic army."

The whispering began to die down, but several students still sat with their heads hanging down, looking at their hands, and texting on their smartphones.

"Due to this crushing defeat, Christian adherents realized they wouldn't be able to retake the Holy Land without a trained army. A hundred thousand soldiers from all over Europe became the first Crusaders and led to the siege and fall of Antioch in Syria in 1097–1098."

Shun was gaining ground. Now more than half of the students seemed interested in what he had to say.

"The battle was meant to be a holy war, but the army began pillaging and cruelly slaughtering great numbers of people in both Islamic and Greek Orthodox countries. Obviously, the Christian Golden Rule—to love your neighbor as you love yourself—only extended to those neighbors who were also Christian."

Students in the front rows stared at Shun with earnest expressions.

"History is the study of the truths of the past, but it is also the study of the human mind. Our conjectures are of great interest and at times even mysterious."

"By the time of the fourth campaign, the Crusaders had managed to invade their fellow Christian nations of the Byzantine Empire and the Kingdom of Hungary. However, in the battles over Jerusalem, the Islamic side did not kill Christians, but instead captured them as prisoners of war and released them for ransom. It is true that there were many truly pious men among the Crusaders. However, there were many fanatics who would destroy pagan villages at random. By the way, there was an instance, called the Children's Crusade, where young boys and girls aiming to reclaim the Holy Land were sold off as slaves."

"That's the legend of 'The Pied Piper of Hamelin,' right?" a female student in the front row spoke out.

"Correct. It's a story of a male flute player who lures children and steals them away from a town."

"I read it. Kind of a creepy and scary story, but I don't really understand its meaning," she shared with the person sitting next to her.

"Generally agreed, the last campaign was the Eighth Crusade of Louis IX of France. But, after that, the crown prince of England, the future Edward I, and his men led an expedition to Akko in Israel. This so-called Ninth Crusade landed in Tripoli in May 1271. However, the Islamic Army could not be defeated, thanks to Mongolian reinforcements. The English retreated in December. In the end, Christian Crusaders failed to reclaim the Holy Land," Shun concluded. But he wasn't finished.

"Do you know what period Japan was in while the Crusades were going on?"

"The Heian Period," several students answered.

"Actually, it was from the Heian Period to the Kamakura Period. What happened in 1274 and 1281?"

"The battles of Bunei and Koan," the girl who mentioned "The Pied Piper of Hamelin" said.

"Yes, those were the two Mongolian invasions of Japan. To tell the truth, there aren't many historical records left about the Mongol invasions. The ones most often cited are the *Mōko Shūrai Ekotoba* hand scrolls, the *Hachiman Gudokun*, and the *History of Goryeo*. However, there is a theory that a typhoon didn't wipe out the Yuan invading ships, as is commonly accepted."

"But wasn't Hojo Tokimune extremely studious?" a student asked. "Didn't he leave behind a lot of historical evidence for future generations?"

"Unfortunately, he died of illness at the young age of thirty-four, three years after the second Mongolian invasion. You could say that he lived his short life protecting Japan from foreign invaders. All foreign invaders. At any rate, this was an era riddled with enigmas. Why couldn't a great empire like Mongolia, which had invaded as far away as Europe, overthrow a small island country like Japan as it had done with countries on continental Asia? Was Japan exceptional in some way?" Shun let out a deep breath.

"During the Kamakura Era, samurai desperately fought to replace the longstanding political system which centered on the emperor and the aristocracy with a system controlled by the samurai. A great number of conflicts ensued, and many people died for the samurai cause. Many doubtless died unobserved and have consequently been erased from history. Never forget this."

Finally, Shun held his students in the palm of his hand.

After the lecture, Shun returned to his office. Exhaustion hit him hard, and he had to sit down. On his desk were two clumps of rusted iron, the same two pieces of sword that he and his students had dug up from the stone wall in Hakata. There was no mistaking the pieces for anything but a Western sword. The box next to the broken sword contained the dagger and cross from his grandfather's storehouse. And, although he needed more scientific verification, he knew in his heart that the crest on the handles of the sword and dagger was the same. The connection between the two was . . . the more he thought about it the more mysterious the connection became.

Shun took another box from his desk drawer. It contained a rusted bundle of chains which could be from a thirteenth-century chainmail hood that Crusaders wore to protect their heads in battle. He had found a child playing with it at the foot of Mount Iimori. When he asked him where he had found it, the child told him he had picked it up near the mountain stream. There was an old legend that foreign soldiers had been buried at the foot of the mountain, but everyone believed them to be Mongolians. Shun had thought at the time he should dig there, but he still hadn't gotten around to it.

"I have time. This is a story from the distant past. It won't run away," he muttered to himself and once again looked at the lion crest on the dagger's handle. At that moment, he felt the strange sensation that someone was trying to speak to him. He strained his ears and listened.